Tunkhannock Pub
Tunkhannock, PA 18657

S0-BRM-019

PRAISE FOR

The Necromancer's House

"[An] eruption of characters who evoke Dickensian whimsy and range from the merely unusual to the bizarrely imaginative . . . An explosion of enthralling fantasy. [A] vibrant, bracing atmosphere."

—*Publishers Weekly* (starred review)

"You find yourself believing the unbelievable and fearing what you thought belonged only in those old-world, pre-sanitized fairy tales."

—Andrew Pyper, author of *The Demonologist*

PRAISE FOR

Between Two Fires

"Cormac McCarthy's *The Road* meets Chaucer's *The Canterbury Tales* in this frightful medieval epic . . . [Buehlman] doesn't scrimp on earthy humor and lyrical writing in the face of unspeakable horrors . . . An author to watch."
—*Kirkus Reviews*

"I was spellbound from the moment I opened the front cover . . . Intense and chilling . . . The ultimate good-versus-evil battle." —*Night Owl Reviews*

"Fans of historical fantasy and horror will find this epic darkly rewarding."
—*Publishers Weekly*

PRAISE FOR

Those Across the River

One of *Publishers Weekly*'s Top-Ten SF, Fantasy & Horror Novels

A World Fantasy Award Nominee for Best Novel

"One of the best first novels I've ever read."
—Charlaine Harris, #1 *New York Times* bestselling author

"What a treat. As much F. Scott Fitzgerald as Dean Koontz. A graceful, horrific read." —Patricia Briggs, #1 *New York Times* bestselling author

continued . . .

"Beautifully written . . . with a cast of Southern characters so real you can almost see the sweat roll down the page. The ending is exceedingly clever."
—*Boston Herald*

"An unsettling brew of growing menace spiked with flashes of genuine terror—do not miss this chilling debut. Christopher Buehlman is a writer to watch. I look forward to hearing from him again. And soon."
—F. Paul Wilson, *New York Times* bestselling author of *Dark City*

"Buehlman's lyrical prose vividly captures a landscape made familiar by William Faulkner and Flannery O'Connor. A delightfully genre-bending juxtaposition of supernatural horror and gothic drama."
—*California Literary Review*

"A horror story that manages just the right balance between building dread and suspense and delivering action."
—*The A.V. Club*

"Sublimely crafted . . . It is clear that Mr. Buehlman brings his poetic background to bear in creating the rhythm and meter of the story . . . A well-crafted novel that is a pleasure to read."
—*New York Journal of Books*

"[A] masterful debut novel . . . Moody and lush . . . [A] spellbinding tale of terror . . . Filled with cowardice and bravery, foolishness and wisdom, grief and grace, and, alas, helplessness and beauty. Buehlman has written one of the best books of the year."
—*Shelf Awareness*

"In its unnerving depiction of small-town creepiness and heathen savagery, this surefooted debut resembles nothing more than Thomas Tryon's *Harvest Home* . . . Viscerally upsetting . . . This is lusty, snappy writing, and horror fans will eat it up (or vice versa)."
—*Booklist*

"Buehlman packs suspense and secrets into his debut novel . . . Keep[s] readers on their toes right up until the big reveal."
—*Publishers Weekly*

"Fans of novels like *'Salem's Lot* or classic radio dramas will find this story impossible to put down . . . [It] feels completely fantastical by our rational minds but believable by our deepest fears."
—*Suspense Magazine*

Ace Books by Christopher Buehlman

THOSE ACROSS THE RIVER

BETWEEN TWO FIRES

THE NECROMANCER'S HOUSE

THE
NECROMANCER'S
HOUSE

CHRISTOPHER BUEHLMAN

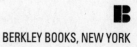
BERKLEY BOOKS, NEW YORK

THE BERKLEY PUBLISHING GROUP
Published by the Penguin Group
Penguin Group (USA) LLC
375 Hudson Street, New York, New York 10014

USA • Canada • UK • Ireland • Australia • New Zealand • India • South Africa • China

penguin.com

A Penguin Random House Company

Copyright © 2013 by Christopher Buehlman.
Penguin supports copyright. Copyright fuels creativity, encourages diverse voices,
promotes free speech, and creates a vibrant culture. Thank you for buying an authorized
edition of this book and for complying with copyright laws by not reproducing, scanning,
or distributing any part of it in any form without permission. You are supporting writers
and allowing Penguin to continue to publish books for every reader.

BERKLEY® is a registered trademark of Penguin Group (USA) LLC.
The "B" design is a trademark of Penguin Group (USA) LLC.

Berkley trade paperback ISBN: 978-0-425-25691-6

The Library of Congress has catalogued the Ace hardcover edition as follows:

Buehlman, Christopher.
The Necromancer's house / Christopher Buehlman. — First Edition.
pages cm
ISBN 978-0-425-25665-7 (hardcover)
1. Magic—Fiction.   2. Witches—Fiction.   I. Title.
PS3603.U3395N43 2013
813'.6—dc23
2013011502

PUBLISHING HISTORY
Ace hardcover edition / October 2013
Berkley trade paperback edition / September 2014

PRINTED IN THE UNITED STATES OF AMERICA

10   9   8   7   6   5   4   3   2   1

Cover illustration © Richard Tuschman; background wallpaper © Dedyukhin Dmitry / Shutterstock;
abstract texture © Alexey Kashin / Shutterstock; border © iStockphoto/Thinkstock;
lace trim © antipathique/Shutterstock.
Cover design by Judith Lagerman.
Frontispiece photo © Dagny Willis / Getty Images.

This is a work of fiction. Names, characters, places, and incidents either are the product
of the author's imagination or are used fictitiously, and any resemblance to actual persons,
living or dead, business establishments, events, or locales is entirely coincidental.

For Ginny

Prologue

The old man walks from the cabin to the porch behind, palming his whiskey glass from the bottom and swirling the ice in it. A drop of water falls from his knuckle, falling on the head of the beagle mix snaking near his feet. This distracts the dog so that it halts long enough to get underfoot, almost tripping the old man, who swears viciously in Russian that Khrushchev might have barked, then apologizes in Pushkin's honeyed tones. The dog wags halfheartedly but steers starboard in case his master kicks at him. The kicks are infrequent and never hard, so the evasion is lazy, and the kick never comes. An observer would note how balletic the interaction is, how practiced each is at his part.

But no one is watching them.

Not yet.

The man lips at his glass and sits facing the sunset.

The dog curls at his feet and begins a snorting, chewing hunt for a flea that has disgraced him near the base of his tail.

"Kill that fucker," the man says in a jovial Slavic growl, scratching under his left tit in sympathy.

The sun has already performed its nightly slow-motion dive into Lake Ontario; it has slipped behind its blue veil like a bulb of molten glass, so beautifully that a man on Fair Haven Beach, one town west, spontaneously proposed marriage to his girlfriend of less than six months, and a group of actors on the McIntyre Bluffs, near the bird sanctuary not a mile away, silenced their chatter about the day's rehearsals and broke into applause. Now the aftershow is wrapping up; the surface of the lake has turned an iridescent color reminiscent of mother-of-pearl, a hue that has proven irreproducible in watercolor; an ephemeral purplish-silver that even the great Eastman Kodak an hour and change away in ashy Rochester has never brought to shore alive.

The old Russian's nearest neighbor, a former comparative religions professor in a nearly identical summer cabin a hundred yards down the ridge, once told him, "These sunsets have been rated the second-best sunsets in the world."

"Rated?" the Russian had said. "Who rates a sunset?"

"The photographers of *National Geographic*."

"Oh," he had said, pushing his lower lip out and nodding. The professor, who is renting long-term and working on some atheistic magnum opus, loves sharing that piece of trivia with other visitors just to see them first reject and then accept the idea that sunsets might be rankable. He had been disappointed that the Russian did not ask the usual follow-up question, so he had answered it unbidden.

"The best sunsets are over the Sea of Japan, looking toward Russia."

Now the lake spreads squid's-ink black beneath a sky like a luminous bruise. The Russian wants a cigarette, but it is a mild want that only comes with inebriation and goes away when ignored. He looks at the dog, at the white in his face that stands out from his black-and-tan body like a cheap plastic ghost mask.

"Go get us a pack of Marlboros, Caspar. Caspar the son-of-a-bitch ghost."

His wife comes to mind.

She had called the dog Caspar. She had made him quit smoking. She had taught him to say *son of a bitch* correctly, separating and emphasizing *bitch* where he had always run the three words together and accented *son*.

This ache for a dead woman will be harder to chase away than the ache for nicotine.

Here is the devil!

It is too beautiful an evening to wallow in melancholy again. Maybe the professor will consent to play chess? The thought bores him senseless; the man is a good conversationalist, but he can't smell a trap, is too lazy to think more than two moves ahead, and understands nothing about keeping force in reserve—he will jabber away about the Upanishads, or about the cowlike stupidity of evangelical Christians, and send his pawns out too far, stroking his orthodox-thick beard while the light shines on his bald dome, crossing and recrossing his legs, and saying "huh" as if surprised that the center of the board, which he thought he had in his fist, is turning into a kill box.

Besides, he is enjoying the night air and doesn't feel like going anywhere.

He toys with the notion of turning on his computer and looking for an escort, but the connection is sketchy at best, and waiting for the pictures to load on the escort site will be purgatorial. Besides, once he has selected one, assuming he can talk her into a last-minute meeting far away with an unknown client, she will have to come from Syracuse or Rochester, and that will be two hours. Perhaps three. Perhaps there are prostitutes in Oswego, half an hour east, but he shudders to think of what one of those might be like; the profile, so poorly written even a Russian could correct it, will lead to some pale, plain-faced girl raised in the shadow of the nuclear plant and plumped on foldable pizza; he can see her now with her bad tattoos and her mouse-brown hair, undressing clumsily, asking him questions about his life and interrupting with "uh-huh" when he answers, then, after ten grim minutes of fucking, slipping one of his liquor bottles into her backpack while he discards the prophylactic and struggles to begin a postcoital piss.

Oswego is for chicken wings and beer.

Oswego is not for pretty girls.

Not that he is any prize himself, with his shirt open on his hard, round, Florida-brown belly and his toenails that barely fit in the clippers, but a man need not be a horse to buy one.

His father said such things.

His father had ridden bare-chested into Berlin on a tank and had paid a month's wages for the privilege of taking a shit in Hitler's bunker.

If his father were here, he would call the Rochester escort *and* the Oswego hooker and send his mother out for cigarettes.

Which is why he loves and hates him thirty years after his death.

He will call no escort.

"Caspar, the son-of-a-bitch dog. Go get us a woman."

Caspar squares his black lips and makes a barely audible whimper, as he often does when a command word like *go* is followed by something he does not understand.

Now Caspar's nose twitches.

The Russian smells it, too.

Foul and tidal, as though something has washed up from the lake.

He had just been remarking how sweet the night air was, and now this.

Has a whale beached itself?

"Lakes have no whales," he tells Caspar, pointing a nut-colored finger gravely at him. The dog doesn't seem to understand, so he tells him in Russian, too.

Now Caspar looks toward the lake.

He wags his tail a little as he does in lieu of barking when a stranger approaches.

"I thought I heard Russian," a woman says, in Russian.

The light from his cabin lights the area of the porch, ending in the sun-grayed handrails at the top of the stairs leading down to the beach.

As though the world ends with those rails.

Beyond is lake and night, as black as the black behind a star.

"Ha!" he says, and then, in Russian, "You did. And so did I. Come up the stairs and say hello."

"In a moment," she says, in accented English. "I'm changing."

She sounds young.

He feels the small thrill a man feels when he is sure he is about to meet a pretty girl. Of course, one can be disappointed making such assumptions, as she will be if she thinks him handsome for his deep, rich voice.

That smell again.

"Do you like whiskey?" he says, matching her English, suppressing the old-man grunt he usually makes when he gets to his feet.

"Oh, very much," she says. "Is it scotch?"

"Oban. You know it?"

"No. But it smells good."

"You can smell it over that"—it wouldn't do to say *shit* before he knows her character—"other smell?"

"I can smell it. It smells like peat and burned seaweed."

"Ice?"

"Please."

He enters the house and fills two glasses, pleased at the turn the evening is taking. He glances at his nearly transparent reflection in the hutch, thinking he doesn't look so good. But not awful for almost seventy. He walks out back again, managing the screen door with more difficulty, burdened as he is with two dripping glasses now.

Still no woman.

The wooden handrails stand out, brilliantly illuminated against the primordial darkness behind them.

He looks down to see if Caspar is still wagging his welcome at her.

But Caspar is gone.

He sets the glasses down and whistles.

He walks to the rickety stairs and hoists himself down to the level of the beach, his back deck bathed in light and receding with each step down. He steps onto sand that soon gives way to rocks, his eyes adjusting to the darkness. He listens for the sound of Caspar's collar, the jingling of the tag with the dog's name and his master's information, and the legend *Help me get home!* but all he hears is Lake Ontario's languid whisper and a gentle breeze in the crowns of the maples and birch trees behind him.

His sandaled foot plunges into a puddle, which some precivilized part of his brain registers as incorrect—the tide doesn't come this far and it has not rained—but he walks on.

"Girl, you didn't take my dog, did you?" he asks in Russian.

Nothing.

He walks farther down the beach, closer to the water, the smooth rocks pushing up against his sandals' bottoms.

"Caspar?" he says, his concern for the dog growing and mixing with anger. Has this bitch with the Leningrad accent taken his dog? Is there a market in upstate New York for old mixed-breed dogs who flatulate like dying grandmothers?

Here is the devil, he thinks.

Now he hears the jingle of the collar behind him.

Is the old bastard actually going up the stairs on his own power instead of whimpering to be carried?

He remembers the smoky amber of his whiskey and feels happy to be making his way back to it.

He climbs up, hearing the jingle inside the house.

"You little fucker," he says, smiling.

Warm light spills from the windows and door of the cabin.

He looks for the whiskey and finds only two wet rings on the table.

That is incorrect.

Another sound registers as incorrect, though familiar.

His shower is running.

A sly smile creeps onto his face.

The girl. What game is she playing? This night will be very good or very bad, but at least it will produce a story.

This was the sort of thing his father said.

He takes his sandals off and opens the screen door, stepping in. He finds the floor wet. He goes to the hallway and stands before the closed bathroom door—God in heaven, it stinks of the lake in here—and then he turns the handle. The shower is running, the curtain pulled back to show the rusty showerhead and the bad grout.

No steam, though.

The water runs cold.

He turns it off.

An empty rocks glass sits in the sink, one very long auburn hair coiled near it. He plucks this from the off-white porcelain and looks at it—how coarse it is!

Hearing Caspar's jingle, he goes into the hallway again, and his heart skips a beat.

A woman stands in the hallway, pale and nude, her hair thick and russet-colored and wetly quilting her shoulders and breasts. His eyes trail down to her tight, alabaster navel, below which a scud of curly hair leads to the kind of prodigious bush one doesn't see on young women these days except on specialty Internet sites.

The second whiskey glass drips in her hand.

With the pointer finger of her other hand, she makes her collar jingle. Caspar's collar, more properly, which she wears on her neck.

The man has bounced between shock, worry, anger, and glad surprise so precipitously that when he speaks he only sounds old and bewildered.

"Where's my fucking dog?"

"Help me get home," she says, showing yellow-gray teeth that don't belong in the mouth of a first-world girl. "That is very sweet, Misha."

The smell that pollutes his cabin is coming from her, maybe from that thick, cabled wet hair, maybe even from her mouth or cunt. How can something so beautiful smell like that?

He notices now how scarred and sinewy she is, how strong her limbs look.

"You didn't hurt him, did you?" he asks in Russian.

"You'll kiss me now even if I did," she says in English, moving the mouth with the bad teeth and the beautiful lips closer.

He thinks to pull away, but he does not.

Something about her eyes fixes him in place.

How green they are.

How cold her mouth is.

He tries to pull away, but her hand has found the back of his head and anchors it where she wants it. His mouth is too full of cold tongue for him to yell.

Past her, he sees his collarless dog pad from the kitchen, squaring his lips and wagging gently, unsure what to make of the struggle in the hallway.

When she drags the old Russian down the stairs and to the lake, the dog follows, even down the stairs, but he only walks to the lip of the water, where he paces back and forth as the woman who does not smell like a woman pushes his master's head below the surface.

He thrashes, but she holds him under with ease.

The dog has enough beagle in him to make him howl.

Owooooooooooo

She howls back at him playfully until her head goes under, and the dog is alone.

PART ONE

1

This is what Andrew does at the AA meeting.

He says his piece when he has to.

He translates the God stuff in his head so it makes sense to him.

He tries very hard to let the new people know he's listening to them—he brightens his speech when he says "Hi, [new person]" and "Thanks, [new person]," and he does his best not to categorize them into will-be-back, won't-be-back, because that feels just a little too black-and-white, sheep-and-goats Manichean to him, and one thing Andrew Ranulf Blankenship is not about is black and white.

He is a calm-eyed icon of gray areas.

And if he does sometimes think, *That guy's just here because it's part of his DUI deal* or *That woman's going to drive into the parking lot of the Driftwood Bar and Grill and back out again three times tonight before she turns her car off and trots in with her head down,* he chides himself afterward.

Who are you to caricature them?

What do you really know, O wise seer?

If you saw someone like yourself walk in, would you know what you were? Could there be two of you within driving range of this rural Presbyterian church? And how did it feel to have them all look at you when you first came? And know that some of them were thinking, Probably a faggot, *and some were thinking,* Belongs in the city with that hair.

Not that new people come in so very often, or that they're really all that new. The woman who'll probably go to the Driftwood buys produce at the Orchards—he's seen her with her faintly electric bottle-red hair and the buzz-cut child who pulls at her sleeve and whines like he's two years younger than he looks. The DUI guy he doesn't know, but a Lexus pulled up and ejected him while Andrew smoked with his friends.

More about them in a minute.

DUI guy probably found the meeting online in Rochester and drove out to the sticks to make damned sure the Anonymous part of Alcoholics A stuck.

Looks like a real estate agent, maybe a high-end car salesman, some industry that's been whomped and he's one of the last ones standing, barely hanging on by his martini habit, which stretched from three after work to four and he thought he was just getting a speeding ticket when the young-enough-to-be-his-nephew cop said, "Have you been drinking, sir?" and his heart skipped a beat, make it two, and he peed just a little in his khakis and tried on his first pair of handcuffs. When we pass the basket he'll be all slick and fold his court-ordered attendance slip in a dollar bill, make it a five because he'll want to show us he's making it okay, and then the basket will come floating back with nothing in it but the signed slip and make its way to him like a homing pigeon and he'll sheepishly pluck it out and pocket it. So much for discretion. I prefer the DUI guys who drop their slip in like an ace-queen in blackjack, defiantly, BOOM, fuck everybody in the ROOM.

I'm doing it again.

Motor-minding, shitty-committee.

Knock it off, Blankenship.

So Andrew blinks his lazy icon eyes and listens to tonight's chairperson (Hi, Bob!) talking about humility, and just for fun (and exercise—the exercise never stops) he dims the good Presbyterian fluorescents above their yellowing Presbyterian screens, stopping before Bob notices, then brightens them again, stopping before any of them pop.

Chancho and Anneke both look at him.

Chancho the honcho and Anneke-Harmonica.

They of the smoking troika that watched the Lexus birth the DUI guy.

Chancho looks at him in a guilty Mexican-Catholic stop-fucking-around way. Because this is *guero* God but still God's house and you're just lucky he doesn't strike you down for being a *brujo* in the first place.

Anneke, who wants to and will be a *bruja* because Andrew is teaching her, side-eyes him as if she's unsure whether he is the source of the phenomenon. His icon eyes reveal nothing. He casually reforks the samurai-style bun on top of his head, though, and she knows he's doing that to fool Chancho into thinking he's too distracted to fuck with the lights and to let her know that he's fucking with the lights.

She wishes he were a woman.

He wishes she liked men.

Chancho wishes the meeting were over so he could go home for another plate of his wife's *mole* enchiladas and an hour of UFC on Spike.

Andrew's only real complaint about this particular group is that they run a more-than-normally religious meeting. Stands to reason, out in the sticks like this. Still beats the darkly secular town chapter with its constant friction between doomsaying bleeding deacons and cigarette-mooching relapse punks.

During the hand-holding Lord's Prayer, only Anneke and Andrew are silent. That was what first made them notice one another, their shared agnosticism. And the fact that, except perhaps for Laura (Hi, Laura!), a runner-up for Miss New York in 1999, they are the two most empirically attractive people in the room, misaligned gender preferences (hers, not his) aside.

2

Andrew and Anneke drive to Dunkin Donuts and have coffee (his with cream, hers as black as a raven's beak), then farther into Oswego to shoot pool at the waterfront bar. They are both far enough along in their sobriety to be comfortable in a bar, and they both enjoy pool enough to tolerate the clientele. In the twenty years Andrew has made his home in nearby Dog Neck Harbor, he has come to Oswego periodically for those things one goes to town for when one lives in a hamlet, pool and bowling being two of them, but he has never understood Oswego's denizens.

Oswego hurts his feelings a little, with its redbrick waterfront buildings still faintly overlettered with hundred-year-old advertisements (*Enjoy refreshing Coca-Cola! It still has cocaine!*) wasted on its aesthetically impaired youth; with just a little artistic *umph*, just a thimbleful of intellectual zeitgeist, just one really banging university, this town could have been a tiny Amsterdam, a waterfront Ithaca. Instead, it . . . well, isn't.

In the twenty years Andrew has been coming here, he has watched the town smother almost every good restaurant it birthed. French bistros, Indian buffets, from-scratch hippie bakeries, quirky greasy spoons. And the names . . . Casa Luna, The Coach House, Wahrendorf's Diner, the Little While. Oh, the closing of the Little While hurt. The seafood marinara fed three; it was so thick with garlic that slivers of it stuck to your fork, and so generous with seafood that you had to push aside the shrimp and fish to get to the mussels, then opened a mussel to find it packed in with more shrimp and fish.

And the pancakes at Wahrendorf's.

"Fucking Wahrendorf's," he says, punching the last word to give his cue more *chi* as he breaks. Sinks a colored and a stripe.

"Fucking Wahrendorf's," Anneke agrees.

A lad in droopy shorts, a wife beater, and a baseball cap (twenty years and the Oswegian wardrobe hasn't changed any more than the appetite for cheap fried food and sports bars) saunters over with three quarters in his hand, but Anneke stacks six quarters on the table and shoots him a look that makes him veer to the jukebox instead. Andrew ignores him and turns his icon eyes to the task of sinking two more solids.

The boy goes back to his friends, also wearing their regulation tank tops and baseball caps, and makes them whinny with laughter at something. Andrew looks too small and exotic to be worth punching, and Anneke looks like she might throw a good punch herself.

No glory there.

"I've been thinking about your middle name. Why Ranulf?"

He pauses, hip on table, just about to take a flashy behind-the-back stab at a tough corner-pocket shot, and thinks about his long-ago ancestor.

"I mean, from what you've told me about your parents, I don't see them pulling out some King Arthury name like that."

Andrew imagines Ranulf Blenkenshope, the first known proto-Blankenship, dodging piles of sheep pellets near the smoky Northumberland hovel in which a wife stirs the bland bubbling blankenfood that will keep them and their wan brood alive through another rainy thirteenth-century winter.

"It beats Randolph. I changed it when I was in college. For funsies."

He misses his shot, his concentration bifurcate.

"And since when is an Anneke Zautke so ready to spar about names? It sounds like you should be wearing clogs."

Suddenly curious about what she *is* wearing on her feet, Andrew glances at her Middle-Easternish sandals, sees the slightly chipped green toenail polish. Anneke has handsomely shaped feet. She has handsomely shaped everything. And she dresses well, not just well for a lesbian.

She hates that word.

3

"I hate that word," she had said. "It sounds like something cold-blooded."

"It is," he had said, and she had frog-knuckle-punched him right between the scant muscles of his arm.

Hard.

That had been the night they first attempted to be lovers; the movie they had watched together was over, the bruschetta she had made all gone save for the sliver of basil and crust of cheese drying to the plate. She kissed him more out of loneliness than passion, finally taking him to bed for a self-conscious romp they both mostly laughed through, especially the application of the condom.

Now I Ranulf, king of the Britons, draw my weapon, sheathe it (lo, it droopeth) (a little help, please) (Ah! Excalibur!), and sheathe it again, as is my right.

Shut up and do this if you're going to.
Verily, Lady.

It was clear that her love for him was above the waist, and always would be, no matter how feminine his bone structure or how exotic the scents he wore in his long black hair. His deeper scent was masculine, his angles too hard, his tongue too big in her mouth.

He knew there were spells he might use to make her burn for him, but burn she would; the further the subject was from true desire, the more damage the incantation would do. Suicide, insanity, and illness were the long-term fruits of love's abuse, by magic or otherwise, as so many had written and so few believed.

Andrew believed.

He had seen what happened to those who loved him over the two decades since the witch's raven had left its peck in him.

Sarah.

Anneke would be safe from the raven's beak.

The curse that murdered those he loved who loved him back.

She would not love him, and if he loved her, that was his blood to bleed.

I guess Papillon *was the wrong movie to try to seduce you with.*
Maybe not. You fuck like you've got money up your ass.
Wait a minute, I thought I was Papillon, not Dustin Hoffman.
You were Dustin Hoffman.

4

She had sculpted him twice.

The first time wearing his Japanese robe and sitting with his elbows on his thighs, head slightly bent and cocked to one side like a bohemian *The Thinker*, and she had kept that one.

It sat on the table by her smoking chair, the chair facing the lake, lording over the camel-bone ashtray her sailor father had gotten in Egypt. Sometimes she stuck incense sticks in the space between the statue's arm and thigh and burned them so they veiled his head in smoke, but mostly she just puffed her Camel Lights and watched sunsets or storms or waves lapping at the weird ice figures framing the beach in winter. He liked it that a smaller version of himself kept her company.

The second statue had been larger, life-sized, a nude, and it was so lifelike she sold it for four thousand dollars at an art show in Ithaca. She had barely had it a month but needed the money, and she would not sell it to Andrew because his offer felt like charity. She wanted to see what she could get from a stranger.

And so a man from Toronto took home her best statue, a statue of one of America's most powerful wizards buck naked in white clay, and put it in his basement near a red felt pool table.

It was titled *Nonchalance*, and the Canadian never lost another game of pool under Andrew's bored stone gaze, even against much better players, nor did he ever guess why.

5

Anneke is not made for interiors; there is something smaller, something caged and wrong about her in the bar, as there is whenever she finds herself beneath a roof.

She is too big for the space.

Andrew's mind's eye favors snapshots of Anneke outside, building something out of wood or sculpting it out of clay and slurry; her shag of dirty blond hair, just beginning to gray, has been woven to drink sunlight; if she carries a hammer, tan suede gloves cul-de-sac her strong, brown forearms; if she sculpts at her outside table, her jeans are crusted at the thighs where she wipes her hands on them, and she does not sit, but circles her creation counterclockwise as she coaxes its true shape and name from it.

Just walking across the lawn she has the air of a lioness whose mate had best not be sleeping in her favorite spot.

Andrew knew he loved her when he first saw sunlight on her.

That had been two years before.

He let himself love her because he knew she would not love him back.

6

Anneke Zautke has been out of prison for six years now, mostly sober for eight. She bought her odd, sloped little A-frame house by the lake so she could be close enough to visit her chronically ill father in the little town of Mexico,

Leukemia? Will you die?
    Eventually.
    It's not fair, Dad. You just . . . retired.
    I sailed nuclear subs. Nobody made me do that. Nobody made me work at the plant. Shit happens.

but far enough away from Oswego and Syracuse not to see anyone she knew before.

She makes a decent living selling statues and earthenware mugs at art shows and Renaissance festivals, and her house, like Andrew's, is hard to find.

Anyone who makes a hobby of harassing sex offenders will have a long, winding drive to Anneke's property and back. Nobody has yet tried, but she has another twelve years to go before her name disappears from the registry.

Shelly Bertolucci had been sixteen.

Shelly had been so relieved to find someone else in Oswego who loved like she did that she didn't care about consequence.

Consequence can be lopsided, though.

Consequence was one thing for Shelly, and quite another for the pretty young art teacher fresh from Cornell who introduced her to cabernet, Rodin, Edith Piaf, and her first thirty orgasms.

Anneke Zautke got the maximum four-year sentence for statutory rape and contributing to the delinquency of a minor. This despite her lawyer's exhaustive coaching.

She was in braces when it started, right?

Yep.

Every time you think about sitting upright and tough, doing that Marlene Dietrich thing, remember they're going to show the jury pictures of a little girl in braces.

So, what, slouch?

Sit like someone who knows she had sex with a little girl in braces. Show me what that looks like.

Will you be funny like that in maximum with girls who shot people?

Anneke had been unable to properly display remorse, because the truth was she felt none.

She wished *she* had had someone to light her way through the purgatory of a homosexual adolescence in west-central New York, and saw her willingness to do the same for Shelly as an act of personal valor.

Anneke had also been drinking a bottle and a half of wine a night and self-medicating, both with cocaine and with antidepressants she got online from India, so her ability to discern between empowerment and exploitation was . . .

Suspect.

. . .

When they're showing the braces pictures, are they going to show any of the sculptures Shelly made in class?

Why?

Because they're not bad. She really started . . . growing. Artistically.

What, because she was having sex with you?

. . .

Actually, yes.

7

Andrew takes her home.

The grass is growing high now that summer has settled in for keeps, and the stars are an opera out here.

He walks around to her side and opens the door for her. The car is a '68 Ford Mustang, so the door is heavy and squeaks on its hinge. She lets him let her out; it is her act of chivalry toward him.

"The stars," he says.

"Yep."

"I have something for you. It's in the trunk."

"Is it a puppy?"

"Well. Actually it's a basilisk, so don't look it in the eye."

"What's a basilisk?"

"Something you shouldn't look in the eye."

She goes to light a cigarette.

"Don't yet."

It hangs from her lip as he opens his trunk and pulls out something book-sized in oriental paper from the card shop in Oswego.

"You wrap like shit."

"I only try when I care."

She likes this.

She pulls a folding knife from her pocket and slits the paper, cigarette jutting upright Franklin Delano Roosevelt–style because she's grinning like a little girl. Because nobody gives presents like Andrew Ranulf Blankenship.

Making Stone Move:
Including Revivification of Living Matter Made Mineral
Michael Rudnick (1990)
Orville Hephaestus Yeats (1867)

The book has a red cover and black print, cheaply glued bindings. Somebody did this at home, or maybe with the help of a FedEx Office. She thumbs through it, squinting in the starlight. The text is two thirds photocopied hand script from the 1800s, one third badly typed Smith-Corona, impossible to read in this dim light, but probably no easy task under a lamp.

"A spell book."

"The originals are more powerful, of course, but that's why they're priceless. With study and practice you may be able to get a few tricks out of this, especially Rudnick's stuff. He started as a potter, too. Working with clay and stone as much as you do should give you that sweet-spot intuition."

"Can you do the things in here?"

"Not easily. Nor well. But I never tried very hard at these arts. Not my specialty."

"How did you get this one?"

"With my specialty."

She knows the answer even as she asks it. They rarely buy any-thing. They barter. They are a community unto themselves, spread out across the globe, known to each other by reputation and now, thanks to the Internet, able to communicate in real time with sci-ence's answer to (and improvement upon) the crystal ball. No doubt Andrew performed some act of film necromancy (speaking with the dead via film media captured while they lived) for another of his kind who rewarded him with this book.

His kind.

A wizard.

But he hates that word.

8

"Thanks for the book, great wizard."

"I hate that word. It sounds like something cold-blooded."

"It is."

He pantomimes punching her arm.

"So what do I call you?"

"There's no good word for it. Most of us say *user*. But that sounds like a smackhead."

"Magic user?"

"That's Dungeons and Dragons."

"Oh. I never played."

"I did."

"No shit, a dork like you. But what do I call you?"

He thinks. Plays with his samurai bun.

"I like *magus*."

"Sounds pretentious."

"I know. But it's better than *wizard*. *Magician*'s a guy with a top hat who fakes it. *Brujo* isn't bad, but Chancho makes a face when he says it. Male witch. Going to hell. Communes with demons."

"Don't you?"

"What? No!"

"What's that thing by the train tracks?"

"Not a demon."

"What, then?"

"An . . . entity."

"That you summoned with a spell to do your bidding, but fucked up and it won't go away now. Sounds like a demon."

Andrew doesn't say anything.

9

(From an Exchange on the MyVirtualAA Forum, June 2012)

Floridachica: I heard about something called a high-bottom drunk & then herd it again. Cab anybody tell me what that is?

BRUTUS: A high-bottom drunk is somebody who thinks his s*** don't STINK.>>>>>>>>>

MikeTinfoil: That's sorta crude but BRUTUS has the right idea. A high bottom drunk is someone who has yet to realize what alcohol means to take from him and tries to pretend he can manage. Can't fully surrender. Will probably quit coming to meetings, relapse, etc.

Wookie: A High Bottom Drunk is like my dad, whose on his third wife and doesn't know that the stuff he says while 'buzzed' is why they keep packing up and leaving and also why I left home in such a hurry-just cuz he keeps his job and hasn't been to prison he thinks he has a handle on it.

PaulaQ: Wookie-Is your dad in AA?

BRUTUS: People gotta LOOSE s*** and thats HARDCORE loss I'm talkin about. We got low bottom meetings here. This s*** is REAL with HORSEMEN all FOUR of them. People think they're all good 2 EARLY and they BLOW UP>>>>>>>>

Wookie: No. Hense drunk, not alcoholic.

Ichthus70: I think there's a lot of confusion about what a high-bottom drunk is, and a lot of people with low bottoms are (understandably) chafed because they had to have such awful things happen to them before they "got it." Everybody in recovery has one thing in common, and that's the realization that their lives have gotten out of control, whatever that means to them. It's like Matthew 20: 1-16. The workers were all called at different times of day, and they all got a denarius (NIV) or penny. Those that showed up early griped because the ones who showed up late got the same penny. AA's like that. Whether you wrecked your car and killed people or just showed up with high blood pressure from drinking, you found you couldn't stop so you came to the program. And you got the same penny or denarius. You got clean. Nothing more, nothing less. Take my buddy Ranulf. He got drunk on really expensive wine (the only kind he drank) and called up something he calls an "entity" (but it's really a demon), and because he had 'glass in hand' the spell to send it back went wrong and, even though he has some control over it (the bigger the command, the more likely it is to be able to disobey-the more it disobeys, the more it CAN disobey) it lives semi-autonomously in a cave near his house. But did he give up tampering with magic? No. He gave up drinking! LOL!

PaulaQ: Are you really saying there's a demon in a cave somewhere? This is a serious discussion, not a joke. But I like the first part of what you said, Ichthus70.

BRUTUS: F*** your demonz and s***. U want DEMONZ, we got em at our low-bottom meetings. >>>>>>

Ichthus70: No, it's really a demon. As in "we are legion." And, Brutus, I can't help but notice you like to put greater-than symbols after your posts, but that the number of them varies. For instance, your three posts have gone from 9 to 8 to 6 >s. Is it that your passion about this thread is diminishing, or are you using a more complex formula obvious only to fellow juggalos?

Ranulf: How did you get a computer?

Wookie: I don't like it when these things get all religious. Can we just stay on topic? And I thought a high-bottom drunk was somebody who

Ichthus70: I know what you thought, Wookie. But you were wrong. Just like you're wrong about the rash on your girlfriend's po-po. It actually *is* herpes-2, and you're now a carrier, and, even though you're lucky enough not to manifest symptoms, you will actually pass the virus on to one partner for every > BRUTUS uses in this thread.

Wookie: How did you interrupt me?

PaulaQ: Where's the moderator?

Ranulf: Sign off, Ichthus70.

BRUTUS: Think your SMART but I DON'T THINK UR SMART. OR FUNNY>>>>>>>>>

Ichthus70: Alas, BRUTUS, that's ten more itchy ladies in the greater Baltimore area. @Wookie: If I told you, I'd have to kill you. @Paula: The moderator actually had his first narcoleptic event, but he should be shutting this down within three minutes. @Ranulf: is that a command?

Ranulf: Yes.

Floridachica: LOL I live in Baltimore, too. Who are you, wookie? Better not be who I think you are ;)

Ichthus70: Protocol, sir.

Ranulf: I, Andrew Ranulf Blankenship, command you by the conditions of your entry into this sphere, and by the power of

Ichthus70: My HUGE penis

Ranulf: such bonds as I have lain upon you to immediately

Ichthus70: display my WHALE of a DONG

Ranulf: sign off this forum and make no further use of the Internet

Ichthus70: (Careful!)

Ranulf: for a period of 40 days and 40 nights.

Ichthus70: As you wish ☺

BRUTUS: F*** BALTIMORE! >>>>>>>>>>>>>>>>>>>>>>>>>>>>>> >> >>

10

Anneke leans on the car next to Andrew, their hips almost touching.

"So if I get good at this stuff . . ."

"Yes."

"Become *luminous*, as you put it . . ."

"You *are* luminous."

"But develop it."

"Yes."

Their faces are close enough to kiss and they probably would, such is the warmth between them, had they not already explored that dead end. The stars sing on, quietly, breaking hearts.

The 302 engine cools and ticks under the Mustang's hood.

"Will I attract weird shit, too?"

A cool breeze makes the trees say *hush.*

Andrew turns his almond eyes up to look at the firmament. As in *see where Christ's blood streams in.* As in *The Tragedy of Dr. Faustus,* by one Christopher Marlowe.

Who also played with.

Fire.

Attracted weird shit.

A murderer's knife in his irreplaceable brain.

A satellite hurtles, a bright grain of fairy dust, a second hand overtaking the flashing minute hand of an airplane far and farther below it. The wonders one sees for the price of a head tilt, a second of humility and presence.

"The entity came because I called it, using a very dangerous spell book I was warned not to use at all."

Why, this is hell, nor am I out of it.

"But you attract other things. Salvador, for example."

"I made Salvador."

"I know. But there's that lady. From the lake. The dead mermaid."

"She's not precisely a mermaid."

"You said she has a tail."

"In the water."

"Not a mermaid."

"Not like the kind you're thinking of."

"But she is dead."

"She died."

"But not really."

"She came back with a tail."

"I've seen her here, you know."

"Are you sure?"

"Am I sure? She smells like fish cunt."

"One gets used to it."

Anneke gives him a raised eyebrow that says, *Oh really? So you're actually fucking that?* to which he flattens his mouth and blinks his eyes twice, thus responding, *What if I am, my Sapphic nonpareil?*

"I've told her not to bother you."

"Well, tell her again. I saw her shiny raccoon eyes in the trees more than once, and she leaves that god-awful smell. She creeps me the fuck out. What's the word again? For what she is."

"Rusalka."

"She better not be fishtailing around here stalking me in some jealous fit or something. Because (a) there's nothing to be jealous about . . ."

"Well, not precisely nothing."

"*Nothing* to be jealous about, and (2)—"

"(b)."

"Right, (b), I'm not to be fucked with."

"What does that mean?"

"Let's hope roosalsa doesn't find out."

"Rusalka. As in 'a rusalka.' Plural *rusalki*. And her name is Nadia."

"Cute. I used to name my fish, too."

"Do me a favor and don't ever confront her. Or threaten her."

"What am I supposed to do if she's creeping around on my land?"

"Just. I'll . . ."

"Talk to her, I know."

"Just don't go near the water if she's around. Don't let her talk you into going near the water. If you're scared, turn on your oven. She hates dry heat."

He's looking at her with serious-Andrew face on.

"Is she dangerous?"

Andrew doesn't say anything.

11

"It's just that I was swimming and I heard Russian. I could not resist. I love to speak Russian," Nadia says.

The next day.

Andrew's house.

"What did you do with him?"

"I took him to the ship, of course, with the others."

The man rolls his long, dark hair into a bun and fixes it in place with a two-pronged little cherrywood fork, samurai-style.

"I thought you agreed only to do that farther away."

She nods gravely, playing with the three-tiered necklace of shells, to which she has added the dog's tag.

Help me get home!

"It is June, you know," she says. Andrew knows she's referring to the festival of Rusal'naya, when her sisters dance in the fields and on the roads from Poland to the Urals, luring young men to watery deaths. "I cannot assist myself."

"*Help myself*, you mean. And the Russian thing is no excuse. I speak Russian. You should speak it with me."

"No," she corrects, holding up a pale finger, "you read Russian. When you force it out from your mouth, it goes unwillingly. Stinking of Ohio."

He smiles at her Slavic palatalization of the *h*.

"What do you know about Ohio?"

"I know Geneva on the Lake. I know Erie."

"That's Pennsylvania."

"Is the same."

He gets up from his couch and goes to the window that gives on the lake, turning his back to her, his shoulders hard and angular as though the antique Japanese robe he wears were hung on a block of tilted wood. She can't see his face but knows he is smiling at the darkness on the horizon. A storm is coming, and he likes storms, especially these nasty little June squalls that form so quickly they shame the weathermen. It will come ashore within the hour, bringing Canadian air with it, and he will put on his leather coat and go out to the balcony.

The coat with the cigarettes in the pocket.

"Is *not* the same," he says, mocking her accent.

"Give me a cigarette," she says.

"You know where they are."

"I know. I just wanted to see if you had become a gentleman yet. But you are still from Ohio."

She gets up and feels around in the pocket of the leather bomber jacket hanging near the door, pulling his yellow packet of American Spirits out and tamping it against her hand to pack the tobacco. Never mind that he has already done this. She redoes everything he does to show that it might be done better. She pulls one out and lights it, frowning at it as though even she cannot believe that something living (or existing, if you prefer) at the bottom of a lake might need tobacco.

"I feel your . . . disapproval," she says. "You have something else to say?"

"You know what I would say."

"That you hate it when I drown them."

"To which you will reply that nothing makes you come as hard as drowning someone, and that you'll come like that for a month afterward. Besides, it's in your nature."

"And you will say go to Oswego to do that. Or Rochester. Or Canada."

"But Canada is so faaaar to svim, and I vill miss you," he says, imitating her again. He takes the cigarette from her mouth and puffs it, ignoring the fishy, dead taste, as he has learned so well to do in other situations. She takes the cigarette back and reaches for the spray bottle full of lake water, misting her dreadlocked auburn mane until it drips.

"Then you will ask," she continues, spearing each of the next words with the end of her cigarette as she enunciates them, "What. Did. You. Do. With. The. Dog?"

"You didn't eat the poor thing."

"I wanted to. He was old, but plump and spoiled with good meat on his thighs. But I knew you would be upset."

"So you ate him and resolved to lie to me about it."

"I cannot lie to you."

"You cannot lie to me and get away with it."

"Is same thing."

"Is not same thing. Is question of intent."

"I left him where he was. The door was open. He can stay, he can go, is up to him. Someone will find him. Maybe you? You want an old shitty dog?"

"Salvador wouldn't like that."

"No," she agrees.

He lights his own Spirit and inhales deeply, exhales slowly, mouth closed, eyes closed, letting the smoke come out of his nose in a luxurious rush.

Poison.

Everything I enjoy is connected to death.

"Did you ever get the feeling that something bad has happened, something just outside your control, and perhaps outside your understanding, which will set in motion a series of events that will lead to deep tragedy? And great loss."

She considers this. Draws smoke with difficulty because she has wet the filter. Lets it out of her nose, as he did.

"Yes."

12

As if summoned, Salvador walks downstairs carrying the soaked and reeking bedsheets from the master bedroom toward the laundry room in the basement. If the framed portrait of Salvador Dalí that served as his head could bear any expression other than the self-consciously crazed eyes of the surrealist, the stick-and-wicker man might raise an eyebrow. He loves to hear his name.

As it is, he swivels his painted gaze at them on his way down, hoping to be called over, but, when he isn't, continues dutifully down the steps on his military-grade prosthetic legs.

Once in the basement, it is all Salvador can do not to spread the sheets out and roll in them; the basket at the center of him holds the salted heart of the border collie he had been before the magus revived him in this form, and that heart still gladdens at strong smells, particularly fishy or fecal ones. He inclines his flat portrait head toward the armful of bedclothes, reveling in their filth. It will be criminal to wash these delicious odors away, but he loves his master as only dogs love, and he sighs a canine sigh and opens the door of the washing machine.

13

The Jehovah's Witnesses come soon after the storm is over. The air is damp and the receding dark clouds in the east make their white shirts pop as they walk up the drive between the young maple trees. Andrew stands on his front porch with his leather coat on, knowing he looks and smells every inch the career sinner, combing out waist-length hair redolent of tobacco and myrrh. He frowns at a new white hair, plucks it, winds it around a finger.

It will take them a moment to make it up the steep walk.

He realizes he is about to sigh, recognizes impatience as a sign of entitlement, thinks he really should read another book about Buddhism and try to meditate. He has a date with being Buddhist, but he isn't there yet.

And here come two of God's warriors, both of them African American, one in his sixties, one about twenty.

At least they mean it, I'll give them that. They wear out a lot of shoe leather doing what Jesus said to do. No Christmas. No Halloween. But this is a little like trick-or-treating. Do they eat candy? Do I even have any candy?

The older one is slowing them down.

That guy doesn't need any candy.

That wasn't very Buddhist, and he's not fat, just a little soft around the middle, and probably a grandfather, so give him a break.

Maybe that kid's grandfather?

The elder raises a hand, smiles a winning smile.

"Quite a driveway you have here," he says. "You must be in good shape!"

"I might be if I ever left. I'm a hermit. All I do up here is talk to God and wait for strangers to come so I can tell them God's plan for them. Didn't they warn you about me at the Kingdom Hall?"

"Well, they did say . . ."

"Where's Barbara?"

"She moved to Syracuse."

"More action in the big city. A rich crop of the godless there, I tell you."

"Something like that."

He stands with his hands on his hips, bent forward just a little, his elbows fanning out his open coat, Sears, granddad gray. Tie the color of an excited brick. He's smiling and panting, catching his breath.

"You okay?" Andrew says.

He nods, still panting.

The younger Witness senses he should say something, but he's a shy one. He's also more than a little distracted by the garden of rocks and rusted-out cars piled in Andrew's front yard. The '65 Mustang he wrecked, an old Chevy truck, a Dodge Dart. All of them wound through with young trees and big, handsome boulders. Its aesthetic leans just more toward art installation than junkyard fodder.

The boy is fascinated with it, especially the bleached longhorn steer skull crowning it all, its dry teeth yellowing in their sockets, its horns leather-wrapped at the base, slightly tilted.

The lad knows there's something more to it than meets the eye.

He knows he's the one who's supposed to break the silence, though, so he speaks.

"Quite a . . . quite a storm, wasn't it?"

"Sure was," Andrew says.

They exchange a look.

The boy glances at the steer skull again, then tilts his head a little bit at the magus, like a dog trying to process a strange sound.

Holy shit, is this kid luminous?

A natural?

Andrew smiles more broadly.

Damn if he isn't. Marching around with armfuls of the Watchtower *when he's just humming with receptivity for magic. Anneke's got a little, but this kid's like I was.*

Ready to explode.

One spell book away from a lifetime of . . .

What?

Now the older man stands.

"Arthur. Arthur Madden," he says, holding out a hand. "And this handsome fellow is Marcus Madden, Jr. No relation. Just kidding."

"Andrew Blankenship."

"Nice to meet you, Mr. Blankenship."

This is a genuinely nice guy. I'll keep it dialed down.

It's hard to keep the mischief out of his voice.

"Would you like to come in?"

They leave twenty minutes later.

It isn't the conversation about the reliability of the gospels, nor is it Andrew's Socratic minefield of questions; it isn't even Andrew's assertion that a God who intended sex for procreation alone would not have built a clitoris, nor made it so compatible with the tongue. ("Must be nice to be so close to the lake," Arthur says to change the subject, although Andrew enjoys the unintended symbolism, as he enjoys that this is how faultlessly polite Arthur chooses to comment about the fishy smell permeating the house.)

It's Marcus.

Marcus sees too much.

First he's distracted, looking out at the lake through the back windows.

"Is there something more interesting than us out there, young man?"

"I . . . thought I saw a . . . dolphin."

"Lakes don't have dolphins," Arthur says.

"We have some very big fish," Andrew offers.

The kid looks at him dubiously.

"Very big," Andrew says.

They return to the topic of whether homosexuality is a sin or a natural state of being. Marcus always lets Arthur (his great-uncle, as it turns out) field the questions, but Andrew drags him in from time to time.

"C'mon, Marcus—you've seen gay kids."

Marcus almost laughs at that and Arthur steers the conversation back around to God's capacity for forgiveness, clearly meaning Andrew.

Offers of Witness literature are countered with offers of Buddhist, Taoist, or Confucian books.

Mutual refusal.

"Or, if you want to come back another time, I've got a reference library that might really interest you."

He directs this at Marcus, trying not to sound creepy, and failing.

When Salvador brings Andrew French-press coffee, the young man goes gray, looks at Arthur, watches Arthur nod at the servant, and doesn't understand why Arthur isn't shitting himself, too.

That's because Arthur sees a young Spanish man who bears a slight resemblance to John Leguizamo. You, on the other hand, see the false human form flicker from time to time, and that's when you see the lacquered branches that make his radius and ulna, the awkward but delicate way his artist's-model articulated hands pluck a spoon from the tray or press down the plunger of the coffee press. You glimpse the steam wafting over the portrait. You see ghosts, too, and hear voices. You think you're crazy sometimes and sometimes you think you're possessed. But really you're just awake.

How unlucky.

"I want to go, Uncle."

Arthur raises an eyebrow at the boy, suggesting that a conversation about manners will take place on the drive back, but then he checks his watch, a big seventies-style Timex on a silver watchband.

Salvador offers them both coffee.

Arthur politely declines.

Half turns his wrist to check his watch again.

Andrew realizes Arthur has no cell phone and loves him for it.

Marcus stares, suddenly peaceful, as though resigned to the mental breakdown he thinks he's having.

"Well, I guess Mrs. Simpson will be bringing the car around soon, and we'd best not keep her waiting. Thank you for your hospitality, Mr. Blankenship."

"Thank you for the conversation."

All three men rise.

Salvador is standing between them and the front door, so Marcus steals for the side door leading from the kitchen.

"Oh, no!" Andrew says. "The stairs over there are dangerous. It's better if you go out the way you came."

Salvador moves aside, bowing slightly.

This is my house, and you must exit the same way you entered.

"Remember what I said about the library," he tells Marcus. "It might explain things a bit."

"Thank you," Marcus says quietly, but he just wants out.

His eyes don't meet Andrew's again.

It is all he can do not to race ahead of his ponderous uncle, race down the wooded drive and into the heated SUV where Mrs. Simpson hums along with 1950s music on the radio and Jesus and the angels still hold fast against the devil's wicked, confusing world.

14

Andrew lights the oil lamps on the big pine farm table that sits in the middle of his library while Salvador hovers near; the magus never lets the wicker man, whose wooden left hand is newer and paler than the right one, handle fire.

The servant writes on the Etch-a-Sketch around his neck, turning the knobs with his clever fingers, his wicker hips moving gently with the ghost of his wagging tail.

HELP?

"Wine," Andrew says, and Salvador turns his portrait gaze toward the hall, starting off in that direction; then he seems to remember something important—he shudders, making a sound like a dry whimper and shaking his flat head. He clasps his hands in supplication and stares at Andrew now, still huskily whining.

"I know, boy. That was mean. I was just testing. Fizzy water will do."

The automaton visibly relaxes and hurries out of the library. Andrew goes to the hanging shelf, a weathered blue bookcase suspended close to the high ceiling by belts, just out of reach, a baby doll with wild hair and no eyes hanging from a shoestring noose nailed to its bottom. An Indian-print blanket veils the volumes waiting within. Andrew stands close to the doll and says, "Hello, Sally. I declare myself to be Andrew Ranulf Blankenship, son of George

Blankenship, grandson of Charles Thaddeus Blankenship, and I am the true owner of this house and these books."

The doll kicks her feet now to start herself gently swinging. After three swings' worth of momentum, she latches onto Andrew's hair with one of her plastic hands. She feels his face with her other hand and, satisfied, kisses his cheek and goes inanimate again, swinging limply from the bottom of the shelf. The belts that hold the shelf loosen themselves now and it lowers so he can reach within. He pulls aside the curtain. The power drill that would have lashed out and blinded anyone but Andrew whirrs once to show it's on duty. The drill sits on the bottom of two levels, next to a rubber cobra and a mummified fist wearing brass knuckles (this Hand of Glory doesn't pick locks or light candles or stop hearts—it belonged to a Cossack pugilist hanged for beating his wife's lover and that man's two brothers to death). On the top level, nine identical-looking huge leather books lie stacked in threes, bindings out. The magus eases his fingers around the second book in the rightmost pile and slides it out from under its top neighbor, which lifts itself up obligingly. Each of the eight decoys holds a nasty surprise for anyone, Andrew included, who begins to pull it out; the book below the actual book, for example, contains several dozen dried, wormlike Amazonian parasites, normally river dwellers, that will slither under the clothes of any intruders and race for the urethra, fighting each other, if necessary, for the honor of burrowing within and affixing themselves in front of the bladder with backward-facing spines. Only a blessing from the shaman of a nearly extinct tribe administered in the actual Amazon would make the thing let go, but this has to happen within a week or the beast will catch fire. Not as immediate as the shotgun shells (once owned by Doc Holliday) that wait in book two, but any spell-caster (and who else would have gotten this far?) will have trouble concentrating on anything above the waist while the wigglers do their wiggly work.

He cradles the book and sets it on the table, now pulling a dictionary of Old Russian from a more ordinary shelf behind him, fetching a spiral notebook and pencils, and sitting down to read. Of the four books he brought home from forests near the Volga (each with its own shelf and booby traps), this is one of the two he understands least.

After *The Book of Sorrows*, that is.

But this one.

*Of the Soul and Its Mutability and
How Best to Survive Death*

He knows, as well, that it is the most precious book he owns, and that any magus who becomes aware of its existence will stop at nothing to get it. It is said that Rasputin was protected by some of the lesser spells held within, and that Koschey the Deathless mastered the whole thing before the crone extorted it from him in the time of the Tsar Alexander II.

So far, Andrew has come to understand parts of it but is afraid to try anything beyond a sort of dream-walking wherein he sends his consciousness, still well tethered to his sleeping body, to roam the beaches of the lake or through walls into the homes of his neighbors.

He gave this last bit up after observing his misanthropic survivalist neighbor John Dawes (across Willow Fork Road, binocular distance) drunkenly shaving his scrotum with a straight razor while watching a *Gilligan's Island* rerun. The sight had so startled Andrew that he experienced a sort of spasm and suspects he nearly snapped his tether. He has seen nothing yet to convince him that an actual hell exists (or that it does not), but leaving his body comatose while his soul haunts the house of a lonely, gun-happy ball-shaver sounds close enough. Now he confines his experiments to beachcombing and low-altitude flight, never straying more than a mile or two away from himself; he intends to push himself further if he can understand how to get back into himself without the comforting astral umbilicus that anchors him. Getting back into your own body without it is the first step. Next and harder will be taking over another body, which is a fearful business that smacks of actual evil. Temporary possession is possible, but the language in *Of the Soul* warns that stuffing two souls in one body is draining to both: The original host might succeed in pushing you out and into death's embrace; if not, the presence of multiple souls in one body attracts "other beings,"

Sign off, Ichthus70

whose company might be undesirable. Permanent occupation is, of course, murder.

And yet, one might use this to live indefinitely, practicing a sort of biological alchemy, transmuting the lead of aging and sick bodies into the gold of healthy, young ones. One might live on in beauty and strength for centuries.

Andrew strongly suspects some are doing this now.

He often muses that if he were to walk into a room full of those who actually run the world, the *invisibles* that heads of state and oil barons take *their* marching orders from, it would look like the audition room for a TV soap opera: They would all be lovely; they would all look twenty-five to forty, and whether this was accomplished by the witchcraft of science or the science of witchcraft would be even money. Those who trade in magic value money less than others, true, because they can always manufacture, steal, win, or conjure it as needed; most really powerful conjurers regard those who hoard money as nothing but glorified squirrels saving for a winter they will never live to see. But when you stack enough zeroes behind an integer, enough, say, to bribe a prime minister or buy a vast old-growth forest, even a sorcerer won't ignore it; a handful of people may well be buying their way into extended youth.

"But not eternal youth," Andrew says at half voice.

Nothing is forever.

A memory makes him almost smile, and he shakes it off, turning his mind to the problem of the tether.

Now Salvador walks into the room and pours Gerolsteiner water from a clay pitcher (one of Anneke's) into Andrew's glass, hoping to receive another command, but resigning himself to being ignored—his master has inclined his head to study, and, although the days are past when the dry man with the dog's heart has to clear two empty wine bottles from the table and cork a third before pulling his sodden master to bed by the heels, it will be nearly dawn before the magus shuts his book.

15

"Get that *pinché* thing away from me," Chancho says.

Ten A.M., time for training.

Chancho has taken the morning off from the North Star Garage, which is his prerogative since he owns it. Todd, Rick, and Gonzo, his three employees who vary so much in height they could be a totem pole, will handle things at a slower pace in his absence, but they will still get the work done well, and God help them if they fart around and charge for the farting-around time. Chancho wants his customers to tell all their friends how cheap repairs are at North Star, how fast the work gets done, how polite the mechanics are. Gonzo, six and a half feet tall but so thin he looks like he stepped out of an El Greco, handles the counter and the phone—he wears his hair long and has a shitty goatee he used to wear a rubber band around

Why the f do you wear that thing in your beard?
You can say fuck *to me, I won't be offended.*

I don't say fuck *no more.*
You just did.
Why do you wear it?
I dunno.
Then stop. I won't make you cut the beard, even though it makes you look like a pimp, but that rubber band got to go. Put it around some money.
I don't have any.
That's because you put it in the pinché *bank. Banks are full of robbers. Put rubber bands around that shit and bury it.*
Why is it okay to say shit *but not* fuck*?*
. . .
I need to think about this.

but Gonzo has a voice like wildflower honey pouring winter-slow from a jar, and eyes like Paul Newman.

Everybody likes Gonzo.

The people of Cayuga County are still a little on the xenophobic side, and the Mexican invasion is only just beginning to lap at the ankles of upstate New York, so bearish, tattooed Chancho doesn't want his brown face to be the first one they see at North Star.

He doesn't need their love.

Just their business.

When it comes to love, he gets all he needs from his wife and Jésus Christ. Consuela got fat, but Jésus stayed skinny; he would have preferred the reverse, since he only has to *chingar* Consuela, but her face is still pretty and he remembers how her body was in Mexico and Texas. Maybe she does the same for him—he's got a bigger belly now, too, and fair is fair.

"No, seriously, *brujo*, get this *cabrón* away from me. He gives me the heebie-jeebies."

Salvador stands with two bottles of mineral water balanced on a tray, his hips barely moving in the echo of a wagging tail. Salvador remembers the big man with his smell of motor oil and cumin from his four-legged days. Chancho used to throw the Frisbee for him, and praise him for how high he jumped, and scratch his ears. His master explained to him that Chancho is afraid of him now, but that he shouldn't take that personally.

Salvador really wants Chancho to like him again.

He moves a little closer with the tray.

Chancho squints, takes his mineral water, crosses himself.

16

Minutes later.

Chancho holds the striking pads for Andrew and begins to call off punches.

"Jab. Jab. Right cross. Jab. Jab. Double jab. Left hook."

Chancho calls these words at the outer limit of audibility, as gently as if he were inventorying flowers at a funeral parlor.

"Now move forward with me," he says, lets Andrew push him across the yard. He no longer calls punches, just holds the pads up and lets his friend improvise.

"Now punch while backing up. This is very important. You can knock a guy out who thinks he has you."

Chancho moves forward slowly but insistently, alternating pads, nodding when Andrew lands an especially crisp one.

The taped-up gloves tattoo the taped-up pads in the backyard,

the staccato mixing pleasantly with birdsong and a tractor straddling asphalt and dirt on the road out front.

"Don't puss out on me," Chancho says, now gently boxing out at
Andrew's ears with the mitts to show him he's letting his guard droop.

"Switch," he says, and Andrew takes the mitts, preparing himself
for the barely padded brickstorm he will now be fielding. He's glad
for the rest all the same; his drills have left him wheezing.

The staccato comes faster and harder now, the bigger man pushing the lanky one back, bobbing his head and shoulders like something between an angry chimp and a piston. Chancho had been a
formidable boxer fifteen years ago, and might have gone professional
had he not been so fond of beer—he had never etched a boxer's six-
pack into his belly. The obvious way to beat Chancho was to wear him
out, and enough of them did to keep him from quitting his day job.

But many did not; to wear Chancho out, you had to be able to
duck his bear-swat punches, which was hard, or absorb them, which
was damn near impossible.

And you had to not smoke a pack a day.

"Okay, enough punching."

"Thank the gods."

"Now elbows," Chancho all but whispers, smiling his big smile
under the uneven, dated mustache, just going gray. Only the soul
patch under his chin keeps him from looking like he stepped out of a
Starsky and Hutch episode.

Chancho throws elbows first, so the magus can rest his lungs a
bit more. The tattooed arms lash out and bite the pads deep, the left
elbow flashing the star tattoo of Texas, where the burly man lived
until he found Jésus and got out of moving drugs. Or, rather, protecting people who moved drugs.

Chancho would always be the first guy you'd want to meet in the
ring and the last guy you'd want to meet in the parking lot. Or see
coming up to your sliding glass door with a *lucha libre* mask on.

Andrew is feeling dizzy with exhaustion, but Chancho wants

him to push through it, so he does, the sweat drenching his long hair even in its ponytail, making his bare chest glisten and soaking the waistband of his jeans.

"Now you. Twist at the hips so I feel it. You're little, so it's even more important for you to get your hips in it. I want twenty on each side."

When the drenched and reeking pads are lying on the table and the panting men sit down on their benches, Salvador walks from the back door carrying Mexican Coca-Cola bottles on a tray.

"Good boy," Andrew says. "Thank you."

Six years now since he used his secret books to bring the dog back. Chancho watches Salvador with a fixed eye; looking away from the clockwork figure is difficult, especially when he swivels his Dalí head around to meet your gaze. The thing moves so . . . fluidly.

Chancho likes Mexican Coke because it's in glass bottles and has sugar, not that corn syrup crap they drench everything in now.

He likes it so much he doesn't cross himself when he takes the bottle from the stick-man.

Instead he turns his gaze on Andrew.

"You've got to quit smoking."

Andrew, who knows how green he looks, just nods, sipping his cola.

"I know. But isn't that pretty pot-kettle? You smoke."

The sweat on the green bottles looks heavenly to Chancho and he studies his, pressing it now to the side of his temple.

"I know."

"You smoke *my* cigarettes, for fuck's sake."

"Your cigarettes are *good*."

"So buy some. They'll sell 'em to you."

"Got to go to the hippie shop for that."

"I'm just saying a smoker ought not tell a man to quit."

"I don't wheeze like a busted vacuum. I ought to quit. You *got* to quit."

"Maybe."

"Ain't there a *pinché* spell for that?"

"Yeah. It's right next to the one for quitting drinking."

Chancho smiles.

"Maybe we could get you a hip'motist."

"Ever seen one?"

"Heard about 'em."

"Well, they scare me fuckless," Andrew says. "I saw one make a guy think he came all over himself right at a café table, so that when the waitress came the guy pulled the tablecloth half off trying to cover up his lap."

Chancho laughs, broadly enough to show the gap where the tooth behind the canine should have been.

"Funny. A man scaring *you*. Just a man, I mean. When you play with dead girls and dead dogs and stuff. That fishy girl, you said she kilt herself, right?"

"Her sister stole her man and she threw herself off the bluffs."

"McIntyre Bluffs?" Chancho asked.

Andrew nodded.

"'Cause I know a guy took his lady there and they both fell off f'ing. Only nobody died. But he got his back broke, but could still walk. I think she landed on him."

"Nadia died. Broke that pretty neck back in 1926."

Chancho squints at him and tilts his head up, assessing.

"You need to get right with Jésus."

"I'm fine with Jésus."

Silence.

"Can I drive the Mustang?"

"If you shut up about Jésus."

Chancho smiles.

17

Years ago.

Night.

Another Mustang, the '65.

Upside down, wheels spinning, engine running. Andrew uncomfortable, scratched, confused. Can't reach the keys to shut the motor off because there's a branch in the way. Led Zeppelin is singing about California but it sounds wrong because only one speaker works.

He climbs out into cool spring air, smelling radiator fluid and oil.

Nearly falls; something is wrong with his leg.

The peasants! The peasants cut my leg off!

He looks down, but his leg is there.

Mostly.

His jeans are ripped and lots of little somethings hurt, far away.

His heart is pounding.

Just breathe.

Just walk.

Andrew walks, his back to the lamplit greenery and spinning wheels of the wrecked Mustang.

Ford.

First on Race Day!

(F)ucked (OR) (D)ying.

Andrew in his snakeskin boots and tight black jeans, walking down 104A, tempted to stop at a house but senses he's done something wrong; he needs to get back to his own house and Sarah. He'll be safe there; he'll sleep and he'll know what to do in the morning.

The left leg hurts; he sits on a guardrail and pulls his boot off, pours blood out of it, it won't go back on.

He holds it and keeps limping, waving off several cars that stop, actually yells at one big, Swedish-looking fellow who insists that he should get in his pickup truck, but he won't go away. Looks like he means to wrestle him into the truck. Until Andrew points at the big man's face and gives him a cramp in the cheek muscles

How Prospero of you oh that wasn't nice he just wants to help but I have to have to just please God get home

and the big man drives off, scared because he knows the wild, injured little man did it to him. Andrew doesn't understand how mud got on him, but mud is drying in his hair and on his face and he pulls at this, spits on his hand and wipes his cheek.

The boot swinging in the other hand, the magus limping.

Only ten miles to Dog Neck Harbor, should be there by morning.

He waves off two more cars, but the third one pulls in front of him, its roof exploding in sharp but beautiful flashes of blue light.

Andrew says some words in medieval Russian.

Andrew disappears.

Knows the spell won't last, hobbles into a soy field.

Invisible.

I don't drive so well but I'm not too drunk to fucking DISAPPEAR!

He curls up in the soy plants, feels something like a beetle crawl on his hand but doesn't slap at it.

Says "I pardon you" in a German accent like Ralph Fiennes in *Schindler's List* and laughs until he passes out.

Dreams his car is radioactive, luminous with it, enough to poison Cayuga County, that he has to shovel enough dirt over it to protect everybody, but he can't. He just can't. And he holds his shovel and cries. Because he really, really fucked up.

In the morning, a trio of dogs sniffing him, a man's good, lined face, a giant looking down on him.

Fu fu fu, I smell Russian bones.

"Ambulance is on its way. You want some water?"

He does.

O God I fucked up I did.

He did.

More than he knows.

He sits up.

He reaches into his pocket, thinking something in there will help him.

A napkin with a note on it, a semicircle of cabernet from where the glass rested on it, a crescent moon of vice and folly.

I want you in the library tonight.
I want you to fuck me in that leather chair.
—S.

When did she slip that into his pocket?

Is it even from today?

Sarah.

"Sit up slow. No hurry."

The farmer again.

He shows the farmer the napkin note.

"Do you know when this was written?"

The farmer shakes his head.

"A pretty girl wrote it. She writes grant applications. And they say she plays guitar. And laughs and sings."

The man smiles, points at the ambulance, walks off to talk to them, leaves a jug with a thumbprint of red paint on it.

Andrew notices the bright red silo.
Nice work, mister.
The water tastes like plastic.
And dirt.
Dirt in my mouth.
La la la la.

18

"Whatcha thinking about, *brujo*?"
    "My personal bottom."
    "Bang!" Chancho says, swerving the wheel just a little, grinning.
    The Mustang is doing seventy on a two-lane country highway.
    Andrew jerks, grabs the door.
    "Whoever told you you were funny was a *pendejo*."
    Chancho corrects his pronunciation.

19

Andrew wears his hair in a ponytail to do yard work at the Zautke house because he feels too effeminate in his samurai bun. He walks behind the power mower trying to look like he knows what he's doing, working his way from the curb to the nondescript blue house, circumnavigating the stone birdbath, jogging it past the flagpole, but Salvador has been mowing Andrew's yard for the last few years, and Andrew's feet aren't practiced at taking the turns. He leaves hand-sized patches of taller grass and then has to double back for them; he looks at the shorn front half of the yard and it strikes him funny because it looks just a bit like Karl's squared-off old-man crew cut.

Karl watches him from the porch for a second.

Wants to shout "Need anything?" at his daughter's strange AA friend, but knows he's on the wagon like Anneke and all Karl has that isn't beer is cheap Pick & Save orange juice just this side of brown or tap water just this side of clear, water that tastes like . . . what the hell does the water here taste like?

Not water.

Goddamn Niagara Mohawk anyway.

Karl Zautke hasn't been feeling well lately, his lymph glands swollen up like acorns, his breath short. Not bad enough to go to the hospital, but bad enough that Anneke is coming every other day now instead of twice a week.

She does his dishes, cooks two days' worth of food for him, does his sour laundry.

But does he even try to take care of his flagging health?

Karl drinks his Pabst Blue Ribbon, enjoying the yeasty, cold, carbonated bite on his tongue. It's a good, simple beer for when you're thirsty, not one of these perfumey, pumpernickel microbrews queered up by guys with sideburns.

Anneke has her big suede work gloves on, balanced on an aluminum ladder that has seen better days, shearing branches from the maple tree that had started flirting with the shingles on the west side of the house. She totters just a little, rights herself. Karl sees this, puts down his beer, comes over, and holds the ladder.

"Daddy," she shouts, just loud enough to get over the mower's chop. She points her gloved finger at the front door, meaning he should retake his place on his sagging chair, but Karl holds the ladder stubbornly, breathing hard through his nose and smiling at her. She doesn't like how red his face is.

It does feel steadier.

If Karl Ernest Zautke is anything, it's solid.

They sit on the porch, the three of them, Karl mopping his head from time to time with a kitchen towel. Karl Zautke is just a little too big for the wicker chair beneath him; Andrew has been watching it collapse in slow motion for a year and a half. Anneke would get him a new one except that she knows Karl finds half-collapsed things comfortable.

Dad.

My same Dad but old now.

Sick.

Doesn't drink like he's sick.

Dad's on his third beer, and Anneke has told herself she'll just pluck from his hand the next one he dares to open in front of her.

Karl senses he's on the last beer he can get away with and knows better than to test her. Settles into his buckling throne.

Andrew feels mismatched sitting on his folding chair, sharing the porch with the two outsized Teutons, like a visitor from a fine-boned, nut-brown little tribe that mows the conqueror's lawns and fetches them PBR against their doctors' orders.

Anneke and he can't share their vulgar wiseasseries in front of Karl, so Andrew confines himself to the practical.

Karl doesn't feel comfortable talking about his illness or the day-to-day problems it creates in front of Andrew. Anneke enjoys having her favorite men together, and if they don't know how to connect, that's their problem.

"Car running okay?" Andrew asks.

Karl drives a Jeep Cherokee Andrew has bewitched to keep from breaking down, and has further bewitched so it will come to a safe stop if the driver passes out. Andrew has a real gift for cars, knows how to improvise automotive magic, massage it into their axles and chassis, synthesize it into their gears and skins. He knows very well the Jeep is running smoothly, but he never knows what to say to the big ex-sailor.

"Yeah, great," Karl says. "Thanks again for changing her oil."

"My pleasure."

Two heartbeats go by.

"Mustang running all right?" Karl says, nodding at Andrew's car.

"Yes, sir."

"Sure is a nice one."

"Thanks."

"Turquoise was an interesting choice."

"That's how she came."

"Paint jobs are pricey."

"They can be."

Two more heartbeats.

"You need any juice or maybe a glass of water? Must be thirsty. Hot as heck out here."

It really isn't all that hot.

"Water would be great."

Both men start to get up, but Anneke gently puts her hand on her dad's shoulder so he keeps his seat.

She goes to get the water.

"So," Karl says, looking back at the door to make sure Anneke isn't coming yet. He's winding up to ask something awkward, and Andrew's skin crawls.

How does he make me feel twelve and tongue-tied?

"Yes, sir?"

Again with the *sir*.

This kid doesn't sir anybody else, I'd bet on it.

Knows I served and wants me to like him.

Kid hell, he's like forty, just wears his hair long so he looks like Pocahontas. Probably puts shoe polish in it.

Probably uses moisturizer and plucks his eyebrows, too.

Goes down to the day spa in Syracuse.

I can see this guy getting a pedicure.

I want to like him, I do.

Anneke sure spends enough time with him.

Guy and a girl don't spend that kind a time together without.

Is he?

I kinda hope he is.

"Are you and Anneke . . . ?"

"Sir?"

There's no way in hell.

A guy like this.

Unless she likes him 'cause he looks a little like a girl.

I don't even know if it works that way.

Shit, here she comes.

"Are you staying for dinner?"

Anneke hands Andrew a water glass with faded sunflowers painted on it, the last one of the eight-piece set from her childhood.

"You know we are, Dad."

But only Anneke spends the night.

20

Night.

Andrew opens his eyes in the near-darkness of his own house, two wicks of his three-wick bedside pillar candle still alight, nearly but not quite drowned in red wax.

His paperback copy of *The Baron in the Trees* lies open facedown on the pillow.

Something is watching him.

He knows what.

He also knows it's three in the morning.

That's when it most often comes.

"Ichabod."

The entity doesn't respond.

"Ichabod, say something."

"Something."

It has chosen a little girl's voice.

"Manifest in a form I won't find disagreeable."

"*Ja, mein* Captain," it says.

A gently glowing Katzenjammer Kid, the blond one, appears, sitting on Andrew's leather chair, its legs primly crossed at the knee. While Andrew appreciates the novelty of seeing the little German cartoon boy in 3-D, it *is* mildly disturbing. Perhaps a cat's whisker shy of being *disagreeable*.

Ichabod has a sniper's precision when it comes to causing unease.

Ichabod isn't its name, of course, but then neither was the long

Sumerian name whose first three syllables sounded vaguely like *Ichabod*.

"Did you touch my foot?"

"Just playing little piggies."

"I don't like that."

"It seemed the gentlest way to wake you."

"Don't do it again."

"Is that a command?"

"Yes. Are you going to insist on protocol?"

"Not this time. It seems a modest enough request. Note to myself: no touching Master Andrew's sleeping piggies. Check. Anything else?"

Andrew sits up, gathering the sheet around him.

"Tell me why you're here."

"What, here?" it says, and now the Katzenjammer Kid is sitting in bed next to Andrew, hands on lap, looking like a child who wants to be read a story. It gives off cold like a ham just out of the freezer. It has chosen to be heavy—it depresses the bed.

Andrew forces himself not to recoil.

"Go back to the chair and remain there until I dismiss you."

It blinks its big cartoon eyes twice.

Andrew draws a breath to begin the formal command, but Ichabod winks out and winks back in on the leather chair, sitting lotus-style.

"Well?"

"Well what?" it says in an incongruously masculine bass.

"Tell me why you're here."

"Can't I just visit? I get lonely in my lair. There's not a great deal to do there."

"Then go back where you came from."

"And miss the rest of your life? I wouldn't dream of it."

Andrew sighs anxiously.

It speaks again, using its fallback voice, petulant intellectual.

"I'm worried about you, Captain. Master. Master Andrew Commander."

"Tell me why."

"You know why."

"I don't."

"It's time."

"I don't know what you're talking about."

"Only because you don't want to know. But you need to know."

"Just say what you have to say and go."

"You might have let me destroy your rusalka. When I offered."

"I don't want her destroyed."

"But now it's too late."

"For what?"

"That Russian she drowned was an extraordinary specimen."

"Fucking tell me."

At Andrew's flash of anger, the cartoon child flushes red as though someone had poured blood into it and begins to flicker.

Becomes a writhing squid for a split second, then reverts to Katzenjammer Kid.

"Some people see God's hand in coincidence. Are you one of these?"

Andrew seethes.

"Just . . ."

It cuts him off.

"Ask your rusalka for the dog's collar."

"Why?"

"You will want to research its owner."

21

"There are two kinds of users," Andrew tells Anneke. "Plodders and intuitives. Also called disciples and heirs."

Anneke is walking a penny around in the palm of her hand. Moving small objects is almost always how it starts; Andrew has told her she has to find something she can move and move it three times a day for at least ten minutes.

She favors the penny.

They are sitting in her inside studio, the one she uses when the weather won't allow work al fresco. Today, through the sliding glass door, it rains in indecisive spits and sputters, bedewing the greenery outside, greenery all the more dazzling when overtopped by gray.

All manner of pottery in various stages of completion crowds Anneke's little workshop; ten whitish-gray mugs rest upside down on a board over a plastic tub of clay. Cedar Heights clay, to be exact, its yellow letters emblazoned on a stack of red sacks upon which a clay-bedabbed tower of DVD cases leans, as if eager to consummate, toward the DVD player and television on high. Everything leans and balances in here. Everything is smeared, dabbed, or stippled with clay, white or red.

Her remote controls, one for TV, one for DVD player, have been wrapped in plastic, likewise clay-smudged and fingerprinted.

More inverted mugs, and a smattering of coffee cups and saucers, congregate on a card table, along with a tall vase topped by a precarious-looking round wooden board. A *quarantaine* of rosettes dries atop this board, the same rosettes that, when fitted with brass pins and painted Tudor red, will adorn the vests and doublets of the acting cast of the Renaissance festival to distinguish them from unpaid costumed enthusiasts. That is to say, when a drunken *Landsknecht* in rather convincing armor barfs on your lady fair, the lack of said rosette upon his breast will mark this as an unsanctioned event and indemnify both the festival and the troupe of professional improvisers that animate its lanes.

"Which kind am I?" she says.

Meaning plodder or intuitive.

"A bit of both, like me," he says. "But more intuitive, I think."

Her brow wrinkles, and although she doesn't look away from the exercise in her palm, it's clear she wants more explanation.

"An intuitive just *does* it, doesn't need as many implements, can do small things almost immediately. Like what you're doing. An intuitive is more luminous, must in fact be luminous from the start."

"And a planner?"

"Plodder."

"Plodder."

"They hate that word. And some of them are a bit contemptful and jealous toward intuitives."

"Sounds like you're a bit contemptful of them. *Plodder* is an ugly word. What do they call themselves?"

"*Disciples* is the preferred term when they differentiate, but they don't differentiate the same way. They see themselves as disciplined and those who don't spend their lives bent over books as lazy. Thing is, they're all geniuses. The plodders. To come at magic without luminosity, you have to be smart enough to work for Apple or IBM or crack codes for the CIA, and a few of them do. Their books are much more complex, more like rocket science; more glyphs and formulas, though one of them would say *formulae*. They *think* their way into belief, crack the code of magic and understanding with brainpower. They aren't all luminous at the start, but they get there; they make a fire with sticks where naturals already have a fire. But the payoff is that they can do really big, astounding things. Think of it as learning a language with books and tapes versus being born in that country. Nonluminous plodders are like non-native speakers. But English was Nabokov's second language, and he wrote *Lolita*. Or was it his third language? He spoke French, too."

"Nabokov, huh? Was that a jab?"

"At who?"

She raises an eyebrow, keeps moving the shard.

"Oh, right."

I forgot you're a sex offender.

"Not consciously."

Anneke is officially a witch, albeit a novice. The first time she jiggled that penny, Andrew felt the small tingle of magic waking up. She collapsed and sobbed afterward, but that was not unusual. He had a similarly emotive reaction the first time he spun a pop top. The first spell is usually some light levitation. Small magic, admittedly, a mustard seed from which some build mountains.

He leans forward just a little so the black iron conical stove behind her appears to top her head like a witch's hat. Sandalwood incense leaks smoke behind her. He leans the other way so it appears to come from her nose.

"What are you doing?" she says, her concentration split, Abraham Lincoln dead again on dull copper in her hand.

"Sorry. Nothing."

She tosses the penny into a broken mug full of coins, lights a cigarette, gives him one. He totters the lighter out of her hand, levitates it into his.

"Show-off. Can you light it?"

"It's a more precise motion, takes more strength."

"Yes, but can you?"

"Burns more gas."

She squints her eyes at him.

"Magic burns fuel. Continuous spells burn fuel continuously. Spikes in magic use can disrupt those spells. Think of an outlet, energy surges."

"Continuous spells? Like what?"

"Health. Youth. Luck. One well-cast luck spell in Vegas and a user can clean up. Only not in the MGM Mirage casinos—Mandalay Bay, Bellaggio, I forget the rest but I have a list—they have users working for them, kicking others out. Or worse."

"Youth, huh? You running one of those right now, Mr. Looks Thirty-Five?"

"You should know. Try to detect it."

She closes her eyes.

"Open them and think about what you want to know."

Now she looks at him, really looks at him. Then she feels it, subtle as cat's breath. The hairs on her forearms stand up just a little.

"You vain motherfucker. So you can't flick the lighter or you'll get liver spots?"

"I'm a bit stronger than that," he says, and the lighter sparks, lights up, Andrew smiling with his hands behind his head. "It's just that I have to focus more. It's easier just to light it by hand. It's like Skype."

"Excuse me?"

"Skype. It's . . ."

"I know what it is, what's the relevance?"

"I used to have a crystal ball."

"Sounds like a song title."

He sings.

"I used to have a crystal ball,
It really was a fishbowl."

He pauses.

"Can't think of a rhyme?"

"No."

"Just say it."

"It was a bit of a pain in the ass. The other person had to have a glass something-or-other with exactly the same spell cast into it, and you both had to concentrate; if you got distracted, the image faded or distorted or went away. You're about to ask if my fishbowl rang, and it did. Really, it quivered when the other person wanted to talk, but I taped a little bell to it."

"I was going to ask if there was a fish in it."

"There used to be, before I enchanted it. I'm not good with fish."

"No, you're good with cars and dead people. And you're intuitive, like me. Who's a plodder?"

"I know one."

"Powerful?"

"Scary powerful. Young, too. Lives in Lincoln Park. Chicago. And she's working on a project for me right now."

22

Chicagohoney85: The Mikhail Dragomirov you're looking for is Mikhail "Misha" Yevgenievich Dragomirov. Born December 1943. He was one of the few non-Jewish members of a crime organization that came over during the détente of the early eighties. He lived in Brighton Beach, which some called Little Odessa, but he wasn't from Odessa. He knew these guys from the army. His family has long ties to the Russian military, most notably with the great-uncle Mikhail Dragomirov he was probably named for, a Sean Connery–looking geezer who wrote extensively on 19th-century tactics. Died of heartbreak in 1905 when the Japanese kicked Russia's ass with 20th-century tactics. The dad, Yevgeny, was no slouch, either. Fuckton of medals in WW2. Tank commander, T-34. Only an efreitor, like a corporal, but survived three bullet wounds, crawled out of two burning tanks and killed more Germans than bad Bratwurst. Serious badass.

Ranulf: Where was he from?

—The great-uncle, the badass dad, or your guy?

—All three.

—Big bear, the Ukraine. Daddy bear, a village near the Volga. Baby bear, Gorky, now called Nizhny Novgorod.

A chill runs down Andrew's spine and he actually leans away from his computer, as if away from the memories the word *Volga* stirs in him.

Fu fu fu, I smell Russian bones.

He feels sweat moisten his palms. He rubs these on his pants.

—Where is little Dragomirov now?

—I should be asking you that. He disappeared from his summer cabin in Sterling. New York State. Like a few miles from you, right?

—Does it look mobbish? Old business coming back for him?

—Not likely. Everybody liked him. He was so good with numbers that three separate bosses used him to help cover their gasoline schemes, and so charming and funny the Luccheses didn't whack him when they got Resnikoff. But he hung on until the early nineties when they opened that big, flashy nightclub, *Rasputin's*. Meanwhile, new Russian mob was coming over in droves, lots of it with ex-Spetsnaz muscle. FBI got interested because these guys were as big as the Italians now, at least locally.

Mikhail Dragomirov felt it getting hot, took off to St. Petersburg (Florida, not Russia), married a stewardess who also modeled at boat shows and bought a couple of condos. She died, he sold the condos, and now he just tools around with his dog gambling and frequenting on-line escorts. He looooves the shit out of Vegas. And Cirque du Soleil. I think he saw Ka seven times. And Avenue Q. If someone was going to make him sleep with the fishes, they would have done it back in the day.

Andrew blinks at the screen, rubs his chin. *"Sleep with the fishes"? Was that intentional? Does she know about Nadia?*

—Jesus, old man, you hang out with a rusalka? I didn't know there were any of those in the west. WTF, he comes all the way to America to get drowned by a Russian mermaid?

—Are you actually reading my thoughts over the Internet? And is this conversation veiled?

—Facebook knows more about you than I do. And computers are my specialty. You'd be amazed ;)

So saying, Radha appears in a box on the screen (half Iranian on her father's side but she says Persian—pale skin, dark hair, she *is* a honey), showing her hands. Text nonetheless continues to scroll.

—And I don't have unveiled conversations, except on BS social media as a front. If I weren't veiling this, I'd Skype you, because you type like a trained seal using his nose. I'm the go-to girl for like 40 of our sort . . . you think I'm going to let homeland security read this stuff? Try to print this conversation, I dare you.

Andrew likes dares. He prints. The printer slowly whines out not text, but a photograph. Him on the toilet, pants around ankles, long hair down, reading a copy of *Timber Home Living*, his favorite magazine. The picture is from this morning, from the angle of the polished brass mirror over the sink. A corner of his cell phone winks on the toilet's tank, just behind him, indicating the electronic fingerhold she used to get in. Normally brass mirrors are safe, can't be used as gates like glass ones, but Radha is so good with electricity and currents that she was able to press the conductive metal into her service.

—You scare me.

—Thanks. So, look, you should know I picked up some magic around him. Strong. Not coming from him, but someone near him, maybe family. Maybe the niece. Some Internet chatter about a niece coming over to help look for him, but nothing specific. I think someone's veiling on that end.

—Someone stronger than you?

Radha crosses her arms and raises an eyebrow.

—I didn't say that.

When she uncrosses her arms, she has six arms, Shiva-style, the hands of which she stacks on her hips defiantly, her six elbows fanned behind her, making a sort of Persian seraph of her.

—I dare you to get me info on the niece.

—Not fair.

—I double dog dare you.

—What do I get?

—What do you want?

—Madeline Kahn.

—Ok. I'll open a trapdoor for five minutes. You know how it works, right?

—Yeah, you send me a DVD of a movie she's in, and I get five minutes to get her to talk to me. Only she doesn't have to. She could tell me to go fuck myself and leave her alone.

—Or she could freak out. No telling with the dead. Most likely she'll use your time asking you about friends and family. You should probably Google the shit out of everybody she knew. And it's going to be VHS. I haven't figured out how to do it on DVD yet.

—Better catch up, old man. Even DVDs are old-school now. What are you going to do when it's all computer streaming? Which it is.

—I guess you'll take over.

—I can't open trapdoors. I tried. Plenty.

—Then I guess you'll have to go to a pawnshop and get a VCR.

—For Madeline? Ok. And send History of the World. I want to talk to her in that Roman get-up. "YES! No,no,no,no,no,no, YES!"

—Are you sure you don't have a family member or friend you'd rather talk to?

—I'm young. All of my friends are alive. Only dead family were crabby old grayhairs. One nice Grandma on Brick Lane in London just died, but I'd rather talk to Madeline Kahn. "Ohhh, it's twue, it's twue!"

—As you wish.

—All right. I'll keep poking. We'll see if comrade witchiepoo Dragomirov has hackers or slackers in her kennel.

23

An apartment in Kiev.

Small and dirty, littered with decades-old Western kitsch.

An Eiffel tower perfume bottle, yellowed and empty, cat hair stuck to its sides, dominates a plastic white end table hash-marked at every edge with cigarette scars.

Next to the table, and taller, stands a Babel tower of books, at the top of which a dog-eared paperback presents a redhead with arched eyebrows, her conical, late-sixties breasts like small missiles all but poking through her bikini as she guns a motorcycle beneath the Czech title, *Angels of Road and Beach*.

Fake German steins made in Japan stand on the floor against a peeling once-avocado wall, like very small counterrevolutionaries awaiting their firing squad.

A curling old poster, its corners peppered with tack holes, features a leering and clearly unauthorized Mickey Mouse pointing a gloved finger back at the legend *ORLANDO*; oranges spill from the first *O*, a dolphin jumps through the second. Behind the huge mouse, men and women in early-eighties hairdos, all of them soft around the edges like someone Captain Kirk is about to inseminate, laugh in a sort of twinkling, painted-in, promlike heaven. Mickey's waist is cut off by a neobiblical invitation, *Come and See, Come and See!* in Russian and Ukrainian. Under this is the Sunny Skye travel agency logo atop a long-dead phone number. The top and bottom of the poster are torn and taped in the middle where the apartment dweller's father ripped it from its thumbtacks, ripped it off of the wall of his illegal Donetsk business in 1986, just ahead of the arrival of the police.

An orange cat with white paws licks itself, ignoring the man hunched over the computer in a sun-bleached pinkish-yellow Izod polo shirt. If it could stand up and look over his shoulder, it would see him typing in English:

> On ffriday, I was at the aunts farm and accidentally saw Huh, just call me, if you really want to join inserting hand up the horses butt, til elbow.
> Hey, have you ever seen something like that?
>
> Just take a close look at that pic:
>
> http:// . . . (etc.)
>
> Tell me please, if you, pervert, want to join me next time I travel to the country side.

The man's spine is curled like a question mark, not from an accident of birth, but from years of hunching before monitors. He leans away from the screen now, his back as close to straight as it will go, and regards his work. He is proud of the commas before and after *pervert*, something only an expert in English would know to do.

He smokes, still poring over his oeuvre, checking it for errors. He catches the double-effed *friday*, balances his cigarette on the table ledge, types jerkily, puffs, and exhales. Soon he will sell "passage" on this spam to various clients, some in Ukraine, some in China, a few in Africa, who will pay him to insert their toxic URLs and launch them at Americans and Canadians by name. Like spells, but in the millions upon millions. Sperm, his sperm, racing for the ova of personal information. Credit cards will be stolen, e-mail addresses hijacked, spyware implanted, oh the lovely chaos! More importantly, oh the lovely dollars! Hard currency will appear in his several dozen false-front PayPal accounts; he will shunt this money to accounts he holds in Trinidad, St. Martin, and the Bahamas; and his retirement will grow.

He is thirty-four, means to retire at fifty.

He has been earning his own money since he was fifteen.

He will live until eighty-five, with the help of Western medicine and his retirement, thus spending thirty-five years working and thirty-five years doing *whatever the fuck he wants*. When he visualizes his savings, he sees a cartoon snowball of dollars growing as it rolls downhill, hitting a valley, then shrinking as it rolls uphill until it is gone, and a tiny pop is heard.

The pop of a .22 against his temple; he means to be so poor at the top of that second hill he has no choice but to shoot himself.

It must be a .22.

Small-caliber so the bullet goes in, but cannot exit, ricocheting around inside, making cabbage of his brains, destroying all feeling, all memory. Leaving just a small, bleeding hole. People who shoot themselves with powerful guns are selfish, vulgar.

Bourgeois.

Someone must clean their brains from the wall.

Cursing them and scrubbing.

The gun will be his first purchase upon retiring.

Until then, he cannot bring himself to spend any more than necessary. He is a miser of the first house, wearing everything out until it simply cannot be used, only buying things that cost so close to nothing they might as well be free.

But when he turns fifty . . .

. . . *the next time I travel the countryside.*

"Perfect, pervert," he says in thickly accented English.

The cat yawns, showing fangs that are perhaps the only truly white things in the apartment, and stretches, walking the crooked back of the sofa before sitting imperiously on the arm.

Now the night breeze, cool for June even here, fingers its way beneath the window, blowing the fly-specked curtains up. The view *en face* consists of yet more ugly block apartments, the lights on in only a few windows, but now these rectangles of light shiver slightly, as though from heat fumes.

No heat here, though.

The room gets colder.

The cat almost hisses, remembers what happened to it the last time it did, and curls itself around its master's feet, its tail flicking between those heels-up feet and the sooty footprints on the pink flip-flops beneath them.

Now the man turns in his chair and looks at the window.

She's here.

He looks away quickly.

His palms grow moist.

He anticipates the sound just before he hears it.

The sound of an iron pot scraping against the cheap stucco below the sill, scraping like a rowboat against a pier.

Baba Yaga riding through the night skies of Kiev, sitting in an iron pot, pushing it with a broom.

Just like in bedtime fables.

But she really is outside.

Some part of her, anyway.

I'm nine stories up.

Yuri . . .

"Yes, little mother," he manages, smoking again.

He is careful not to show his teeth when he speaks.

Put on your kerchief.

The cat shivers violently.

He pulls the sticking drawer out, pulls out a blue terry cloth hand towel. Is repulsed thinking about putting this over his eyes but does so anyway, tilting his head back, holding it in place because God help him if it falls off and he sees her.

The crunching sound as the iron pot crumbles stucco.

Is there really a pot, or do I hear one because I expect to?

A bare foot on his gritty linoleum floor.

She is in the apartment now, he knows.

Yuri, you bought the ticket?

"Yes. One ticket for Marina Yaganishna, first class. Nizhny to Moscow, Moscow to JFK, JFK to Syracuse."

She will not want to sit next to anyone fat.

"I already looked. The seat next to her on the long flight remained unsold, so I moved a skinny man there."

Good.

A long moment passes.

There's something you're not telling me.

I don't like that.

An acrid smell as the cat pisses on the floor.

"Sorry, little mother. I . . . There was someone poking around my curtain. In America. Chicago, I think. Magic."

Find out who.

Find out why.

She comes closer.

The cat jerks from below the table, sprints for the bedroom, something else moves faster than the cat, which shrieks.

Yuri dares not look.

"I . . . I was working on this. I wanted to have the answer before I told you."

And this is why you spend your time on filth?

A bony finger ticks on the screen of his computer.

Hands in horses? You think this is what happens in the country? I can show you what happens in the country, but I think you will not like it.

He doesn't know if she is reading the English on the screen or just peering into his head. He isn't sure she can do this, but neither is he sure she cannot.

He doesn't know what she is.

Nobody does.

He smells her scent of iron and cookfat and pepper, undercut with dried blood, mold, fear.

She smells like fear.

He presses hard on the towel over his eyes, frightened his shaking hand might betray him, that it might fall away. His urine fingers at its gateway, wants to leak out. He controls it.

He breathes through his mouth, awkwardly shielding his teeth with his lips.

She lets him stew for a moment.

Yuri . . .

"Yes, little mother?"

You have needle and thread in this shithole?

"Yes, little mother."

Use it to sew the cat's tail back on.

"Thank you, Baba."

Somewhere in his head, she grunts.

Now the sound of a twig broom, sweeping away her footprints.

She mounts the pot, which scrapes noisily against the bricks.

The woman in the apartment next door calls through the wall.

"What have you got over there, Yuri Denisovitch, an African rhinoceros?"

Then, more quietly, he hears her exclaim, "Shit! Spiders! So many!"

Now the sound of a broom (cheap, modern) whacking at the floor, a hurried prayer.

The cat yowls miserably from his bedroom.

The breeze stops.

The room warms, if it can be called that, from cold to merely cool.

Half an hour passes before he dares remove his terry cloth blindfold.

It is soaked with sweat.

But he did not piss himself this time.

24

An older man on a wide-screened television is speaking in a broad New England dialect that recalls the unhurried pace of a dray horse. The man's head is long and horselike, handsome even though he is in his late sixties. He looks down at a paper, then up at the viewer.

Up at Andrew.

But he doesn't see the younger man.

Not yet.

It's still just a tape.

". . . His life actually *depends* on obedience to spiritual principles. If he deviates too far, the penalty is sure and swift . . ."

The man drops his eyes to the paper.

"Bill."

"He sickens and finally dies."

Andrew knows the man will look up at the camera before speaking again.

"Bill Wilson. It's Andrew Blankenship."

"Andrew Blank . . . ?"

Recognition steals across the older man's face.

The trapdoor is open.

The dead man in the grainy color home movie becomes a little blurrier. But now he is awake, aware. He pokes his horn-rimmed glasses up on his nose and squints at Andrew through the television. He is off-script now. His surroundings are frozen. The tape stops turning in its machine.

The lights in the media room are warm and reassuring, not bright, but neither dim. Andrew doesn't know what he looks like through the television, from *there*. Neither does he know if he is communing with a soul or if he is somehow snatching conversation with the man in his own time.

What he does know is that the dead souls, or the encapsulated intelligences, or the shades in Hades, or whatever they are, remember him when he finds them again.

There is continuity.

"Where are you?" Bill says, squinting.

"I'm at home."

"That's right. You do this from your basement, right?"

"Yes."

Bill chuckles agreeably. He is an old man in this 1964 clip Andrew got on eBay and converted to VHS from eight-millimeter. He is speaking at a meeting in a private home in Philadelphia. He largely reads from the work of the "first hundred drunks" in this piece, and Andrew has found that this point, where he talks about death, is the easiest point at which to interrupt him. The visible half of a stainless steel water pitcher gleams below Bill, but it gleams like a still photograph.

He knows the man could touch the pitcher and the condensation would bead again; a droplet would run down the side. He could wake the pitcher up. But he would *see* the pitcher only if Andrew told him it was there. If he asked the dead man what was around him, he would say it was blurry, or foggy, and then, very probably, cognitive dissonance would rear its head and the dead man would start to get upset. When speaking with the dead through film, it is best to keep their attention on you.

They've already been through this.

Bill knows he's dead in 2012.

Andrew told him.

Bill knows, too, that Andrew is a sorcerer, but he doesn't hold that against him. Nor does he seem to mind Andrew's long hair and odd clothes. Bill is perhaps the least judgmental dead person with whom Andrew has spoken.

"The last time we spoke," Bill says, "you told me you were sponsoring a young lady from Wisconsin."

"Her father's from Wisconsin."

"That's right. How's she doing?"

"She's got six months now. And her slips aren't so bad, so she's been effectively sober for eight years. Although I don't think she's really hit bottom."

"How long ago did we speak?"

"It's been . . . months."

Bill wipes his eyes under his glasses like he's tired.

"Seems like five minutes ago. Time doesn't make any sense here."

He begins to look around.

Begins to look agitated.

"Bill."

Bill looks at Andrew again.

"Yeah, sorry."

"Nothing to be sorry about. I was just wondering if you're still comfortable being my sponsor. This is a . . ."

Andrew trails off.

"Highly unusual situation, I know," Bill finishes for him, "but, sure. I'll keep meeting with you. What else have I got to do with myself, after all? And I say that without asperity."

"Great."

"So what's on your mind?"

"I . . . wonder if giving up magic and giving up drinking are similar things."

"Sure they are. Thinking about going back to church?"

Bill is in earnest when he says this. Andrew suppresses a laugh but acknowledges that it would have been a sorry, yellow little laugh anyway.

"No."

"That's up to you, of course."

And where did church get you, old man? Is that heaven? Is that even you?

"Yeah. I just wonder if I could give it up now. If I wanted to."

"Not alone, certainly."

What exactly is my higher power, anyway?

"I'm sorry. It just. It feels good to talk to you."

"Lost your dad young, did you?"

"I did."

"It's a hard thing not to have your dad. You look for what you're not getting from him in other people. And that's okay. Love is always A-OK."

Andrew nods.

Tears are close.

He fights them back.

And here sits the magus in a dim room, using dirty tricks to disturb a dead man's rest, crying because he wants his daddy and his mommy.

Boo fucking hoo.

"We have sponsors in the world of magic, too. Mentors."

Bill just listens.

"Mine lived in Ohio."

25

1977.

Near Xenia, Ohio.

The last warm day of the year.

"I'm not queer," the driver says.

"That's not my business," Andrew Randolph Blankenship says, although he *has* just begun to wonder why a bald, bearded man with his shirt unbuttoned to show his potbelly might slow his big, blue Impala to a crawl next to a teenaged boy walking his bicycle.

"You always walk your bike past this house."

The man points at a lopsided 1890s two-story with peeling blue paint and a sun-faded *FOR SALE* sign.

Andrew doesn't say anything. He just furrows his brow as he often does when he is processing a lot of information.

Watching me? Is this guy dangerous? Does he know why I walk my bike here? Does he see her, too?

"You know there's a ghost in that house, don't you?"

Andrew feels his heart thudding in his chest.

There is a ghost and it scares the shit out of me.

I walk my bike because I've wrecked twice knowing it was looking at me.

"Yes, sir."

"Don't *sir* me."

"Okay."

Andrew scratches at one of the sideburns he has begun to grow in emulation of his older brother. Although Charles will soon shave his because they look too "hippy-dippy."

But this dude.

Who is this dude?

"She swells up like a balloon when you ride your bike past it because she has a crush on you. She was seventeen when she died. Your age now, if I'm correct?"

"Yes s— Yes."

Andrew peers into the car, which is closer now. He is relieved to see that the driver is wearing pants. Dungarees, to be precise.

"Do you know why you can see her?"

Andrew shakes his head.

A car horn blares because the older man has let his Impala wander into the other lane. He looks at the road again and corrects his path as a mud-colored flatbed pickup truck stacked with pumpkins goes by, losing a pumpkin, its driver half-unfurling an arthritic bird-finger.

"Do you want a ride past the house? I'll take you the rest of the way to Enon."

Andrew does want a ride.

He doesn't want to see the floating girl in the window leering at him, her head as big as a head on a parade float.

And he doesn't want to spend forty minutes pedaling when those forty minutes might be spent napping. He got almost no sleep last night and the girl he made love to in the cornfield got grounded.

It was worth it.

The lovemaking, quick and earnest, was after they tampered with the letters on the Xenia Baptist Church marquee so that *REPENT, MY PEOPLE, YOUR TIME TO SIN GROWETH SHORT* now said *GO SIT ON PETERS HOT POLE.*

Now a pale yellow station wagon underbellied with rust the color of Chef Boyardee spaghetti sauce swings around the Impala, the driver barking some hostile syllable through his open window.

The bald man's eyes stay fixed on Andrew.

"And I'll tell you why you and I can see the dead girl and that guy can't."

The boy stops.

A turkey buzzard kites lazily overhead.

"Is there room for my bike?"

"There is."

Now the man who will teach Andrew his first spell pulls his car over in front of the boy. He opens the huge trunk so the Impala looks like a whale opening its mouth.

Its mouth is very black.

Its tongue a spare tire.

Andrew feeds the whale his Schwinn and prepares to go to Nineveh.

26

"Is he still living?"

"No."

Silence.

"He taught you what you're doing now? With me?"

"Yes," Andrew says.

"I'm sure it occurred to you to try this with him."

"He asked me not to."

"Why's that?"

"He didn't say."

And yet I do it to you.

Bill nods inscrutably. Then says, "There's something else, isn't there? You're not just lonely. You're scared."

"Yes."

"And this fear's got you missing John Barleycorn."

"More like Gilbert Grape for me, but yes."

He won't know that reference.

"I'm glad you sought me out."

"Are you really?"

"I am."

"Are you really *you*, Bill?"

"I don't know how to answer that."

Bill wipes his eyes again.

How many alcoholics would like to be able to do this? Would give anything for this chance? To talk to HIM. Thank HIM personally. Why is it fair that I get to have this to myself? And if I let Anneke see him, what is that? Showing off? I should let him go. Burn this tape.

"Andy."

Only he gets to call me Andy.

"Yeah."

"Don't send me back yet."

Andrew raises his eyebrows in place of asking *Why?*

Bill W. says, "The next time I'm awake . . . talking . . . I'll be talking to you. I'm always the same, but you . . . I'm a little concerned about what you'll have to tell me when I see you again. There's a cloud over you."

"A cloud?"

"I don't know how else to put it. Just . . . sit with me here for a minute. Is there music there?"

"Music?"

"You know, a phonograph?"

"There's music."

"Play me something. Please."

Andrew goes to his stereo.

Turns on satellite radio.

Turns on the forties channel, turns it up good and loud.

Betty Hutton's "Blue Skies" pours from the speakers in no great hurry.

Bill W. closes his eyes, leans toward the screen.

Moves his head in time to the music, subtly, reminding Andrew of a cobra coming out of its basket for a snake charmer.

Now Andrew cries.

"There it comes," Bill says, eyes still closed.

And then he says, opening his eyes suddenly, fiercely,

"You're the one who needed the music. It's a shoehorn for your feelings, like the booze used to be. Shut me down when you want to, son. Everything's A-OK."

27

Early evening.

The barn behind Andrew's house.

Anneke belches and excuses herself, moves away from the warm pocket of garlicky air she has just made. The ghost of the penne, spicy sausage, and basil Andrew sautéed for them earlier can't over-power the stronger odor of hot, raw walleye.

"How lonely and deranged do you have to be to want to blow-dry a fish, anyway?"

He touches the yellow pike's side with the back of his hand, decides it wants another blast. He flicks the on switch and wands hot air back and forth over the fish. Wrinkles his nose as he detects her belch and aims the dryer at it, making her laugh.

"Better than hot fish. It smells like your dead mermaid friend in here," she says, raising her voice over the dryer's petulant whine.

Andrew smiles.

"It makes the skin thirsty so it drinks pigment," he says.

"I'm not five. I know why you do it. I'm just saying it stinks."

She sips her diet soda.

Now Andrew brushes a brownish, mustardy shade of yellow on the fish, which sits almost flush in the fish-shaped niche Andrew cut into a silvery panel of insulation foam.

"I thought you said you wanted to watch me do this."

"I do. I'll be good."

Andrew grunts skeptically, begins swabbing rusty orange ink onto the fins he pinned in place against the foam. She looks up and around, taking in the twenty-odd fish prints he has framed and hung out here. Sturgeons, carp, black bass, coho salmon, in many colors, some naturalistic, some fantastical, all swimming north, as though toward the lake they were pulled from.

One Prussian blue octopus from a trip to Florida drifts amid the school as though lost.

"Gyotaku?"

"Gyotaku," he corrects, but she can't hear the difference.

Now he takes a piece of rice paper and lays it over the walleye, tucking it under and around the fish, massaging the color up into the paper. He details the fins with a plastic spoon.

"Okay, I like this. I'm not saying I want to learn. But I like it."

He grunts again, his barely blinking eyes fixed on his work.

He pulls the paper off.

"Nice!" she says.

"I'll let this dry for a bit and then I'll do the eyes. I'm not much of an artist, but I can handle fish eyes."

He clothespins the paper to a line, then sits down on the moth-eaten Goodwill couch next to the dorm-sized fridge he used to keep stocked with German and British brown ales.

He pulls a fizzy water out instead.

They both just sit for a long while.

The sun goes down and moths wheel and flutter around the bare bulb overhead.

"Are you nervous?" she asks.

"No," he lies.

28

Full dark.

The fireflies outside have largely given up.

Andrew has spread himself lengthwise on the couch, hands on chest like a pharaoh ready for the wrap. Feet bare. Blue jeans. No belt. No shirt. His hair a dark pillow under his head.

He asked her to watch him, so she sits opposite, on the rusty folding chair.

She bats a moth away from her eyes.

Another, larger moth crawls on his face, but she is afraid to touch him now, so the moth remains.

Andrew watches the moth, too.

He's next to her, out of his body.

When he realizes this, his body gets goose bumps.

He sees his body get goose bumps.

29

He turns now—it feels like turning his body but he believes this is just how he explains it to himself—and looks at Anneke. He wants to put his nose in the hollow of her ear and smell her unadorned, slightly spicy scent, but the part of him that wants that has no nose. Her neck is tan and lovely, and her eyes shine with curiosity and concern as she looks down on his body. He sees

with what eyes?

the fine hairs on her cheeks, sees her pulse gently thrumming in her temples, feels the rhythm of her heart. He moves closer to her, almost mingling with her, begins to feel that he is putting off what he fears to do. But it's so *good* to be this near her. Is this what it is to be a ghost? No . . . he is still connected with his body. He tries to breathe in her scent, hears

with what ears?

his lungs fill where he lies on the couch, thinks he can smell her now. *Anneke.* She smiles a little, looking down at him, turns down the corners of her mouth trying to suppress the smile, so he follows her gaze and sees why.

He's getting an erection, bulging at the zipper of his faded jeans.

Oh, that's great.

Just great.

He has the urge to cover himself, and now his hands obey the impulse, his face flushing red, a worry line on his half-sleeping forehead. Anneke bites her knuckle to keep from braying laughter, but the laughter wells up in her. Andrew-on-the-couch now half turns his body away from her, makes an involuntary growl like a frustrated bear.

Anneke turns away, too, laughter escaping in hitches around her fist. She fishes out a cigarette and puts it in her mouth, but she doesn't light it.

"Say," she stage-whispers between laughs, "I can light this even if you're floating around, right? You're not flammable or anything? Like methane?"

She's laughing so hard she's almost crying.

"Help! My friend turned himself into a fart and I burned him up!"

Now Andrew laughs next to her, his belly hitching where he lies on the couch. He reaches out

with what hand?

and tries to light her cigarette for her, his physical hand twitching.

She steps farther away from the couch now, moves *through* Andrew, who, almost against his will, allows himself to be dragged along *in* her.

He has never felt anything like this—it is electric, delicious . . . it feels like burnt caramel tastes. He senses that if he lingers, he will soon be the one feeling through her skin, moving her limbs,

and what will happen to Anneke?

but this is only for an instant—he pushes out of her.

And that sensation of pushing makes him remember something from the text . . . the *push* can be turned around so it happens entering the body. If you *push* while entering, snapping your own tether, you can knock the other soul completely free and into death. If you try and you're weak at it, if you don't believe, you'll be the dead one.

But Andrew did not push.

He melted into her like liquid caramel, and it was hard to leave.

All Anneke has time to feel is a flash of numbness, as though her heart has skipped two beats, and she understands what has happened. Her laughter dies like a caught breeze. She shivers. Fear winks in her eye, then turns, as it always does with her, into curiosity. She turns to where she thinks he is and says, as if she has dared herself to speak before she can take it back, "Do it again."

She heels a tear of laughter from under the corner of her eye.

"Do it again, I want you to," she says, and looks down at his body. His head is gently shaking *no*.

She lights the cigarette.

30

Andrew-out-of-Andrew rushes away from the barn, at the speed of a sprint, faster than a sprint, now at a gallop, and he takes off. He looks back at the barn below him, only it isn't precisely like looking behind him, as he has no neck to swivel; it feels a bit like he's a nautilus, jetting backward through inky water, tentacles trailing behind it. Nothing trails behind Andrew. He is nothing, has nothing.

The barn recedes, light bleeding through the pineboard walls, etching the high grass and short trees around it in faint gold. Anneke is in there, smoking her Winston down to the filter, mantling her consciousness over his half-vacant body while his consciousness soars over Cayuga County. He turns now, the nautilus transforming to owl, attention cast forward. Trees loom at him and he pushes through them, feeling their slower, muted rhythms, rustling their leaves as if he himself has become a breeze.

No drug can do this.

Now he follows the coast south and west, away from Dog Neck Harbor, skimming low over the water, watching the lights in the windows, the bluish glow of televisions anesthetizing tired fishermen and waitresses, and one winks out—there!—where young parents begin to caress each other in earnest now that their children have gone to sleep.

Don't look in that window, you pervert.

He knows his body chuckles in the barn behind him, miles behind him now, but he can't think about that or his tether, stretched like a rubber band, might snap him back into himself.

He sees something over the water.

Reddish light collected in a form that moves on the lake, its nucleus a ball of white. It is the size of an oil tanker. He moves away from it.

What is that?

Don't let it see you.

No, really, what the fuck IS that?

This is not the first strange thing he's seen while traveling out-of-body. Nor is it the scariest. But it might be the biggest.

It roils and rolls in on itself, moving slowly, flashing as if with internal lightning. He thinks that he will probably never know just what it is. He senses it, senses neither malevolence nor goodwill, just power. Indifference. A god? A devil? An alien? None of the above?

If you sense it, maybe it can sense you.

His tether spasms, nearly whips him back into his body, then nearly . . . what? Breaks?

Not out here.

Not with that.

It stops.

It starts to drift toward him now.

He thinks of the *Titanic* steering away from its iceberg, slowly, too late.

Only I'm the Titanic *and that's the iceberg.*

Oh, fuck that.

He flies lower, skimming the water like a pelican.

He knows he is moaning in the barn.

The tether pulls at him, but he resists.

Not yet, I haven't learned enough yet, and I'm not going to let that thing scare me off; even if I'm what it's looking for, even if it eats souls, I defy it to find me.

(Careful!)

He moves over the shore, up a small bluff, into the woods.

He moves now as if on legs, down a fire trail.

A bat flutters near him, *through* him, reaping mosquitoes and moths. He flinches, his body jerking on the couch, but then it flies through him again, then again; it knows he's there, it likes the feeling like Anneke did. He relaxes, lets it. Feels the purr of its tiny heart beating hundreds of beats per minute, feels the craving for moth in its mouth, the dusty, gritty joy that moth flesh is, and then he wants the bat to go away and it does, careening off into the night.

Behind him, a reddish glow on the water, still far away, but he moves faster now. The fire trail becomes a paved road and he moves along its side. A cabin looms on his left, light pouring from its front window. Inside, a sixtyish bald man with a beard and small glasses hunches over a chessboard, his legs crossed at the knees European-style, but he senses that the man is American, has trained himself to do that. He moves a white pawn, consults a book, then moves a black pawn. He lifts a glass of wine to his lips, a rubyish droplet spilling down his beard, then disappearing within it.

Now the glow is over land, but farther away, heading toward Rochester. It moved fast when he wasn't watching.

Or there are more than one of them.

That's your fear talking. There's only one. It doesn't see you, doesn't want you.

He flies again, moving left, back toward the water.

To his right, a dark cabin, wooden stairs leading sharply down from its back deck.

Beneath him dry sand becomes wet sand becomes rocks, here and there punctuated with driftwood or seaweed. He pelicans over the water again, and then he sees it.

It sees him.

A ghost.

Under the water.

A bloated older man's ghost floats under the surface of the lake, its form luminous gray-green, like algae, its eyes two holes of starlight, locked on Andrew.

It surfaces.

Oh shit, it's time to go.

The tether jerks.

A luminous hand rises from the water, grabs something.

Grabs the invisible umbilicus anchoring him to his body.

Shakes it savagely.

NO!

Shakes it harder.

PLEASE!

The puffy phosphorescent head of the dead man comes out of the lake and bites at the air with black teeth. Andrew feels something like pain where his belly should be.

Now it is pain, excruciating pain.

The tether is down to threads, but the last threads are tough and the thing can't quite sever them.

Cold I'm cold!

Andrew tries to move away, but he is pulled down *by his tether* until a fatty dead arm loops around his neck, pulls him under the surface of the water.

How do I have a neck? Oh fuck my soul is almost all here now, I'm about to die. Help! HELP! PLEASE!

The dead face leers at him.

No bubbles.

It doesn't breathe.

But it speaks.

In Russian.

"It is an unpleasant thing to drown."

The eyes are not starlight anymore, just milky white lamps, like the lamps deepwater fish use to lure prey.

Panicked, Andrew tries to think of what to do. He cannot escape the half headlock he is in, the soft but insistent mass of it somehow handling his nonmass, nor is his tether strong enough to snap him back.

"With your permission, I would like to show you my new home."

Dragomirov!

And now they dive.

Down and down.

Past a school of fish, just dark, blunt shapes moving around and through the diving souls.

A ship comes into view on the bottom, lit only by the witch-light given off by the ghost.

"Isn't it pretty?"

Andrew is shoved now, pushed through a tear in the hull.

He sees a quintet of skeletons through the murk and detritus, all sitting at a table with plates and cups near them, the remains of their clothes around them.

The rusalka had been busy.

Maybe only one drowning a year, if all of them were here, but since this had started before 1930, she had brought a lot of lives to their end.

She is a one-woman disaster, played out in slow motion.

She is a monster.

Now Andrew is held by the nape, brought face-to-face with a skeleton sitting in the corner.

"Look. This one is me. You can see my clothes are in better repair, and those fucking mussels haven't had time to grow on me like the forgotten ones in the engine room. She tends us, you know, the recent ones. Keeps us clean, like dolls in a dollhouse. I bought those jeans at the Nordstrom, International Mall, Tampa. One hundred fifty dollars. And now, look. Look at the dental work I had done in Mexico, such art, these crowns, art by Dr. Hernan Rodriguez of Leon, and for what? For your pretty bitch to drown me for a joke in a cold lake."

I'm sorry.

"The devil take your sorry."

The fatty thing holding him shudders violently, begins to come apart, bits of its not-flesh drifting off it. Andrew can see through parts of it now, but also its witch-light is fading. It is getting dark in this ship.

"I have to go now, the bitch is coming back."

Nadia!

"But let me tell you something, Mister Andrew. You'll be sorry soon. I know who you are now, and I will tell *her.*"

Your niece?

"You poor fucker!"

It laughs now, shaking itself to pieces, its light almost completely gone. Its voice is strangled, as if it is drowning again.

"But I'll tell her to make it quick. If you do something for me."

What?

"Find my dog. Find my little Caspar."

31

Complete darkness.

Cold.

Andrew screams.

Cold arms find him, cradle his head, a stiff, cold nipple brushes his cheek down in the dead ship.

"You idiot," the rusalka says, kissing his mouth.

32

Light.

Warmth.

Andrew screams.

Warm arms find him, cradle his head, a soft breast beneath the cotton of a T-shirt.

Anneke is crying.

"You idiot," she says, kissing his mouth.

33

"I thought you were dead. You looked pretty dead."

She uses a roll of paper towels and a bottle of rubbing alcohol to swab his upper lip and chin. While the weightless parts of Andrew were touring the depths of Lake Ontario, his body sprung the mother of all nosebleeds. It dropped its other ballast, too, but Anneke won't let go of him yet.

He is lying under a blanket, the blanket topped with his leather jacket.

"I need to change my pants."

She hugs his head to her chest one more time.

Salvador paces behind her.

"Send Jeeves for new pants. I don't want you walking yet."

"Salvador, please get me a pair of jeans."

Happy to have a task, the wicker man disappears from the buggy barn and heads for the main house.

"Well, since you're my sponsor, I guess you're the one I tell I really want a drink right now."

He nods his head, shivering.

The lake's cold is in his bones.

"You know what the worst thing was? When I thought Elvis had left the building for real, my first thought wasn't, 'Oh God, my friend is dead.' My first thought was, 'They'll think I killed him—I'm going back to prison.' How's that for sucking? As a person, I mean. Who's that selfish?"

She won't let herself cry.

He wrestles free of her, goes to the barn door, leans over, and vomits. Cold lake water comes out of him.

She brings him a paper towel for his mouth.

"I don't understand half of what happened tonight," he says. "But somebody's coming for me. Somebody dangerous. And I think I know who's sending her."

"Who?"

"I don't want to say her name. But I think it's time I gave you a proper tour of my house. And I think it's time I told you what happened to me in Russia."

It stinks of lake now, worse than before.

"Is time you were telling me, too," the naked woman with the dreadlocked auburn mane says. She walks dripping into the barn, eyeing Anneke territorially.

Anneke does some eyeing of her own.

"You have cigarette for me?"

"You know where they are."

Nadia pads across the barn floor, reaches into the jacket pocket.

Anneke watches her, willing herself not to react to her smell.

Nadia pulls out a bright yellow cigarette pack, but the cigarette she pulls from it is broken in half.

"Shit," she says, smelling the blond strands of tobacco.

Anneke offers her a Winston.

The rusalka takes it.

34

He tells them what happened to him in Russia.

PART TWO

35

The man who forgot his own name has been living on the street in Syracuse since March. March was a hard, miserable month to be outdoors, but, with the help of the blanket from the Salvation Army, the down vest from Goodwill, and the shoplifted sleeping bag, he made it.

He's caveman strong.

A tribe of one.

He is proud of the sleeping bag. Not just for the tactical skill he showed in getting it past the sensors before the stock boy saw him or the sheer athletic prowess that left the pudgy employee huffing and puffing on the wrong side of a wall; he is proud he had the foresight to swipe it while he still looked okay. He knew it wouldn't be long before he smelled like Dumpsters and had a beard, and that people like that get watched the minute they enter a place of business.

He is proud, too, of the fight with the shower-cap man. Shower-cap wanted that sleeping bag; it was a hunter's bag, camouflaged, rated all the way down to ten below. You don't need to tuck tail and run for the mission in a bag like that. Shower-cap pushed a shopping cart full of stuffed animals around, held the stuffies up, and made them wave at cars before he showed his *HUNGRY NEED A DOLLAR GOD LOVES U* sign. Kids made their parents give him the dollar, and he smiled his gap-toothed smile at them. But not everybody who plays with teddy bears is nice. Shower-cap thought because he was big and had a pipe he was going to get that thermal sleeping bag and make the new guy push on to another on-ramp. Shower-cap was wrong. Shower-cap pushed on. Shower-cap's smile has more gaps now.

The young man has always been a good fighter.

Going into the infantry seemed right, even though someone he cared about asked him not to. Begged him not to that day on the couch, lying on him and crying down into his eyes.

He had to go, and at the time he thought she didn't understand, but he has come to believe that maybe she did.

He came back from Afghanistan after only a few weeks in country. He came back different. Not better different. Traumatic-brain-injury-and-severe-tinnitus different. The IED had spun the Humvee like a soda can, popped it in half, killed the lieutenant and the Mexican outright, blinded the guy who played hockey. He didn't remember names so well anymore, but he knew that guy played hockey. He himself was the luckiest guy in the limo that day, but he wasn't all that lucky. Kept all his outside parts, but now everything sounded like whining, and he got mad fast. Yelled when he argued, which didn't play well at the smartphone sales kiosk in the Carousel mall. Or at the Catholic high school that took him on as a janitor. Or at the car wash, where he worked for six hours.

That he grabbed arms and squeezed to emphasize the yelling hadn't played well with sparrow-tattoo girl. And it was sparrow-tattoo girl's apartment.

Had been before he left for the army, when he had his own place, too. He had known her for years. Three? Four?

She had cried down into his eyes.

He used to have some letters she wrote.

She was right to kick him out.

He stole the sleeping bag the very same day.

Never went back for his stuff.

He is a caveman now.

.   .   .

It's a warm day and he's wearing the video game T-shirt, his favorite shirt. He has already gotten thirty-three dollars and fifty cents from the good motorists heading away from the airport onto Interstate 81. He has just lain down to nap when he sees a woman walking up to him, a pretty, older woman.

He sits up on one elbow and smiles at her.

He still has a good smile.

He watches her.

It isn't every day that someone bothers to get out of the car and come over to him here, although it has happened.

She has a carload waiting for her, calling to her in another language. One of the men gets out, starts toward her protectively, which is completely unnecessary. He's harmless to women unless they argue with him, and then he just squeezes their arms. He doesn't even mean to do that.

She takes something from her purse; a vial of water? Three ounces, just how they like it at the TSA.

She unscrews the cap.

He just stares at her beauty mark, her pretty, fair skin.

She's prettier than sparrow-tattoo girl, even though she's old enough to be her mom.

A MILF.

He hates that word.

"Your name was Victor," she tells him. She has an accent.

Her voice cuts through the whining in his head, and the whining stops.

Nobody ever did so much for him.

Tinnitus comes and goes as it pleases, doctors can't help, the VA can't help, but this woman made it stop.

He wants to cry.

"Victor," he says, agreeing. "That's right."

He remembers it sometimes on his own, but it's good to have it in his mouth again.

He hears the soft rush of cars, the delicious music of birds.

No whine.

"You are too young to live so hard. Are you thirsty, Victor?"

Come to think of it, he *is* thirsty.

He licks his lips and nods.

What is it? he thinks.

"Melted snow," she says. "From home."

She gives him the vial and he drinks it.

It's cold, colder than he thought it would be, and clean.

"Don't waste any," she says, and he doesn't, he even licks the back of his hand after he wipes his beard.

Now the foreign man is descending on them, speaking their language.

It's Russian.

He understands them, though he doesn't get how.

"This sort of thing is not done here, these people are dangerous. Please, Marina."

"He's not dangerous to me," she says, still kneeling, and winks at him.

She hands him a twenty-dollar bill, but he understands that it isn't really for him, that it's just *pokazukha*, a show she's putting on for the cousin.

He won't need money anymore, and the thought makes him smile.

He smiles at this woman, whom he loves with all his heart, whose arms he will never grab and squeeze, and she smiles back.

She gave him his name back, but it was just to let him know how special she was, how right it was for him to trust her.

He isn't Victor anymore.

He isn't a caveman anymore.

He doesn't know what he is, but he goes to sleep under the overpass for the last time before his great adventure, and he dreams of his blind friend playing hockey. He has his sight back, and he's skating with his stick low, skating fast, skating with agility and grace.

Once-Was-Victor has to look up to watch his friend skate.

He is watching him from under the ice.

36

Morning.

The necromancer's house.

The birds had been chirping before, and he guesses they still are, but Salvador now fills the house with the sound of vacuuming, perhaps the most domestic sound on the American Foley board.

The previous night had been full of horrors, but the morning seems so placid it all might have been a bad dream.

Awful, really awful, but I learned a lot.

I'm ready to try more.

Maybe today, after I show the girls the house?

He rubs his navel, remembering how much it hurt when the thing from the lake bit down on his tether.

To hell with that.

Nadia smokes and lounges on the patio below, outside.

Anneke isn't here yet.

Nothing makes the world feel mundane like a nice, soul-numbing dose of social media. Andrew plants himself in front of his desktop Mac, logs in to Facebook, and scrolls down the news feed on his home page. He watches the Honey Badger for perhaps the fifteenth time, chuckling at it anyway. He scrolls past event invites, Farmville crap, the obligatory feel-good story soured at the end by "share if you're not a bastard" or the like, and then finds the pro-Obama photo he reposted. President O in cool shades, smiling big, extending a hand in a walking drive-by hello, captioned.

SORRY I TOOK SO LONG TO SHOW YOU MY BIRTH CERTIFICATE—
I WAS BUSY KILLING BIN LADEN

Thirty-seven comments.

He knew when he reposted it that it was a bad idea, a little more wrong than funny, but he had been tired. Unsurprising that it generated a thread with thirty-something comments; most of his friends are liberal, and most of the conservative ones are polite enough not to start a donnybrook on someone else's post, but some people enjoy charging into a hostile audience.

Andrew calls this belligerent Facebook sport "Red Rover," and, although he never plays, his brother Charley should be in the social media asshole hall of fame.

Along with John Dawes across the street.

The two of them actually found themselves facing the shield wall of Andrew's friends so often they friended each other, though they would never meet in person, and wouldn't like each other if they did.

Charley is a big-money infomercial pitchman for Jesus (BMW Jesus, not donkey-and-sandals Jesus), and Dawes owns a vintage German sniper rifle and keeps a balls-mean dog on a run that only just stops him before the road. It's a three-legged dog (Dawes's one inarguable virtue is his volunteerism and advocacy for rescued pits), but the fucker really moves. Andrew hates biking past that house, knowing he is one chain link away from hospitalization and that Dawes would treat the whole thing like his fault. Charley would think Dawes was dangerously unbalanced (he is), and Dawes would think Charley was fake and a huge pussy (he is).

Andrew really wants them to hang out sometime.

In this thread, John Dawes (who, it must be said, has never been in the military) is explaining the operational details of the bin Laden mission, while Charles Blankenship is questioning Andrew's patriotism, which he does about once a month.

Andrew wishes he were better at casting spells over the net—that's Radha's thing—because he would cheerfully cause two photos to appear:

1. John Dawes shaving his nuts during *Gilligan's Island*.
2. Charley Blankenship, age ten, holding his eye and running away from the black girl he tried out the N-word on in 1965. (Ironically, this was at an all-Dayton Halloween Fair and Charley was dressed as an Indian, feather and all.)

Anneke knocks.

She has gone home for the night and then returned.

Andrew answers the door wearing his Japanese robe, wool-lined Ugg mules on his feet.

A vacuum cleaner is running but cuts off a second after the door opens.

"This is my house, and you must exit the same way you enter. It's important."

He says this to her every time she comes over.

"What happens if I don't?"

"It's important."

Salvador crosses behind Andrew, carrying the vacuum cleaner in one wooden hand, winding the cord with the other.

The rusalka is already here, wearing a dress, almost certainly at

Andrew's request. A simple summer dress that's a bit short on her, damp at the top where she keeps wetting her hair.

He really is fucking her. Nose, meet clothespin.

French-press coffee first, Sumatran.

Black for Anneke.

Honey for the rusalka.

Hazelnut syrup for Andrew.

Salvador knows the drill.

He keeps himself out of the way when the tour begins.

First, the staircase.

"All right, this one's cheap and basic. I'll just show you."

He stands at the top of the steps.

"Anneke, you up for a stunt? It might hurt."

She smiles at that.

"Yes."

"Come on up."

She starts up the stairs.

Andrew says, "*Slippery-slope.*"

The stairs turn into a very sleek, polished ramp.

She falls forward, slides down, lands on her feet.

"Nice!" she says.

"*Ziggurat.*"

The stairs reappear.

"Care to try again?"

She nods, grinning, starts back up.

"*Flytrap,*" he says.

Reality seems to blur.

Anneke has the sensation of falling, stopping.

At first she doesn't understand why she seems shorter, but when she tries to take a step, she realizes she has sunk into the wood beneath her, as if into quicksand that set and became hard again instantly. Everything below her knees is caught fast.

Without even thinking, she glances back to note the location of the rusalka.

Nadia's eyes are narrow and shining faintly luminous green.

"Don't do that," Anneke says.

"Do what?"

Sounds like *Vaht?*

"Look at me like prey in a trap, or whatever that raccoon-fishy look is."

"Oh. Is reflex."

"We'll do this top down," Andrew says as Nadia and Anneke ascend the ladder after him. A bare lightbulb comes to life overhead. "This is my attic. Most of the things up here have to do with keeping the house safe, so please don't touch anything. At all. And don't ask very specific questions about items. Once an aggressive spell is loaded into a physical object, explanation dilutes its power. Sometimes even triggers it."

"How would it trigger it?"

"Intent. Visualization. If someone other than the creator knows exactly what it does and imagines it happening, it might happen. 'Someone' meaning a user. Or anyone with a particularly vivid imagination. It's supposed to be rare, and I've never seen something go off because it was discussed, but I've read about that happening."

Everyone is up.

The girls look around.

The attic is much less cluttered than Anneke expected.

A few cardboard boxes and several sealed plastic tubs sit against the walls, but those aren't what draw the eye.

The owl stands out.

A great horned owl, glass-eyed, the kind that's big enough to drive eagles off their nests, stands atop a long shelf also inhabited by a blue jay, two crows, and a hummingbird.

Both Anneke and the rusalka next notice a vaguely animal-shaped form sitting atop a huge, old steamer trunk, draped with a dusty sheet.

Whatever it is has a long, reptilian tail.

Andrew sees them looking, steps over to it, pulls the sheet back.

"What the fuck is *that*?"

"It's a Tri-Star vintage rolling canister vacuum cleaner, of course. Slightly modified."

"*Slightly modified*," Nadia says, displaying her rotten teeth in an appreciative grin. The bulldoggish, triangular canister forms the base for a disturbing amalgamation of tools and taxidermied animal parts; the wheels that would normally support the larger rear of the appliance (now reversed to serve as the beast's puffed-up chest) have been replaced by a chimpanzee's arms, currently resting on their elbows, hands folded as if in prayer. An especially large alligator donated the tail snaking from the tapered end of the wedge, where the hose once attached. Said hose has been grafted to the larger end and pressed into service as the neck supporting the head, a sort of welded brass-and-metal rooster head with gogglish eyeglass lenses for eyes and the tips of kitchen knives for a crest. The beak looks fully capable of biting through a truck tire. For good measure, folded vulture's wings perch on the slanted back.

"Does he have a name?" Anneke asks.

"Actually, she does. And I know it's in the form of a rooster—I thought about calling it 'Billy' after the guy who welded it for me— but something about it strikes me as feminine."

He whispers the name to her.

"*Electra*."

Next the trio considers a sort of standing fish tank with a great mound of dirt coming halfway up. Crisscrossed coat hangers frame the top, and from this frame, supported by golden threads, hangs a scale model of the necromancer's house, exact in every detail.

"What . . . ?" Anneke starts.

"Don't ask about this one," Andrew says. "Let's move on."

"The bedroom," he says as neutrally as possible.

"Stand at the door," he says to Anneke.

"Why always her?" the rusalka pouts. "When do I get to do something?"

"I'm not sure how this stuff will work on you."

"Because. I'm not. A person," she says, with more than a dash of hurt pride.

Unimpressed, Andrew says, "That's. Exactly. Right."

He lies down on his bed, stretches out.

"Come to the bed and sit down," he tells Anneke.

She does so, looking around, wondering what the trick will be.

Nothing happens.

She just sits.

"Now go back and do it again, only this time think about hurting me."

"Gladly," she says, laughing.

Now she crosses the room at a slight crouch, her hand held up dramatically as if holding an invisible knife, ready to stab him *Psycho*-style.

When she gets halfway there, the door to the walk-in closet opens.

"Oh shit," she says.

Takes another step.

Everything happens fast.

The telephone on Andrew's nightstand rings.

Serpentine objects fly from Andrew's closet, brown and black, four of them, whipping at high speed.

She tries to cover her face with her hands.

Not snakes.

Belts.

The leather stings when it hits her.

"Ow, fuck!"

Andrew swears in surprise and mild pain as well.

The belts wrap around Anneke's hands and feet, bind them together, hog-tie her. A fifth belt loops around her neck, but only tightens enough to let her know it's there.

The reason Andrew swore is that the belt he was wearing whipped off him, gave him a nasty burn on the side, dinged his hand good with the buckle as it shot itself at Anneke.

The phone rings again.

Levitates off the bed, floats over to her.

The speaker cozies up to her ear.

Andrew's voice, prerecorded.

"*Honi soit qui mal y pense!* Try not to move too much, as the belts tighten when you struggle. Especially the one around your neck. I'll be with you at my earliest convenience."

The phone dies, thunks to the floor, lies still.

Nadia gently applauds, as if at the opera.

The magus helps Anneke off with the belts.

"Why did you waste a big one like that?"

"I'll load it up again tomorrow. It's not the only one in here."

"What was the French?"

"Basically, *Think good thoughts.*"

37

"This is my bathroom. These silver fists you see holding the roll of toilet paper make the roll inexhaustible. Very popular with the ladies, as is the lid, which lowers itself when the room is vacated. Subtle magic, that. Less subtle is the claw-foot bathtub. If you dive into it headfirst, hard enough to break your neck,"

(Nadia winces at this)

"it will send you to a bathroom in whatever place you say and think about. If you say nothing, it will send you to the last place it gated to."

Anneke thinks about this. It makes sense . . . bathrooms are private. One wouldn't want to appear in the middle of a public fountain or even a kitchen. If Superman had been real, he would have changed in a toilet, not a phone booth. Maybe he uses a toilet now since phone booths are nearly extinct. Andrew might know—he seems dork enough to have a secret comic book habit.

"Do you get wet?"

"Only if the bathtub's full. The water in the pipes conducts, it doesn't immerse."

"How do you get back?"

"Any fixture in the bathroom you got sent to will send you right back to this tub. Another tub is best; toilet works, too, though the idea is off-putting. The sink will stretch wide enough to accommodate you if you believe it will, though I once cracked a rib on the spigot when I wondered if I was going to clear the spigot. Belief is more than half of all magic."

"What is the last place it gated to?" Anneke asks.

"I don't remember," he says. "Would you like to see for yourself?"

She gives him a you-must-have-forgotten-whom-you're-daring look and dives. Nadia, startled (and a little impressed), swears in Russian, stepping back so as not to be clipped by Anneke's foot.

38

Anneke finds herself in a bathroom, painted green from the waist down, white on the top half. She's on the can, the lid of which is thankfully down. A startled young man with a sandy white-boy Afro was washing his hands at the sink. His mind can't deal with the idea that she suddenly appeared, so it performs a kind of emergency rewrite.

"People knock, you know. I'll be done in a minute."

She's in shock, too, though, so all she does is blink at him.

He wonders if she has a head injury.

"Are you all right?"

She nods.

The paper towels are out, so the young man wipes on his pants.

It doesn't even occur to him that he has to draw the tiny bolt to open the door because nobody came in that way after him.

"Want it closed?" he asks.

Sweet kid.

She nods.

She stands up on shaky legs and locks the door again so she can gather herself. Sits back down. A water heater dominates the cramped bathroom, a yellow sticker warning her that gasoline should not be stored nearby as the pilot light will ignite the fumes. The walls are hung with memorabilia from a cable mafia show.

She thinks about just jumping into the toilet and returning to the house, but doubt strikes her. The fixture looks harder somehow, more *real* than the one she launched herself into in Andrew's house. She imagines braining herself in the old commode. Afro-boy would tell the paramedics she looked confused, walked in on him, didn't seem right to begin with.

And there she is, rolling around at an LGBT mixer in a wheelchair.

"How did you get paralyzed?"

"UTI."

"Urinary—"

(She cuts off her imaginary interlocutor, who looks strangely like Shelly Bertolucci.)

"Unfortunate Toilet Incident."

She doesn't know how long she stands looking at the toilet (which could use a brushing), but a timid knock shakes her from her reverie.

"Just a minute."

"No problem," a girl says.

Wherever she is, they're nice here.

She leaves the bathroom on weak knees, walks into a bright room—a coffee shop—filled with kids studying, old hippies talking politics, a mean-faced woman in line crossing and recrossing her arms, impatient to order her complicated drink. A reflective red truck goes by on the street outside and the whole room flashes red. Anneke opens the door, the little bell on top of which jingles, and the affable man making the cappuccino machine hiss says, "Come back and see us."

"Thanks," she says, walking onto the sidewalk.

Where am I?

How do I get back?

Am I really going to jump in a toilet?

Yes, I am.

Then you had better just go in there and do it because the longer you think about it, the worse this will be.

She glances back in the picture window of the coffee shop, sees an abandoned newspaper on a table. Makes the door ding-a-ling again. Looks at the paper. *USA Today.* Not helpful. Where did it come from? She sees the rack now, near the counter, approaches it as cross-arm-woman eyes her, suspicious she'll try to cut.

The New York Times.

USA Today.

Ah!

The Dayton Daily News.

This townlet looks too small and clean for Dayton, though.

She spots a small rack on the other side of the coffee line, cranes her head to look; the woman winds up to say *Excuse me*, but the pleasant fellow at the counter shuts her down with, "What can I start for you?"

Anneke excuses herself behind the woman, plucks a paper, looks at it.

The Yellow Springs News.

Yellow Springs, Ohio.

Jesus Christ, this is real!

I should get out of here.

They're waiting.

Are they?

Is this happening in real time?

She contemplates another trip to the bathroom, but a heavily bearded poet-type shuts himself in.

Fuck.

I'm not ready to jump in the toilet yet, anyway.

She gets in the coffee line.

Looks behind her, out the front window.

A saloon across the street, all wooden and old-timey.

Oh, that's all I fucking need.

No, that's EXACTLY what you fucking need.

Nerve.

She feels herself start to sweat.

Stays in line, gets a hot chocolate with the cash in her front pocket.

Sips the hot chocolate primly, looking now at the bathroom, now at the saloon. Drums her fingers on the table.

Okay, this isn't your fault. You're in a situation. You have to do this.

Wow, you're cunning.

You're through a magic portal. Whatever happens here won't count.

[Yawn] Wow, you're baffling.

You already know you're going to do it. That, or head to the bus station and get yourself a ticket to Rochester. All you're doing now is wasting time. Yours, Andrew's, and fish-cunt's.

Okay, that was powerful.

Higher power time.

I haven't really got one.

I'm a phony in AA.

I'm only six months in since my last slip.

What's six months?

During the next half an hour, Anneke uses the remaining ten in her pants to order one more hot chocolate and a decaf hazelnut latte. She moves her lips while talking to herself. After her third trip into the bathroom to stare down the throat of the potty, she says "Fuck it," marches out the door,

Ding-a-ling!

and into the tavern across the street, where she orders three shots of Jack Daniel's, only to be told they don't serve hard liquor. She asks who does. Walks the block and a half to the Dayton Street Gulch, looking pissed about it.

Now she orders her three shots.

"Fifteen dollars," says the bartender from a very red mouth sunk in a white-blond beard.

She reaches for her pocket.

Out of bills.

She sees herself tucking her wallet under the front seat of her Subaru.

I don't have my wallet!

The bartender turns to the fridge, fetches out a beer for the fedora-wearing black man who had been wiping up the pool table with a college kid in an ironically name-tagged mechanic's shirt. Anneke slams the first shot. She goes to the bathroom of the saloon (just to pee). Returns to the bar. Slams the second shot. Watches the soundless television, where some daytime TV judge reprimands a woman with an improbable weave. A series of commercials follows:

Detergent, with smiley MILF and smilier babies.

A self-help tape for getting rich through faith, presented by an oddly familiar-looking smiley hypocrite.

Diapers.

More babies.

Fuck daytime television anyway.

She downs the third shot.

"What's your favorite brand of diaper?" she asks the bearded young bartender.

"No preference."

"Very diplomatic of you," she says.

He grins.

She used to be able to outdrink men, but now she's a lightweight. The whiskey slips its hairy fingers around her heart.

It's good.

Here comes the buzz.

It's *really* good.

Maybe he'll pour me two more.

I'll ask if they take Visa first so he thinks I'm okay.

I want them.

But then I'll be shitfaced.

Magic is dangerous enough sober, eh, brujo?

Now or never.

Anneke slips out the door, is nearly struck by a van, runs across the gas station parking lot, nearly hits a stroller, sprints past the tavern and into the coffee shop,

Ding-a-ling-a-ling!!

finds the bathroom door latched!

She glances at the window.

Glimpses the bartender's head between trucks and over cars. She could have played that cooler, acted like she was just going to her car, but adrenaline got her. He looks purposeful. He'll vault when there's a break in the traffic.

Anneke says "Fuck!" and kicks the bathroom door open, the tiny bolt tinkling on the floor.

"Fuck!" echoes a peaceful skinhead type with quarter-sized wooden disks in his ears. She yanks him out from in front of the toilet just before he starts urinating, then pushes him into the coffee shop, his pierced cock a-jiggle.

"Wh'th'fuck, man!" he says.

The counterman sees the push, starts to say "Hey!"

Before he can, both counterman and baldy see Anneke jump into the toilet and disappear.

More properly, she jumps *at* the toilet, but no part of her touches it.

Her cracked oxblood Docs vanish last, flailing.

Both men instantly forget her.

When the exasperated bartender flings open the door of the coffee shop—*ding-a-ling-a-ling!!!*—the counterman asks if there's a problem.

The bartender scratches his beard.

"I'm sorry," he says, realizing he was rough with the door but absolutely blanking on why.

He covers.

"Do you have any fives?"

39

The cabin is full of Russians. They have come from Florida, New Jersey, Little Odessa. A few Americans, stunned-looking relatives of Dragomirov's late wife, all tall, sandy-blond, and blue-eyed, sit in their own corner of the back porch, almost on top of each other because there is no room. The intensity of the Russians scares them, these Lutherans whose stewardess-model married a man of dubious past employment and dangerous associations. This Dragomirov tribe is wild-eyed, dark-haired, quick to laugh, quick to anger.

They read poetry to each other.

Who reads poetry at a party?

This isn't precisely a party.

Neither is it *not* a party.

This is something like a wake, but darker.

Singing, stories, jokes, hints at vengeance to come, these followed by knowing looks between men that suggest more will be said when the women and children have been packed away.

Mikhail Yevgenievich Dragomirov, "Misha," has been gone one month.

The family came today to take possession of the cabin, which has been paid up through the end of August.

One would think the patriarch of the American wing of the family, Georgi Fyodorovich Dragomirov, cousin of the vanished man, would be the one to dominate the room, but he is old now, he dyes his eyebrows, and his heartburn bothers him when he forgets to take his medicine. He has forgotten to take his medicine.

Next in line might have been the half sister, Valentina Fyodorovna, at whose request the icon of the virgin appeared on the corner shelf, replacing Misha's whiskey. She expatriated most recently, but she is too sad to speak at any length, and blows her nose often, always into two tissues, always behind her liver-spotted hand, the nails of which shine with the best burgundy nail polish.

The one who captivates them is not even fifty, and none of them have seen her for years. Little Marina, who had such a hard life. Marina of Nizhny Novgorod, the girl from the woods, saved from prostitution by her Baba, then sent to university. For poetry. How she stunned them when they fetched her at Hancock airport in Syracuse.

She is the brightest of them, seems to shame them with how America has diluted the Dragomirov stock.

She is petite, toned, pretty; they have seen the video she sent them as an introduction, to show them she had her uncle's sense of humor, a video of her working out with kettlebells in the forest to the tune of the Volga Boat Song.

Now she stands before them in her stylish peacoat as evening comes on, her pale, healthy skin, accented by the beauty mark on her cheek, making her look like some lost Romanov.

"My uncle would not want tears," Marina Yaganishna says.

"Bullshit! He cried at movies. He cried at poetry," says a nephew-poet.

"He cried at *your* poetry."

They laugh.

They love her.

They have eaten the funerary blintzes she cooked in the cabin,

"Marishka has taken the stove's virginity—Misha used only the grill and the microwave!"

smeared with the quince jam she learned to make in the forest,

"Her Baba must have taught her this before she died!"

and they have plied her with Stolichnaya only to find themselves drunk before a bright-eyed, clearheaded girl

"Girl my ass! She is a tank soldier like her great-uncle Yevgeny!"

who teases with the best of them.

"Alexandr Nikolayevich, will you dishonor your great-uncle's memory with such a weak fart? Eat more sour cream on your chicken, and fart like a Cossack."

This boy is twelve, and laughs and blushes like beet juice to have his strange Russian aunt spear him so deftly. Earlier, she had stolen the smartphone from his hand and said, "No man under forty should play with a phone more than his *zalupa.*"

His father had made them laugh more with, "But I tell him all the time, drop the *zalupa!*"

One of the American Lutherans, relieved to have something to talk about, explained to Marina what a chalupa was, the dated commercial with the talking chihuahua.

Now, when the last light is gone from the sky, the Lutherans say their good-byes through big-teeth smiles. Marina comically shields her eyes, saying "Your smiles are so perfect in America, you blind me!"

Women and children leave the cabin until it is only Marina and the men who knew Misha. She will be staying—they have all agreed that she can have the cabin as long as she wants it.

But now it is time for men to speak.

They look at her meaningfully, perhaps a bit apologetically, and she understands that they will now fill their glasses more rapidly and exchange oaths of vengeance should the disappearance turn out to be murder—the police said there were signs of a struggle, that DNA evidence of several women has been found, two of them known prostitutes, one of them an unknown. The cousins and nephews of the missing man know his habits; there will be talk of pimps, jealous lovers. The hot-blooded men will vow to handle it personally; the wiser ones will mention, not by name of course, old associates of

Misha's who could be brought in, men who know their way around a Makarov, men who know how to leave a mystery.

She lets herself outside.

She laughs a little when they cannot see her face.

They will be right in their assertions that Dragomirov was the wrong man to fuck with.

They will be wrong as to why.

Marina Yaganishna goes down the stairs, leaving behind the wash of light that bathes the patio. She takes her boots off and walks barefoot out to the edge of the water, barely swaying despite the amount of vodka she has poured into herself. She carries a nearly full bottle with her. Now she removes the rest of her clothes, wades out into the lake with the bottle.

She stands for some time, looking down, as though listening to the waves.

Old Georgi, indicating the nude woman, rubs the burning stomach he knows will kill him soon, says quietly, "Good thing the Americans left."

They laugh.

"She's got the devil in her," one of them says affectionately.

Now they watch their estranged kinswoman upend the bottle, pouring it into the surf.

"Ha! She's giving Misha a drink!"

"Someone should tell her he likes whiskey better."

A silence, as the men continue to watch, despite themselves.

Marina Yaganishna looks thirty-five, not almost fifty.

"I think menopause will be late for her," Georgi says.

They laugh themselves sick, then go back to talk of vengeance.

Out in the lake, the woman pours vodka into the mouth of a kneeling, dead old man with dim lamps for eyes.

"You're sure?" she says.

He nods.

"It will be done, then."

"And I will be free?"

"I think so," she says. "Revenge is liberating."

He opens his bloated mouth for more vodka.

She got it from the freezer, where one of the Lutherans had stashed it in mock ignorance when clearing the table.

She pours again.

"Sorry it's cold."

Misha doesn't care.

Everything is cold now.

He swallows gratefully.

Sinks.

40

Andrew hears Anneke throwing up in the sink, goes to find her.

The stink of hot whiskey, coffee, and chocolate assaults him as he steps into the guest bathroom.

"You've been to Dino's," he says.

She nods, bent over, wiping her mouth.

"And to the Gulch."

Nods again.

Looks at him, eyes glistening, whether from shame, heaving, or both he can't tell.

She becomes aware of the sound of a vacuum cleaner.

"Tour's over for now."

The shame of relapse starts to steal upon her, but she boots it under.

"What about the roosalsa?"

Anneke was gone for an hour.

Nadia got bored and left after ten minutes, but Andrew just ignores the question.

"Are you okay?"

"No."

More okay than you should be because you haven't really crashed yet. This is going to keep happening until you do.

"Are you off the wagon?"

"No."

He looks into her eyes.

Her eyes say yes.

She looks back, fighting the urge to look down.

The Anneke Anneke wants to be doesn't hang her head.

"Well, maybe the tour's not completely over. I want to show you a movie."

"Okay," she says. "As long as it's not *Papillon*."

Down the stairs to the media room.

He turns the lights on, dims them, actually uses the wall switch.

He goes to the combination-locked cedar trunk wherein fifty or so cassettes stand in alphabetized rows, bearing strips of Scotch tape; the tapes on the left are for the famous—*Muhammad ALI, Isaac ASIMOV, Sir Winston CHURCHILL, Harry HOUDINI (no sound), John LENNON*, et cetera. The ones on the right, fewer in number, are not alphabetized, and many have no last name: *Marisol, DAD, SARAH, Aunt Katie, Bill BARNETT*.

A separate locked box sits at the bottom of the chest.

"What's in that?" Anneke says.

"You always want the forbidden fruit, don't you?"

"Don't you?"

"Yes. I guess we all do. All of us who do this. The box has tapes of dead users."

"Why is it locked?"

"They're dangerous. They can still cast spells. One of them's actually not dead—he just left it as an insurance policy. But you need a different kind of magic, I think."

Andrew takes the tape reading *Bill WILSON* from the bottom left.

"That's not . . ." she says.

"Yes."

She looks at the tape.

Shakes her head no.

Andrew sets it on the VCR in front of the television.

He puts his arm around her and she allows it.

They snuggle in on the leather couch, the needle of the intimacy meter moving further away from "buddies," but stopping shy of "lovers." He just holds her, pets her hair, until at last she nods.

He puts the tape in.

Bill speaks.

"Every AA member knows that he has to conform to the principles of recovery. His life actually depends upon obedience to spiritual principles . . ."

"Can he hear us?" she whispers.

"Not yet."

Andrew kisses the top of Anneke's head, separates himself from her enough for decorum, prepares himself to open the trapdoor.

". . . If he deviates too far, the penalty is sure and swift. He sickens and finally dies."

"Bill Wilson. It's Andrew Blankenship."

Bill continues, oblivious.

"He comes to understand that no personal sacrifice is too great for the preservation of this fellowship."

"Bill, can you hear me?"

Apparently not.

"He learns that the clamor of desires and ambitions within him must be silenced whenever these could damage the group."

"Bill Wilson."

Bill ignores him.

Andrew stops the tape.

Rewinds.

Plays.

The same thing happens, or, rather, doesn't happen.

"Something's wrong."

"No shit," she says.

He goes through the song and dance again, gets a little further.

". . . It becomes plain that the group must survive, or the individual will not."

"Bill Wilson, hello."

Bill continues.

But something changes.

His New England accent goes Slavic.

". . . And when the individual doesn't survive, ho, hey! This is a tragedy, small in the grand mechanic of things, but signifying to those who know and care for him . . ."

Andrew blinks dumbly at the screen.

He senses magic.

She does, too.

"Fuck," he says.

"What's happening?"

He grabs her knee, leans forward, intrigued and spooked.

". . . and if there is a God, perhaps signifying big deal to him. But there is no God."

Bill is angry—his head whips and spit flies when he says *God*.

Andrew says, "*This isn't the same tape. He doesn't say these things.*"

Anneke feels gooseflesh ripple down her left side.

". . . Of course, a man doesn't say, never, is no God. A man does not say that he is denying of God if he wants to farm the benefits of 'polite' society."

Bill gets up from his desk, walks over to a curtained window.

The camera follows him.

"Ichabod?" Andrew says. "I command you to stop tampering with this tape."

Nothing. This is not Ichabod's doing. The entity doesn't leave the warm tingle of magic in a room; rather a sort of dead, flat emptiness.

This room is tingling.

On the television, Bill grabs the cord to the curtains, turns to address the camera.

"But when a man knows heartfully how society can be not polite, hey, sometimes fully rude, we are forgiving him for crying himself atheist."

Bill pulls the cord.

The film jerks, jumps out of frame, goes white, comes back on.

A bad splice.

Bill is standing in the same spot, but the colors have shifted.

Orange and red light tints everything.

The sound of propeller planes outside.

Bombers?

Help me, bomber!

Out the windows, fire.

A city on fire.

Stalingrad?

The window Bill opens is on the third or fourth floor of a building that shakes now as a bomb explodes nearby.

A chorus of screaming rises up.

"Oh God," Anneke says.

Now the film jerks again.

The tame, grainy interior colors from the original tape return.

The curtain has been closed, or was never opened, and Bill is sitting at his desk again.

Only the silver water pitcher is gone.

A nearly empty bottle of vintage Soviet vodka has replaced it, a darkly handsome Joseph Stalin leering on the label beneath the Cyrillic legend *NOT ONE STEP BACK!*

Bill's necktie hangs sloppy and loose, the first buttons of his shirt undone. His hair uncombed. He is drunk.

The sounds of war have gone away.

A musician of small talent plays a violin in another room.

"Do you see what you have driven me to?" he says, in Ukrainian-accented Russian, looking at Andrew.

"Stop it," Andrew says, pointing authoritatively at the television.

"Stop it!" shitfaced Bill Wilson says, in English, mocking him, laughing, pointing.

Andrew presses the power button on the remote.

The television flicks off.

Then turns itself *back on.*

Bill points at Andrew, says, in Russian, "You think you got away with something, don't you? But your time has run out. We know where you are. And we are coming."

Subtitles appear in yellow, doubtless for Anneke's benefit.

"You will die, you sloppy little shit. Sloppy. Weak. Little. Shit."

"Who are you?"

Bill W. smiles, but it's not a pleasant smile.

The image freezes.

The celluloid burns exactly where his mouth is, burns in the nearly flat U of his smile. His eyes burn, too.

The violin stops.

Now the television screen begins to smoke where the mouth and eyes were.

Anneke jumps to her feet, puts the couch between her and the Sony.

"Christ!" Andrew yells.

The television catches fire.

41

The fire is magical in origin, but thankfully not in nature; an ordinary extinguisher stifles it in seconds. Not that the house would burn; Andrew set very powerful dousing wards at every corner of the property. The smoke alarm goes off, hurting their ears with its shrill chirps. Andrew sets down the extinguisher, silences the alarm. The room is murky with smoke and nitrogen. Anneke, her stomach still queasy following her belly flop out of sobriety, fights the urge to heave.

"Well," Andrew says, "this is what magic looks like when used as a weapon. It's not pretty."

"Nothing's pretty when used as a weapon."

"I love your zero-tolerance approach to bullshit."

"You're trying to sound authoritative, like you're in control. But you're not, are you?"

"Not entirely."

"Not entirely? More bullshit. Do you even know who did this?"

"I think so."

"How did they get into the house? *Your* house?"

He notices the cord connecting a MacBook Pro to the television from his last streamed movie.

"Through that," he says, pointing.

He disconnects it, handling it like a snake that might still bite.

"I need to e-mail somebody."

42

Chicagohoney85: You're going to owe me big for this. I don't know if you understand how hard something like this is.

Ranulf: It can't have been that hard if you're already getting back to me.

—Difficulty is not measured in duration.

—It took you 24 hours.

—Labor can take 24 hours. Or it can take two. I've never popped one out, but word on the corner is that it sucks either way.

—Point taken. But it's going to take me some time to trick out a car for you. That's what you want, right? A car that cops, thieves and meter maids don't notice?

—Yep. Tell me what else it'll do again . . . City car stuff, right? I've got no use for big or fast.

—Runs on water. I know another user who can do that, but fitting in extra-tight spaces by making them bigger is mine alone. So far, anyway.

—Sounds awesome! Parking sucks here. That's exactly what I want!

—So be it! But I'll need a week or two to find the right car, and another week to do the work. Twenty four hours, my ass!

—What, should I have acted like it took longer? Mechanics always make less per hour than IT people. And you like working on cars ☺

—No more than you like solving puzzles ☺

—You got me. I do! And this one was a bitch. Here's what you gave me—a hut somewhere in rural Russia, probably the Volga region, but maybe anywhere in Russia. Maybe Belorussia, maybe the Ukraine, maybe Poland, somewhere Slavic. Real specific, right?

—I gave you more than that!

—You did & I'll get to that; I'm just pointing out that I had to search a pretty big chunk of the earth's total land mass.

—But you have some way to detect magic, right? Some tweak to Google Earth or something?

—Yes, something like that. But I told you before she's got somebody veiling her. Another techno-savvy user. And a good one, spooky good.

—I think I got a taste of how good he is.

Andrew remembers the burning smile, the burning eyes, how they stuck to the glass, then burned out the other side.

—You're sure it's a he? I'm not a he.

—I think he's a he. I think you're a she. I don't know either one for sure.

—If you were ten years younger, I'd tell you to come to Chicago so I could show you. I've seen old pictures of you, you know. I Facebook stalked you. Hot! But you're too old now, so you'll have to take my word for it. I'm just saying don't make assumptions-that can kill you in this game.

—True enough. But my point was that however good he or she is, I feel good having you in my corner. You're spooky good, too.

—I am! Which is why I think I found her anyway.

—May I ask how?

—You just did. And, yes. I found her with shadows.

—I'm not sure I get it.

—First I used the magic-detection, then flagged areas that looked indistinct; veiling draws a screen, and a lesser witch wouldn't even see the screen. But I can. I pick up a slight blur. Flagged all the blurs in Slavic countries. There's a fuckload of magic over there, BTW. You were brave to go over there, what, during the cold war?

—You say brave. Some would say stupid.

—Now I took something else you told me. She eats kids, right? Actually eats them.

Andrew leans back from the screen, rubs his eyes with his hands, as if to massage away the pictures in his head.

—You there?

—Yes. She eats them.

—I hacked police records. I don't speak those languages, so I had to outsource the translations. These people aren't luminous, they just want money, I sent you an invoice. It's a bit steep. Good, fast and cheap, you can't have all three, right?

—I got the invoice.

—So I looked for reports of missing children. Infants. The Volga lit up, just like you said it would. But so did a few other areas where I saw blurs. Now we've checked for magic, hidden

magic and missing kids. Still a bit of crossover. But the Volga stuff
was old, like a few years old. You know what lit up since 2008?

—Tell me.

—You're going to like it. Not that kids are missing, I mean,
but where I think she is. It fits. But let me tell you the third thing
I looked for, cause I'm proud of it.

—Shadows, you said.

—Shadows, sure, but what kind?

—I give up.

—So now I bring in the military eyes-in-the-sky. Hacked the
shit out of them, and they're mighty. Hi-res satellite images. I
can find a fly sitting on poop in Mongolia.

—Ha!

—Now I think about the physical structure. You said the hut
stands on chicken's feet, right? Big ones, like taller than a man.

—Not everybody can see them.

—Film still records things like that. It's why we sometimes
see ghosts in photos. The camera doesn't lie-the lie happens in
our heads.

—But the angle? A satellite wouldn't see feet under a hut.

—Think.

Andrew furrows his brow, taps his index finger on the table like a
woodpecker seeking grubs. It's easier for her to puzzle things out—she's
a plodder, not a natural. She worked her way into magic with brains.
But Andrew is far from stupid. The last tap is hard, a percussive *Eureka!*

—The shadow! The hut is higher, as if on stilts.

—And stilts aren't a big thing in these countries. Louisiana,
Indonesia, Southeast Asia, sure. But, aside from ice-fishing huts,
it's not a Slavic thing.

—But I remember it was in forest . . . it was dark. She likes
dark. What about the trees?

—You also said she had a garden. Gardens need sun. She's not going to park herself in total darkness. There'll be a break in the canopy.

—There was! There was a patch of sunlight.

—Now we've got three criteria . . . magic, child disappearances, and a hut with a shadow that suggests 6-10′ clearance. One match. Check it out.

A photograph appears.

A straw-roofed hut, not big.

Not on the outside, anyway.

Fu fu fu, I smell Russian bones!

And then a second cursor appears.

Points at a hunched figure carrying a pan of what look like pork bones, mostly in shadow. Indistinct.

Andrew shudders.

Do not look at me with your eyes or I'll take them.

Do not smile at me with your teeth or I'll take them.

Piss squatting or I'll carve a cunt on you.

—You there?

—Give me a minute.

—K

Andrew feels himself begin to shudder, an involuntary response he can observe, as if it were someone else's shudder, but which he cannot stop.

—Is that her, Ranulf?

The cursor wiggles over the crone.

Andrew feels his testicles ice over.

His palms go clammy, he wipes them on his jeans.

—Is that Baba Yaga?

He can't seem to will his fingers to type.

Her name has been invoked.

He glances behind him at a handsome brass mirror, terrified he'll see her image, but his own scared face looks back at him.

Brass mirrors are safe, can't serve as gates for her.

He notices the tension in his mouth, how carefully he keeps his lips pressed together.

Radha is waiting.

She wants to know if the hunched shape with the pan full of bones is the ancient thing that kidnapped him twenty-nine years ago.

—I think so.

—Awesome! I think so, too. Now you wanna know where she is? Not exactly where she is, but what she's pretty close to?

He envies Radha her fearlessness, how casually confident she is of her own power. He was the same way before he went to Russia.

—Where is it?

—It's pretty creepy. And pretty perfect. Nobody will fuck with her there. By the way, Madeline Kahn is kind of a bitch.

—Where is she, Radha?

Radha types.

Andrew knows what word will appear, knows it a microsecond before it appears on his screen like a name on a map of Hell—

Gehenna.

Dis.

Tartarus.

Acheron.

—Chernobyl.

In the other room, Anneke's phone rings.

43

Karl Zautke lies on his side with the breathing tube in.

His pillows are damp beneath him. The lymph nodes in his neck hurt him, have grown from acorns to grapes, but he can breathe a bit better, well enough to sleep. He fights it, though, his big blue eyes rolling back, the lids closing, and then he forces them open again for another bleary image of his daughter, her faggish but nice friend sitting next to her.

He feels so bad he doesn't even want a PBR.

His left foot sticks out, pink and huge, the flesh swollen around the little yellow nails.

Karl is far too big for this place, hates his hospital gown, hates how wet it is. One of the minor nasties (among many nasties, great and small) about leukemia is how much laundry you have to do, how much you sweat. *Like a whore in church* is his default cliché. His girl has been doing his laundry for him, doing everything. He can't stand being a burden. But the sweating. He soaks his shirts and underthings so easily he keeps his three window AC units thrumming at sixty-six degrees from June through September.

They're running now in his empty house.

This is Karl's third hospitalization for pneumonia in two years, and he knows as well as Anneke does that this is what kills most people with his kind of leukemia. Chronic lymphocytic leukemia, the slower kind. It wears you down. Erodes you. He's had it for eight years, several stretches of remission making him hopeful he might live long enough to die of heart disease or something that wasn't so damned . . . *nagging*. This is no way for a man to live, constantly tired, afraid of infection. Purel in his shirt pocket. Waterpik-ing his goddamn teeth like a supermodel, crossing the street away from anybody coughing, especially kids. And Karl *likes* kids. It just isn't fair he's had to stay away from them now when he hasn't done anything *wrong*.

He looks at Anneke one more time.

An unpleasant thought crosses his mind; he puts that away.

Thinks instead about her learning to ride that powder-blue bike with the streamers on the handles. The face she made (teeth bare, mouth half open, a lion cub about to bite) when he picked gravel out of her scraped knee, sprayed cold Bactine on it. How proud he was of her for getting back on the bike immediately, how he knew she was doing it for him, for that extra scrunch in his eyes when he smiled down at her.

Nothing pleases Karl like watching someone he loves be brave.

This is why Anneke.

Won't.

Fucking.

Cry.

Her eyes are moist, but that's as far as it goes.

Father looks at daughter, daughter at father.

Their Germanic blue eyes hold communion for another few seconds before the big man rolls his eyes back under his lids and sleeps.

. . .

"I don't feel good about this one," she says.

Andrew holds her hand. She allows this but squeezes his every few seconds as if to show him the strength in her hand, as though she is too proud to just let her hand lie in his, take warmth and love from him.

"He's seventy now. He's tired," she says.

Andrew nods, looking at him.

His beard, mostly white with hints of the reddish blond that made him look like a stout Robert Redford in his youth, seems itchy and wrong on him. He only grew it to hide the lymph nodes so nobody asked about them.

"He hates sympathy. Can't stand people fussing over him," Anneke explains. She's taking on a teacher's voice, assuming an in-control role so she doesn't have to feel quite so much.

Andrew already knows this about the big ex-navy man, not only because he waited until he had almost suffocated before he phoned his little girl for help, but also because Anneke could have just as easily been describing herself.

The man never thought much of Andrew, never knew him well or wanted to. He was pleasant enough, just didn't know what locker to put him in so radiated a benign neutrality toward the smaller man. Not his daughter's boyfriend, she didn't have those. Effeminate, probably somebody she met in "gay circles," whatever those were. Andrew always felt vaguely ashamed around him, even now, looking at the faded blue anchor tattoos blurring his forearms, the hint of a sparrow peeking from his chest through the open gown. Karl is all man, and nobody ever doubted that about him. The small, insecure, fatherless part of Andrew wants Karl's approval and sees the last chance for that slipping away, feels selfish for thinking about himself.

He just sits there, feeling Anneke's pulsing squeezes, letting her talk about her dad from time to time. Wishing she would put her head on his chest so he could stroke her hair, soothe her. But she rarely shows him that side of herself, and never in front of Karl Zautke.

Andrew wonders, not for the first time, what good it is to fool with magic when this lies at the end no matter what or who you are.

Except perhaps for her.

She's old.

So old.

Don't think about her now.

Are there mirrors in here?

He's relieved to see there aren't any. Of course there aren't—the sick don't like to look at themselves.

Soon Anneke dozes, her head touching Andrew's shoulder.

The sound of the ventilator makes him drowsy, too.

She enters the bathroom through the mirror.

Andrew hears her, hears the sound she makes coming through, a sort of creak that suggests glass about to break.

I have to put my kerchief on!

Now!

He takes a hand towel from the bedside table, one that Anneke had been using to soothe her father's sweating head. Lukewarm now and faintly sour with Karl's sick smell. No matter—Andrew tilts his head back, rests it over his eyes.

The shaking starts.

He wills himself to be calm, but it only partly works.

Fu fu fu.

She's in the bathroom!

The ventilator stops.

The heart monitor goes wild, flatlines, the long beep announcing another death in the land of air conditioners and SUVs.

Nobody moves.

No nurse comes.

The bathroom door opens; he feels the air get colder.

With a gasp and a sudden full-body clench, Anneke dies next to him.

Baba has used the Hand of Glory he took from the witch's hut, the one that stops hearts.

Anneke is unimportant to her, so the old thing discards her.

Baba only wants him.

She will not stop his heart.

She will take him back now, back to her hut.

Back to his kennel.

Back to be leeched.

"Hey! Shh! You're making noises."

Anneke looking at him, exhausted, irritated, afraid.

He nods.

Sits up straighter.

Feels his heart racing.

The sound of the ventilator confuses him.

She pets his hair.

Soothes him.

44

Day.

The necromancer's house.

Andrew stands in the front living room near the unlit fireplace watching the feral man crouching in the tree line. The feral man wears a T-shirt of indeterminate color, so torn his bony shoulders and one nipple show—the ring of the collar is most of what holds it together—the image on the chest picturing what looks to be a faded Pac-Man being chased by his ghosts. His legs are sheathed in a pair of muddy jeans that look ready to slough off him and show thighs that might be satyr's thighs. His matted hair and unkempt beard mark him as some sort of latter-day John the Baptist, or more boyish Manson. No thread of silver shoots through that black mane. He is young. By his movements, less catlike than monkeyish, Andrew guesses the boy to be about twenty. He arms aside the bushes and walks in a crouch, sniffing and listening as much as looking. But it is the looking Andrew likes least.

He sees the house.

Nobody uninvited sees the fucking house.

That was the point of the three-month-long spell he wove around it, burying mirror shards and the dried skins of chameleons in a circle, painting the walls with paint he'd hidden in public for a month and added octopus ink to, intoning both the *Iliad* and the *Odyssey* in Homer's Greek to provoke a benign blindness in those who climbed the hill and looked at the house. Sure, people who knew he was here could see it. But since he kept his address unlisted, the only people who knew the house was here were people he told and people from the neighborhood who knew the house before he bought it all those years ago.

This young man looks right through his window and *at* him. Even without magic cloaking, the angle of the sun should make the windows reflective, should throw so much light back that the panes become shields of trees and sky that let no gaze past them and into the house's cool heart.

But this man sees him.

Andrew walks backward, out of the picture window's frame— the boy seems to track him as he moves, and he waits by the fireplace before continuing to the second picture window. By the time he gets there the boy is gone. Utterly gone. Had he even been there? He licks his lips and looks at the space on the mantel where his best scotch used to sit before he emptied the house of booze.

Wish a bottle there you have a spell for that six sentences and a pinprick and a bottle will sprout where the blood drop falls.

He shakes that away and goes back to the left-hand window, peering into the woods where he saw Pac-Man boy, using a hunter's patient eyes, and he sees no movement, no line of shoulder or haunch breaking the bloom of foliage. But now he wants a drink, and he wants it bad.

One remedy works better than any other for chasing that particular noise out of his head.

The room of skins.

He goes to the raw oak door and closes his eyes, remembering his first hunt, remembering the sliver of raw stag heart his uncle had offered him off the knife.

This door will open for you only if you have eaten the heart of something killed with your own hand.

He slides the brass handle into his palm and turns, feeling the door open easily on its hinge. This is a small room, its walls hung with stags' heads and hide maps and an antique wardrobe on either side. One window gives on a sort of brambled alley leading down the hill toward the forest path, and he goes to open this.

I'll kill two birds at once here; I'll have a boozeless run in the brambles and see if I can find the Jesus-looking boy.

Should I go scary or fast?

Does the boy have a gun?

It didn't seem so.

What if he's watching me change?

Fuck him, then. Let him watch. Maybe he'll shit himself.

Andrew opens the window as slowly and quietly as he can; it is always best to open the window first, while one still has thumbs.

He opens the left wardrobe now, its door cutting off his view of the window, and he regards the selection of furs hanging from their iron hooks. Fox. Wolf. Bear. Stag. Bobcat. All the indigenous beasts, safest to run in these woods. The right-hand wardrobe holds more exotic skins, skins for special occasions.

No, he will run a New York beast today.

He runs his hand on the black bear pelt.

He killed this bear with an Osage orange longbow and a flint arrowhead made by a master fletcher in Pennsylvania.

He has named the bear Norris.

Norris will do.

Now he sticks his thumb in his navel and pushes, saying in old French, "I open myself." He imagines his thumb slipping bloodlessly under his skin, and so it does. It doesn't precisely hurt, but the feeling is deeply creepy. He works the thumb under and skins himself. He hangs his skin from the one bare hook in the wardrobe. He has to be quick now—one can't just hang out skinless—so he takes up the black bear skin and puts it over his flayed shoulders, feeling it grab him, feeling it wrap all of him so his legs are bear legs and his cock a bear's cock and his snout smells berries and sap and he chuffs his bearness and climbs comically out the window.

Let's see how Pac-Man shirt likes this.

Picking up the boy's scent is easy with the bear's nose; the smell is tangy and human and strong, innocent of soap. He dips his head and trundles into the underbrush, his shiny black bear-shoulders working as he tracks. Not far from the house, near the strawberry patch he has to put off foraging from by sheer force of man-will over bear-will, he smells out a pile of shit. Human shit in the woods doesn't seem odd to the bear, but Andrew-in-the-bear is mildly offended that somebody would not only come slinking and spying near his actual house, but would have the territorial nerve to leave droppings.

Odd droppings for a man, too.

This boy clearly eats fast food like many boys, cheap mash of discarded, hormone-bloated cow full of preservatives and despair, but he doesn't chew much before he swallows. He also eats beetles. He had fingered cicada larvae out of the ground. He had eaten earthworms raw and had cooked beetles in squirrel fat, and had gorged on squirrel and even fine squirrel-bones.

Very fast, or a good trapper.

Or a good shot.

But I smell no gun, or gun oil.

A man can kill a bear without metal.

You did.

This is more boy than man.

The boy has also eaten strawberries.

My strawberries!

Oh, this will not do, not by half.

He snuffs and makes his way around to where the boy had been crouched in the woods, looking at the picture window. Tracks and scent loop back into the woods, so he follows, and soon finds himself looking back at the window leading to the room of skins.

The boy is halfway between the tree line and the open window, contemplating a dash for it. He not only sees the house, he is about to go in!

Fuck this!

Andrew-in-the-bear chuffs and lopes at the boy, who turns and looks passively at the bear. It would be fair to say the boy looks curious, but he does not give off the satisfying rush of fear-smell Andrew-in-the-bear hoped for.

The bear four-legs up to the boy, then stands.

Only a little taller on his hind legs—Norris had not been a huge bear—but still lethal.

He breathes his hot bear-breath into the boy's face, but the boy just blinks at him.

Why doesn't he run?

He pushes the boy's chest with his forepaws, not hard, but more than gently. The boy staggers back, but still makes no meaningful move to retreat.

Okay, you want it rougher? I can do rougher.

Now he grabs the boy's pants with his jaws, slipping his fangs surgically under the waistband, and he throws the boy back, half tearing the jeans. The boy falls but gets to his feet again. Beginning to walk away, but not frightened.

Faster, you little shit.

Now the bear swipes at him, curling his claws back so he doesn't lay him open, but heavily enough to send him sprawling.

To Andrew's surprise, Pac-Man shirt doesn't stand up this time, but breaks and runs on all fours. The bear shuffles after him on two legs, Andrew-in-the-bear dimly aware of the irony.

Just before the feral young man makes the tree line, he stands again and gives the bear one more longish look. A look of assessment, calculation.

Calculate this.

The bear charges, and the boy sprints away.

Who was that boy?

No, really, who the fuck was he?

The bear lumbers back toward the house, checking over his shoulder and sniffing the air once or twice to make sure the interloper is really gone.

Then he waddles over to the strawberry patch and eats himself almost sick.

Too dominated by bear-hunger to notice or care that the berries are frozen.

45

This is what Andrew does at the AA meeting.

He greets Bob, the chair, on his way in, remarking once again on how happy Bob is. How goddamned, unassailably *happy.* The man went to jail four times for DUI and involuntary manslaughter, got evicted, lost two marriages, a boat, and a career as a charter captain; now he works at a church resale shop, hasn't got a pot to piss in, and yet . . .

"Andrew! Haven't seen you in a week or two. We missed you!"

"I must have felt you missing me, Bob. Here I am."

Bob hugs him like Andrew's his little brother, nothing fake about it.

Unlike when his own brother hugs him, though that hasn't happened for a while.

Maybe fifteen years since Charles gave Andrew something other than a perfunctory manshake.

Bob has fifteen years sober, a bona fide elder statesman.

Bob's nothing like Charley.

Bob went for donkey-and-sandals Jesus, knows Charley's BMW Jesus is something else.

Bob's eyes twinkle like he figured out God's his secret Santa and he knows you'll figure out he's yours, too, in your own sweet time. Early on, Andrew swung between feeling inspired by Bob and really resenting him; where does a beat-up old fellow who isn't much to look at, can't do magic, can't afford a restaurant meal, and hasn't gotten laid since the Berlin Wall fell get off just *glowing* like that? It's a little like being luminous, only Bob will never learn magic out of a book and make things happen in the world. All the magic happens in Bob's head—he stopped trying to change the world and just changed how he looks at it.

It's genius, really, if you can manage it.

Why make a big house for yourself when you're happy in a shack?

Why lust for a new car when your crank-handle windows work fine and Chancho fixes your rusted-out old beater at cost?

You could shit in Bob's shirt pocket and he would run to spread it on his blueberry patch.

Between her introduction to the hostile side of magic and the coming death of her father, Anneke needs Bob.

With the ancient Russian crone who captured and tortured Andrew twenty-nine years before now stalking him, the magus needs Bob, too.

Bob doesn't know exactly what's wrong in their lives, they don't share tonight, but he's glad they came. He reads from the Big Book, and then he talks about forgiveness.

Andrew has trouble staying on message.

He's not thinking about forgiveness.

He's thinking about self-defense.

He's thinking about revenge.

46

New Orleans in June is a sort of bright, dangerous sauna whose steam seems to come from the crotches and armpits of its citizens; its nucleus is a tangle of colonial streets where tourists tread on bones; they drink liquors distilled from the sweat of dead West Africans, the grandchildren of whom have been pushed to low ground to await their centennial drowning, but some of these don't wait quietly. It is easy to get shot here, or stabbed, or clubbed toothless, even in the bright places that smell of rum and fruit juice, even as rotten cops look down at you from the saddles of their horses and fat Iowans and Michiganders sleep above them in overpriced hotels, dreaming of the morning's beignets.

Haint likes this about the French Quarter; he likes walking among the entitled and the blind and feeling their condescension toward him; he is another curiosity in a city teeming with them, an intentionally scarred and branded black man with skin that looks almost indigo, his crown of graying hair horseshoeing a balding dome that bears a front-to-back row of scars he inflicted himself with a hot razor.

"I liked your letter," Haint says to Andrew as both men sit sweating in Coops. "You write your words tight and plain and press hard with the pen, none of this loopy shit."

"I e-mailed you," Andrew says.

Haint enunciates each of the next words carefully, as if explaining things to a well-meaning but disappointing child.

"I am talking. About the way. I saw it in my head. I saw your e-mail as a letter."

Haint is one of those half-mad users whose conversation must be sifted to separate delusion from actual magic. This is often difficult.

"You press hard with the pen," he continues. "*You mean what you say*'s what that says, and I keep such men close to my heart."

He wipes his ridged dome with the greasy and formless bicycle cap he carries more than wears, then takes another bite of the jambalaya he has rendered lukewarm in temperature (if not in taste) with Crystal hot sauce that pools like orangey blood around its rim.

"Will you help me?" Andrew says.

"Another thing I like 'bout you is you don' try and act like you ain't scared."

Andrew nods.

"Anybody smart's scared of that ol' . . . her. Her, I mean. I didn't even know she was real. Heard bad stories, figured they was stories. But if she is an actual *actuality*, and she *is* that old, she gonna make Marie Laveau look like a Girl Scout, home team pride aside and all. Yeah, I'll help. But keep the book. I ain't got no use for books and I don't read English so good's I got any hope of readin' Russian."

The part about not reading English is a flat lie. Haint reads like an Oxford scholar but hides his brilliance behind a hedge of *ain't*s and *cain't*s.

Andrew's e-mail offered one of the treasures he brought home in 1983, a beautiful tome on invisibility written in the time of Peter the Great, a remarkably valuable book for reasons both aesthetic and practical.

But what Haint says next tells Andrew the hoodoo man already knows how to disappear and isn't interested in acquiring something to barter with.

"I want that hand."

"You already have a Hand of Glory. Hell, I heard you had three of them."

"Not like that one. Mine open locks and turn lights on and off. Useful as hell, don't get me wrong. But you know what that Russian hand does, don't you?"

"Stops hearts."

"Works, don't it?"

"It works."

"How do you know?"

"It works."

"Prolly you knocked a squirrel out of a tree with it. Only you ain't never tried on a person 'cause you ain't like that. Me, I'm like that. That's why you want me."

Andrew nods. Of course Haint had heard of Baba's lethal Hand of Glory; Haint is a collector of murders, a man who has gathered an arsenal of artifacts that take life. He is rumored to have a Turkish knife that, when used on a piece of lambskin the user has bled on, will cut or stab whatever the user thinks about cutting or stabbing, even across the sea, provided he has seen it and can picture it clearly. Years ago he carried a Polaroid camera around his neck in case he wanted to capture your image.

Now Steve Jobs has armed him with a smartphone.

If you are on Facebook, or if your image can be Googled, it is said this man can cut your throat no matter how far away you live from his warehouse apartment on Frenchman Street. Or Carondelet. Or wherever it is this week—it is also rumored that Haint's apartment is actually in a black trash bag he can blow up into the window of any abandoned place, and leave with in minutes.

He received Andrew's e-mail under the name hoodoohowdo-youdo@gmail.com. Until 2000, when he finally went digital, he used to get letters through a PO box under the name Sam E. DiBaron. It was the same PO box he used to arrange killings, but never for money.

Always for things.

Never yet for anything he wanted as much as Baba Yaga's Hand of Glory.

"Can you do it?"

"If I cain't, you cain't."

"That's not an answer."

"No. 'Cause I don't have one. I don't know if she can die, and if she cain't, I don't know if I can stay hid from her."

"I did."

"I know. That's the only reason I'm thinking about trying this crazy shit. How's your boudin?"

Andrew nods appreciatively.

"They don't put it on the menu; never on the menu 'cause they cain't sell enough for how fast it goes bad; just on special sometimes. Normally you don't want restaurant boudin—what you want is gas station boudin somebody's mama boiled up in a Crock-Pot out in Grosse Tête or Scott or Breaux Bridge, if you can stand them coon-asses out there. But it ain't bad here. They know what they doin' here. Dreddy white fella in the kitchen plays a mean fiddle, too. I'm goin' to hear him tonight. You wanna come?"

"Love to. Thanks."

Haint now swigs his beer and uses a thumb-struck stove match to relight the reeking stub of cigar he has rested on the crown of his bottle cap. At his third puff, a woman at the booth to the right issues a dainty cough behind a dainty hand, at which the polo-shirted man with his back to them turns and throws a disapproving glance.

It was probably this fucker who stacked Jack Johnson songs on the Internet jukebox.

Haint discreetly raps the table with his knuckle and a car alarm goes off on Decatur Street outside. The man looks doorward now and excuses himself, fumbling with his keys. As he crosses the threshold, Haint deftly snaps the matchstick between two fingers with his thumb and the big man trips, foolishly trying to break his fall with his hand. His wrist snaps audibly and he issues a gagging cry. The woman gets to her feet, her distaste for cigar smoke and shirtless black men forgotten. The waitress runs to help, wiping her hands on her apron. The dreddy bearded fellow peers out the kitchen door, and a teenaged boy begins to film the incident with his phone, ignoring his mother's admonitions. The jukebox sputters now, aborting the song it had been playing and starting up Billie Holiday's "They Can't Take That Away From Me."

Haint keeps eye contact with Andrew throughout, puffing contentedly on his cigar. Mismatched earrings shine dully in the hoodoo man's ears.

"Maybe you can."

"Maybe I can," the man agrees, his eyes twinkling.

47

Andrew has some time to kill before night comes down, so he walks around the Quarter. Construction everywhere, as usual; torn-up roads blocked off with orange webbing, tourists filtering by one another on what's left of the sidewalk, stepping carefully around piles of shelving for this or that new store. On Royal Street, women in Mardi Gras feathers dance in the heat while cameras turn and film crewmen detour folks up Orleans, some of these pooling up in the margins and holding up phones to film or snap stills of the dancers.

On Dauphine, the woman who runs a perfumery is yelling at the owner of the tattoo parlor next door because the new electric purple paint job smells like paint. He nods at her briefly, then goes inside. She yells at his retreating back, is still yelling at the door when he comes back out holding a ukulele, which he plays in accompaniment to her oration, driving her volume up and making her widen her eyes with fury. Andrew is nearly jabbed in the eye by her gesticulating finger, laughs as he continues past them, has the good sense not to answer when she screams, "What's so funny!" at his back.

Andrew's shirt is good and soaked by the time he gets to his former apartment on St. Ann, a small second-floor flat now annexed to the Sanson boutique hotel. He stands below it and looks up, noting how much neater and more inviting it looks now. Hanging plants cascade from the balconies thereof in majestic gouts of green. A woman in a turquoise bathrobe stares unashamedly down at him, a sort of bright balcony house cat drinking something red from a clear plastic cup. Her colors go so well with the aqua stucco behind her that she might have been paid to hold that post.

"Afternoon," he says to her.

She raises her glass and inclines her head slightly, with the gentility of diurnal inebriation.

He misses his Vieux Carré flat but cut it loose after Katrina. He wasn't really coming here often enough to justify the expense, after all, and it's normally not too hard to find a hotel.

Normally.

He heads south again, then left on Bourbon, right on Frenchman.

The Frenchman voodoo shop sits beneath a wooden sign depicting a bat in an eighteenth-century powdered wig. The bat holds a tiny skull in one foot and a tarot pack in the other, echoing the American eagle motif with its olive branch and quiver. Miss Mathilda, an enormous black woman in an Indian-print dress, advises a pinch-faced man in a tweed suit.

"Now, this kind of service is not cheap because it is real. Do you understand me, sir? This is not a joke."

She cuts her eyes to Andrew when he enters.

The man in tweed does, too.

She winks at Andrew, looks back at the man, actually uses her finger to turn his face back toward hers. He suffers this. She goes on.

"You will need to bring me film of your father, plus one or two personal effects of his, preferably things he handled frequently."

The man looks at Andrew again.

Miss Mathilda says, "He's a friend, we can speak in front of him."

She can barely contain her smile.

She turns the man's face once more with her finger, swallows him with her eyes.

"In two weeks or thereabouts we will receive the tape and call you. About the tape; it must be VHS."

"Yes, ma'am."

"Do you have VHS footage of your father?"

"Doing what?"

"Anything."

"Christmas. Is Christmas okay?"

"We love Christmas at the Frenchman voodoo shop."

"But I only have one copy. And nobody makes VHS anymore."

She plucks a business card from between the teeth of a cat's skull.

"This man on Tchopitoulas does. Ring the bell downstairs. And don't be alarmed if he answers in his boxers. Just between us, he's a little touched, but he's the best man in the city for vintage electronics."

"How do I . . ."

"Know it's real?"

She uncurls a finger, points a black fingernail with a triangle of diamond chips in it like stars. Points at a red door hung with testimonials.

"That room. You'll watch it the first time in that room. If your father does not speak to you, you will not be charged."

His eyes dance over her face, looking for the scam.

"I won't?"

"Of course not. I told you, this is the real thing. We have no need to cheat anyone."

"Three thousand even? No tax?"

She nods.

"Where does the tape go?"

"I'm not at liberty to say."

"Is this legal?"

She smiles broadly.

"My friend, nobody has ever asked me that before."

When the man leaves, Andrew and Miss Mathilda bear-hug each other, laugh together, talk.

"How long are you here for, pretty man?"

"Not long."

"You smell like hoodoo."

"Guilty."

"And boudin. Have you been eating boudin?"

He nods.

"Where's mine?"

He shrugs, smiling. She's younger than him by a decade but always makes him feel twelve. He resolves to bring her boudin when he leaves.

"But how about that? That guy. You think he'll want a trapdoor?"

"Could be."

"What a coincidence. Walking in just then, I mean."

"Not as much as you might think."

"How so?"

"My dear Mr. Blankenship, I offer your service several times a day most days. To anyone who lingers at the altar of the dead with hope or sadness in their eyes. And of course to anyone who buys a candle to light or hangs a photo. Look how many!"

The tin tree standing over the waxy altar blooms with pictures of the dead. Incense lingers.

She goes on.

"It's just that so few people have that kind of money now. Even for parlance with the blessed dead."

"I'm doing all right."

"If you were doing all right, you wouldn't have given up that sweet little apartment."

He blinks twice, squints like he does when he's about to ask a favor.

She anticipates him.

"Seeing a friend, huh?"

"Yep."

"Gun show this week," she says.

"Uh-huh."

"Hotels all booked."

He's ashamed of his poor planning.

"That's right."

She fishes around near the register.

Holds up three brass keys as if fanning three cards.

"Pick."

48

Andrew opens the door to room 373 of the Brass Key Apartments, his left hand flipping up a dead wall switch, his nostrils flaring to take in the damp air. Hot and dark. It smells of nylon stockings and stale semen, the nosegay of adultery, but why shouldn't it? Adultery is his business here, too.

He crosses to the AC unit beneath the window and turns the

knob, glad to hear it sputter on. The air coming from the cross-hatched mouth is dog's-breath warm, though, and turning the loose temperature knob all the way into the blue only cools it marginally. A drop of sweat milky with salt runs down his nose and disappears into the vent.

He tries the window and it refuses to rise, so he braces himself and pushes up hard. Painted shut. A young couple on the street below whinnies self-conscious laughter, and he laughs, too, as he imagines himself pawing at the glass at them like a dog stuck in a hot car. His guayabera is beginning to stick to his back again.

Across the street, a balding man in suspenders and a blood-soaked shirt looms behind a filthy window, fanning himself with a fedora. His look suggests mild curiosity, incongruous with his recently cut throat. A ghost. So many of them here. Andrew suppresses the urge to wave and turns from the window.

Lights from the bars on St. Louis wash the room in red light that recalls the engine room of a World War II submarine, even through the flimsy curtains. He sits on the futon and feels the cord of the table lamp until he finds the switch, which he is immediately sorry to have pushed. Now the gaudy purple and gold wall hanging, bearing the obligatory fleur-de-lis, pounces at him. Now he sees the truly impressive cum stain on the futon cover, as big as a map of Cuba. He has the impression its author is a minor league baseball player, but has no idea where that comes from.

He notes a filmy glass ashtray near the lamp and decides to give the window another try before he lights up.

Brace.

Strain.

Window still shut.

Drop of sweat in the eye.

An idea comes to him then.

He is reluctant to bother Haint again, having left him at the Tin Shack to listen to the fiddler's second set, but Haint is the best man he knows to solve this problem; the only one who might be able to do it remotely. Miss Mathilda gave him the key, but she will already be settling down to sleep, having read her autistic girl an article from *Scientific American* or *Popular Science.*

He texts Haint a photo of the window with the message:

Painted shut. Hot as fuck. HOG?

Less than a minute passes before the "Ring of Fire" ringtone goes off and he sees Haint on his screen. He enables the camera. Haint is drunker than hell, holding a dead cat by the neck with one hand. He holds a tiny, gnarled claw-hand in the other. Haint gestures with the claw-hand that Andrew should point his phone's camera at the window.

"Tap tap," his phone says, and Andrew taps the phone twice on the glass.

A chip with a crack for a tail appears in the pane as though a small rock has hit it. Flakes of paint fly as a seam gouges itself furiously in a square circuit defining the frame, as though the window is unzipping itself, as though a very strong hand wields an invisible putty knife. The whole assembly shudders and the window pops, easing itself up an inch. Andrew pushes up with his free hand now and the window opens as if on greased rails.

Air comes in, not cool air but fresh.

He turns the phone's screen faceward to thank Haint, but the man is dancing in the candlelight of his mobile brick apartment, slow-dancing with his limp cat and kissing its dead mouth, holding the Hand of Glory up in the other. Etta James plays tinny and small through the phone's speaker.

"Good night, Haint," he says, and the man dips the hand in his hand twice in acknowledgment.

Andrew hangs up and sits back on the futon, well away from the map of Cuba. His cell phone tells him it is 12:22 A.M.

He lights a Spirit and inhales gratefully, blowing smoke in a drowsy billow toward the window that yawns subtropical night on the other side of the room.

Althea.

She will be here in eight minutes if she keeps her word, but she never keeps her word.

"Did you find a meeting?" she asks him as they lie on the damp bed. He is still panting. She is already toeing around in the sheet-nest for the panties she will be slipping back on soon.

It is nearly three A.M. and she will want to welcome her man home after his shift. Then sleep from morning until nearly five P.M., when she will make some weird vinegary salad with apricots or strawberries or pomegranate seeds and run off for three hours of teaching Kundalini, Hatha, and hot yoga, if she is still doing that.

"Not here," he says. "I'm not in town long. Like a day."

"But you've been to one recently? A meeting?"

"Last night."

"Good. So you're feeling strong?"

"Don't start that," he says, instantly regretting it. Telling Althea not to do something is like pressing the accelerator to stop a car.

She takes a small bottle of Jack Daniel's out of her tin purse and sips it, straddling him and bending down to put her lips to his. He turns his head away.

"C'mon," he says, "it isn't funny."

"Who said it was?" she says, swigging again, loading up with a mouthful she will now try to squirt between his lips.

He jabs his thumbs roughly just under her armpits and wiggles, causing her to laugh and cough, whiskey spattering from her mouth and down her chin. She tries unsuccessfully to catch it in a cupped hand.

Pleased, she bends to kiss him and this time he allows it, her shag of curly brown hair engulfing him along with her riverbed scent while the forbidden taste of booze rides her tongue into his mouth.

And just like that it is awake again.

The big electric animal under his skin that doesn't understand the word *no*.

You're in trouble.

He breathes hard, wanting to take the whiskey bottle from her and swallow until a big warm pond pools around his heart, but he concentrates on her tongue. It is a dirty tongue, always coated with something; it feels the way your skin feels when you shower somewhere with soft water, always slick, always filmy.

The Jack Daniel's bottle lies on the bed, its handsome black label and the good feel of it in his palm only a scoot and a reach away.

Fuck your way out of this.

Andrew looks down past the twin hanging cones of Althea's breasts to where her belly rolls, pale above her dark bush and only just beginning to dimple as she approaches her fortieth year.

He begins to harden again, flicking her oily nakedness with the top of his shaft.

"Hmm," she half growls, reaching down for it, but he dumps her off him and holds her down. She snakes her legs around him now, high up around his ribs, and wiggles, waiting for him.

Definitely still teaching yoga.

He hardens to three quarters.

Closes his eyes and sees Anneke.

Wanting me, naked and eager.

Except that Anneke already loves me.

Just not sexually, "as a wife loves a husband."

Or the raven's beak would kill her.

As surely as cancer is killing her father.

Stop sabotaging this, you need this.

Why?

What happens when you get too old to hide in a cunt?

And it's just you alone with you.

Andrew opens his eyes, sees the beautiful, eely woman beneath him; he flares his nostrils and takes in the punk aroma of her excited sex. Althea has a strong smell, but mild and sweet compared to the rusalka. He closes his eyes again.

Karl Zautke is dying.

Anneke is relapsing.

She needs you, and you're here.

Opens his eyes.

"You don't love me, do you?"

His own voice surprises him.

Althea brays a laugh, then shakes her head slowly and wickedly at him.

"I love my husband," she says. And she does. She loves her husband so much, in fact, that she will strap him down when he gets home from the bar and tell him in luxurious detail about her unprotected sex with her gris-gris New York lover. He will want her to ride him while she is still full of his rival, emasculating him until he is half sobbing, and then, when it's over, turning mommy on him, cleaning him off and cradling him until sunrise. You would never look at the big, dangerous-looking bouncer with his bald dome and huge biceps and think, *This guy only gets hard when he's being ground down*, but that's how it is.

"I know. I just wanted to hear it."

"Stop talking," she says.

He stops talking.

He puts a coin between her eyes that lets him think thoughts into her head, and he shows her a dream where she is raping men on a Persian slave galley—she yowls so hard at the end of it that one of the neighbors accompanies her vocals with the percussion of shoe on wall.

Someone outside and below claps.

49

Andrew emerges from his bathroom, carrying the little duffel he took to New Orleans. No baggage claim, no bored security guards watching you walk past the point of no return; fuck you, Homeland Security. The day a user decides to go terrorist is going to be a bad day indeed.

His phone, temporarily confused, and perhaps insulted, by the rapid shift from Central to Eastern Time zones, resets itself and chimes the arrival of a text message it had temporarily misplaced.

Anneke Zautke
Dad's on the way out. Don't come. I'll keep you posted though.
Sorry & thanks. God damn this anyway.

Und zo.

He goes upstairs, sits on the edge of his bed, and peels off his Old Gringos. The warm, animal smell of his own feet hits him—it was so hot in the Quarter—and he notices a hole that will soon allow his big toe to peep through his sock.

Time to get rid of these.

Knot them together and give them to the dog to chew.

Only the dog isn't a dog now.

As if summoned, Salvador knocks at the door frame, keeping politely out of sight, the clack of wood on wood startling the tired magus.

"Come in," he says, almost adding *boy*.

Isn't a dog.

Then what the fuck is he?

A monster. You've turned him into something unnatural, as you do with everything. He should be a handful of ashes on the breeze. He should be chasing rabbits in Elysium.

Will you put Karl Zautke's heart in a basket and make him wash your boxers, too?

Salvador walks in, the Etch-a-Sketch he uses to communicate hanging by a leather cord around his wicker neck. The knobs turn themselves, and black-on-gray letters appear.

"Closer, Sal, I can't see."

The automaton lopes close, the knobs still turning.

TV IN DOWN.
GARLIC CHOP IN BOWL.
WHO COOKS?

Salvador has cleaned up the media room and put in a new television.

He chopped garlic because, even though he doesn't know what Andrew wants to eat, it will certainly contain garlic.

"I'll cook. Thanks."

Boy.

I can't even scratch your ears now.

The picture frame cocks, Salvador Dalí's head now at a quizzical angle. He wants further orders. Just like a border collie, happier with a task.

He always asks who cooks even though Andrew hasn't let him near the gas range since he caught himself on fire two years ago. But he's not afraid of fire, not afraid of anything except displeasing his master.

What else has he got?

Me.

He just has me.

. . .

Andrew stands up, puts on the orange running shoes Anneke teases him about, and grabs a tennis ball from the closet. They go into the backyard. For the next half an hour, Andrew throws the ball and the wicker man sprints on his synthetic legs to grab it, scooping it with his wooden hands as nimbly as an outfielder, then throwing it back to his master. When it goes into the brush, Salvador turns his framed head sideways so it doesn't drag branches.

John Dawes, the neighbor across the street, watches with military binoculars, can't figure out for the life of him why the Spanish-looking butler would play catch with the strange bachelor, both of them laughing, only one of them soaked with sweat when they go back into the house.

It isn't the strangest thing he's seen at 4700 Willow Fork Road, though.

Not by half.

Dusk is coming on.

Andrew's fingers are yellow with turmeric and his squash soup is boiling when the phone chimes again.

He knows what it says.

Anneke Zautke
Dog tell, og tell.

Let Go, Let God.
Elvis has left the building.
Out of nowhere he cries.
For his dead policeman father.
For his dead user mentor.
But also for Anneke, who'll have to learn for herself how hard it is

when the second parent goes. How real it gets when you're sweating down into the cardboard boxes bound for Goodwill and the Salvation Army. When the other parent isn't there to tell you stories from before you were born. When you go in the attic and the plastic tchotchkes crumble in your hand, and you sob like a bitch when you realize your mom saved a little bundle of report cards from third and fourth grade because they said something nice about her kid.

About you.

And that those cards waited in that peeling old folder for your adult hand to fish them out and throw them away because there's just nobody else in this world who'll ever give a damn about them again.

Maybe you really and finally grow up when you see the wall behind the last box of mysteries and it's just a wall.

Your wall now.

50

Andrew drives with the foreknowledge that he will see at least one deer, which has nothing to do with magic; these farm-mottled woods are teeming with them, and they fling themselves across the roads with such abandon that wise drivers scan the margins of the trees. Their once-balletic bodies lie strewn from here to Buffalo, and if more of them are visible on the great deer-killing buzz saw that is Interstate 81, that's only because the highway department cuts the grass there. Here in the sticks they tumble into ditches choked with greenery, hidden from the eyes of motorists, but advertising their spoiling perfume every few miles to those who go on foot or bicycle or in the slow, open tractors that beetle along between farms.

Andrew is not beetling tonight.

He has opened up the Mustang's 302 and it roars like something hungry, like something that has been waiting too long to run.

It is the day after Karl's death, two days before his funeral, and Karl's daughter is drunk. She has a lapful of her dad's PBR and a bottle of Tullamore Dew between her feet, and she has turned the volume knob up almost as high as it goes. One of the classic rock stations; Andrew switches between them at every commercial, so he rarely knows which one he's listening to. Whichever one it is, "From the Beginning" plays so loudly Andrew has to shout to speak to Anneke.

"Look!" he says, pointing across the road to his left, where a doe stands so still she might be made of felt, her eyes blazing Coke-bottle green in the headlights, a tiara of fireflies winking about her head. Anneke does not look, just hangs her heavy shag of hair down and does her best to sing along with the radio. Ignorance of a song's lyrics is not proving to be an impediment to Anneke tonight.

Andrew readies his hand above the horn and readies his foot for braking, but the doe does not stir, and, as always with her kind, he wonders afterward if he has really seen her.

Now he relaxes.

He *has* seen his nightly deer.

Anneke is watching the road now.

Andrew is tempted to do that naughty thing he used to do quite often in the days before sobriety—the very thing he had been doing when he wrecked the '65.

Yes, let's do this.

When he sees that the road is empty of traffic both coming and going, he slows to twenty miles per hour. He cuts his headlights now so they can see the ballet of fireflies where they twinkle in the low places on the farms to right and left.

Showing off.

Anneke loves it, smiles with her cheeks shining, her eyes big like the eyes of a little girl at the circus. Emerson, Lake, and Palmer still pours from the speakers, unaccompanied now. How beautiful the fireflies are, a small galaxy of them signaling to one another as the last violet light fails above them.

"Exquisite," he breathes, unheard under the music, then pulls his lights back on.

"More!" she shouts. "Encore!"

Instead he speeds again, and she honks the Mustang's horn, then howls from the window like a wolf.

At the bluffs.

The whispering of the surf makes him think of the thing that came from the water at him in a dream.

Not a dream.

You were flying without your body and you almost didn't make it back.

But he loves these bluffs and so does Anneke and he'll be damned if he'll let some bloated nasty in a sunken ship keep him away. The ship's far out, and the Russian's cabin is a good mile away.

They're safe.

The two witches, master and apprentice, are alone.

The two recovering alcoholics, one holding on, one in full relapse, are alone.

The grieving daughter and her best friend are alone.

And kissing.

When they arrived he spread an Indian throw over the high grass and they both comically rolled on it to flatten it out; it's still lumpy beneath them, but they want to be off the main trail in case some other celebrants arrive. The Sterling Renaissance festival is opening soon and musicians, actors, and vendors wander out here in the summer months to sing, drink, and couple. Oswegian teenagers also frequent these bluffs, breaking into parked cars, smoking pot, drinking hooch. But now nothing stirs but the lake and the breeze. Andrew and Anneke lie together, cocooned in their small, grassy cell.

Hidden.

Occult, in the original and medical meaning of the word.

And kissing.

They had barely spoken on the walk from the car, just trudged out here, hopped the rusted guardrail, hiked the rise that, by daylight, gives on the lake and the little promontory one dare not walk now. They had just gotten the blanket down when her mouth was on his, hot and boozy.

And the kissing was good.

Is good.

She fumbles for his belt, and, to his utter surprise, he stops her, playing goalie like a good Catholic girl.

She stops, squints her bleary eyes at him.

"Don't you want this?"

He sees that she's crying.

"I'm just afraid *you* don't want this."

"You're wrong."

Her strong hands on his belt again, more insistent; she unbuckles it. He scooches back away from her.

"Are you fucking serious?" she says, wristing a tear out from under her eye.

"Anneke, you're plastered."

"So?"

"You'll regret this, that's all."

She pushes him down.

Holy shit, is she actually stronger than me?

"I don't know if you've noticed. But regret?"

She's too drunk to say the words she wants to say, but shakes her head. He gets it. Anneke doesn't do regret, or at least she tells herself that enough that it has become her mantra. If she were in *Game of Thrones*, her household words would be, "Yes, I did do that. And fuck you."

"I need this," she says.

She's straddling his hips now, towering over him, the horns of the moon behind her and an embarrassment of stars about her like a fay court, bearing witness to her need and to her primacy in this.

My father is dead and you're going to help me fuck some of it away. Just that first little bit of it. Because when the tribe shrinks by one, the sons and daughters go into the fields and make increase.

This won't be *Papillon*.

She's not laughing with him now.

She's fearsome.

Will this bring the raven down?

"Do you love me?"

Her silhouette nods.

"Brother. Not husband. But we're doing this tonight."

She bends down, a tear falling ridiculously into his nostril, but this is still not funny, and she grabs two fistfuls of his inky hair, painfully, the hair at the temples. She kisses him softly, though, wetly, until the tension leaves his body. He feels it in the crotch now, that first twitch, and she feels it, too.

Off him now, and down with his pants.

She has never put her mouth to him before, perhaps never to a man before; she doesn't entirely know what she's doing, hurts him a little, but it doesn't matter.

It feels to Andrew like that warm, wet contact point between them is the geographical center of all creation.

This is so unlike Althea—he *feels* this; his heart is as warm as the marrow of a roast lamb's bone, melting like that, and she could beak under his sternum and lick it right out of him.

They both know it's going to happen.

And it does.

Urgently.

Quickly.

She barely gets her jeans off.

He spends around her navel, in it, abundantly like a twenty-year-old, and gasps as he does.

She clenches her teeth to keep from sobbing, not with pleasure, he's sure she didn't come, but with grief and thwarted love and mortality and gratitude for this little bit of warmth, this sliver of divinity, and she holds him, her wet belly hitching.

He knows he'll hear the sound a second before he does, and it seems so clichéd and awful and obvious that he's angry at whatever passes for God that he should have to hear it, that the gears should move so predictably and so intractably toward sorrow.

Always sorrow.

A raven in the trees.

Kwaaar!

He tries to tell himself it's a crow, and maybe it is.

He only hears it once.

And he isn't sure.

51

Noisy crows in the trees greet Jim Coyle, former professor of comparative religions at Cornell University, as he clambers out of his Toyota. He arms up his modest bag of groceries—important not to overshop when you're about to leave a place—and heads for the cabin.

He has mostly enjoyed his half-summer on Lake Ontario. The

landlady lives in Pennsylvania, does all her business by mail and over the Internet; nobody disturbs him out here, and he is halfway through with his manuscript, working title *The God Mechanism: Making Friends with Death*. He's ahead of schedule and still has most of his advance in the bank.

The time away from his wife has been restorative, too. The system they've used since her son moved out is simple: When we need space, someone leaves. When we miss each other, we reunite. The "Don't Ask, Don't Tell, Use Protection" rule has, at least on his end, been vestigial since he turned sixty—he just doesn't care about all the wrestling and sweating anymore, and has no feelings approaching jealousy regarding Nancy. He half hopes someone is paying attention to her that way—she's still aesthetically attractive enough—as long as she doesn't give him permanent walking papers; he would really miss her, even if he doesn't easily respond to her below the waist these days. Truth be told, he feels guilty about his apathy in that department. Hormone therapy has occurred to him, but it would undoubtedly involve testosterone, and testosterone is his prime suspect in the case of his assholish youth. Interrogating girl-friends about past lovers, obsessing over sophomores and freshmen and sometimes bedding them, getting in loud fights on pay phones, it was all a ridiculous storm of ego from which he was glad to feel himself emerging in middle age. He began balding young; he purses his lips, remembering how carefully he used to hide his patchy tonsure in the days before baseball caps were cool for adults.

Nancy had been good for him—sane, unromantic, cerebral. Easy to laugh, slow to anger. An early music professor. Unsure she wanted to marry at all, but finally consenting on a trip to Chicago when he asked her on the Navy Pier Ferris wheel after a live taping of the NPR show *Wait, Wait, Don't Tell Me*.

If only he still wanted her.

That way.

"You know who I *do* want *that way*," he mumbles into his elbow-crooked reusable Pick & Save grocery bag (plastic is *not* okay) while he fumbles his key at the lock, "that Russian tea cake who moved into Dragomirov's place, that's who."

The crows yap at him.

He unsacks whole-wheat linguine, *alla vodka* pasta sauce, cold-pressed olive oil, half a gallon of organic skim milk, and a half dozen other items one might expect a health-and-environment-conscious upper-middle-class intellectual to unsack, smirking at his own bourgeois habits as he cabinets and refrigerates his goods.

"Not my fault," he tells nobody. "I ate enough beanie wienies and mac and cheese growing up. I get artisanal Tuscan boules if I want them."

But back to the niece of the unfortunate Mr. Dragomirov.

That mole on her cheek drives him to distraction—a classic beauty mark worthy of Marie Antoinette—and she has the firmest body he's seen on someone her age who wasn't a movie star or aerobics instructor. He half imagined she had smiled at him *that way*, but knows better than to embarrass himself. She's way out of his bald, myopic, professor-bearded league, no matter how well-stocked his cabernet shelf may be or how close he came to beating her brilliant uncle in chess. All right, he wasn't actually close to beating him, not once in their half dozen games, but he made him *think*.

Now that the locust swarm of Russians has dispersed, she seems to be on her own. Good riddance to that horde, too. He actually caught one of them, a man the color of ashy leather wearing socks and sandals, standing in his yard, swaying drunk, blatantly pissing on his basil plants.

But it was a funeral, after all.

Too bad about Dragomirov.

A likable fellow.

With an eminently likable niece.

Who enjoys swimming in the lake.

It has occurred to him to offer his services as guide, maybe take her to the McIntyre Bluffs for one of the world's second-best sunsets, but he knows that she'll be laughing inside, even if she treats him politely.

No, he'll steer wide of that Charybdis, and count himself lucky to return to his pragmatic Penelope and her excellent collection of viola da gamba CDs.

As he muses on these things, he plucks a sweater from the back of a chair.

Cold in here.

Isn't it July?

He thinks about checking the air conditioner to see if he left it on, remembers that there isn't one. It's just cold. This makes him feel a spasm of anxiety—just one cold summer day arms his über-Republican lich of a dad (eighty-eight and still shoots trap) with enough anti-global-warming jokes to last through a whole snowless winter and an Easter in T-shirts.

But it's warm outside.

Isn't it?

He walks outside again, and feels sunshine on his face, feels the pleasantly warm lakeside air. A little cool in the shade, but downright cold in his house. He walks around the side of the house now, crows a-caw behind him, and sees that there's something odd about his bedroom window. It takes him a moment to register what it is.

Condensation?

Water has beaded on the panes, trickles down in rivulets.

His bedroom window is sweating like a Pepsi can on a picnic.

"Curiouser and curiouser," he says, heading back into the dark mouth of the cabin's front door. He goes to his bedroom, finds the door to that shut. He never shuts interior doors.

He grabs the knob.

Cold.

Ice-cold.

And locked.

He never *locks* interior doors.

It occurs to him to call the police, and then he chuckles at his own cowardice.

Hello, officer? Yes, I'd like to report a suspicious locking and a temperature anomaly. Is there a squad car in the vicinity? With a thermos of hot cocoa and a trauma counselor?

He goes outside again.

The crows are quiet.

He glances at their tree, thinking they'll be gone, but they aren't gone. They're just quiet. And watching him.

He looks at his Toyota.

Just get in it and go—something's wrong.

Hi, Nancy. I left all my clothes and books and my computer in the cabin because my room was cold and locked and birds were looking at me.

I know, but it's the WAY they were looking at me.

He looks at the crows again.

Still watching him.

Get stuffed, birds.

Jim gives in to a juvenile impulse and flips the branch gallery off.

He walks across the yard now and looks at the window.

He can't quite see inside his bedroom for the condensation.

He uses his sweatered elbow to wipe a pane dry, looks in.

Someone's in there!

His heart skips a beat, then hammers.

A strange man is sitting on his bed, reading something.

A strange, feral man in a filthy T-shirt.

Is that my manuscript?

He calms down a bit—people who read aren't dangerous.

He knocks on the window.

The young man turns around.

Wild-bearded, black haired. Wild-eyed, too. Probably one of the damned Russians. Not the one who pissed on the basil, though. That one had a potbelly and this one is skinny. Emaciated, even. The front of the T-shirt is visible now.

Pac-Man?

The man smiles at him, but it's not friendly.

"Excuse me!" he says.

Call the police, this is trespassing and it's legitimate to call.

Hello, officer? Yes, a badly groomed boy is reading on my bed. Does the National Guard have a spare tank it can send by? This looks dangerous.

He taps again.

"What are you doing in my house?"

Jim shields his eyes against the glare, peering through the dry pane. He watches the man go into the bathroom, fish around in a drawer, come out with a hair dryer. The dryer he uses to dry the henna dye he puts in his beard.

The boy returns with the dryer, points it at the pane the man squints through. Turns it on—he hears it whine.

But he didn't plug it in.

A patch of fog appears on the glass where it was heated.

No, really, he didn't plug it in.

Now the boy's finger traces letters in the fog.

Why didn't he breathe on the pane?

HAVE YOU

Because he doesn't breathe.

REALLY

Get in the car.

MADE FRIENDS

Just get in the car figure it out later you're hypnotized this is dangerous what about the birds and the dryer HE DIDN'T PLUG THE FUCKING DRYER IN! RUN!

WITH DEATH?

When the youth's finger dots the bottom of the question mark, the windowpane cracks. The professor backs up, backs straight into his nightstand.

He is inside his bedroom now.

Somehow the room and outside switched shell-game fast.

Like teacups, one of them poisoned, in a spy movie.

He feels dizzy.

He sees his breath.

It plumes from his open mouth.

So cold.

He can't seem to shut his mouth.

None of this is real.

I was just at the store!

He can only gape and shake his head as he watches snow begin to fall from the roof of his bedroom.

52

Andrew appears in the bathroom at Dino's coffee shop in Yellow Springs, Ohio. A fortyish woman sits on the commode next to him, openmouthed, smartphone in hand, confused. He wouldn't have guessed her as the type to enjoy Angry Birds, but that is in fact what she is playing. She begins to pull her pants up over her knees, moves her mouth as if to form a word. It looks like it's going to be *Who*. Before she can speak, however, he smiles disarmingly and says, "I know you're a bit startled, but there's nothing to worry about. I'm not actually here."

"Of course you aren't," she says, as if confirming the innocence of a wrongly accused child, and goes back to her game.

Andrew steps into the hallway, shuts the door behind him, peeks into the back room. His friend Eric, an eminently likable red-bearded poet and musician who serves as the unofficial mayor of Yellow Springs, says "*Paisan!*" when he sees the magus, stands up and gives him a back-slapping, fraternal hug.

"Can I borrow your car for two hours?"

Eric hands him the keys.

The borrowed car smells like kids.

Andrew loads his bouquet of sunflowers and single bottle of Yuengling into the backseat, next to a toy hammer and a tiny pink sock.

He drives to Enon.

He drives home.

. . .

The sky shines with the kind of bright, sunless gray made to punish hangovers. Luckily, Anneke is nursing hers two states away, and Andrew hasn't got one. He's just exhausted.

The Enon cemetery is one of three in Enon; Mud Run and Prairie Knob (behind the Speedway corporate office) are closed now, stacked thick with Civil War–era dead. The Enon cemetery holds a number of these, mostly resting under tombstones, but a few dozen of the white obelisks favored by the nineteenth century's wealthier dead stick up like fish spines; the largest spire pokes heavenward from atop a hill and reads:

IN MEMORY OF THE PATRIOTS
OF MAD RIVER TOWNSHIP
WHO DIED FOR THE UNION
1865

The second largest remembers one Leander J. M. Baker and his wife, Martha. An Ed Baker's phallic monument juts nearby, both of these overtopping a sextet of smaller spires in the foreground, all belonging to the fun-loving Funderburghs. Andrew follows a sort of reverse Mohawk of shorter, darker monuments plowed between the old obelisks and tombstones, these dating from the middle eighties when it was decided to eliminate the walkway that used to bisect this part of the boneyard and to start planting Enonites between their forefathers.

Andrew kneels before and kisses his mother's small stone, then lays his armful of sunflowers down, not bothering with a pot or water. This was how his mom left flowers for Grampa John Standingcorn.

The flowers are for the dead, not the living. All these folks who stand 'em up in water's just showing off. Sooner these flowers brown, the sooner Grampa gets 'em.

ELIZABETH
STANDINGCORN
BLANKENSHIP

The letters crowd awkwardly on the pinkish-gray stone, and he furrows his brow remembering the fight he had with his brother about including their mother's Shawnee maiden name.

She never went by that. It's too long. And it's not Christian.

He sees Charley standing in front of him, pointing a finger for each of these arguments until he has made a proper pitchfork of his hand, the irony lost on him.

Charles Stewart Blankenship doesn't do irony.

He also doesn't do follow-up, which was why Andrew's last-minute call to the monument company decided the Standingcorn matter.

Charley hates his Indian blood and probably thanks his beefy white Jesus every night that he inherited his father's pink tones and brown hair and left Andrew with the nutshell complexion and inky black mane of his grandfather.

Charley wants nothing to do with his "occult-dabbling" Indian-looking brother.

The elder Blankenship sibling has made himself rich on a series of instructional CDs about how to make oneself rich. With Jesus. It's called *The Catch*, and it tells the listener how to focus concentration and will on making wealth appear. To say certain ritualistic things every day and to believe and visualize. To implore the Fisherman for a bountiful catch.

It works.

At least, it does for Charley, who is mildly luminous.

And probably for anybody else who is, too.

That his magic-hating older brother has made himself a millionaire by unwittingly practicing low-grade magic is one of the most beautiful ironies Andrew Ranulf Blankenship is aware of.

Charley would argue that it's not magic because he calls on Jesus to make the money roll in. Andrew doesn't know much about Jesus, if there is a Jesus, but he doubts that the guy who said it was easier to get a camel through the eye of a needle than a rich man into heaven would be shoveling Benjamins at his believers.

Charley is tone-deaf to hypocrisy.

Charley doesn't do irony.

Their shared father did, though.

Their father the cop, the actual fisherman, not of men or Benjamins, but of river trout.

Andrew opens the Yuengling and pours it into the grass before the stone just next to Elizabeth's, which says simply:

GEORGE
BLANKENSHIP

"Sorry it's warm, Dad."

He drives Eric's car a few blocks from the cemetery, parks it on Indian Drive just off the roundabout that encloses the mound. The mound is Adena Indian, not Shawnee; the Adena were all done here by the time Jesus popped his first pimple.

He hops the little fence around the base of it, remembering how irreverent he and the other kids were to it, how he dubbed it the "earth boob," smoked his first joint on it on a moonless night in November 1975, its three trees holding on to the year's last leaves. That wasn't so bad, but then he took a good long piss against one of those trees to make his friends laugh.

They did, but they didn't mean it.

He made himself laugh, too.

He remembers the dream he had that night. He was tied to the tree he had pissed on and a man with actual strawberries for eyes danced around him, periodically jabbing at his face with a dead porcupine on the end of a spear. The porcupine smelled rank. He was sure he would be blinded by a final, decisive thrust, and then, suddenly, painfully, he was. Apparently he had not fully voided his bladder earlier, because he woke up in cold, pissy sheets.

He never urinated on the Adena burial mound again.

He just sits there for ten minutes.

The sun warm on his face.

Warmer here than in New York.

And then he goes.

53

Haint's picture comes up on Andrew's phone.

He's smiling, leering toothily at the camera on his computer.

Standing far enough away so Andrew can see around him, behind him—he gets his best view to date of Haint's portable apartment.

The dreddy violin player lounges behind the hoodoo man, smoking an immense, poorly rolled joint that looks like it wants to fall apart. An iguana watches from the arm of the sofa, serenity made flesh. Bricks behind the couch, a shelf with an altar of sorts, big leather Bible, a jar of dice. Candles. Four Thieves vinegar. Junk-sculpture art on the walls. The most clearly visible piece looks like an iron sun—chains of different gauges and states of oxidization arranged in rows forming a ferrous circle, at the center of which hangs a malign, rusted bear trap, cocked and ready.

Isn't hard to guess what that thing does if the wrong person comes in.

Neither Haint nor Andrew speaks for a moment.

"I like it that you don't say hello. You're waitin' for news and that's all you want to hear, and anything else is bullshit."

Andrew blinks his icon eyes, feels the stirrings of elation; Haint seems pleased with himself. He has good news.

Could it be?

Haint holds up a lambskin covered in dried blood, a smile-shaped gash letting a flap of it hang. Haint begins to dance, showing off the skin, then begins to sing.

"Ding-dong, your bitch is dead, she's really dead, I killed her dead, ding-dong, your Russian bitch is deeeeeeaaad."

The man on the couch blinks through the cannabis smoke wreathing his head, as if it has only just occurred to him that his eccentric host might really kill people. He seems to reject the idea, takes another puff, leans close to exhale his smoke in the iguana's face. As if doing it a favor. Only makes it blink.

Andrew's heart is racing; his breath comes in little hitches. He remembers the hut, the last time he thought she was dead. The ancient, ghoulish thing. You don't get ancient being killed easily, but this is a new age. Technology just might have made her vulnerable. Haint's cursed Ephesian knife married to satellite photography, swooping down like some drone's missile to kill the witch in her own garden.

Help me, bomber!

He pushes his old fear down, clings to the hope Haint offers him. The evidence on the skin.

So much of it.

"You're sure?"

Haint doesn't speak.

Then he does.

"That little smudge there, that's my blood, to prime the knife. The rest of this, *all* of this, come outta her. I seen it in my mind. She was hunchin' in her garden, digging up a turnip or something, and she didn't even see the shine on the knife blade. Not that there was much shine, man, that's some hunka deep dark woods. But I went *zip* and she went *gaa!* And it wasn't no harder than this—"

So saying, he lunges fluidly backward, plucks up the iguana by the tail, and whips it hard against the floor, holding it up so Andrew can see its last spasms. He forces himself not to show disgust in his eyes, his calm eyes. The dreddy man is not so poised. Haint's speed and brutality have startled him, made him drop the spliff all over himself, burn himself, say "FUCK, man!"

"FUCK, man!" Haint mocks him, throwing the limp reptile on him now, causing the musician to leap to his feet, still swatting at the ember on his pants.

Drops of blood from the lizard's head have spotted his T-shirt.

"Not COOL!" he says, looking less frightened than he should be.

This is so much worse than not cool!

Get out of there!

Haint looks at Andrew, eyebrows comically raised as if to say, *Can you believe this guy?*

"Verify, then bring the hand," he tells Andrew.

Sounding happy with himself.

Andrew nods.

Should turn off his phone but can't.

This is a user's biggest weakness: the need to know what happens, how things work, to see what others don't get to, no matter how cruel and ugly it is. *Especially* if it's cruel and ugly.

The dreddy man gathers up his canvas bag, stomps off behind Haint, then stomps back in the other direction.

"Where's the fucking door?" he says.

Haint raises his eyebrows again.

Rubs his hand front-to-back along the neatly scarred ridges of his scalp.

Turns off the camera.

Leaves the sound on.

Knows Andrew will listen.

Is doing this *for* Andrew because he likes him and wants him awed and uncomfortable and repulsed.

Haint only respects other users.

"Are you really telling me what's cool and what's not cool in MY house?"

"Just where's the door, I'm outta here."

"You THINK you're outta here, but you ain't gone yet."

"Look, we're good, man, I just want the door."

"We ain't good, *man*. It's my door, *man*, and you only gonna use it when I say so."

"Put that down."

Andrew's finger hovers over the end call button, but of course he can't press it.

"There you go, tellin' me what to do in my house . . ."

They speak over each other.

"Please, just . . ."

"In MY fuckin' HOUSE!"

"I want to go . . ."

"A man's home is his castle, and you are in my CASTLE . . ."

"Okay, okay, calm down . . . I mean let's . . ."

"And in my CASTLE, you do not refuse my HOSPITALITY."

"Okay, please don't . . ."

"Eat it."

Silence.

"I like your cookin' and I like your playin' so Imma give you this chance. Imma make the door come back and let you outta here if you eat this motherfucker. All of it."

"Please."

"PLEASE NOTHIN' I AIN'T IN THE PLEASE BUSINESS YOU EAT THAT FUCKIN' THING."

Silence.

"Here's some hot sauce."

Call ended.

PART THREE

54

Michael Rudnick drives his old pickup truck to Anneke's house, following a small, golden finch. It perches in trees near the turns he's supposed to take, flutters around and flies on to the next turn. The birds he charms to guide him fall behind him on the interstates, but he doesn't need them on the interstates. Maps work just fine there. He only calls a guide bird on the sort of rural roads so many American users choose to live near. Users are a solitary breed, after all, more big cat than wolf.

"Andy was right. You do look like a lion. I'm Michael Rudnick. Mike's fine."

Anneke stands on her front porch, perplexed.

She only got the text this morning.

Andrew B-ship
MAN WHO WROTE THE STONE BOOK COMING TO MENTOR
YOU. LET HIM IN. HE'S THE REAL THING.

Mike Rudnick offers his big, tough hand and she allows it to swallow hers.

Tough, calloused hands with small thick nails.

Worker's hands, not reader's hands.

And he's had so much sun on him that the white in his mostly white beard almost glows. He looks like a less self-indulgent Hemingway, harder and leaner. Michael Rudnick is the last guy you'd look at and think *user*. He carries himself like a rancher, or maybe a circus man—someone who works with large animals and makes them do what he wants because that's the only way.

He looks seventy.

"Nobody calls him Andy," she says.

He ignores this, except to smile at it. Paternally, somewhat amused. She's not sure she likes him.

She's not sure she doesn't.

But still.

A bird sings.

What the fuck was Andrew thinking, sending this old geezer here like some kind of replacement dad?

She knows she's surly, knows the booze does that, feels good and surly anyway.

His truck cools.

Her hangover throbs like a bass line to the duet of chirping finch and ticking truck.

"So you're good with minerals."

"I sculpt."

"That's something. That's really something. I sculpt, too. May I see?"

"Uh . . . now's not . . ."

"Pottery, too, right? Mugs. Cups."

"You know, I'm not sure this is going to work. This is a bad time for me."

"It's actually a good time."

She blinks twice.

The balls on him!

"Says who?"

"Grief is a catalyst for magic. We get growth spurts when we're hurting, and the worse we're hurting the faster we might grow. If we push it."

She looks at him, her mouth opening a little but not settling on a word. Her teeth are still dark from last night's boxed wine, a thin line of dried cab/merlot circumnavigating her lips.

She looks rough and knows it.

Remembers spitting into the toilet last night, her spit nearly black from tobacco and wine.

He takes her hand again; she almost pulls it away but doesn't. With his other hand he pulls a small pair of reading glasses from his shirt pocket. Inspects her hand, looking for calluses. Like it's a tool he might buy if the price is right.

"I'll go away," he says, turning her hand over, letting go of it, taking up the other one. Now he looks at her, over his glasses. "But I won't come back."

She returns his gaze, unblinking.

"Look, Mr.—"

She blanks.

"Rudnick," he says, unoffended.

His face a brown-red mask, deep lines around his mouth and eyes.

"Nobody asked me about this. I appreciate you coming all the way out here."

He just looks at her.

The bird chirps.

He waves a hand at it, a subtle gesture, and it flies away forever.

"But I just lost my father, days ago, and I can't focus right now. All I do is turn pieces, play Sudoku and. And nothing. Sudoku is pretty much it."

He looks at her.

He doesn't know or care what Sudoku is.

"I know you're the best teacher I could have, if I'm really doing this. I read your book. I can do a few of those things. But if now is the only time you have for me, I have to say no."

This is where he should say graceful words, shake her hand, and get back in his truck.

Or tell her to fuck off, turn on his heel, and get back in his truck.

But he doesn't move.

Just looks at her, like he's waiting for her to realize she's fucking up, and that makes her a little mad. Even Karl Zautke knew better than to patronize her; he learned that when she was a little girl. One may disagree with Anneke Zautke, but one *must* not treat her like she's stupid.

Big mistake, rock-mover-old-man.

"Well, enjoy your day," she says, and shuts the door.

Not a slam, but neither an apologetically slow close.

Shuts it like she would if nobody was there at all.

Yeah, a bit rude.

She breathes for a minute, still looking at the door, knowing he's just standing there. She doesn't think he's a danger to her, but she does wonder if she's making a mistake. What does she really have to do just now but turn mugs for the festival and play number games until she can sleep? And wish she could cry for her daddy, drink, and then cry for her daddy. She nearly opens the door, then remembers his wizened, sure-of-himself half smile and gets pissed again.

Turns decisively away from the door.

Says *Haaa!*

She has been walled in. By her own stock. Every mug, bowl, and plate she has, finished, unfinished, purchased, every one of them, stands stacked before her. From floor to high, A-frame ceiling. A frozen waterfall of clayware. All precariously balanced, some pieces on their corners, the whole thing ready to fall. If she removes one cup, it will pour down like a dynamited chimney. On her. A month's hard work wrecked. Black eyes, lacerations, worse perhaps, and a herculean mess of shards and clay dust instead of half a summer's income.

Kat, the multiply pierced woman who manages Anneke's booth at the Renaissance festival, is coming tomorrow in her bumper-stickered van with the dried roses on the dashboard to get the finished pieces. With her father's illness, Anneke has put Kat off several times, and now her booth has bare shelves. Will have nothing but bare shelves if this deadfall crashes.

Fuck that old guy.

She breathes hard.

She turns to open the door.

Can't.

It has been mortared shut, concrete caulking the jamb, the hinges. A tongue of poured stone licks down from the wrecked lock. The only part of the door not slathered with freshly set concrete is the brass mail slot. Which now opens. She steps back a half step, which is all the room she's got if she doesn't want to bring down the wall of pottery.

A Snickers bar and a small box of raisins slide through, fall on her hickory floor.

"What the FUCK!" she says. "You let me out of here, you old COOT! DO YOU FUCKING HEAR ME?"

The pottery wall shudders, a saucer slipping headily close to falling out, nearly releases the threatened avalanche.

"Temper," he says. "Ask me a question civilly and I'll answer you."

She makes an uncivil noise.

Stamps the Snickers bar flat, pushes it flat through the slot.

It comes back.

"Try not to step on your food. You're going to get hungry. Probably very hungry. Depends on how good you are and how well you listen. I'm going to tell you how to unstack that wall, if you want to know. But you're not to use your hands. You'll have to start from the top."

She seethes.

He waits.

"What if I can't?"

"After a day or two I'll let you out if I have to."

"Do it now."

"Sorry. You were ready to waste my time by sending me away;

now I'm wasting yours. If you can pull that wall down, I'll be happy to teach you more. If not, well, it was nice to meetcha."

She seethes, cools down.

"I'll get thirsty before I get hungry."

Silence.

"Well?"

Silence.

The garden hose pokes its snout through the slot, hangs there.

Waits.

55

The tailpipes really draw the eye.

Two perfect holes on a tight little rear end.

The car Andrew will give to Radha.

First, a distraction.

His phone chimes.

He pulls it out.

Anneke Zautke

Your friend is really an asshole.

He texts.

Andrew B-ship

HOW?

Anneke Zautke

Just is ☹

Slips the phone back in his pocket.

Andrew and Chancho stand under the Mini Cooper on its elevated lift. Chancho raises a stubby finger, crescent-mooned with oil on the cuticle, and points.

"The cat-back exhaust, that's performance, like a double-barrel shotgun, BANG! BANG! 'Cept a quiet shotgun, she's got a sweet purr, kitty-cat purr. This is a nice car, man. 2003, but cherry."

"Dude came from Arizona."

"Yeah, eff that road salt. What you get her for?"

"Six one."

"I give you seventy-five hunnert right now."

Andrew shakes his head.

"Eight."

"Not selling. I have to fix her up."

"You mean *brujo* the *chicharrones* out of her, right?"

Andrew smiles.

"Yep. Woman did me a favor, I do one back. Did you find why she was pulling?"

"Yeah. Strut towers are shroomin'. 'Specially the right one. Must be potholes in Arizona. Got Rick runnin' back from Syracuse with parts, picked a coupla plates up from the import place. All polished and all. Bling."

"This girl won't care about bling. She probably won't even pop the hood."

"Yeah, but whoever does, BLINGITTY BLING!"

Gonzo looks over from the reception desk, where a big-eyed woman is mooning at him, about to hand over her keys.

Andrew's smile widens.

"But she passes? The Cooper?"

"More than passes. You screwed that guy."

. . .

—*It was generous of you to advertise such a nice car for six thousand. Is everyone in Arizona this good-natured? And do you play tennis professionally?*

—*Professionally? No.*

—*You look like a tennis pro.*

—*I think you read it wrong. No Mini in this shape is going for six. It's ten thousand. Have anyone you like check it out. Did you see the exhaust? The alloy wheels? The stereo alone is worth a grand.*

—*You're right. It is a sweet machine. Sorry to hear you've been ill.*

—*Excuse me?*

—*All this damp New York air, a guy from Arizona's bound to have a bad reaction. Even an athlete. Of course you're under the weather.*

—*What are you talking about?*

—*Am I mistaken?*

—*Actually, yes. I never felt better.*

Andrew blinks, looks confused.

—*What did I say?*

—*That I was sick.*

—*What?*

—*You said I was sick.*

—*Six will be fine.*

Now the young man looks confused, comes almost back to himself.

—*I can't . . .*

—*You're what, five eleven?*

—*No.*

—*What then, six feet even?*

—*Six one.*

The young man puffs up proudly.

—*Sorry?*

—*Six one.*

—*Five ten?*

—Six one, goddammit, six one!
Andrew smiles disarmingly.
—Sold!
He offers his hand.
The young man shakes.

"Just charmed him a little."
"Effing *brujo*."
Chancho smiles despite himself.
Claps Andrew on the back.
Leaves a smudge.

56

Andrew drives the Cooper down the farm roads from the North Star Garage, admiring the handling, the clockwork feel. A little rough on the bumps, but damned fine on curves. It doesn't gobble road like the Mustang; it ticks off distance (the damned thing clearly thinks in kilometers, whatever the odometer says) like seconds on a runner's watch. Radha is bound to be pleased. Six hours' worth of incantations and directed thought, a pinch of hummingbird feathers in the gas tank, a good massage of the body with prepared wax.

Wax ingredients: beeswax, badger hair, ground snail shells, filings from a Slinky, ash from thirty burned parking citations. Getting the badger hair was going to suck until Andrew remembered that old-timey shaving brushes use it and rush-ordered a Vulfix #403 Best Badger from the mildly luminous but untrained young owner of Classicshaving.com.

Now the Cooper runs on water and will fit into any parking space so long as the owner believes it will.

Perfect for Chicagohoney85.

She believes any story that involves her success.

It's why she's so fucking powerful.

Andrew pulls up to his house, sees a man waiting on his porch.

An older man.

Michael Rudnick.

They exchange brief waves.

He pulls the plum-colored Mini in beside his Mustang, keeps going until he's just in front of his separate garage.

Cuts that sweet watchmaker's motor.

Michael is already walking over to him.

"You look the same," the older magus says as Andrew gets out, stands.

It's not a compliment.

Michael knows Andrew is burning magic to make himself look young.

Probably a lot of magic.

Michael doesn't look the same. His hair was still mostly dark the last time Andrew saw him. His skin looks blotchier, too, the browns and reds more separated, less the healthy rancher's tan Andrew remembers.

This man looks like a candidate for skin cancer.

"It's good to see you, Michael."

Andrew's a bit of a hugger, but Michael isn't, so Michael offers him a preemptive shake in the driveway, moves up to the porch.

"What do you think of Anneke?"

"Luminous as hell."

"I thought just a little."

"Just a little to you. Mechanics and the dead on film are your specialties. When it comes to stone, you're just a little luminous. How big a rock can you move?"

"Maybe a brick."

"She'll be moving bricks by the end of the week, if she tries. Maybe more. I see what she can do with minerals, and it's kind of scary. You were right to call me."

"Where is she? Is she coming?"

"Not tonight. I gave her some homework."

The two men don't go inside just yet.

Michael walks to the installation of junk cars and boulders, lays hands and cheeks to the rocks.

Twines his fingers in the vines and touches the saplings and the shoots on the tree.

He climbs up and touches the horns on the skull of the longhorn steer. Wiggles one flat, yellow, herbivorous tooth in its socket as the skull grins, tied to its post, an out-of-place western exile in this damp, northern province.

Back to the biggest rocks, three of them: one the size of a large old-style television; one the size of a love seat; one the size of a Volkswagen Beetle, a proper boulder.

A scattering of smaller rocks, still too heavy to lift.

Cheek and hands on all of them, like a doctor.

Like he should have a stethoscope.

No hurry, maybe ten minutes of this.

"How is it?"

Michael smiles.

Whistles in appreciation.

The way older men do to say *damn*.

"Still there. Still all there."

He looks as proud of himself as he ever lets himself look.

It had been ten years since they built this.

Since they put a spell in it.

Salvador had still been a dog.

Andrew had still been drinking.

Sarah.

Let's not start thinking about Sarah, now.

This spell.

This big-ass spell.

Evidently he didn't mess everything up in those days.

"Really?" he asks the other magus.

But he knows.

He puts his hand to the hood of the wrecked Mustang, feels the thrum of buried ferrous magic.

This is really mighty stuff.

"Probably still be there in another ten years. We did good."

57

Anneke joins them at breakfast the next day, her hair frosted with clay dust, her eyes baggy from poor rest. She smells like sweat and anger. Andrew cracks eggs and tips their treasure into holes in sizzling French bread while she glares at Michael Rudnick. Salvador brings the coffee press, pours coffee in her cup. She reaches for it, but Michael wags a finger at her.

"What?"

This is the first thing she's said since she entered.

"Use your hand to touch that mug and I'll pop it in your face."

She blinks twice to keep herself from flinging it at him.

She really wants to fling something at him.

Speaks instead.

"*You're* using your hands. You're lifting that mug to your face just like everybody else."

He takes a sip of coffee just to rub it in.

Looks at her, eyes twinkling like flaws in quartz.

He doesn't need to say it; she gets it. He has nothing to prove. He has his own regimen, has cracked the foundation of his house and fixed it six times this year, juggles forty bricks as high as a Ferris wheel every Sunday, turns rabbit, squirrel, or doe to stone in midrun then animates it again. He's a mighty motherfucker with eyes like Medusa and a geologist's heart, and he'll use his hands if he wants to.

She's the one on coffee cup detail.

She swivels her angry glare from Michael's eyes to the steaming earthenware mug in front of her. Terra-cotta colored, artsy, from an art fair in Ithaca. She feels the clay in it as if it's an exiled part of her, believes it's part of her, feels the heat of the coffee in the cup that is now her own brittle flesh somehow, but the feeling is muted, fades in and out.

The cup is like an extremity that has gone to sleep. It is a struggle for her to move it; her arm tingles in sympathy.

This is harder than lifting the empty pots and plates, which actually got easy at the end; by the time she was near the bottom of the wall, she had two pieces in the air at a time.

The first one, though. It hurt her between the eyes, like an ice cream headache in the wrong place. Took her two hours to wiggle it, and then it slipped immediately from her phantom grasp and broke. Almost brought down the whole wall. Michael peeked through the slot, helped her a little by nudging the wall back and into a more solid configuration. The second item, a wine goblet, had been hard, too, had also broken. The third thing, a beer mug, made it, also slipping from her grasp, but in a controlled descent that she could not stop, but managed to slow enough, just enough, so it survived its landing. It had been like watching a skydiver fall a little harder than he meant to.

That had been her first significant act of magic.

She had been doing exercises with a penny, then a pot shard, had moved sand around as gently as a kitten pawing at it, had managed to put a crack in a thin wineglass.

Taking that mug down from on high was a different thing.

She would save that mug.

Drink Mountain Dew out of it one day when she got back into recovery.

This, though.

A full coffee cup. And she didn't make this cup, hasn't already got an intuitive connection to it. The weight of the liquid confounds her, has multiplied itself like weight at the wrong end of a lever. It's heavier, yes, but she's stronger than she was a day ago; this is a fair fight. She clenches her teeth, feels something coiling inside her, getting ready to expand.

She sees the coffee cup lifting, manages to jog it, sloshes a *plap* of coffee onto Andrew's table.

Grunts.

Tries again.

It wobbles, coffee spilling over its sides, dribbling onto the table.

She brings it to her lips, starts to incline toward it, sees Michael gesturing for her to sit back.

Make the cup do the work, she thinks, then remembers his words as he stood outside the door instructing her.

Let the cup move, don't make it move. Like archery, or golf, or bowling, it's a relaxing, not a stiffening.

Something in her relaxes.

The cup drifts closer, drunkenly, uncertain it wants to stay aloft. Now it trembles at her lips, quivering so fast the surface of the coffee ripples in intricate patterns.

She sips.

The hot coffee on her lips jars her out of it.

The cup falls, makes a *thunk* but doesn't break, coffee splashes on the table, her lap, everywhere.

Michael nods in lieu of saying, *Nice job.*

He says, "Next time you'll be ready, won't let the heat shock you."

Andrew, who has just taken breakfast off the burner, comes over with a dishrag.

Why is he handing me a dishrag?

Oh, the coffee.

Drops of blood patter on the table, mixing with coffee.

Not just the coffee.

Nosebleed.

Magic made me bleed.

The first time was just messing around, but now I'm in.

Cherry popped, as the boys who helped me prefer girls used to say.

She takes the rag.

"Welcome to the club," Andrew says.

Breakfast is good.

Before they leave the kitchen, Michael makes Anneke change a cherry tomato into a rock. This takes half an hour. Her period, which isn't due until next week, comes on hard, sending her running for the tampons she left behind for herself in the guest bathroom.

She lies down in the spare room, meaning to rest her eyes and her throbbing head, but she falls asleep and stays that way for two days.

When she wakes up, Andrew hands her an envelope.

The rock is in it, and a note.

IF YOU WANT TO LEARN TO
MAKE THIS A TOMATO AGAIN,
COME TO VERMONT FOR A WEEK.
NO BOOZE, THOUGH.
I NEED YOU CLEAR.

Michael Rudnick's address.
She takes the stone cherry tomato with her and leaves.

58

Chicagohoney85: This is pretty cool if you like dark stuff. But I don't think you do as much as I do. You sure you want to see this?

Ranulf: Just show me. I need to know.

—What, don't you trust me? I'm not going to say I know if I don't know. And that's one dead witch. Deaddity dead dead dead.

—Cute. Just show me.

—How's my car?

—You'll splee.

—I think you're trying to say squee. As in, make a squee noise. Because splee is more like have a male orgasm which is anatomically misplaced, and just a little off sides.

—I meant squee.

—I know. A guy like you can still get action and doesn't need to be a creeper. There's nothing I hate like a creeper.

—Understandable. Are you going to show me?

—What color is it?

—?

—The car!

—Plum. A Mini Cooper.

—*SQUEEEEEE!* Okay, here's your morbid little treat, and it's weird. I didn't know things like this happened. Pretty f'd up. The images were shot at two-second intervals.

A picture loads. Black-and-white, military satellite photography. The hut, the garden, hard to make out. Early morning. An old woman's foot, a slipper near it. The echo of *The Wizard of Oz* is impossible not to notice.

Ding-dong, your bitch is dead.

—Can you get a closer shot of that shoe?

She zooms in. It gets grainy, but he thinks it may be an old-timey slipper. Not ruby. Embroidered.

He can't be sure, but he thinks he's seen it before.

His stomach does a slow roll.

—Just click when you're ready to see the next one. This'll flip your shit.

He clicks.

A wolf crouches on the path. A skinny wolf, not like the ones you see in pictures from Alaska or Yellowstone—this critter is gray and ratty and hungry-looking.

Small.

Nose pointed like a gun at the owner of the inanimate foot.

(Click)

That wolf is nearly out of the shot, its tail all that's visible; it's sniffing her. Perhaps doing more to her than that. Two more wolves have appeared on the path before the hut, coming to share the prize.

—Now watch the house.

(Click)

The house has turned.

He sees one of its windows like a dark eye.

It has turned ninety degrees toward the wolves, the dead woman.

(Click)

Fully turned, facing them.

More wolves have come, two of them crouched and growling at the house, the rest circled around her.

Feeding.

—You won't believe this. Are you sitting down?

(Click)

Motion. Things get blurry now. Something has flashed from beneath the house; the wolves have reacted. One was too slow. The blur has the wolf.

(Click)

A huge chicken's foot.

That's what has the wolf.

Still blurry, but less so, still in motion.

The wolf struggling, trying to twist out.

(Click)

The wolf is dead.

Its brains dashed on the ground, as dead as Haint's iguana.

Two others are growling at the house, front halves low as if salaaming, like dogs at play but not playing. Not surrounding it as they might a giant elk, but blocking it while the others retreat.

The rest are dragging the old woman away, about a third of her in the shot now, swathed in dried blood.

(Click)

Everything blurred, house twisting, motion beneath it.

(Click)

The house turning away, just a corner of it in frame.

Two dead wolves as limp as dishrags.

The woman and the other wolves have gone.

(Click)

Just the garden.

The path.

One of the wolves trying to get up.

Wasn't dead after all.

Will be soon.

Too much of its insides outside.

That is the last image.

He clicks back through them two more times.

—What do you think?

—I think maybe you're right.

—I am right. She's deader than hell. You're in the clear, my man.

—Thanks. Really, Radha. Thanks.

59

Andrew feels pretty good as June gives way to July and July sheds days.

Baba Yaga is dead.

He has Radha's car to work on, and it's a damned fun little car.

The woman he loves is newly confirmed in witchcraft and studying for a month in Vermont.

Chancho, who has family coming up from Texas, has invited him to a fiesta, and that means piles of oily tamales and pans of enchiladas and bowls of the best guacamole this side of Austin.

Who cares if his cousins move drugs for the Zetas?

He can almost completely ignore the tinny little voice in his ear saying

Something's wrong,
Something's coming.

60

July 14.

Bastille Day.

Anniversary of the storming of the Bastille in Paris, of course, but also a very personal anniversary for Andrew Blankenship.

Seven years exactly since Sarah collapsed at Darien Lake.

Aneurysm.

Just after she rode the Mind Eraser.

One of life's stupid, mean little jokes.

Enough to make one conclude there is a God and he isn't all that nice.

He was handing her her earrings to put back on when she said she didn't feel well.

Wanted to sit down.

Slumped over like a kid playing a prank.

And that was it.

He had just started looking for a ring, was thinking about asking her on Halloween.

Now he hovers at the top of the stairs that lead down to the media room.

I shouldn't be doing this.

Why am I doing this?
It doesn't hurt her.
No, but it hurts me.
I just have to see her again.
God.
God.

Downstairs.

Quickly, before he loses his nerve.

From the box of VHS tapes, one tape marked *SARAH*.

In it goes.

Stop.

He does stop, but only because he has to shut the door to the media room and lock it.

Salvador cannot, must not see this.

Sits back down.

Pushes play.

Push stop.

No, really. PUSH STOP.

The woman throws a Frisbee, probably an hour before sunset.

The McIntyre Bluffs.

2004.

Eight years ago, before the path to the promontory had eroded into a crumbling saddle, when a brave or foolish soul might still skitter upright over something of a spine to the platform of turf that remained.

But the woman.

Thirtyish, sandy brown hair cut into bangs.

That smile would melt an iron heart.

That smile could stop evil itself.

It is the sun on toast, it is the sun on Christmas morning with all wars over.

It is a smile to give up magic for.

Her faded jeans, all the rings on her fingers, one a teaspoon ring.

Should have thrown myself from that promontory.

Just like the rusalka did all those years ago.

What have I done with myself since Sarah?

She hated this part of you, this self-pitying part of you.

No she didn't.

Sarah didn't hate.

Now the camera follows something flashing through the high grass.

A swatch of the lake behind it.

It's really tearing ass.

A dog.

A young border collie, not a year old, already an acrobat.

It leaps, yanks the red disk from the air as if tearing it from the swatch of blue sky hung behind the cliff.

The camera dips back to where the woman laughs and claps.

The trapdoor is coming.

"Good Sal! Good, smart Sal!" she says, and the dog drops the Frisbee in the grass at her feet. Her lace-up thrift store boots. Sarah is a thrift store empress, five foot four, size seven shoe, tiny through the waist, fucking everything fits her.

And the thrift stores took it all back.

Here's the trapdoor.

The drop of the Frisbee marks it.

He can call her name, have her lock eyes with him, speak to her.

He has done it exactly three times.

Only once sober.

Not today.

Not never, it doesn't work like that.

Just not today.

"That's my boy," she says, and gives the Frisbee a lusty throw.

"Some arm on you," younger Andrew says.

His one contribution to this tape.

She looks at the camera.

Looks at the younger Andrew she loved like that.

The trapdoor is still open.

If he speaks.

If he says *Sarah*.

She is about to speak to younger Andrew.

Her eyes cut left and she smiles that smile instead.

Now Salvador bounds into view but doesn't drop the Frisbee.

Wants to play chase this time.

The hump of his running back in the high grass.

Whatever she was going to say goes unsaid, turns to laughter as she runs after the dog. Out of frame. Young Andrew is smart enough to stop filming, put the camera down, join the chase. Live. Soon the young couple will pack their dog and blankets and empty wine bottle into the Mustang, go home, back to this house, and make love.

Older Andrew isn't welcome to that party.

Let's say now-Andrew, *shall we?*

Now-Andrew isn't welcome to that party.

But that's okay.

He's not entirely sure he believes in time anymore, and if there is no time, he is making love to Sarah even now.

He often thinks of the Russian word for *wing* when he thinks of making love to Sarah. *Krihlo.* Said with that little Russian vowel that sounds like *i* but in the front of the mouth, like you're trying to sneak a *w* in there. That *o* that opens the lips instead of closing them.

God Sarah God Sarah God

Her rings on the nightstand.

Her boots on the floor, making a sort of happy swastika with his.

Her soft, joyful whimpers.

Salvador the dog crying to be let in with them.

. . .

Salvador the wicker man taps on the door to the media room.

Let's say now-Salvador.

Now-Salvador, then.

Now-Andrew sleeves his cheeks dry.

Puts the tape away.

Opens the door.

61

The UPS man has arrived with a parcel Andrew must sign for.

A parcel from Frenchman Street in New Orleans.

He can tell by the weight of the package.

He recognizes Miss Mathilda's squared-off, careful print.

Three tapes.

The dead in their black plastic shells.

Souls trapped in amber.

He can't free them, but he can make them dance.

Oh God, he wants a drink.

The house is quiet with a quiet that television and music are powerless to interrupt. The night groans by on rusted wheels.

62

The dream is the same dream.
Always the same dream.
The Soviet dream.

He is twenty-three again, arrogant, strong, as pretty as a girl, irresistible to girls and women of every stripe. He travels easily through Soviet Russia, using magic to outdance its bureaucracy, its lethal but ponderous bureaucracy, clever in places but cold. Secular. Unable to allow for the impossible. He is playing chess with adversaries who cannot see all the pieces, who might beat him if they allowed for the *possibility* that they could not see all the pieces.

His papers say he is a Soviet citizen.

Magic gives him flawless Russian.

Magic summons perfect answers to his lips.

He is too light for the police.

He is too clever for the KGB.

He is looking for treasuries of magic tomes lost since the days of the tsars.

"Of all of the spell books and relics known to exist, whether seen by reliable witnesses or referenced in other works, only a quarter or so are in known hands," his mentor had told him; on mention of secret magic books, Andrew had sat like a cat before a can opener. "Of the remainder, it is believed that a disproportionate amount have accumu-

*lated in what is now the Soviet Union. Some hiding in plain sight, no
doubt, waiting in bookstores for the first luminous person to buy them
for less than an American dollar. Most will have been hoarded and
stored."*

"Hoarded and stored by whom?"

*"We don't know. Various users, even more deeply hidden than
Western ones, perhaps more powerful. I know a man, a Walloon Bel-
gian, who went to Leningrad in 1973 and came back with a book on
traveling underwater, a bit redundant in the age of scuba, but still. I
also know a man and wife who went together to the Volga and never
came back. The Volga's probably where most of it is."*

"When did they go?"

*"1975? Jesus, three years ago. I saw them get married the year be-
fore."*

Now, in the 1983 dream, Andrew has left the city of Gorky, in the
Volga region, and makes his way by train and bus into the countryside, hitchhiking rides from farm trucks, beat-up Zaporozhets with
their goldfish-eye headlights, even a horse-drawn cart full of bar-
reled milk.

And then.

And then.

Andrew has been hitching all day, with mixed success.

He just realizes how hungry he is, how long it's been since he ate,
when he finds himself looking at a scene from the nineteenth century.

Two men in baggy shirts, short woolen vests, and brown pants
swing scythes into the high grass, looking for all the world like they
had stepped out of *Fiddler on the Roof*. They work their way down
the side of a hill, the sky chalky blue above them, one of them humming to keep his time, the younger one swinging less rhythmically,
fighting the scythe, tired. Maybe sixteen years old.

"I see you have made an enemy of the grass, Lyosha," the older man says from beneath a tsarist mustache. "This will not do. Make friends with it. Let it know that you only want to let it lie down and rest."

He goes back to humming his song, but still the boy chops and sweats, stopping for a moment to wipe his brow with his cap.

"Call your idiot brother and see if he can show you how."

"He will not come, Uncle. He is lying on the stove."

"Call him anyway."

"Ivan!" the boy calls.

Andrew keeps walking down the path, keeping an eye out for another potential ride, but this.

This is something else.

He slows down a bit because he wants to see how this idyll will play out. Do they still make idiot brothers who like to lie on the stove in Cold War Russia?

Clearly they do; the large man who crests the hill and lopes down at the other two has the characteristic eye tilt of Down syndrome, and he breathes through his mouth as he says, "What do you want? I was catching flies."

"You caught no flies unless they landed in your mouth," the mustachioed man says. "Now show your weakling brother how a man mows hay."

The boy hands the scythe to his brother, and Ivan whacks at the grass like a mad thing, shearing great armloads of it down with each stroke, giggling. Soon the little brother takes up a fistful of grass and throws it at Ivan, ducking back out of range before the scythe's blade swishes down again. It becomes a game. The older man sets down his scythe and joins in, baiting the laughing peasant with flung grass and dancing away from the flashing blade. Andrew now has to turn his head back to watch, so he stops walking altogether and slides his arms free of his backpack. He lights a shitty Soviet cigarette so he will not appear to be nosy, just a man having a rest and a smoke, and he sits on the big canvas sack he has been lugging.

A flight of sparrows wheels about, lands briefly on the road near him, and then takes off again.

And then.

It happens.

The younger boy takes greater and greater risks with the scythe, forgetting the grass-throwing, just leaping in and out Cossack-style while his uncle claps and shouts in time. Andrew knows what is going to happen an instant before it does; at last the idiot brother swings faster than the boy anticipated and lops into the acrobatic youth's leg.

It comes off just below the knee.

He collapses into the grass with a look of astonishment on his face.

How pale his face is!

How dark the O of his mouth!

Andrew's own mouth hangs open, the cigarette stuck on his lower lip.

The injured boy howls in pain; the older man goes to him.

The idiot stares openmouthed, a long strand of spit reaching down to the grass.

Andrew's paralysis breaks, and he says, "Jesus."

The boy goes silent.

The uncle had been removing his rope belt to tie off the boy's leg, but he stops and turns his head toward Andrew. The idiot brother looks at him, too. Now the boy sits up, holding his bloody stump, less concerned with the blood fountaining through his interlaced fingers than with Andrew.

"Can I help?" Andrew says in decent but accented Russian, his own Russian, Russian that stinks of Ohio, walking toward them now, his hands open in a timeless gesture of harmlessness.

He doesn't even notice that his fluency charm has failed.

All three of them look at Andrew with flinty, suspicious eyes. Their gazes are so malevolent, in fact, that Andrew stops coming toward them. He isn't sure this is what it appears to be.

Then it hits him.

Magic.

It has been so long since he felt the flutter of magic that he has now been blindsided.

He didn't see the pieces.

Fear wakes up in him.

This could be bad.

This could be very bad.

"Can I help?" the uncle says, mocking Andrew's American accent. "Who could help *this*?"

He gestures at the boy's gushing leg.

"Or this?" he continues, nodding at the idiot brother, who draws back his scythe.

Strikes off the uncle's head.

O mother of fuck fuck fuck

Andrew's legs buckle in fear.

He begins to back up at something more than a leisurely pace, unable, however, to turn his head from the scene in the field.

Now the big idiot bends over, legs splayed, the crack of his ass winking below his too-short shirt, and delicately picks the cap from the uncle's head so he can get a handful of his hair. He lifts the head, the white and rolled-back eyes of which now slot into place.

Fix on Andrew.

A few yards away, the uncle's body sits up.

Then it stands up, arterial blood jetting.

It takes the rope belt between two fists and pulls it slack.

"Now do you want to help? Does Jesus Christ want to help?" the head asks from the idiot's huge fist, now hawking and spitting out a bright clot of blood. The idiot takes his scythe up in the other hand and begins to stumble toward Andrew.

"I think he wants to hear American, Uncle," the bleeding boy says, using a scythe as a crutch and standing on his remaining leg. "Two kopecks says he does."

The head hanging from Ivan's hand now opens its mouth and a sound like television static comes out of it.

The *chunk chunk chunk* of a television dial being turned, and then . . .

News.

A newswoman speaks through the uncle's open mouth, in perfect midwestern American English.

"The remains of an American backpacker missing in the Soviet Union since June were returned to his family today. . . ."

Andrew backs up faster.

He spits his cigarette out.

"The young man's mother and elder brother flew to Wright-Patterson Air Force Base to claim the body, which had suffered great violence at the hands of unknown assailants . . ."

The idiot holding the severed head, the bleeding boy hobbling along with his scythe, and the headless peasant with the rope belt between his fists advance on Andrew.

Andrew feels backward with his feet, terrified to fall.

" . . . His hands, feet, and genitals were cut from his body by what appeared to be a farm instrument, although the cause of death has been established as strangulation . . ."

Andrew keeps backing up, not wanting to take his gaze from them. As long as he looks at them, they aren't closing distance.

"General Secretary Andropov has promised a full investigation into the killing, which he will see to personally as soon as his nagging cough goes away."

"Help," Andrew shouts. "I need help!"

"HELP!" the head screams, much louder than Andrew had, making wide eyes at him.

Oh, to turn and run.

He dares a glance behind him and sees that the road keeps straight, intermittent trees punctuating pastures in which sheep and the odd cow walk, heads bent to the grass, chewing.

When he turns his gaze back to them, the three peasants are yards closer, though he can see no difference in their gaits. He notices now their grass-stained boots.

"You owe me two kopecks, Lyosha. The man did not want to hear American."

The head hawks and spits again.

I'm dreaming.

This is 1983 and I'm dreaming.

Look up!

A series of very tight jet contrails etch themselves in the clear summer sky.

Bomber

"BOMBER!" the head screams, never looking away from Andrew. "HELP ME, BOMBER!"

The idiot likes this, says it also, as if to himself.

"Help me, bomber."

They continue down the road for some time, Andrew sweating more than the cool day should call for.

He hopes to hear a truck behind him, all but prays to hear one blow its horn. No sooner has he thought this than the uncle's head blares the *AH-ooo-GAH!* of a farm truck.

Mustn't look away again

"Hey, Lyosha," the head says to the hobbling boy, "I don't think he means to look away again."

"I think you're right, Uncle."

"It's no good if he sees us; he can just keep the same distance all day long."

"Right again, Uncle."

"He is young with long legs. Not like you since your accident, stupid boy."

"You had an accident, too, Uncle."

"But mine did not slow me down, as you see."

So saying, the body walking with the strangling rope executes something between a spasm and a *tour jeté*.

The simple man laughs, then bites the head's ear to hold it so he can clap his pancake hands together.

The body leaps again.

"Vanka," the head says, rolling its eyes dramatically back to look at the simple man carrying it, "how many flies did you catch?"

The head goes back to the fist so Vanka can reply.

"Many."

"Enough to bring on night?"

"Night! Night! Night!" the big man chants, and it is clear he would clap his hands except for the head he carries.

"Do it, then, big boy!"

Now the idiot opens his mouth and what looks like a big, black pudding begins to emerge from it. He vomits this into the road, where it writhes and undulates, weak light from the sun playing on its slick surface.

Now the boy hops up on his remaining leg and uses his scythe to take a huge swing at the pudding, which bursts into a swarm of blackflies that cover the sun.

And it is night.

Night without stars.

Andrew runs.

The dream changes so he finds himself in a nest.

Or perhaps a bed of dry hay?

Something woolly nuzzles his arm aside, chewing.

He pushes at its head to get it away from him, but it baas explosively, showing him its black tongue.

A sheep.

Where the fuck am I?

A crude wooden roof stands above him.

No walls.

A stable?

The sun is setting, or perhaps rising, casting a dim violet light. A pitchfork stands up from the ground, backlit, tines up, two of those tines spearing an oblong, head-shaped something, also backlit.

Oh, it is a head

It hawks and spits, then speaks.

"Our little baby is awake now, yes?"

Husky laughter comes from near the water trough, against which the idiot brother sits, Andrew's backpack spilled out near him. He unrolls a pair of faded blue jeans and marvels at them, a lit cigarette in his mouth.

Wait until he finds the Playboys

He shouldn't smoke

Why, because he's retarded?

Special, we say special *now because it's nicer*

"Don't burn a hole in those, Vanka—we can sell them to a party member for a lot of money," the head says from its perch. "So, little baby, you like Jesus, yes?"

Andrew says nothing.

"You like him so much we put you in a manger."

The sheep baas again, as if prompted.

He looks into the field, where the headless body jerkily brushes down a plow horse, who stands placidly, swishing its tail against flies. Clearly headless bodies groom horses all the time in this hellish fairy-tale Russia.

Maybe I am in hell?

I ran into something hard in the dark.

A fence?

A plow?

Maybe I died?

"What, you have nothing to say?"

Andrew just blinks.

The head hawks and spits again, excusing itself.

A dream that's all just a dream

But I thought that when it happened

And it was real

"Even in a dream, one must be polite. But no. You are badly raised in America. Even if you did speak, all I would hear would be the sound of America coming from your mouth. Do you know this sound?"

Andrew says nothing.

"Would you like to hear this sound? The sound of America?"

Andrew shakes his head weakly, causing his head and neck to hurt.

"At last! The baby has an opinion! Well, here is the devil, baby, you will hear anyway."

The head growls then, showing the crooked teeth below that thick mustache. The growl grows into the sound of an engine starting up. A helicopter engine. It opens its mouth as the rotors of the unseen helicopter spin more rapidly, then, as the rotors chop and roar at flight velocity, it opens its mouth impossibly wide and blows a jet of wind, hot and stinking of gasoline, blowing the straw in the stables about furiously, frightening the sheep away and scattering a trio of hens. The idiot brother shields his cigarette with his cupped hands, but it blows away anyway, and he cries.

The head shuts its mouth now, cutting off the roaring wind.

"It's all right, Ivan. America is gone now, and it is time for hot towels."

"Hot towels? I like hot towels."

"I know. Hot towels feel nice."

Now the boy comes from behind Andrew

Neck hurts too much to turn and see where he came from

somehow carrying a bucket, towels, a lit oil lamp, and a shaving box. The boy has his leg back on

?

but limps slightly as he sloshes the steaming bucket along.

His big brother fetches himself a stool and sits, chin poked forward, loosening his collar. The boy packs a steaming towel around the simple man's neck and he coos.

The headless body now comes, washes the horse sweat from its hands in the soapy water, unwraps the towel, and then soaps and shaves Ivan's face, gently slapping a cheek when it wants him to pucker and tighten.

It wields the straight razor expertly.

Andrew shudders.

If they were going to hurt me, they would have done it already
Says who?

"Hurt you?" the head says from its tines, squinting with concentration at the remote-control shaving job its body undertakes. "More light!" it barks, and the boy winds the tiny knob that adjusts the length of the wick, leaning the lamp closer.

"Now you're in my way."

The boy steps to one side.

"Good. Stay there."

It hawks and spits a black clot and then addresses Andrew again.

"Hurt you? Why would we hurt you when you do such a good job hurting yourself? You should see the goose egg on your head. No, we want you well. We have many accidents here. Farmwork is perilous— but what would you know about it with your supermarkets and whores and ghettos? We want you safe and sound so you can heal us, little Jesus. See how you helped Lyosha?"

I want to wake up

"Wake up, then!"

I want to go home

"Who is stopping you? Go!" the head says, looking at Andrew

now. The body has turned his way as well, and gestures with the razor as if to indicate the road Andrew is welcome to walk.

With some effort, Andrew swivels his hips over the lip of the manger, but something is wrong, something more than his throbbing head and ground-glass-packed neck.

He tries to stand but collapses to the ground, knocking his chin and biting his tongue. A startled rooster flaps its wings halfheartedly and continues to strut.

Of course he has fallen.

He has only one leg.

Andrew wakes up.

Adjusts the sweat-dampened pillow beneath him.

In the distance, a train.

63

"Ichabod."

Nothing.

"Ichabod, I command you to appear to me."

Nothing.

If it isn't listening, it isn't disobeying.

He'll have to formally invoke it or go see it.

The idea of going to see it in its cave makes him shudder.

Its cave by the train tracks.

And formal invocation is a pain in the ass.

He looks at the antique clock on his nightstand.

One ten A.M.

Just after midnight in New Orleans.

He has a debt to pay.

He appears in the restroom of a fine-dining restaurant off Chartres, one he knows keeps late weekend hours. Knows also that it won't be so busy he's likely to have company in a private stall. He gets lucky, appears in front of the sinks, sees himself in the mirror.

Looking older.

Looking fortyish, not thirty-five.

Hair still black, skin tight, but there's something.

Still beats looking fifty-three . . . what would that look like?

Before his eyes, his hair goes mostly white, loses its luster; deep lines bracket his mouth; his eyes get crow's-feet.

Not ready for that. Not yet. Go back.

He concentrates, believes himself younger.

Gets younger, thirty-five again.

Pops a blood vessel in his eye.

"Ow, FUCK!"

His left eye goes red; he bends over.

A waiter peeks in the bathroom door.

"You all right, sir?"

"I'm perfect, thanks."

He's far from perfect, but people don't press things in this city, and the waiter disappears.

His sclera will clear up; he'll still be younger when it does.

It gets harder every year, though; they all lose this battle.

He feels the bulge in his coat pocket, wonders if the waiter thought he had a gun.

It's worse than a gun!

. . .

He goes by the zinc bar where a bartender with retro-lacquered hair cracks an egg, looks at Andrew, looks back at his work, finishes making the pre-Prohibition fizz for the rich young lady in the antique silk stockings. It could be a scene from 1935 until her cell phone buzzes and she looks down at it, smiles privately.

Now his phone is out, dialing Haint.

It rings five times, and then he hears the message.

"You know who this is if you got this number. Don't fuck around."

Now the sound of something small and squeaky getting killed by something hard and heavy, underscored by Haint's gravelly laughter.

Beeep

"Andrew. Call me back. I'll be at Lafitte's. For a while."

He's there for longer than a while.

A bearded boy in a bowler hat tears up Zevon's "Werewolves of London" in the back, fenced behind listeners perched directly at the piano, wobbly on their stools. The pianist's buddy leans against the wall near him, accompanying him on harmonica. Everything is dim. Everyone is drunk. The steamy little building reeks of whiskey and sways with inebriation.

If Dionysus came back, this would be his temple.

No sooner has Andrew thought this than Dionysus walks in.

WTF?

Did I just think WTF instead of what the fuck?

Is that fucking Dionysus?

Andrew relaxes a bit when he realizes the grape-leaf-crowned figure moving through the crowd is wearing a papier-mâché mask. He tenses again when he notices that nobody else looks at it. It's looking at him. No, correct that; it points its eyeholes at him, but those holes are black and eyeless. Sleeves hang past where the hands would be, but he is nauseatingly sure it has no hands. It floats rather than walks.

Andrew white-knuckles the table.

Now the piano man aborts the Doobie Brothers song he had just started, bangs his hands discordantly on the keys, looks at Andrew, and says, "May I sit?"

Nobody else notices.

They sway and drink and talk as if they're still hearing the song.

The harmonica man plays on.

"Sure," Andrew says.

The chair opposite him pulls out on its own and the empty Dionysus collapses into it, the grape leaf garland and mask landing on top, the eyeholes fixed on the ceiling.

The waitress, a depressive woman with a lazy eye and a *Who Dat?* T-shirt, plucks the crown of grape leaves from the chair and walks it over to the piano player, fitting it down over his hat.

"Thank you, Felicity. Your next period will be crampless."

"Awesome," she says, sounding upbeat for the first time tonight.

The piano player tickles the keys and speaks to Andrew again.

"I believe you're the only person in this establishment drinking virgin soda water. You profane my temple, sir."

"Ichabod?"

"At your service, as ever."

"I called you hours ago."

"You commanded me to appear before you. You did not specify a time."

Everyone around the piano claps and cheers.

A man in a ridiculous toupee reaches past other celebrants to tuck a fiver in the well-stuffed tip pitcher.

The waitress points at the musician's near-empty glass by way of asking him if he'd like another drink.

"Absinthe," he calls to her.

Looks back at Andrew.

"What is your pleasure, O magus?"

"I have a question, but I'd like to ask it in private."

"Ask away! Nobody's listening."

Now everyone in the bar turns and looks at Andrew.

"Ichabod."

"I know. The manners in this city aren't what they used to be. Friends, might we have a little privacy?"

The drinkers all put their fingers in their ears, still staring at Andrew.

Andrew's fear grows, but then he remembers he's in charge.

Sort of.

"That was good," he tells it.

"They're easier to control when they're drunk. But you know about that."

He plays a little piano riff.

"Make them stop."

"MAKE THEM STOP!" they all say.

"I command you."

"I COMMAND YOU!"

"Do you really?" the piano player says.

His buddy starts making a train noise with the harmonica.

"Yes," Andrew says.

The harmonica *choos* like a train whistle.

The harmonica player now lowers his harmonica, looks at Andrew, too.

Silence.

The piano man spins his garlanded hat, puts it back on his head at a more rakish angle.

"I choose to interpret 'Make them stop' as 'Make them stop living.' That's a tall order. Forty souls in this room, including the piano man. I'll have to tamper with a gas line."

"That's not . . ."

The waitress comes back with a glass of liquid that glows green like antifreeze. The piano man takes it.

Nods at her and says, "Forty-one!"

"My life sucks anyway!" she says.

"Forty-one dead in New Orleans gas explosion, America's oldest bar destroyed. You and I will survive, of course. But this is going to be on CNN!" says the piano player.

"That's not what I meant and you know it."

"I don't have to know what you meant. I only have to know what you said. Now either you insist and they all die, or I disobey. Your call entirely."

Now everyone in the bar drops to both knees, bowing their heads, their hands extended palms up in supplication.

"No, that's more classical, isn't it? Let's do something modern."

Now they all look up, interlace their fingers, tears streaming down their cheeks as if they were all attached to the same irrigation system.

Andrew can't speak.

"Just say 'live' or 'die.' I won't insist on protocol."

Andrew's mind races. He can't think of a way out of this.

"Friends," it says. "I believe the wizard fears to slacken my leash, even just a little. If you have any last words, now would be a good time to say them."

They speak in chorus.

"NOW I LAY ME DOWN TO SLEEP
I PRAY THE LORD MY SOUL TO KEEP
IF I DIE BEFORE I WAKE
THE PIANO MAN MY SOUL TO TAKE."

All eyes rest on the magus.

The sound of gas hissing rises up.

One of the candles leaps.

"Live!" Andrew says.

The hissing stops.

The candle leaps again, throwing too much light, casting the piano man's shadow against the brick wall behind him, but of course it isn't a man—tentacles, a writhing squid, just a split second of that.

Now he bangs out "Happy Days Are Here Again" on the piano.

All the drinkers look at each other, reach out to each other. They kiss indiscriminately, with no regard to age or gender. They begin to reach down pants, up skirts, fish out breasts.

A wild-eyed Asian man on his knees begins to stroke Andrew's thigh. Andrew moves away forcefully, stands up. The Asian man attaches himself to another couple, pets them, is petted in return.

"Shall I make them *stop*?" asks the grinning piano man.

Andrew speaks slowly, considering every word.

"I, Andrew Ranulf Blankenship, command you by the conditions of your entry into this sphere, and by the power of the words I here intone, which bind you to my service, to release all men and women currently in your power from said power, and to restore them to the state of independent thought and action in which you discovered them upon your entry to this building."

The piano player stops playing.

"Nicely done."

Raises his glass to Andrew.

It's going to leave before I can ask it if the witch is really dead.

"To you, sir. And to wormwood."

He knocks back his absinthe.

"Ichabod, wait . . ."

The room blurs.

The bearded boy in the bowler hat belts out "Werewolves of London," his friend accompanying him on the harmonica.

The entity

it's a demon just say it

is gone.

It came on its own terms and fucked with him until it got him to make a mistake.

It inched that much closer to liberty.

It kicked his ass.

Haint never comes, does not answer subsequent texts.

When Andrew gets back to the restaurant, he finds it closed and locked.

He will sleep among the crypts in the cemetery north of the Quarter, not far from Marie Laveau. He will sleep there, unafraid of molestation; he will make himself invisible.

Failing that, he has other means of self-defense.

Very persuasive means, indeed.

It will be the next day before Andrew takes his Hand of Glory and his unanswered question back through the rabbit hole, back to Dog Neck Harbor, New York.

To you, sir.

And to wormwood.

64

Cayuga County Deputy Brant McGowan follows the red Toyota on a hunch.

Just slips behind it as it pulls out of the Fair Haven gas station, decides to try to get a look at the driver.

A child abduction in Syracuse has everybody from here to Watertown on edge. This is the second one in two weeks, but the only one they've got a lead on. First one was an infant snatched from its stroller, just gone and nobody knows when or how, and that was in Red Creek. Mother is the primary person of interest. This time, some creep yanked a toddler off his sister's arm while they were walking back from the park just two blocks from home. The suspect appears in flashes on a security camera, swooping up from his parked red Toyota Prius, the action reminding Brant of a trap-door spider he saw at an insect zoo when he was a kid. Not so long ago. Deputy McGowan is a young man.

So was the perp in the video. Young, and dirty to be in that kind of car.

Deputy McGowan is off duty, coming home from Auburn in his own Saturn—not the kind of vehicle to draw attention, although he would freely admit his sunglasses look a bit coppish.

He doesn't think the driver knows he has a tail.

He's seen maybe three of the distinctive Toyota hybrids in red since he saw the footage, but this is the first one driven by a male. Also the first one that makes his guts crawl. He has only seen the driver from behind so far, sees that it's a bald or short-haired man, indeterminate age. He needs to get up beside him for a proper peek, but the one-lane roads here in farm country won't allow for that unless he goes to pass.

Might as well stick with him for a while.

As it turns out, he sticks with him all the way to Marsh Road.

When he sees the Prius slow down and signal to turn off 104A, he has to decide whether to turn with it; if he does, there will be no ambiguity. The guy will know he's being followed. If it's *the* guy, that is. Most honest citizens don't notice shit unless they've got a good reason to.

He turns, too, keeping a good distance behind, almost letting him get out of sight.

Got a glimpse of him as he turned.

Older guy, big beard.

Too old to be the perp.

But maybe he's not the only one who drives that car.

When the beardy guy turns up the dead-end road leading to the cabins, the game is definitely up; he can't just swivel in there after him. He drives past the turn, pulls in the driveway of a house, sits there until the Toyota is out of sight.

Wasn't there a disappearance out this way, maybe these cabins?

Yeah . . . German tourist or something. State police said they got some weird DNA, but no body, no suspect.

A woman peeps at him through drapes.

He pretends to be checking something on his phone, pulls out, parks a bit farther down.

Heads down the road to the cabins on foot.

Just a guy taking a stroll.

In cop glasses.

I really suck at this.

I left my gun in the car.

I'll never be a detective.

I need a story in case he talks to me.

He sees the Prius now.

Walks closer to the trees, in shadow now, pretends to look at his phone again.

Sees the man getting out.

Kind of a smarty-arty-looking old dude.

Getting something out of the back now.

A cage?

A cage.

With a rooster in it!

Flapping its wings halfheartedly, feathers floating.

The man wrinkles his nose.

Takes the cage in the house.

What does a latte-drinking guy like that want with a rooster?

Should I go talk to him?

I'll say I'm looking for a buddy's cabin.

Bob?

Too generic.

Kyle.

Big guy with a red beard, having a keg party.

He'll hate that, he'll be so busy hating it he won't stop to wonder if I'm a cop, if he's not involved.

If he's not, who cares?

Might tip him off if he's involved.

Looks twitchy, wonder if he's scared about something.

I'd like to know what.

If anyone else lives there, I might see who.

Movement behind him.

He turns around, but whatever it was is still or gone.

Squirrel.

No, bigger than a squirrel.

He looks back toward the house.

All still and quiet.

Don't think anyone else lives there.

This is stupid.

He stands with his arms folded, weighing the pros and cons of approaching the house.

Something weird's going on here, but weird isn't illegal. I don't think this is the guy. And if it is, I'm more likely to fuck things up than make myself useful. Still, I'll tell Syracuse about the car and chicken-man, see if they want somebody on duty to roll by and ask questions.

He senses motion behind him now, turns around just too late again.

Birds flutter near the crowns of the trees.

His hand strays to where his gun should be.

He decides it's official.

He's creeped out.

Hell with this.

He walks back down the road now, feeling watched.

He walks more quickly.

Strong late-afternoon sun, not even close to dark, and he feels like a teenaged girl in a graveyard.

Laughs at himself.

Still walks fast, though.

He sees his car.

Something's different.

I had the window up.

Now it's down.

Did I have it up?

He approaches the car from the blind spot just in case.

Pops his trunk with the fob.

A slate-gray Volkswagen Jetta slides by, the driver eyeing him suspiciously.

He waves without meaning to, an instinct.

Puts on his gun belt.

Feels better.

Looks in the window, sees nobody, relaxes a bit.

Sits down, a chill going through him.

Damn it's cold in here, I was running the air but damn.

Freon leak or something?

He starts the car.

Cocks the mirror to look at himself, thinks he looks ridiculous in his badass shades.

Opens the glove box to put them away and get a piece of gum.

Sees it.

The antler.

He checks his windows and mirrors again to make sure there's nobody near the car, then looks at it again.

It's a goddamned antler, an antler from a young buck.

He nearly picks it up, then thinks about DNA and prints and decides not to touch it until he has a sandwich bag.

It really is cold in the car, cold enough to make him put the heat on.

He closes the glove box and drives off with his sunglasses on, chewing no gum.

65

The men in the slate-gray Volkswagen Jetta don't talk much.

They are on their way to avenge Mikhail Dragomirov, whom Georgi believes was murdered by a female associate of one Andrew Blankenship, who lives on Willow Fork Road, but whose dwelling should be identified by a turquoise Mustang from the late sixties, what Americans of a certain age call a muscle car.

Sergei Alexandrovich Rozhkov doesn't like this.

He doesn't like Georgi, either.

Sergei is nearly seventy-seven, but still vigorous. Still dangerous. His son back in Brooklyn looks older than he does now, ever since the liver problems turned him the color of bad salmon.

Georgi is not his son.

Georgi is the nephew of an old friend, the kind of friend you do inconvenient things for.

Even when that friend is dead.

Georgi has stumbled into his midthirties, neither fully American nor truly Russian, too scared to join the mob, an honest citizen who doesn't notice shit. The man they passed on the road was a policeman putting on a gun. Georgi looked at him obviously, drawing his attention. Getting his own face looked at. There would have been no room for such a man in the Odessa operation, but that was a long time ago now.

What's more, he's clearly in love with his estranged cousin, the niece, and wants to impress her by killing those who may or may not have killed Misha. The little niece believes it was this Blankenship, a man of small consequence, who killed Misha over a whore, and she won't say how she knows this.

Sergei is all but sure Misha drowned.

It's always this way. When we lose someone we love, we want a villain. What if the villain was the whiskey Misha was drinking and the currents in the lake? He should shoot a bottle of scotch, empty a clip into the lake, and go home.

Misha was a good man, strong at chess, a genius with numbers, but he comes from a degenerate tribe with their best days behind them. Everybody's best days are behind them. The world has become a playground of idiots and zealots, where the ever-shrinking center of reasonable men must work harder and harder to keep the lights on and the bombs from going off.

Sergei wants to go back to Brooklyn and get out of this paradise of horseshit and apples where you must drive everywhere.

He misses the pastrami at the deli on the street full of Greeks.

Now they wind their way up Willow Fork Road, looking for a house that doesn't seem to be there.

"This address she gave us is correct?"

Sergei speaks English because Georgi spends too long searching for his words in Russian and this is annoying.

Georgi answers him in Russian anyway.

"I don't know. She says so, but his address is not listed. The Mustang is known; the . . . what is the word? sales record has been found. On the Internet. And this color, blue-green and bright."

Sergei says the Russian word for *turquoise*.

Georgi switches to English.

"Yes, *biryuzoviy*. It's an unusual color, and an unusual car. Look," he says, showing him a cut-out page from an auto sales magazine, a 1968 Mustang circled in red pen, a tiny skull drawn badly near it.

"It's a nice car," Sergei says.

They come to the end of the road, execute a three-point turn, and go back.

And then, good luck!

The turquoise Mustang appears from a tree-hidden drive that seems to lead to no house; it has to be the same car. And it *is* a magnificent beast. It takes a right onto the road and tears out, using its big, Vietnam-era motor to vault down the winding road. The motor is louder than those in modern cars; it sounds powerful, like a predator. And classic. The man who owns such a car will be good with his hands, a good worker. It occurs to Sergei that he may like the man in the Mustang more than the nephew of his old associate.

But a promise is a promise.

They follow the Mustang out of Dog Neck Harbor all the way past Fair Haven, where it pulls off 104A and parks behind a barn that has been converted into an auto garage across the street from silos. North Star. Nice name.

The driver has already gone into the garage when they pull around.

"Remember," Georgi says, "he has long black hair like an Indian and he is thin."

"Am I a man you must say things twice to?"

"Sorry."

"Let me see your gun."

Georgi looks around, then removes his snub-nosed .38.

Sergei takes it from him, opens the cylinder, spins it, his heart gladdening at the sight of brass. Shell casings are his favorite jewelry.

"This is ready. Try not to shoot me."

He now pulls out his own Makarov, flips down the safety, puts it back into his coat.

They get out.

Open the door, walk in like they know what they're doing. Sneaking is for idiots; people who look as though they have a purpose rarely get questioned.

They find themselves in a back room, an employee room of sorts, where a number of heavily tattooed Mexicans sit around a table littered with tequila bottles and half-eaten plates smeared with brown and green sauces.

The place smells like chocolate, cinnamon, and garlic.

Now a voice behind them.

Mexican accent.

"Keep your hands out of your pockets."

They do.

"Why were you following me?"

"I like Mustangs," Sergei says. "I was hoping that one might be for sale. Is it?"

Chancho grunts.

The men at the table look at the Russians with eyes like brown stone. Several of them have their hands ominously under the table.

"Why were you coming in the back door to talk about buying a car?"

"That's the way you came in. We wanted to talk to you."

Chancho grunts.

Gonzo walks in, sees guns, puts his hands over his eyes like the see-no-evil monkey, and walks briskly out.

"Why the *pistolas*? You know, it's not nice to bring guns to the back door to ask about buying a car."

"Please," Georgi starts.

Sergei says, in Russian, "If you beg I will shoot you myself."

Then, in English, "This was our mistake. I apologize for disturbing you. With your permission, we will leave now and we will not return."

"Give me your wallets," Chancho says. "And put your guns on the table. Like slow, though. Super slow."

They do.

Chancho looks in the wallets, grunts.

"Lotta money in these wallets. If I still stole I'd be real happy about these wallets."

The Russians stay quiet.

"But I don't steal, not no more," he says. "Not money, anyway."

He takes the driver's licenses out of both wallets, gives the wallets back, always behind the Russians, and they do not look at him.

Now he tosses the driver's licenses on the table. Georgi's lands in pico de gallo.

"My cousins, they gonna keep those. They could be fake, but I don't think so. If something bad happens to me, something *real* bad's gonna happen to you. *¿Comprende, pendejos?*"

"*Ponymayu,*" Sergei says, nodding.

The Mexicans walk them outside.

Chancho asks them to open the car doors.

They do.

Chancho pulls out a large, brutal-looking knife and cuts long slashes in the upholstery. He does this impassively, taking his time, like fucking up car seats is just another service they offer at North Star, like it's something he wants to do well.

He motions for them to get back in their cars.

They do.

"*Adios, pendejos.* And don't come back."

Before the disgraced Volkswagen pulls out of the North Star Garage, Sergei Alexandrovich Rozhkov looks at Georgi.

"You let a woman tell you what to do, and this is what happens."

"But . . ."

"Be quiet. Misha drowned. You're an idiot. I'm going back to Brooklyn."

66

Night.

A new moon, the sky and the lake beneath it as black as oil.

The woman stands naked atop the cabin, naked but for a canvas bag slung over her shoulder. She readies two bottles, vodka bottles now filled to the neck with blood.

One contains rooster's blood.

One does not.

She takes a swig from that one, then empties both into a bucket from which a birch broom juts. She ties the empty bottles together and hangs them around her neck. She uses the broom to drizzle and flick the blood on her roof, knowing she'll have flies tomorrow, but there's nothing for it. This is how it's done. She doesn't have to coat the whole roof—there isn't enough for that anyway—but she must not leave two handsbreadths unbloodied.

This is an old spell, and the old spells are particular.

She walks backward toward the ladder, walking the bucket with her, sweeping behind so she doesn't get any on the bottoms of her feet. Every yard or so she rests the broom, takes hen feathers from her shoulder sack and sprinkles these on the roof, repeating a verse in Russian and concentrating on what she wants.

The bottles knock together tenderly sometimes, reminding her how testes, breasts, and ovaries—all the genitive organs—come in twos. Three is the number for gating, invocation, and killing. Four is for protection and weather. But two is for creation.

Two babes, a boy and a girl.

Two chickens, a rooster and a hen.

Down the ladder now, and she gives the Man Who Will Not Look At Her the bottles. He puts them in the garbage bag with the bones. The hen and rooster bones, and the bones that are not hen or rooster bones.

And the clothes.

The little clothes.

In the bag that will be rowed out to the lake.

She stands now on the porch watching the Cold Man row.

Moroz.

The Man Who Will Not Look At Her will not row—he will go back to his room hooded like a bird and sitting somewhere between sleep and waking. He learned quickly, hoods himself obediently, goes to town to run errands and never dares to run. Knows the Cold Man would come for him, and for his. He took to it so naturally because he is a coward. Not like the thief.

Things are beginning to move against the thief.

He is strong now, not like then.

He has killed the Baba in the woods, or caused her to be killed.

His bitch in the water killed sweet Misha.

His house is full of tricks.

He has friends, many friends.

First, the friends.

Then the fear will come to him, weaken him.

And then she will close his eyes.

Take back what is hers.

He hid himself, but that magic is waning.

She knows his town, even what road.

He has spread himself too thin with other spells.

She will find him soon.

Tonight's magic must sleep, but it will awaken when the moon waxes fat and full.

"Wait a moment," she says. "The potatoes."

The Man Who Will Not Look At Her is tying up the bag, putting it in the boat. He hears her, says, "Potatoes? Do you need potatoes?"

"Yes. That might be enough for him. You will go tomorrow and find me a bucket of potatoes. Other things, too."

"Of course."

"Are you hungry?"

He shakes his head, looking at his feet.

"You'll have to eat."

He shakes his head again.

A tear falls on his feet.

"Go to your kennel."

He leaves, still looking down, his shoulders folded in on themselves.

She smells the air.

Smiles.

Garlic, rosemary, wine, black pepper.

And meat.

She salivates.

The first roast is done.

67

Andrew drives Salvador to the North Star Garage, where Radha's car waits to be driven north to Chicago. Salvador will drive it in a day, needing neither rest nor sleep, looking to all but the very luminous like a handsome young Latino. And the very luminous will be used to seeing strange things; will not think much of seeing a portrait of

Salvador Dalí swiveling in the window of a Mini Cooper, checking the blind spot twice as it changes lanes. He will return through Radha's shower, perhaps in time for lunch tomorrow.

Chancho shows Andrew the final touch. Zebra skin seats. He had seen on her Facebook page her post about her new zebra-skin pillow, how much she liked that particular pelt.

She's going to squee.

Chancho looks ashen, distracted.

"You still thinking about the Russians, Chanch?"

"Them? No. One was a pussy, the other didn't care. Not enough to tangle with us. They ain't comin' back."

Andrew is thinking about the Russians, though. He thinks it might be prudent to acquire a pendant that turns bullets, a lovely bit of sorcery made from Kevlar, lead, silver, armadillo blood, and the ground tooth of someone who died of natural causes, but the user who makes these lives in Rio de Janeiro and doesn't care for tapes of the dead or cars.

What the Brazilian wants is a cloak of feathers that will change him into a hawk. Andrew could make such a cloak, but it would take him weeks, maybe months. Birds are hard, and this is not his specialty. The user in Brazil doesn't know Andrew and has a reputation for being kind of a prick—very QPQ. *Quid pro quo.* Reputation is everything between users, so they tend to trust each other. Not bullet guy. QPQ. He wants payment upon delivery. And Andrew wants the protection pendant stat.

The best shapeshifter, the one who taught Andrew, lives near Québec; she could make the hawk cloak in days, probably has one or two ready for trade. He doesn't know what she might want, other than a really mighty youth potion, and those are in high, high demand. She has asked for stone spells before, though. If so, back to Michael Rudnick, who is sequestered with Anneke until the full moon. Luckily, the *Québécoise* trusts other users, knows Andrew, and would be willing to wait. Unluckily, she's old, very old-school, and doesn't use the Internet. Thinks it's evil. So he'll have to call her on her landline. Again. She didn't answer last night, but that's not unusual; she shifts and spends days at a time as an animal. It's widely thought she's close to opting out permanently, rebooting into a young critter and spending her last years on earth flying or running on all fours.

There's a man in the city who knows about birds and shapeshifting, but he's old, too.

And he helped Andrew once before.

The kind of help you can't pay back, and you can't ask other favors after.

Back to Chancho and his ashen face.

"What's wrong?"

"Saw something messed up this morning."

"You've seen plenty of messed-up shit."

"Not like this."

"Not like what?"

"You wanna see?"

"No. Yes."

They walk through the employee room. An AK-47 leans in the corner looking insouciant.

"State police brought it in; I'm supposed to clean it up. They took the *muerto*, left the deer. Effing big effer. Look at this *pinché* deer."

First he's looking at the car.

The crumpled, dirty mess of a car.

Now he looks at the beast stoppering the hole where the windshield should be.

It *is* an effing big effer of a *pinché* deer.

Two hundred twenty-five pounds or better. Fifteen points or more on the rack, if the rack were intact. But it's not. It's through the windshield of the Saturn that clearly also hit a tree. The stag is practically *fused* into the car.

"You can see where they had to cut the poor dude out on this side, cut part of the deer's horns off, too, where they were through him. *All the way* through him. Look at this seat."

Andrew suppresses the urge to gag.

"But this is what I don't get . . ."

Now he points at a hole in the deer's rear shoulder, another flowering out of the back of the neck.

"Bullets. Homeboy shot this deer. Probably through the glass, but the glass is gone. They took the gun, too. He had it in his hand. They asked for pliers to get it out, that's how tight he had it."

Andrew tries to process this.

"Yeah, I know. Messed up. But look at this . . ."

His strong, brown finger indicates a broken headlight, blood, fur.

"And this."

Muddy hoofprints on the roof, scratches on the door.

"More than one deer," I say.

"Yeah, and it's the *tree* that crunched in the front end, not the deer. Not *this* deer."

"He didn't hit this deer?"

"Nah. He hit another deer. Wrecked his car. Then deer come along . . . Maybe more than one. Look . . . hoof-ding, hoof-ding. Coming out of the woods and going at the car, looks like. Then the big boy came like a cannonball, ran through the effin' windshield so fast it broke it and put its horns through his heart. Even though he shot it, shot it good. Look."

He points again at the lethal bullet wounds.

"This is *brujo* stuff, isn't it?"

Andrew touches the car.

"Isn't it?"

Andrew nods.

Brujo stuff of the first order.

Slavic forest magic.

And very, very strong.

Then it happens.

A young man appears, pale, speared by the deer, writhing in his seat. He wears aviator sunglasses; blood comes out of his mouth, makes bubbles every time he says the word *please*. He says it several times.

Chancho can't see it, is still examining the hoof and antler gouges in the Saturn's finish as if they were a rude hieroglyph that might explain how such things happened in the world.

The ghost starts to swell up.

Take it easy, Andrew thinks. *I see you.*

THEN HELP ME

The pallid young man puts the phantom of his gun in his mouth, pulls the trigger impotently, coughs blood all over the gun, and cries.

Help me

How?

It shivers. Points the gun at him. Spasms its fist as it pulls the trigger. Nothing happens, but it shoots Andrew several times, then Chancho, then itself.

Get Them.

Who?

Them, it wheezes.

Becomes frustrated that Andrew doesn't understand, begins to get tired. New ghosts get tired easily.

It vomits black liquid all over itself and fades away.

The dead deer jerks, kicks.

Chancho jumps, crosses himself.

The stag deflates a little, lies very still, won't move again.

Andrew rubs his temples.

"Headache?"

Andrew smiles, shakes his head, closes his eyes.

"I'm in trouble, Chancho. Bad trouble."

Chancho nods.

"I told you not to eff with this stuff anymore. *¡Cabrón!*"

Chancho hammer-fists himself in the thigh, looks angrily at Andrew.

"This is from before, Chancho. From before I met you."

"Yeah, but you're still *in* it. Don't you see? It's why they can get to you, still. Get *out* of it."

"It's not like that."

Chancho throws his arms up.

"No, it's like *this*," he says, indicating the wreck, the improbable deer, the bloody seat.

Andrew nods.

"I'll stay away from you until this is over. After I help you clean this up. This isn't your mess."

"Nah, go home. You'll get in the way. And don't stay away after. Just quit with the books and the *chingada brujerías*."

Andrew laughs a little, still rubbing his temples.

Looks at Chancho.

"I've noticed that you say very bad things in Spanish but not English. Why is that?"

Chancho pauses.

"Because I'm American now. Them other words are in my blood. I can't help it. But I got to start over with American."

"Ah," the magus says, clearly unconvinced.

The bigger man walks over, encircles Andrew with a mighty arm.

"I'll ask the boys to stay around," Chancho says. "I'll pray, too. Get some Jésus down here."

If only.

Andrew doesn't know if there is a Jésus, and, if there is, whether he was God or man.

If he was a man, though, he must have been a user.

Water into wine sounds really.

Fucking.

Good.

68

Early evening.

The doorbell rings.

As Salvador is engaged in the garden, Andrew opens the door himself to find Arthur Madden and Mrs. Simpson standing on his porch, Mr. Madden panting somewhat more than usual, Mrs. Simpson smiling broadly and holding a paper plate covered in tinfoil.

"Good evening, Mr. Blankenship," she says, her massive, jacketed bosom forming a sort of brooched cliff. "Sorry to drop by so late. I hope we're not disturbing you,"

She's doing the talking so Arthur can catch his breath.

"Not at all."

He thinks quickly, trying to remember if he has anything controversial lying about in the living or dining room.

He thinks not.

"Would you like to come in?"

Now Andrew sees why the older Jehovah's Witness is huffing and puffing so much—a produce basket and two full grocery bags stand on the porch behind them. The climb up the drive is nearly too much for Arthur without sacks to carry, so these really tested the poor geezer.

"Oh, we couldn't impose on your hospitality so close to suppertime," she says.

A second and a half ticks by like an awkward musical pause.

"We were just in the neighborhood and thought we'd bring you some leftovers."

Leftovers?

Andrew attempts several polite refusals, but Mrs. Simpson is expert at parrying these. She wears him down. He takes the plate, peeps under the foil.

Looks like pot roast, creamed corn, and coleslaw.

"It's pot roast," she says. "I made it myself, so you'll have to eat it all up."

"Mmmm-mm," he says. "Well, thank you."

Arthur has enough wind back in him to speak.

"We also brought you some groceries."

"Mr. . . ."

"Madden, it's okay."

"I really don't feel comfortable taking groceries from you. I have plenty of food, and I'm sure you can think of someone in need who would love to get these."

"Well, here's the situation, Andrew. I am too tired to carry these bags back down your drive, and, may the Lord forgive me, too proud to let you or Mrs. Simpson do it. So you are just. Going. To have. To take. The groceries. Call it a favor to me."

This guy could charm the mustache off a gay trucker.

What the hell is going on?

"What's the occasion?"

"Call it a random act of kindness. Have you seen that bumper sticker? Perform something-something-beauty and random acts of kindness?"

"All right," Andrew says. "You win."

"I usually do. I mean, is this stuff that you will eat?"

"I'm sure it is."

Andrew peeks in the first bag.

First item, weirdly, a ziplock bag holding about half a dozen pickled eggs.

A block of sharp cheddar.

Canned goods.

Tomatoes, peas, chicken soup.

Creamed corn.

"And don't you worry about a thing. I know things may seem tough now, but with the Lord's help, all trials are temporary, and all burdens bearable."

He peeks in the second bag.

Rice. Mac and cheese. Dry spaghetti noodles in their long, coffinish boxes.

"Trials?"

"It's nothing to be ashamed of, Mr. Blankenship. This recession is very real, and jobs are hard to come by, and hard to keep. A good many of our congregation are also unexpectedly seeking new employment, and I understand you've been off the job for a while."

Andrew pauses. Looks at Arthur. Looks back down at the produce basket and then pulls the cloth off the top, revealing a prodigious heap of potatoes.

And a mirror.

A small hand mirror.

Sitting on top of the potatoes.

He sees his own reflection in it.

A spell.

His heart skips a beat.

He throws the cloth back over it as if covering a snake.

"She said you might be reluctant to accept help, but I assured her . . ."

"She?" Andrew says a little too loudly.

Heart skidding.

"Why yes. Your mother's friend."

"My mother's friend who?"

"You know, she didn't tell me her name. The Polish lady."

"Russian," corrects Mrs. Simpson.

"That's right, Russian. Very nice. She said she was just speaking with your mother . . ."

My mother's dead.

"... and told her she was bringing you potatoes from her own garden because homegrown food tastes best. And promised your mother you would visit her soon."

"Forgive me, but you have to go now."

"Pardon?"

"Please go," he says, gently pushing Arthur just a little, then calling, "Salvador!"

"Well, yes, all right, but if there's anything we can do to . . ."

"SALVADOR!"

Andrew takes the mirror from under the cloth, breaks it violently on his porch.

Mrs. Simpson takes her colleague by the elbow and begins to lead him down the long drive.

"Good night, Mr. Blankenship," she says. "God bless."

Salvador comes trotting around the side of the house, holding a pair of pruning shears, his prosthetic knees smeared with dirt. Some sort of weed is caught in the wicker of his left arm.

His framed head cocks to one side, awaiting instructions.

Before Andrew can issue any, however, the produce basket turns over on its own and the potatoes roll and bounce away from it like so many tailless rats escaping a ship.

Their paths cone away from Andrew and diverge; he dives, grabs one, but then it flips out of his hand and keeps rolling.

"Find out where they're going!" he shouts at Salvador.

The wicker man obeys, trailing the biggest group of them.

Andrew follows the one he grabbed.

It heads east, into the patch of woods near his house. He sees others moving in the low brush; to his left, one stops rolling, begins spinning in place. Burrows underground with a distinctive skirring noise.

He hears this happening all around him.

"Oh shit."

His does it, too, as soon as it gets half a dozen yards away from him.

Planting themselves.

I don't know this spell.

I don't like this spell.

Salvador finds him, points urgently, in several directions.

"Okay, okay. Thanks, boy. First, get me a shovel. No, a spade. No, I'll get the spade, you pile firewood in the pit."

Salvador tilts his head and moves his thumb and forefinger as if measuring an inch.

How much?

"All of it."

69

This was Andrew explaining fireglass to Anneke last month when he let her watch him make it:

"Any glass will work, but I like yellow glass so I know what it is. This wineglass will do fine. Smoky amber like. You break it. When you enchant it, you'll instruct the pieces to fold in on themselves, become smooth and handleable, like little stones. So when you first break it, gather just the bigger shards, and for God's sake don't cut yourself—if you make fireglass with your blood in it, the fire will try to find you, will creep out of the fireplace toward you, on the carpet, up your clothes. You get the point."

"Could you kill someone with it? Like put their blood in a lightbulb,

turn it into fireglass, and put it in their bathroom? Instruct the glass to
ignite not on a voice command but when the filament gets hot?"
He just looks at her.
Gets a little more frightened of her.
Falls a little more in love with her.

70

Andrew runs to the barn, grabs a few fireglass stones from their
vase, runs back, and throws them beneath the first load of wood Salvador has stacked teepee-shaped. He says *bhastrika* and they jet
flame and hot air like small torches until they are spent and a good
fire blazes in the pit. He passes Salvador on his way with another
double armload of wood, tells him, "Be careful!" and runs for a spade
and gloves.

And a flashlight.

It's not dark yet, but it's getting late.

He finds the first one by its telltale mound of dirt.

Uses the long-handled, leaf-bladed garden spade to lever it up.

It's bigger than it was, just slightly bigger than a big potato, and
has sprouted tendrils.

He fishes it up with his hand, wary that it might sprout thorns or
something.

At exactly that moment, it sprouts thorns.

"Fuck!"

He drops it instantly, only just manages not to get jabbed as one of the spines catches and breaks its tip off in his glove.

He quickly pinches out and flings down the point.

The thing rolls back into its hole, starts using its tendrils as sweepers, covering itself with dirt.

"You little fucker."

He jabs at it with the spade, finds its texture not wholly potato-like, tougher on the outside, slimier inside.

Probably turning animal, probably full of blood.

It writhes away from the jabbing spade but can't escape. At last he strikes it hard enough to make it rupture, and bleed it does. It's still writhing and dripping, like a spiny liver or other organ, as he waddle-runs it around back to the fire.

He braces himself for a sound.

It shrieks when he throws it in, high and infantile, though not exactly human. Outraged that it never had a chance to do its job.

To kill me.

But how?

It was growing.

The fire is huge now, and here comes Salvador with another arm-load of split logs, like the sorcerer's apprentice, literally ready to throw all the wood in.

"That's enough, Sal."

Sal puts the wood down.

"Help me find them now."

He holds the spade up; the portrait head inclines slightly, the automaton's articulated hand touching the spade's blade almost tenderly, as if it were a flower.

The fire casting amber light on the painting's glossy finish.

Dalí's nostrils appear to widen just a bit as Salvador takes in the scent.

His wicker hips waggle just a little.

Smelling things is so deliciously doglike.

All right, you anticipated the thorns and the blood and the shrieking. You have her number, know how she thinks. What's next? Prepare yourself. The next one will be bigger.

Salvador points at the ground where a quartet of tendrils are carefully smoothing down the mound the thing made burying itself.

Clever, awful little things.

Andrew spades up the dirt.

This one is the size of a small squash, not a potato.

It starts burrowing farther down.

He spades the hell out of it until it, too, bleeds, burbles, and weakens.

No thorns on this one. Could they all be different?

Now a tiny mouth, like a baby's, forms, bites feebly at the blade.

He grimaces, strikes a few more times.

Ruins the tiny mouth.

Pulps it all.

Shovels that out and takes it to the fire.

Have to work faster, they're growing.

The next one, the size of a cat, has enough tendrils to try to fight him for the spade. It loses.

The sun has gone down.

Think!

The next one must be carried into the fire in a bucket.

When the blisters begin to weep and sting within his gloves, Salvador digs.

The one after burrows farther down before he spades the life from it, and he gets an idea.

When the next one goes deeper, Andrew flings fireglass into the hole.

Bhastrika!

Fire gouts up from the hole, licks Andrew's jeans.

The potato-thing screams and dies.

His nonluminous neighbors don't hear a scream.

They hear a train.

. . .

The work goes on into the night.

He digs them up, finds abominations ever larger, stronger, harder to look at. He burns them, they shriek or squeal, he shovels out the smoldering mess and buckets it over to the bigger fire.

The last one Salvador finds is as large as a bear cub.

When the magus shines the light down into the hole, eyes shine up at him. He pauses, stunned. The eyes look human. It starts covering itself back up.

He runs for the house, gets his revolver, a .357 Smith and Wesson, and a fire extinguisher. Salvador is losing the garden spade to it, holding the light on it with one hand, clutching the spade with the other, digging furrows with his planted prosthetic heels.

A whitish vine has snaked around one of Sal's legs.

He's whimpering and growling.

Andrew levels his magnum's six-inch barrel at the thing in the hole.

It blinks at him.

I wonder if it knows.

It lets go of the spade, covers its face with the larger tendrils, tendrils that look suspiciously like hands.

Andrew fans a hand over the gun, imagines a kid banging on a metal garbage can lid. When he fires, that's what the neighbors will hear.

I wonder if it's going to say please.

It says *please*, or tries to, its mouth full of dirt.

"Prease."

It sounds a lot like the ghost in the car.

Slavic forest magic.

Very, very strong.

It almost has a hand-tendril around the barrel when Andrew recovers from its mild charm.

The trash can lid bangs six times.

A train whistles.

The thing in the hole mostly dies.

"Stand back, Sal."

The wizard throws so many fireglass stones into the hole that when he says *bhastrika* the flame burps up, makes a ring that lights brush and lower branches.

He uses the extinguisher.

Turns around to find Nadia looking at him, pleased with him.

It is near two A.M. when he satisfies himself that he has found them all. Salvador covers the whole property. They trespass onto the neighbor's land, Nadia holding the light, all of them invisible; if they are spotted, they will look like errant fireflies. This spell strains the already weary magus, but it must be done.

Slogging up to his front door, he sees a raccoon running off, dragging the bag of pickled eggs.

Just a raccoon.

Just eggs.

This strikes him really funny and he laughs the way people do on the subway sometimes when they've stopped caring who's looking at them.

Just as suddenly, he stops laughing, remembers what he was just doing. Shudders to think what those things might have grown into.

Before the shower, he looks at himself in the mirror over the sink.

He looks at the wall behind his shoulder, happy it's just wall.

Happy there's nobody behind him.

Is the old witch really dead?

What the fuck is after me?

He is filthy, his hair flecked with something like potato, his skin stippled with blood.

And then there's his eye.

He has popped the blood vessel in his sclera again.

It hurts.

He decides to let himself get a little older, at least until he has his strength back. Gray runs down his Indian-black hair in several fine skeins, like runs in a nylon stocking. The lines around his mouth deepen. He looks fortyish now, feels sixty. But his eye stops hurting, clears up.

His muscles are so sore he can barely turn the knobs, but the shower is good. Grime and blood run down across the Italian tiles and down the drain.

He's watching the last of the night's dirt swirl into the plumbing when he sees her long, pale feet step just behind his. The rusalka can't resist the water. The smell of deep lake and tide overwhelms him, but seems oddly pleasant after the high, seminal smell of the potatoes. Odd how their scent changed as they grew, became bloodier, more mammalian.

He doesn't look at her, just her feet. Probably a size ten? The men in her family must have had gunboats. He remembers stories she told him about their boots, the high, black boots of her uncles who worked in the New York workshop where they painted silk ties. She was a teenager when they fled the revolution, but the clomp of those boots had reassured her, had made her feel comforted and homesick all at once, certain at least that she was part of a tribe. Russian intelligentsia. People who wanted to keep their nice homes, couldn't pretend to love the wild-eyed prophets the bastard Lenin sent out like dirty angels to raise the farmers up in anger, making demands, standing on things to talk.

So they fought alongside the whites.

The losers.

But civilized losers.

Romans fleeing before Vandals.

Romanovs dying in the yard.

The first time he's connected those words, Roman, Romanov.

Like *tsar* comes from *Caesar*.

Did Nadia ever see the tsar?

Who cares?

She drowns people.

They say please and she drowns them.

And I fuck her.

He feels soap slide across his hips, his navel.

She touches him more intimately, takes it in her hand, slicks her thumb expertly over the head.

He moves away.

"Not tonight," he says.

"When?"

Sounds like *Venn?*

"I don't know. Maybe when I forget that ship full of dead people you keep. Or those things in the holes out there. Fucking awful, it's all so awful."

"You want I should go?"

He pauses.

She starts to leave.

She's a monster.

But I am, too.

As long as I do this.

"No," he says.

"Good. You shouldn't sleep alone anymore."

He shakes his head *no*, as if in agreement.

"In fact, I won't let you," she says in Russian.

She dries him off and puts him in bed.

He lets her do that.

She tries again to do the other thing, but he curls up into a ball.

Please, it said.

With dirt in its mouth.

And then I shot it.

He doesn't sleep so much as passes out.

She remembers the part of herself that used to care about more than fucking and swimming and killing and eating fish cold in the lake.

She enfolds the sleeping magus in her arms, remembers other warm arms that held her once, long ago.

Clinically notes that this is where she would cry if she did that.

71

Andrew wakes to the sound of Salvador barking.

He had been having a particularly nasty dream in which malign and malformed versions of himself were trying to get into the house.

"The dog is barking," he says to Sarah.

But it's not Sarah, warm Sarah with her scent of sandalwood.

It's a foul-smelling woman with cold feet.

And Salvador isn't a dog anymore.

Except when someone's trying to get into the house.

Because that's part of the spell.

Glass breaks.

"Oh fuck!"

Andrew and the rusalka both sit upright.

The closest thing Andrew ever saw to this was *Night of the Living Dead*, when the zombies surround the house and stupidly batter their way in. He's not sure how many there are, but they are most certainly surrounding the house, and one has broken the window in the kitchen door.

How did it break the window?

I charmed these windows against breaking.

Did I drain the magic using other spells?

The thing is now fumbling with the knob, just about to open the door.

Salvador, a border collie again, but bigger, more the size of a German shepherd or a big wolf, prepares to lunge.

Gets confused.

Because what steps through the door is his master.

Or, rather, what his master would look like mutated, or slightly melted, naked, dumb, and strong. The thing coming through the door is rippling with muscles.

And so are the ones behind it.

This is why Salvador missed them.

Their smell changed.

When they smelled like me, Sal couldn't find them in the ground anymore.

How to fight them?

Room of skins.

"Sal! That's not me! Get 'em!" Andrew says. "Don't let them get around you!"

Salvador knocks down the first one, shakes its arm.

The second one hammer-fists the dog hard enough to make him yelp and let go; the huge dog beats a retreat into the living room.

Andrew sends Nadia out the way she came, by the front door, but she doesn't go alone.

She grabs a not-Andrew by the hair and runs with it for the lake.

The rest of them mob in.

"Don't let them get around you," one says clumsily.

"Get around you!" one echoes.

Andrew runs into the hall, into the room of skins.

Shoves his thumb under his skin, unzips himself, working as fast as he can.

Good thing you don't drink.

You couldn't move, think fast enough drunk.

Move!

Think!

"Don't let 'em get around you," one says, pounding on the door now. Pounding *hard*. That's an oak door, solid, but the frame can't take much more of that.

BAM! It goes, and the room shudders.

"Don't let them get 'round you!" one says from the kitchen, and lots of things break.

They're trashing the fucking house, hurry.

His skin is off.

He doesn't usually have to do this fast.

He opens the wardrobe on the right.

Knows which one.

It burns a lot of magic fuel, though.

"Don't let 'em get around you!!!"

BAM!

(shudder)

"'Round you, 'round you!"

Now out in the living room, a fight in earnest.

Growling, snarling.

Get 'em, Sal!

The flayed man is about to put it on.

It's a heavy skin.

He remembers to open the window.

One looms in front of the window.

"Don't let them get around you!" it says, lunges for Andrew.

He steps back, sees its fingernails flash, dirty from clawing its way out of the ground.

It picks up its foot to come in, but a fast, white arm is around its neck. Its eyes bug, a pretty face terrible behind it framed in red dreadlocks, her teeth gritted in pleasure. She giggles while she runs with it, bigger than her, but it might as well be a doll.

My friend the monster.

Like me.

Andrew picks up the skin again, is about to put it on.

Can't resist while he still has a mouth, but has to hurry—soon you start to feel your skinlessness and that REALLY hurts, your whole body an open blister.

But he does say it.

Yells it through the door.

"Whoever made me is a giant asshole!"

On with the skin now.

His favorite one.

Oh, it feels good.

Three of them have gathered in the room of skins.

One stomps on the pelt of their father.

Two have cornered Sal, are beating him and getting savaged in return. The lake-woman has drowned two and is loping up, hoping to take a third.

One has gone upstairs.

"Whoever made me is a giant ASSHOLE!" one says, kicking in the door to the room of skins. The other yells, "Asshole!" in agreement. They are supposed to kill their father. But this room is empty, except for a human pelt that looks strangely like their father.

In the living room, the dog fights hard but has been injured.

A broken foreleg.

One of them gets an idea, sacrifices itself, lets the dog tear its belly open so its brother can grab the dog's neck.

Fighting hurts, but it's better than being in the ground, which is all they have to compare it to.

The one who got torn open is dying but still kicking at the dog.

The other is about to kill the dog by twisting its head.

Although it senses the dog has already died before.

If the dog dies again, the magic in it will go out; the other thing it is will not move again.

That would be good.

Except that it can't feel its arms or legs anymore because something has it by the neck, yes? Yes. Something much stronger than the dog has broken its neck.

It sees a piece of the thing, consults its father's murky bag of facts.

Dog?

No.

Tiger.

Bengal tiger, native to India.

They can get up to ten feet long, tail included.

This one is ten feet long.

"Whoever made me . . . giant asshole," it complains.

And dies.

The tiger goes through the three in the room of skins like they're nothing. They *are* nothing next to the five-hundred-pound cat, which twists heads, rakes out insides, and bites off limbs with the ruthlessness of a wild animal and the tactical savvy of a man. It takes less than a minute.

Worrisome that one of them had the man-pelt in its hand, but Andrew-in-the-tiger will think about that later.

Thinking like a man is harder in the tiger; tiger essence is truly dominant, and much less manlike than bear is.

Andrew-in-the tiger licks his gory chops, yawns a big, tongue-curling yawn (it has been a *very* long night, after all), licks the injured dog in the living room, who licks him back, and then smells with his tiger nose.

One more.

Upstairs.
In the library!
Must kill it!
Big books there!

Up the stairs.

Library door is open.

The last not-Andrew stands there, dirty and nude, looking around, not touching anything.

Its eyes shine blue.

It isn't like the others.

When it sees the tiger stalk in, it smiles.

The tiger was about to launch itself on the little monkey-thing, but something about its smile, its luminous blue eyes makes the tiger stop.

Andrew-in-the-tiger growls, though it feels doubt.

Like it hasn't felt since it met an elephant in 1913, the day it was shot.

"Congratulations," not-Andrew says.

Andrew's voice, but thicker.

Slavic accent.

The tiger's growl rolls on, continuous.

"You passed the test. Now the fight begins. You are a very pretty man. I wonder if you are too pretty to fight? Pretty or ugly, here is what you have to look forward to."

It reaches down now and, with some difficulty, *yanks off its own testicles.*

Begins to eat them.

Holy shit! NOOOO! Andrew-in-the-tiger thinks.

Tiger-around-Andrew thinks *I was going to do that!*

The tiger pounces.

Finishes things.

Drags it out of the library.

Down the stairs.

Outside.

"Oh no," Andrew says, looking in the mirror.

Even in the yellow brass he can see how bad it is.

"Oh Christ."

72

"What happened to you?"

This is Bob, just outside the church before the AA meeting.

His normally huge smile has been shelved, his twinkling eyes now radiating sincere concern. A few of the others hover near.

"I got mugged."

He looks like he got mugged, all right.

On his way back from getting run over by an ice-cream truck.

"Where?" the bottle-red mom asks.

"Syracuse. Clinton Street."

They all nod.

When the others walk away, Bob says, "If you need anything, and I mean anything, don't be shy about asking me. Okay?"

"Thanks, Bob."

That night is an open meeting. Friends, the curious, anybody who wants to show up can. Not the best night for Andrew to come in looking like a lopsided eggplant who ran halfway out of hair dye, but he needs this tonight. Now. He had slept all day, nearly got talked into going to the emergency room by Chancho, decided against it, but then Chancho mentioned the meeting and Andrew had nodded, holding frozen peas against the side of his face and drooling.

The bruising was wretched, covered what seemed like a third of his body. Getting his cast-off epidermis stomped against the hardwood floor by a Neanderthal version of himself had spared him broken bones and damaged connective tissue, but when he suited back up he started bleeding in six places and the swelling was horrible. His left eye swelled shut, the right one nearly so. He looked a bit like the raccoon he had seen running with the bag of eggs.

First he had seen to Salvador, who swiftly ran out of alarm-triggered dog-magic and changed back into wicker. That had been hard to watch, but then so had a lot of things. At least a wicker arm was easier to fix than a dog's broken foreleg.

Then Sal helped him, got him ice, a bag of frozen peas, and ibuprofen, sat with him, rotating the ice and peas.

He watched Nadia drag one lumpy, dead Andrew after another out into the lake, far into the lake.

Tiger-killed bodies make a big mess.

Salvador mopped first, and that took some time. Then he spread stain-removing goop on the oriental runner rugs in the hallway, only one of which would probably be salvageable. In the kitchen, he gathered the broken shards of the coffeepot, plates, and glassware, trashed the wrecked blender, as well as the coffee table and several nonmagical statues. He had just been duct-taping plastic sheeting over the kitchen door window when Chancho came over.

Made a face when Salvador opened the door on Andrew.

Some at the AA meeting had made the same face when he walked in. He felt like the Elephant Man.

The looky-loos are thinking I've been in a car wreck, gotten in a drunken fight. Okay, I have done those things, but not last night. It's okay. Let them look. Let them think they're not as bad as me, therefore they're just fine, because if you're still playing that game you probably haven't hit bottom yet, won't make it stick. Some can, but not most.

I almost died last night.

Would have died if I had a bottle of wine in me.

That was.

Awful.

I need to get out of this.

But first I have to get ready for her.

The niece, the relative.

She's so fucking strong.

And she found me.

How?

His eyes widen as far as they can in their catcher's mitt of bruises.

The Jehovah's fucking Witnesses.

She saw them canvassing, maybe they even ding-donged her wherever she is and she charmed them.

Got them to deliver her magic payload.

It's only starting.

I could run, but where?

She found me here, she'll find me again, only next time I won't be in my own house, on my land. Terroir isn't just important for grapes; it's important for users. We take strength from our own land; it's why so many here have at least a pinch of Indian blood.

Flee or dig in?

I could abandon my books, give up magic, go back to Ohio. Or anywhere. She'd like that . . . to take my library without a fight, then find me cowering in Enon and pinch me between her thumbnails like a flea. Crucify me and hang me upside down at the Apple Butter Festival as a big Fuck you *to Christ, Ohio, and apple pie. I could fight her on the Adena mound, but with what? Dead porcupine guy wouldn't help me; I peed on his grave.*

Chancho nudges Andrew, whispers in his ear.

"Hey, *brujo*, you dreamin'? At least look like you care—this guy's talkin' about his mom who beat him up."

A guy with a curly red frizz of hair and one of those necks that looks like it has an extra joint in it

a neck like the pipe under a sink

is talking about his mom who would huff gas and drink cheap gin and sometimes work him over with a toilet plunger, but he got away from her and went to college, where he, too, started drinking and found out he couldn't stop.

Andrew writes on his coffee napkin.

Chancho grunts, then writes back.

Andrew flips the napkin.

Toilet plunger mom?
wtf is wrong w/people?
THEY <u>SUCK</u>!!!!
ALL EXEPT JÉSUS
he's not a people
PAY ATENCION TO DUDE
he looks like Art Garfunkle
YOU LOOK LIKE A TURD
A Turd? Really?
PORPLE TURD

Now they're both trying not to laugh.

Chancho bites the inside of his cheek so hard a tear falls down his face.

. . .

After the meeting, the DUI guy from before, the ejecta from the Lexus, approaches Andrew at the doughnut box. Andrew isn't hungry, but he's standing next to Chancho, who is tucking half a cruller into his mouth.

"Andrew? Right?"

"Yep."

"I don't know if you remember me, but I'm Jim. Here's my card. Let me know if there's anything I can do for you."

SIMKO, MOSS and MCALLEN

Jim Simko, PA

When you need a voice

Now it clicks.

He's seen this guy's obnoxious commercials; his billboards are all over Rochester.

An ambulance chaser of the first house.

Probably sidestepped the DUI conviction, used his own dark magic to transmute it into reckless driving, but the AA meetings?

Judge wouldn't budge.

I got a card because I look like a PORPLE TURD.

He manages not to laugh.

He manages not to say three words in Aramaic that would make Jim Simko have a minor seizure in court tomorrow, voiding bladder and bowels.

Ten years ago he would have said those words.

Last night, in his tiger suit, he would have cheerfully batted half the lawyer's face off, then sat on his legs and watched him expire, because tigers are all about impulse.

Now he just takes the card, puts it in his back pocket where he knows it will get mushed into a ball in the washing machine.

I don't like this guy, I don't have to like this guy, but I have no right to judge him. He's doing the best he knows how, just like me.

Oh, but he is a smug bastard, isn't he?

Stop hanging good *or* bad *on everything.*

He just is.

Like that killing bitch who's after you.

No, you can't suburban-Buddha your way out of this one.

No gray area on her.

She's bad.

She's really, really bad.

And she's not going to walk away from this unhurt.

He should give her *the card.*

"Thanks, Jim," he says.

Follows still-chewing Chancho outside to smoke.

Pats Bob gently on the back on his way out.

I'm not running.

I'm digging in like a goddamned badger.

73

Andrew hasn't been on the Internet in a while.

He logs in, holding frozen okra to his head.

He's had the okra for a while because he's meant to make gumbo, but hasn't gotten around to it. Okra works almost as well as peas, but he ate the peas.

It delights him to see an e-mail from Radha in his inbox.

Chicagohoney85: The car is bombdiggity. Radha is a happy girl. Do you know, I parked it past the 'no parking to corner' sign right on Clark Street and left it ALL DAY. No tickets, nothing. Just some dude who saw me going into the coffee shop left me a note on the wiper, drew a flower on it, a good flower, and his phone number and website. An actor. Has his own website but hasn't really done anything yet except for some wretched naked musical at the Bailiwick. Which my friends call the Gailywick because everything there is Gay-oriented and sucks. Not very PC, but it's kinda funny. Gay people call it the Gailywick, too, so it's probably OK.

Anyway, the Cooper?

You killed that car.

The zebra skin seats really gave you most favored nation status.

And this is how Radha does gratitude.

INFORMATION!

And you want this.

It's interesting.

This is about Daddy Bear, Yevgeny Dragomirov.

Two things.

One: I dug around in Soviet military archives, not the kind of thing Americans get invitations to see. But I have inroads and people. Dragomirov fought in Stalingrad and Kursk, really heavy fighting, really nasty, some of the most brutal stuff of the war. Kursk was huge, 5,000 tanks mixing it up, more than two million combatants. Hitler was trying to double down after losing his ass in Stalingrad, but he lost more ass in Kursk.

My point is, this was survival of Mother Russia shit, not the kind of fighting you get leave from, and Yevgeny and his T-34 were tangled up in it from November 1942 until at least August 1943. Mikhail Dragomirov was born in December 1943. You might think you see where this is going, but you don't.

I don't think Mama Dragomirov had herself a fling; she was a mousy little thing loyal to her husband and scared of him, too.

Busted her ass in a factory that made soldier's boots, belts and satchels.

No, it wasn't her.

There's a twist.

I found record of a soldier, a Gennady Lemenkov, an illiterate farmer from the Urals, who, with the help of a friend who could read and write, sent a letter of complaint to a superior officer about comrade D.

Here's the letter:

Comrade Junior Lieutenant,

I know the danger to our beloved country and so I would not waste your time with small matters. Please believe me when I say, however, that our comrade Efreitor Dragomirov, Yevgeny, steals away from his post to have relations with a woman. This woman follows the column. She may well be a spy for the fascists. She comes and goes as she pleases, and knows tricks only a spy would know. I saw her bring him wine, which he shared with us, but when she left, there was only one set of tracks in the mud, belonging to a snowshoe hare. I saw her come to him as a beautiful woman where he slept in a stable. When she left the moon was out and I could see that she had become an old babka. A costume trick! I know that comrade Dragomirov has been a loyal soldier. I wish him no ill. But please, for the sake of our lives, come to investigate this matter of the woman. Before she can betray us to our enemies. Which I believe she will. Others believe this, too. One simple Cossack whose name I forget said she is a witch, a very bad witch, and that she pulled dead men from tanks and cooked them as her meat, and that was whose smoke we saw in the trees though the scouts found nothing. Another man agreed that she was a witch, (Baba Yaga herself, can you believe it?) but said that she was against the Germans, that she had brought a hard winter to kill them all and that frost went with her in the form of a starving wolf. I do not believe such childish things. But I know she is bad for morale. And I believe she is pregnant now. And even if she is not a spy and not a witch it is not fair that one man should have the comfort of a woman when the rest of us do not.

There's no record of follow-up, at least not from the Soviets. I'm sure they laughed their dicks off at this guy.

But someone wasn't laughing.

This Lemenkov went chasing a doe a few days later and disappeared. They thought he deserted. But they found him dead, naked, holding a tree. He had been crying; they know this because his tears were frozen on his cheeks.

His eyes were frozen in his head.

The dude who told on Dragomirov froze to death.

In June.

And nobody fucked with Yevgeny Dragomirov again.

Are you following this? He got some spooky witch pregnant at the same time his wife supposedly got knocked up. But his wife took no time off from the factory. Even hardcore soviet chicks take a little maternity leave. Nothing. Nada. Nyitchevo.

You know what I think?

I think that was Baba Yaga, in the woods, with the smoke and rabbit tracks.

I think she walked right up to Dragomirov's house with an infant in her arms and made Dragomirov's wife raise the baby.

I think your rusalka killed Baba Yaga's son.

*   *   *

Two:

I attached a one-paragraph article about a grave-robbing near Nizhny Novgorod.

A body was taken last week.

It probably would never have made the paper, but it was the body of a heavily decorated hero of the war against the fascists.

Even in these days, you don't fuck with Second World War heroes. You know how protective we are about ours? The Russians are even more hardcore about their WW2 vets, they worship those guys, and for good reason.

I'm getting off topic.

The point is, it was our guy.

Yevgeny Dragomirov got exhumed last week.

* * *

I didn't advertise a three, but there's a three.

Three:

Somebody's trying to hack me.

Hack ME.

Seriously?

I tracked the probable source to the Ukraine, and it shouldn't be long before I have a name and address.

And then?

I bring the whoop-ass.

I'm thinking maybe a . . .

But I'll keep that a secret in case he or she intercepts this.

I REALLY don't think there's much chance of that.

But.

* * *

If you ARE reading this, cocksucker, you should think about taking a little vacation, and not going near anything with a screen and a plug until Carnaval season. Or until the Mayan apocalypse comes.

Which it won't.

Except for you if you don't go low-tech, and I mean now.

Which I hope you don't.

I'VE GOT SUCH A COOL SURPRISE FOR YOU!

74

Vermont.

Anneke squats froglike, fingering the leaves of the maple sapling she just petrified.

"I want to rest," she says.

Her head hurts and she's nauseated; the living tree fought with all its sap and chlorophyll and nonverbal stored-up common sense against the unnatural thing she was doing to it. It felt like having an argument in which you knew you were wrong but won because you were better at arguing and eventually, unjustly, wore your opponent down. She wrung the juicy and vibrant parts of it out with an ugly, strong hand she never knew she had, and now it stands before her white and bleached and dead; still beautiful, but beautiful because it is impossible; no sculptor could carve or shape such thin and perfect leaves from granite. Even as she thinks this, a leaf falls from its branch.

It's exquisite, she thinks.

This would sell for twenty grand.

Michael just looks at her, sitting in his camp chair, drinking his coffee. The lesson takes place in a patch of woods between the farmhouse and the quarry.

This old bastard's not going to let me rest.

He sees her looking at him and just nods at the tree.

"I don't feel good," she says.

"You're not supposed to. You just broke the laws of nature. Now make it right."

She bites her tongue.

Broken laws of nature surround them; Michael Rudnick appears to live in a quaint New England farmhouse neighboring an old quarry, but really he lives in the quarry. A perfect overhang of granite hung with vines shields a vintage Airstream trailer. Doric columns modeled after those supporting the Athenian temple of Hephaestus seem to prop the ledge, and brick walls of varying heights partition the space, keyholed with nooks and alcoves wherein unquenchable oil lamps glimmer by night. Stone benches and chairs surround an impressive fire pit topped by a chimney in the shape of a human mouth open to breathe in smoke. How the trailer got into or is supposed to get out of the neoclassic wonderland is not apparent. Rock stairs lead down to the opening beneath the ledge, and another set leads to water.

The trapezoidal lake that has collected at the quarry's bottom half submerges an outsized sculpture and cypress garden: a granite elephant jets water from its upraised trunk, cyclopic giants, Atlas-like, hunch beneath gardens erupting from stone troughs, a mischievous-looking cherub crouches on a pedestal above the waterline, holding a stone to its chest in the posture of a pitcher, a pile of other such stones at its feet. It seems to be eyeing the steps. The stones are the size of volleyballs. Woe betide anyone approaching Michael's cave with fell intent.

She looks at the stone tree.

Feels the echo of its vanished life, how surprised it was to find itself so violated, cut off from water, numb to sunlight. Dead. When she touches its trunk she feels its absence.

"Put life back into it."

She tries.

"See it happening."

She pictures the breeze blowing through supple leaves.

Nothing happens.

"It's not like moving rocks," she says.

"No. It's intimate."

She tries.

Her head throbs.

"Why are there no schools?" she says. "Harry Potter and all that."

He just looks at her.

"Are there?"

"You're in one."

"But a big one. Like a university."

He shakes his head.

"Magic is artisanal. You apprentice. One at a time. You'll teach somebody, too, one day. I'll make you promise before you leave here."

"Somebody must have a school."

"Workshops go on in some actual universities. Grafted to them, working veiled. Antioch College in Yellow Springs is a fine example. They had three users in the faculty at one point. They made students they wanted to teach magic get accepted in other fields, fields they taught in the system."

She remembers her embarrassing introduction to that town, how she hurled herself into a bathtub, off the wagon, and at a toilet.

"Andrew went there?"

Michael nods.

"Studied Russian. And more."

"I still don't get it."

"There's talk every few years. But everyone's scared. Three's the most users it's wise to gather at one place for very long."

"Why?"

"Something changes."

"So nobody ever tried to found a big, dedicated university?"

"Schools were founded. Couple of times."

"What happened?" she says, absently touching the leaves of the dead tree.

"Different things."

"Bad?"

"You could say that."

"Tell me."

"Most successful one was in England, started in the 1580s. Hid in plain sight. In Deptford, just down the river from London. Did some big things. You know how Spain could never seem to land an armada? It wasn't just once. They tried three times, got swamped by storms three times. That was no accident."

"And?"

"They kept killing each other. The survivors determined that too many users together makes it turn dark. They agreed to separate."

Now she just looks at him. There's more, and she wants to hear it.

"Last big one was France, outside Paris. Between the wars. Like a dozen users, thirty or so students. They exchanged oaths of fraternity, made loyalty and friendship more important than the magic, drummed out anybody who seemed greedy. Called themselves The Order of the Duck. I saw pictures. Real cute with the short pants and tall socks, even berets and sacks of baguettes, like the stereotype."

"And then?"

"Something came and killed them."

"A demon?"

"Sort of. Hitler."

She furrows her brow.

"Couldn't they fight, or hide?"

"Can't fight an army. And it's hard to hide from other users."

"Hitler had users?"

He looks at her.

She remembers a picture she saw of Adolf Hitler, surrounded by wide-eyed adorers, all of them half mad. Hitler calm in the middle of the storm of madness. They were looking at him like they were starving for something, something in his words and eyes, something only he could give them. They were addicted to him.

"Oh my God," she says. "He was one."

Michael nods.

"Only the very luminous can make it out, but those tapes of him ranting in German? I've listened to them. It's not German. It's not a human language at all. Something taught him those words. Something he conjured. And you can only hear it for a moment. Because it starts to work on you, starts to sound like German. And if you speak German, it starts to sound like the truth."

She goes pale.

Wonders what she's gotten herself into.

Wonders if she wants to know these things.

Thinks *it's too late*.

"Don't worry," he says. "It's not all rotten. Now fix the tree."

She looks at one stone leaf.

She plucks the leaf. Holds it by the stem, holds it up to the sun. So thin opaque light filters through it, lights up its veins and capillaries. You could almost shave with its edges.

She'll need a word.

Ancient Greek is best for stone.

"*Pneuma*," she says.

"*Ezasa*," she says.

It liked *pneuma* better.

It tingled.

She concentrates on the part that glows with the sun behind it, sees the glow turning maple-green.

"*Pneuma*," she says again, and breathes on it, as if kindling fire.

Green glows where her breath touched the leaf, starts to creep out toward the edges as fire would creep on paper.

"Ah! Ah!"

The leaf is almost a leaf again.

"Hurry," he says.

She understands.

She touches the leaf to the rest of the tree, watches the green catch, spread. She blows on it as one would blow kindling, watches it move from leaf to leaf, revivifying the sapling until at last it trembles in the breeze again, at last the sapling winks back into life. Exists again. It wasn't there, and then it was. As her father had been there, and then gone, in the length of a breath.

75

The beautiful girl furrows her brow, looking at her phone. The handsome man sitting across from her at the hip Lincoln Square sushi restaurant says, "Everything okay?" She nods, still looking into her palm, but the furrow remains. She pockets the phone.

"Sorry. I know that's rude," she says, still not looking at him, but she's said it before, and still keeps checking her phone. When she does this, he doesn't know where to rest his own eyes. Sometimes on her cleavage, sometimes on the restaurant's expensive-looking water feature. He knew she would be high maintenance; she looked high maintenance strolling down Clark Street with a bag full of shoe boxes and mustard-yellow pumps, but he took a sheet from his sketch pad, drew a flower on it, wrote down his information, and left it under her windshield wiper anyway because she also looked smart. Girls who aren't that smart can be fun, but they're not impressive. This might be the most impressive girl he's ever brought to Fugu Sushi.

He's brought seventeen girls to Fugu Sushi.

He calls ahead to get the window seat. Figures everybody wins because he gets a nice view, the restaurant looks hip because he looks hip, and the server always gets twenty-five percent. Twenty percent makes a server happy, twenty-five gets you remembered. The staff remembers him.

Not the way he thinks, though.

They call him manwhore, as in "I'm cut for the night, you've got manwhore."

Always a two-top.

Always by the window.

Staff sympathies turned decidedly against him when, on companion number eight, he left his website and e-mail address for the waitress, along with a pen-and-ink sketch of an octopus (he had dined on tako that night), which he had prepared in advance. He managed to do it while helping that evening's date put her coat on, did it with the skill of a cardsharp.

The waitress showed everyone the octopus, and now an octopus-like wave of the fingers means *manwhore.* Thus, pointing at oneself and waving the fingers, with a gently repulsed lip curl, means "I'll take manwhore." The bartender's in on it, too. Finger wave followed by cup-to-lips uptilt gesture means, "What are manwhore and the young lady drinking?"

The exotic-looking number seventeen, sipping Bride of the Fox sake, would have already figured out manwhore's deal except that she has been too distracted by computer problems to vet him pre-date, and, tonight, so distracted by her phone that she's not plumbing his charmingly self-deprecating monologues for sincerity or spontaneity.

"If there's a problem and you need to call it an early night, I understand," he says. He knows that's what he's supposed to say, but he doesn't want an early night—he wants to get her back to his loft, put on Portishead, and send a finger up under that orange suede skirt to test his theory that small-boned women are tighter and full-lipped women are wetter.

The phone hasn't been in her pocket a minute when it buzzes again. She decides to let him in on the problem.

"Somebody's sending me odd texts."

"Why don't you turn it off?"

"Good idea," she says, and starts to, then doesn't. "Only I'm intrigued."

"By what?"

She considers him; he only just clears her threshold for minor confidences.

"What do you see?" she says, showing him her phone.

"A horse."

"Yeah. A horse."

She scrolls down.

"More horses," he says. "Are you an equestrian?"

She shakes her head no.

He sees them.

That's something.

Now she knows the texted photos are not themselves magical, though she's picking up magic around them, and the sender's number is blocked. She's sure that if she saw it, it would be international, originating in Ukraine. It's the middle of the night over there. She turns the phone back to herself, scrolls down the photos, all twenty-something of them showing different horses: bays, roans, and blacks; Arabs, quarter horses, and Belgians.

This is an attack.

This is how wizards fight; they begin by psyching out their opponent.

It's not going to work on me.

Horses?

My hacker must be a man, and a very silly man.

"May I try your sake?" her date says.

She looks at him as if only just realizing he's there.

She gets a tickle in her ear, telling her there's a conversation she may wish to eavesdrop on. She swivels a sort of invisible cat's ear toward the kitchen.

. . . way too hot for that creeper, I don't know how he even gets them here.

Well he's hot, hot's not his problem. Kinda looks like a watered-down Johnny Depp. He's just clueless. Wonder what he drew for this one.

Do you think they sleep with him?

Some, I'm sure, or he wouldn't keep dropping Benjamins. Must be a trust fund kid. Told me once he's an actor, his Visa has three first names like an actor, Michael Oliver Scott or something, but they don't make that kind of money, not in Chicago. Unless it's commercials.

She listens for another moment, making eye contact with Michael Anthony Scott.

She smiles at him.

He's still waiting for an answer about the sake, wondering what game she's playing.

As he'll find out in less than a minute, she's playing the "finish her sake and leave her date at the restaurant" game.

She's also playing the "steal his wallet with a spell" game.

She's also just about to play the "what's in its pocketses?" game.

When he fishes for his wallet, he'll find a piece of paper with a child's crayon drawing of a crying man getting arrested outside FUGU SOOSHI. When he shows it to the manager as evidence that somebody must be playing a prank on him, the manager will not see the child's drawing. What he will see will be a newspaper blurb about local actor Michael Scott's dine-and-dash arrest at a Ravenswood pizza parlor, complete with mug shot.

Radha, sitting on the zebra-skin seat of her idling Mini Cooper, dictates the nature of the drawing, the photo and text of the article, and where she wants these articles placed into her phone, into an app she made for herself, clicks Preview, giggles, then presses Cast.

She drives off toward home.

As she turns onto Damen, she sees a homeless man sitting on cardboard, two dusty-looking heeler dogs napping near him.

She rolls down her window.

5454545454545454

Throws the wallet.

It skids to a stop between his legs.

"Do as thou wilt," she says.

He grins, gives her a thumbs-up.

Plays a peppy version of "Blue Skies" on his kazoo.

76

Later.

Radha sits before her computer.

She wears her *Muppet Show* onesie, a footed onesie with Animal on each foot.

Her roommate, a flamingly, fabulously gay dancer, a Michael who spells his name with a *Y* and has no idea she's a witch, won't be home from rehearsal until well past midnight; *Equus* opens in less than a week. She designed the poster graphic, three dancers in horse masks frozen in synchronicitous movement against a pear-green backdrop. The masks have a dystopian look, something H. R. Giger might have designed, and they appear off-balance, about to topple. She's really proud of this graphic.

She is less proud about the persistent low-grade infection her computer seems to have. No amount of flushing, warding, or spell encryption seems able to do more than keep it busy. It has interfered with her ability to track the Ukrainian, it won't let her corner it, and it finds and infects any other devices she tries to use the web from.

I'm the vector.

It hides in me somehow.

This is masterclass cybermagic.

How's he doing this?

She's working on a spell to create a sort of antibody for the system, and she's pretty sure it will work, but writing the intruder-specific code takes time; and she has to get the blood of a watchdog. She has the dog picked out, a German shepherd that has barked at her from behind the white wrought-iron gates of a house two blocks from her complex, on the way to the chocolate shop. She can make the pooch take a nap with a spell, but she's not good with animal magic and it will cost her juice she needs to find the computer bug.

She'll go no-frills on the tranquilizer, get it from a vet.

But she really hates needles.

Maybe she'll charm or pay a phlebotomist to come with her.

And once the infection is flushed, she'll be able to take the offensive. She found a really ugly Brazilian spell that liquefies bones, and she's already practiced on a lamb shank. The poor thing actually danced a spastic little dance and smoked from its holes before it balloonishly collapsed; she's more than ready to try it on her Slavic friend.

She's never been in a duel with another user before, and, if she's a little scared, she's even more excited. Americans have the best computer magic, and she's one of the best in America. It's a game for young witches. Maybe only sealiongod@me.com is better, but he's out in San Francisco.

All right.

A Greek yogurt with almonds and honey.

A glass of Gewürztraminer.

An hour of code.

Then another glass of Gewürztraminer while Mykel rubs his calves with tiger balm and bitches about the director's choices.

When she comes back from the kitchen, something's wrong.

The screen saver with the three horse-men has turned into a GIF;

the figures now move in a loop, executing a plié and scoop over and over again.

Fuck! He's through!

She spits the yogurt-covered spoon out of her mouth.

One of the horse heads now noses against the screen, bulbs it out like soft plastic, pokes through.

It happens slowly, then fast, as if someone sped a film up.

A real horse's head, a real man's body, and the monster births itself through her computer, knocking over her chair.

The other two simply appear behind it, piggybacking on its magical entry.

She's about to use her Brazilian spell when it occurs to her she's not sure what these things are made of, if they even have bones.

Now the first one lunges for her, grabs her shoulders, drives her back against the wall.

The violence shocks her—*nobody* manhandles her.

So strong, so fast.

I'm really in trouble.

No.

I AM trouble.

The first rule of magical combat is *Be the most dangerous thing in the fight.*

Believe it and it's true.

She relaxes as best she can, feels the tingle of magic waking up in her, but before she can pronounce a spell, the horse-man's hand is in and on her mouth. She bites, but it doesn't seem to care. It begins to choke her. The second one ducks under its fellow's arm and bites her.

Bit my fucking nipple off!!!

She can't even scream.

Tears of pain well in her eyes, blurring the image of the thing killing her, the third one behind it picking up the baseball bat she keeps by her bed.

They have bones

Mistake not to use the spell

Dying

She remembers another spell.

Imagines her left footie ripping, and it rips, exposing her bare foot. She probes for the outlet, but it's too far.

So she stretches her leg out magically, the length of two legs, finds the outlet, lays the sole of her foot against it.

Imagines herself made of copper.

Becomes a conduit.

The second one has started biting her ear off.

Bad timing.

To touch her just then.

She dumps so much electricity into the horse-men that they scream horse-screams, hop on their flexed man-feet, convulsing.

She smells equine hair burning.

They drop.

Her windpipe is damaged, but not crushed.

She sucks air.

Coughs.

The third one is almost on her now, bat upraised, a second and a half away from staving in her skull.

It doesn't get that long.

She cables out her forearm, slamming her palm into its muzzle, grabbing.

She hears a *pop!* And watches an almost comical plume of smoke ascend from its head as it, too, jerks stiff, then drops and twitches.

Now she's angry.

She looks at the computer, sees an eye in the corner of the screen.

It blinks twice and vanishes, but too late.

Radha runs at the computer.

Sees her reflection in the black screen, dim, getting larger, blood from her insulted breast blotching the onesie.

She leaps.

. . .

Yuri has prepared this spell for a week.

He made the horse-head men in 3-D using the woman's art as a model. He taught them to kill, taught them not to let her speak.

Now it is time.

He must succeed.

His veiling spell can't hold much longer, burns too much fuel, and if she finds him, she will destroy him. He knows he's not as strong as she is. Knows he's only strong because Baba made him strong, dumped magic into him that she stole from others.

One chance only.

He watches the monsters come to life, sends them through the screen, thinks he has Chicagohoney85. Thinks she needs her computer, like him, that she will be weak without it, like him. Such creatures would have torn him apart with little difficulty.

But she is not weak.

The spell with the outlet is superlative.

Genius!

"Xhm," he says, watching it all like a video game that has taken an unfortunate turn. He realizes, intellectually, that he will be in danger now, but he doesn't feel it in his gut until he sees her notice him, see the eye, feels her lock on to him.

He clicks the camera off, but it is too late.

She pushes a hand through the screen.

He clicks the camera back on, leans away from the grasping hand.

He senses the electricity stored in her, knows she'll fry him like a herring if she touches him.

He squeals, rolls his chair away.

Now her head is pushing through.

Slowly, as if through clear taffy.

She sees him!

Behind her, one of the horse-men, the one that bit her, is on its knees, puking, barely alive.

But alive enough.

"Plug!" Yuri says in Russian.

It shambles that way.

Radha's head is halfway through.

He senses powerful magic, knows he'll die if she speaks.

Now her mouth is through.

Behind her, the monster in her room disappears as it crawls under her computer desk, whinnying in pain.

She hears the whinny.

Hears it crawling, hitting its head on the desk.

Knows what's about to happen.

No time to reverse direction.

She fucked up.

Instead of saying the Brazilian word that would have made the small man die horribly, she says "No."

Just says it.

Like a disappointed child.

The monster pulls the plug.

Most of her head and one hand, neatly shorn, fall onto Yuri's keyboard, the head continuing on to the floor.

Yuri watches the head empty itself on his linoleum, a pool spreading, the girl's pretty, terrified eyes looking up at the ceiling, seeing it, then not seeing it.

The cat comes to investigate, then skitters away, its one wet paw leaving prints on the floor.

Yuri passes out.

Back in her room, the body, missing one hand, cropped above a severe diagonal line starting at her chin and continuing up through her ears, falls onto the horse-headed man, releasing its stored charge.

Both bodies burst into flames. The one that shouldn't have existed disappears, as do the other two like it.

The police will say Radha Rostami died in a freak power surge.

Her roommate will tell his boyfriend it was spontaneous human combustion.

He will never sleep in that apartment again.

77

Andrew finds this on his Facebook events page.

THE THEIF ANDREW BLANKENSHIPS' BAD DYING

 Soon!　　🕐 until ???

📍 online

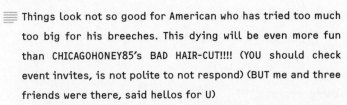 Things look not so good for American who has tried too much too big for his breeches. This dying will be even more fun than CHICAGOHONEY85's BAD HAIR-CUT!!!! (YOU should check event invites, is not polite to not respond) (BUT me and three friends were there, said hellos for U)

Result: No more help hiding money$$$ for taxes, no more histories from long ago, but, Hey! Still pornography is available! Until ????

This will also be for killing of good man, Mikhail Yevgenievitch D.

And killing of old babushka in Ukraine.

(You've been a busy boy!!!!)

To Bring: Just yourself! Books and relics stolen long ago will go back to there true home and if any are missing or destroyed—more people on friends list have similar event planning as yours! (I hope it is so)

Going: Andrew Blankenship

Maybe: Everybody on Andrew's friends list.

Declined: Radha Rostami

Andrew can't raise Radha by computer or by telephone.

He doesn't know if this was a lie, meant to off-balance him, but he suspects it's not.

This makes him blearily angry where he should be sad.

It puts him in a very bad mood.

He calls Chancho.

Chancho drills him hard, makes him knee the kicking pad in his yard until he feels like he can't lift his leg again.

Makes him work on "the plum," wrestling your opponent's head forward in the A-shaped trap of your arms so you can knee the face and head.

Chancho leaves.

The coin that turns bullets arrives by UPS.

The driver honks cheerily as the brown truck lumbers off.

Morning.

Andrew stands before his brass mirror, surveying himself. His bruising has mostly gone greeny-yellow or faded out. He heals quickly with the youth magic running. He's about to amp that up, ink in the runners of gray that he allowed in.

Then he remembers a sound.

The sound of glass breaking.

The glass that he charmed not to be broken.

This is what's draining the magic.

My vanity.

He knows that youth spells burn a lot of fuel; he's had to finesse his apparent age up a bit—looking twenty-five burns almost everything you've got when you're over fifty, but thirty-five is doable.

Was doable.

It gets exponentially harder every year.

I wonder if you're too pretty to fight?

He lets a little more gray in.

Feels the house get stronger around him.

It had weakened by degrees, so slowly he hadn't even noticed.

Only things he used stayed strong, like the gate in the tub.

Would the things in the attic still work?

The vacuum-cockatrice?

The doll's house?

And now he is going to need offensive magic.

As much as he can muster.

Where else could he economize?

The hiding spells.

I spent months on those!

They'll be so hard to raise again.

But you know good and goddamned well she's the one you're hiding from.

She already knows where the house is.

Fine.

Fine.

I'll make the house visible.

I'll shut down the youth spells.

What you see is what you get.

He lets himself get older.

Feels his body stoop just a little.

Feels his muscles thin, develops a pain in his knee.

He sees the fifty-two-year-old smoker with the long hair looking back at him, bruised and hollow in the jaws.

He wants to pin his gray, dry hair up with his cherrywood fork, samurai-style, but sees this as vanity, too. Hair is an antenna for magic; Indians knew this.

Wizards know it.

He leaves his hair down, fans it over his shoulders.

I'm older than my dad ever got.

I'm an old man.

But I'm strong now.

Stronger than ever.

I'm not a fucking user.

I'm a warlock.

He spends the next three hours unweaving the spell he cast to hide the house. The neighbors could already see it, but now passing motorists and kids on bikes would see it, too. Anyone can find it now without first being told or shown.

But if they have bad intentions toward Andrew Ranulf Blankenship, they might wish they hadn't.

It's high time to make war magic.

78

1978.

Yellow Springs, Ohio.

October.

The wizard with the potbelly and the bald head has his shirt open even though the leaves in Glen Helen have yellowed. He and the boy and the girl can all see their breaths.

Andrew's in sweatpants, wearing a terry cloth headband.

"Try again," the older man says.

Andrew doesn't want to try again.

A big, dirty smudge on his left buttock and thigh evidence the outcome of his last try.

He steels himself, runs at his mentor again.

Runs like his brother used to run at tackle dummies.

When he leaps, he leaps at waist height just to the right of the shorter, stockier man, seemingly at nothing, his face scrunched up for impact.

He makes impact in midair, and the world around the three jerks with the characteristic bad-splice jerk that happens whenever reality and illusion collide. The man winks out from where he was, winks in again falling with Andrew, going "Whooof!" but it looks like he was always in Andrew's path.

The mind smooths things out.

The instructor's false teeth come out.

He puts them back in, untroubled.

He also picks up three quarters that fell into the grass.

Leaves the penny because it's tails up.

Stands up.

"That's it!" he says, claps his meaty hands twice. "Well done!"

Addresses the girl as Andrew brushes himself off.

"How do you think he did it?"

"Listened for sound? I'd say watched your breath, but your breath was coming out of your mouth. I mean, where your mouth seemed to be."

"Was it sound, Blankenship?"

He shakes his head, pulls a twig out of his hair.

"I watched the leaves. You crunched leaves under your actual feet."

"Good," he says. "Can't argue with results."

They wait.

"Displacement works nicely against human, nonmagical attackers, and it's a cheap spell. Not much gas. You should be able to run a couple of other things at the same time, once you practice."

He lisps a little.

Adjusts his false teeth.

They wait.

Cats before a can opener.

"Now," he says. "If you should chance to tangle with another user, what's rule number one?"

"Don't," they both say quickly, as they've been taught. Not because they mean it, but because they want to get to the good stuff.

"Right. Don't. And why not?"

"Both are likely to die," they say in stereo.

"Yes," he says. "Fighting another evenly matched user with magic is like driving head-on into another car. You might come out a little better, but, unless you get lucky, you won't come out well."

"And if you're not evenly matched?" Andrew asks.

"Then it's either stupid or unsportsman-like, and I disapprove of both qualities. Sometimes, however, stupid and unsportsman-like conditions arise. And so, your third lesson to date on black magic. To the pine grove with you, and find the most swordlike stick you feel you can levitate nimbly. We're going to do some fencing."

79

Dog Neck Harbor, New York.

Today.

Andrew jabs his index finger with a pub dart, old-school, wooden handle. He bleeds twelve drops into a hole he cut into an apple. He sings "The British Grenadiers" as well as he can, trying to really boom out the *With a TO-RO-RO-RO-RO*. Any pub song would work, but he rather likes that one.

He eats the apple.

Andrew goes to a farm on 104A, a farm where he knows he can buy a live chicken. Butchers it. The farmhand asks if it's for eating, and when he says "yes," the kid offers to butcher it for him.

"Prefer to do it myself," he says.

Something about the way he says it makes the kid look at him funny.

He takes the hen home, cores her eye out. Pronounces a spell in Russian, the words of which he has to rememorize from a book. Burns the eye on a sliver of wood taken from a lightning-struck tree, mixes the ash with rainwater and magic oil, smears the grimy black balm on each of his eyelids. The spell calls for the eye of an eagle, owl, or hawk. Bald eagles nest near the bluffs, but he just can't bring himself to do that to an eagle.

"Ethical wizards get their ass kicked," he tells Salvador, pulling chicken feathers. But he thinks a chicken will do.

Range might suffer, but this is a fuck-all mighty spell.

He bakes the chicken.

Salvador remembers the smell of roast fowl, wiggles his hips the whole time.

He used to get the gizzards.

Evening.

Andrew takes the walking stick down from over the fireplace.

Oak with an iron tip and an ovoid iron knob on the end, a knob that fits smoothly into the hand, but that is obviously a perfect shape for thumping. A silver collar sits under the knob, inscribed with Gaelic words reading, *Think while your skull is sound. Drink while your mouth is whole. Shake this man's hand while he offers it.*

He rubs it with walnut oil.

Kisses it.

Takes it out back to the fire pit, puts the iron tip into the embers, says words in Gaelic that make it glow red-hot. Walks it over to the turtle shell he found—it was no easy thing finding a dead turtle with a whole shell by the side of the road—and punches the cane's tip through, loading the trigger word.

Buckler.

Andrew goes to the thrift store.

Buys a set of six yellow glass tumblers.

Not enough.

Drives to the Pier 1 just north of Syracuse.

Buys a dozen yellow wineglasses.

Makes a whole vase full of fireglass stones.

Puts it in the attic.

Fishes a trumpet out of an attic tub.

The next one's his favorite.

His mentor invented it.

He rubs six pennies with magical oil, puts them heads up on a tree stump, arranged like a tiny audience.

Plays the trumpet loudly (and poorly) down at the sextet of Abe Lincolns for better than an hour.

Puts the pennies in a leather pouch he hangs around his neck.

80

Nadia courses under the water, following the *Jaybird Sally*. She has been tailing the boat since it left the Oswego Marina around noon, partly because she likes the boat's name, partly because one of the two men who periodically fishes from the stern is handsome in a craggy way; his short beard covers the kind of chin one mostly finds on soldiers and athletes.

She's very good at going unseen; dull people will see her as driftwood or a fish unless she wants their attention. For the sake of sharper ones, she knows how to stay in a boat's shadow, she knows how to use chop and murk and to anticipate a glance in her direction, how to submerge before it comes.

When the boat stops, she catches pieces of the conversation between the two men as she floats, her ear overlapped by waves.

"Going to Rochester tomorrow . . . that three-bedroom house we got at auction. I'll be . . . flip it the week after, put some new carpet . . . stripped copper . . . else it needs."

"It burns my ass that . . . things like that . . . plumbing and mark up . . . out of spite because . . . get their shit together. No class."

"None."

The men talk business and switch to women and Nadia begins to regret eavesdropping; it was better when she didn't know how ordinary the handsome one was, when she could pretend he was a cavalry officer with a bright saber and a wool coat, not a house-flipper with a motel mistress and an unobservant wife. She's about to swim off in a state of helpless ennui when the men reel in their lines and the motor starts up. Another race! But it isn't much of a race. She follows the boat, easily keeping up with its drowsy chug, swimming serpentine beneath it.

Then it happens.

A glass bottle hits the water, bobs there.

She doesn't know if anybody on the boat sees her white hand reach up and pluck the bottle under, but she doesn't care.

She's pissed.

She didn't spend all morning breaking those disgusting zebra mussels off her shipwreck just to let these inconsiderate swindlers pollute her lake. So bourgeois. She knows that's a Bolshevik word and she hates Bolsheviks, but *bourgeois*, with its suggestion of new money and bad manners, best describes the specimens on the *Jaybird Sally*.

"Sam Adams," she says, looking at the little brown-vested colonial on the blue label, air escaping from her mouth in a wash of small bubbles. Stale air. She uses her lungs only to smoke and to speak.

When the *Jaybird Sally* stops again, she sees the hooked bait-fish plop into the water, watches a gorgeous chinook salmon swim toward it. She waves it off, still holding the beer bottle.

No fish for you, bourgeois!

But that's not enough.

She bangs the bottom of the boat with her fist, hard.

Not hard enough.

She gets some distance, swims into the hull.

Likes the way that feels.

Attacks several more times, battering the *Jaybird Sally* with her shoulders and head; two of the blows open gashes below the water-line.

Especially the last head butt.

That hole is serious.

About the size of three strips of bacon laid end-to-end.

The lake starts pouring in.

She peeks through the hole, sees the startled captain see her.

He takes the Lord's name in vain.

The alarm sounds as the first float switch is tripped and the pump starts.

She puts her lips to the hole now and says, "Don't litter," swims off.

Realizes she was so mad she said it in Russian, swims back and says it in English now, adding, "Bourgeois assholes" for good measure.

The handsome one, still on deck, gripping the rail in anticipation of another collision, sees the rusalka's pale, slender arm throw the bottle, watches it spin, watches it land amidships with a clunk.

He'll forget he saw this by the time the others come up and the captain starts barking "Mayday" on VHF 16.

By the time the deck of the *Jaybird Sally* starts to tilt, he'll put on his life vest, text wife and girlfriend, put his cell phone in a baggie.

"Don't worry," the captain says. "We're not going in the drink."

He points.

They would have already heard the helicopter but for the alarm.

The helicopter from Canada is coming with a P250 that will flush a thousand gallons a minute out of the ship.

Of course the rusalka could put her fingers in the gash and yank it so large that even the Canadians' pump won't help.

Or she could roll the boat; this would be hard, but not impossible.

No.

Not for one bottle.

But if so much as a cigarette butt hits the water.

When the *Jaybird Sally* finds suitable, safe mooring, she will put in for repairs. The diver will pull several long, coarse red hairs from the gash in the hull.

The boat will not be lost today.

The man who flips houses will fish again.

But, without remembering exactly why, he will never again toss litter overboard.

Skinning below the water like the dangerous thing she is, Nadia passes the Coast Guard ship coming to escort the listing *Sally* in.

Salutes it.

Later.

Nadia snatches down a placid seagull who stopped to float on the lake, so smoothly its fellows don't even fly away.

She feeds violently at first, blood and feathers everywhere, then delicately, picking meat from bones like a girl on a picnic. She means to swim back to the wreck, and police it one more time before heading in to grow her legs back and spend the night protecting her magus.

She's looking forward to growing her vagina back.

She hopes he'll be ready for sex.

Drowning all those lumpy miscarriages of Andrew Blankenship *really* turned her on.

So much, in fact, she decides not to wait.

Swims down to the Niagara Mohawk nuclear plant, turns girl, and floats in the warm discharge current.

Pleasures herself.

Cries so loudly a custodian at the plant scans the water.

Sees only driftwood.

When she gets near her wreck, the sun is going down, throwing lavender and pink all over the sky, the water reflecting it on its gently rippling skin.

A silhouette in black stands out.

A boat.

Very small this time.

A rowboat, the kind you can rent at Fair Haven Beach State Park.

Whoever brought it here must have rowed for hours.

She makes out one shape.

A man.

She dives and swims under the water, comes up near.

He's playing the guitar now, playing well.

He sings a song in Russian.

Improvised, perhaps, no rhymes, but sung in a gravelly voice full of pain and sweetness.

> *"I loved a girl who wore sparrows on her breast,*
> *Two sparrows on her breast.*
> *She tried to love me back, but it was hard*
> *To find my heart*
> *My heart could never fly like hers*
> *I had no sparrows on my breast,*
> *No sparrows on my breast."*

The man in the boat is young.

Not much light left in the sky, but her eyes are quite good in the dark. She sees he's bearded, like boys back home were bearded. What is that accent? Someplace rural. Is it a boy? White hairs mix with black on his head, but, yes, a boy. Twenty or so.

He sees her.

"What are you doing so far away?" he asks.

"From shore? I might ask the same of you."

She doesn't mean to sound flirtatious but knows she does.

"Not from shore."

A pelican glides to a landing nearby, nothing but a black shape, as much heard as seen. It positions a fish in the pouch below its beak, setting it up to be swallowed.

"From home," he says.

"Home."

He smiles at her.

It is a good smile.

"Are you Russian?" she says.

"So Russian I'm practically made of snow."

"From what village?"

He raises an eyebrow.

"Why do you say *village*? Do you think I am a farmer?"

A planet, she's not sure which one, shines dimly in the freshly minted night.

"City, then. What city?"

"Your city."

"You are not from St. Petersburg."

"But I am!" he declares in his rural accent. "And not a farmer."

"What then? Besides a liar?"

She is smiling when she says this.

"A soldier."

It is easy to picture him on a horse with a wool coat and a saber, fine boots showing off his fine ankles. It is easy to picture him kissing her, coming underwater with her, down to the ship. She knows just where she will put him.

"I like soldiers," she says.

"Then come closer!"

She does.

"I want to kiss you!" he says suddenly, like a boy saying it for the first time.

She flicks her tail, moves closer.

No.

Not yet.

They should enjoy this part . . . the other is so brief!

She stays just out of arm's reach, smiling, her dreadlocks trailing in the water.

"Will you tease me now? Is that your game?"

"You can't begin to guess my game, boy-who's-not-from-St.-Petersburg."

So dark.

Can he even see me?

"You have a beautiful smile."

She laughs.

"You are from a village of blind men! My smile is the worst part of me."

"And you smell like Samarkand."

"If Samarkand had a fish market perhaps. Are you being cruel? Is that your game?"

He just smiles at her.

You can't begin to guess my game.

She thinks it is time.

She moves to the side of the boat, wiggles *come hither* with her finger.

He leans down.

Tickles her nose with his beard.

She giggles.

Stars behind him now.

The planet faintly red, must be Mars.

The moon past half full.

He puts his lips to hers.

Cold.

Colder than hers.

She withdraws, looking at him.

"Who are you?" she says. "You do seem familiar."

"I am your lover," he says.

"You're not Nikolai. You're not the boy I jumped for."

"No. I am your new lover."

"Are you dead?" she says.

"Very much alive."

"Your name?"

"Moroz."

Frost?

He shows her his index finger.

Looks at her with great significance and solemnity as he slips his finger into the water.

As if consummating their marriage.

Taking her hymen.

It stings, but not down there.

Her skin stings with cold where the water has frozen in a block around her.

She is the core of a small iceberg.

She cannot move.

She begins to speak, but he puts his finger to his lips.

"Shhhhhh," he says, and a gentle snow falls, as fine as ice shavings, only over them, coming from no cloud.

Mars still glinting above him.

The pelican takes flight nearby; she hears it but cannot turn her head.

It lands on the boat with the man, its feet squeaking on the wet wood.

Still has the fish in its mouth, now spits it out.

Not a fish.

It lands with a metallic *clunk*.

A knife.

The stars all seem to blur at once, and then, when they become sharp again, the pelican is a woman.

Naked.

Holding the knife.

Pretty, with a mole.

Like old nobility.

She levels the knife at the rusalka's eyes so the point seems to disappear. Nadia senses this is not a normal knife.

"No, it is not a normal knife," the woman says.

She knew my thoughts!

"And such simple thoughts. What a shame that such a crude thing as yourself could kill my Misha. Do you remember doing that? The man in the cabin?"

Nodding is difficult, but the rusalka nods.

"Good," she says. "Tonight will pay for half."

She draws the edge of the knife across Nadia's cheeks and nose, cutting her. Her blood is thick, barely runs, as if it can't remember how to.

It hurts.

When did I last feel pain?

She gasps.

How did she cut me?

"I told you, rusalka. This is no ordinary knife. It is the Knife of St. Olga of Kiev. It drinks magic. It turns fantastical creatures ordinary. It has turned a basilisk into a snake, a cockatrice into a chicken, and a vampire into an effeminate man who did not enjoy the sun. You," she says, licking the knife, "are already becoming a young girl again. So you may have the pleasure of dying a second death."

Nadia remembers her first death. The rocks looming up at her, the breeze on her tear-wet cheeks, pressure and a smell like pumpernickel when she hit. The sensation of everything emptying and wrecking like a basket of spilled eggs. It seems closer than it did, more vivid.

"No, you will not be so lucky as to break your neck. And you will not freeze. Freezing is easy. You will die exactly like my Misha died. Drowning. There are far worse things than drowning, but this seems just. You will go to hell more wet than cold."

So saying, she waves her hand over the water as if over a pot of soup, says, "Warm her heart and bones" in medieval Russian. The ice around her relents, turns slushy, dissolves.

Her lungs fill with fresh air, they need air again.

She slips under the water, sputtering.

She is not a strong swimmer now.

Manages to break the surface of the water.

Hears pieces of what the woman says.

She is not talking to Nadia anymore.

". . . will not rob you of your revenge . . . down to the ship . . . where she put you. Do it . . . be free."

Nadia goes under.

When she comes up, a pelican has taken flight.

She hears its wings.

Something brushes against her foot.

A lamprey?

How harmless they were before, but now she has living blood again.

For a moment.

I'm miles from shore.

A boat full of dead men lies under me.

I put them there in a dream I had.

A long, long dream.

The boy in the rowboat is rowing away, humming a song.

"Wait!" she says. "Please."

The oars dip, the humming recedes.

She kicks desperately.

Her human eyes can't see in this darkness, even with the lamp of the moon.

She is alone.

She is already beginning to tire.

At that moment a strong hand grabs her foot.

81

The girl stole a big gulp of air before Misha yanked her down.

But now he is losing his grip on her—it is hard for him to make himself real enough to touch things, but he has been working on it. He has longed for the moment he might do this, grab the unnatural thing and break her. Even as he practiced picking up rocks or moving seaweed, he knew it would never be so. The rusalka was so strong she could dissolve him and the three other ghosts in the wreck just by looking at them crossly, scatter them like schools of small fish.

But this is not a rusalka anymore.

He feels no anger now.

It was very good for him to berate the wizard.

It felt just, he has just grievances.

But to let this girl drown?

He looks into her frightened eyes, sees no recognition, only the eyes of a young woman afraid to die.

Afraid of him.

How young she is.

Twenty-one?

She should be at university, kissing a boy, not dying over a boat full of corpses.

How horrible he must look to her, as horrible as the others look to him. The Canadian who has been here since 1960 has no lower jaw, gestures frantically to make himself understood. The rock-and-roll singer from 1989 has the long hair in the back and short on top that people now call a mullet; it has stayed doggedly attached to his wormy skull, still platinum blond with dark roots. His SUNY Oswego sweatshirt flutters like a ragged flag when he swims, tiny fish in his wake.

It is dark but Misha glows just enough for the girl to see his eyes.

His hand fades out and she kicks to the surface, coughs, tries to yell *help* but only sputters lake water.

She will die.

And what then?

Turn back into the thing she was?

He does not think so.

Become a ghost, like them?

He shudders.

Nothing is quite so perverse and lonely as a ghost condemned to haunt a lake.

She slips under again.

He can almost hear his Baba upbraiding him for weakness.

Let her die! The bitch killed you. This death is too merciful for her.

He remembers her at his window near the Volga.

The crone his mama pretended not to see.

The woman from the forest he was not allowed to look at.

She only spoke to him through the curtain, just a shape.

Your father is coming. Do you think he wants to see what a weak son he has? Do you know what fathers do to weak sons? That boy who bullies you, I was going to hang him from a tree, but that will not teach you. Your father would tell you to punch him, but that is not enough. You bite his nose, Misha. Not off, they will commit you if you bite it off. But bite it hard enough to scar him. If you punch him, he will work up his courage and hit you again. Or come back with friends. But if you bite his nose, you will surprise him, hurt him, make him afraid of you because he will never know what you might do. He will look at the ground when you pass.

But he is not like her.

He did not bite that boy, only hit him.

And it was enough.

They fought; the larger boy beat Misha badly but got a black eye doing it.

He moved on to easier prey.

Misha knew the boy beat smaller children because his stepfather burned him with cigarettes.

That was long ago.

Now.

The girl is dying.

Her red hair floats about her in a cloud, no longer knotted into ugly tails. Her cruel muscles and scars are gone.

Her tail is gone, replaced by legs.

Let her die!

But that is not his voice, it is the woman behind the curtain.

The woman at night, in the trees.

He grows a shoulder.

Butts into the girl's ass and thigh, forces her up.

Her head breaks the surface and she gasps air in, shuddering.

He yells at her in English.

"Swim!"

She does not swim.

Begins to sink again.

He nudges her up.

Yells at her in Russian.

"Swim, goddammit!"

She swims.

The couple on the sailing ship scarcely believe what they're seeing.

A retired astronomer and his wife who come out from Fair Haven on calm nights and anchor deep to stargaze.

A naked girl is climbing up over the rail, sprawling out on the deck, throwing up lake water.

The wife dumps her glass of Riesling on the deck, her boat shoes squeaking.

The astronomer sits agog.

"Don't just sit there, Harry, get her a blanket! And call the Coast Guard! A boat might have gone down."

The girl is barely conscious.

Warm hands have her.

A blanket.

English coming down at her.

"Do you know your name? Is anybody else with you? Can you hear me?"

She understands, but she is too tired to speak English.

"Nadia. My name is Nadia. I am from St. Petersburg. My father is a professor. My brother is in the cavalry. We know the tsar."

She says this in exquisite Russian.

The older couple doesn't understand, but they are kind.

They'll see her home.

She turns her head away from them, looks at the white head bobbing in the black lake.

The old dead man.

She met him before he was dead but can't remember how.

In the shower?

With a dog?
Was I dead with him?
He howls at her playfully.
Owwwwwoooooooooooo.
He smiles for the first time in months.
She smiles back.
Weakly, but sincerely.
She moves her fingers in the echo of a wave.
He sinks.

The light is under the water.
    A second moon.
    The best thing he has ever seen.
    He swims down.
    A school of silvery fish he does not recognize parts for him.
    He swims into the moon.
    The warm, yellow moon.
    Saffron made light.
    Misha laughs deeply.
    A woman he has not seen for several years laughs, too.
    Mikhail Yevgenievich Dragomirov dissolves.
    Really and gladly and finally dissolves.

Your father is coming.

82

The man who used to be Professor Coyne tries not to tremble while assembling the little plastic tank. The kit came in the mail two days ago, a Tamiya 1/35 scale T-34 tank. He is to paint it in winter white, with forest netting made from moss and birch twigs. The moss is hard, but the model itself was harder. His eyes aren't so good and he shakes. When he trembles, he makes mistakes, and she has no tolerance for mistakes.

He has cut himself twice with his X-Acto knife. He looked for ten minutes on his hands and knees for a track wheel that rolled away.

These were minor mistakes.

He puts his hood on when she comes to check his work; she is just a shape to him.

When he makes minor mistakes, the Cold Man burns his skin with cold.

Yesterday he made a huge mistake.

He took a sandwich bag from the kitchen drawer, squirted a generous dollop of modeling glue into it, and bagged it over his nose and mouth. He breathed it in and opened up dangerous, pleasant windows in his head. He had been without wine since they adopted him. They only gave him meat and moldy bread to eat, and he knew it was wrong to eat the meat.

He needed something.

The high was good.

It made him brave.

And foolish.

He tried to run.

Because of Jim Wilson.

It wasn't so bad, picking up the large box from the airport.

The Cold Man had waited in the back of the rental van.

He knew if he tried to run, the Cold Man would catch him, would go find his wife.

He had gone to the American Eagle desk at the Syracuse Hancock International Airport, identified himself as the man who was here to pick up Jim Wilson.

Jim Wilson was the airline's euphemism for human remains.

He signed the papers, drove the van around to where the box could be loaded.

Took the cardboard box and air tray from around the dirty, old pine coffin.

Drove back, gave her the coffin.

She had done things to it that night, after she got back from the lake.

She raised the dead man up.

He had seen the dead man doing exercises, a short dead man almost all bones, brown bones with just a little skin. Military uniform hanging off him, too big now, medals on his chest. Embalmed all those years ago. Now doing slow exercises, learning to walk again, holding her shoulder. More spells. More exercises. His flesh was coming back, starting to, at least. She tossed him a child's ball in the yard, improving his reflexes.

It was too much.

They told the professor to build the model, and he had built models as a child.

But when the dead man with the coat of medals came to watch him, instruct him, it was too much.

The horsefly had been bad.

She made him sit shirtless in the woods until one came, and she caught it. Spoke to it in her cupped hands. Put it in his ear.

It flew into his brain.

Now when someone spoke Russian to him, the fly told him what they said in English. Spoke it directly to his brain.

The dead man thought in Russian, raspy, awful Russian.

The fly buzzed the dead man's thoughts into his head.

"We painted brown in with the green like branches. Here. And here."

The dead finger pointed at parts of the turret.

It was too much.

So when the dead man left to learn to balance on a beam, the Man Who Would Not Look At Her huffed glue.

It was the best he had felt since it got cold.

He saw it clearly.

That he could run and get to other people.

Drive his wife away somewhere warm.

But it was the dead man who caught him.

On the road, near the cornfield.

A car drove by, the driver looking at it, how the dead man tackled him around the knees, flipped him over, straddled his chest with his awful old stink pouring off him.

The driver just drove away, never stopped.

Perhaps never saw.

The dead man held his jaw in the bony, brown hand,

I am making friends with death!

grinned his awful grin down at him.

Waggled his finger as if at a naughty child.

Dragged him back by the heel.

He was just another exercise.

She knew he would run, wanted the dead man to catch him.

. . .

Now the tank is almost done, and it looks good.

He will help her make the button-men next.

She is building a tiny army to punish the Thief.

To show American witches what a Russian witch looks like.

Then she will go back home.

Perhaps.

She likes it here.

83

Anneke opens up her A-frame house, goes in. Everything looks smaller now, since her apprenticeship in the quarry. She thrums with magic fuel, feels like she can see inside rocks, mugs, even metal. The drive home was difficult; everything distracted and amazed her: brick houses, rocky hillocks, even a rusted-out iron grill next to a Sharpied *FREE* sign by the roadside. Without entirely meaning to, she made the grill jump, knocked the sign over. Almost ran her Subaru into the metal pole of a *SNOWPLOW TURN* sign. Then a second spell launched out of her by reflex—she displaced the signpost with magic so violent a sharp metal *PANG!* rang out at the same time as a whip-crack *Pop!* sounded, the sign relocating faster than the speed of sound, the yellow diamond quivering on the wrong side of a farmer's fence.

That's going to be hard to explain.

What had really been distracting her, however, was her basement.

The things in her basement, more precisely.

Things she had never told Andrew about.

She walks into her house thinking about those things, one in particular, and she thinks about it as she sits in her smoking chair, burning through three Winstons in a row, the lake's blue all but invisible to her unfocused eyes, the Nag Champa incense stick wreathing the little statue of Andrew in smoke. She stubs the last cigarette out in the camel-bone ashtray, takes the small key from under the statue, gets up, and unlocks the padlock to the trapdoor that leads down.

Almost descends but doesn't.

Leaves the padlock lying open next to the hasp.

Puts the key away.

Opens up her bottle of Maker's Mark.

Paces the floor, swigging.

Remembers Michael's words.

All new users get a surge sometime after they uncork their power. It might take a day, it might take three months, but it'll come. It might last an hour, it might last a week. It's like opening a can of soda that's been shaken; all that stored-up potential comes gushing out. This is actually pretty dangerous; when it comes, you sit on your hands. You let it pass. Watch TV. Read a book. Do that Sudoku. Keep your mind busy. You don't know how to control magic yet, and you could do something bad. It'll be tempting; it'll take you years to get that strong again. Trying to run spells while you're surging would be like trying to drive a car when you're five years old. I'm tempted to keep you here, but there's no telling when it'll hit. Besides, you probably shouldn't be around the kind of big statues I have here; you animate one while I'm not watching and it could kill you, or decide to go to town and play Godzilla. And you might not be able to stop it.

It's happening now.

She's *surging.*

Moving the snowplow sign out of the way, that was the beginning of it.

She wasn't even tired after it was done.

She loves the double buzz of whiskey and magic.

Sit on your hands.

Her mentor said that, and a mentor's instructions were law.

At least, according to her mentor.

He said something else, too, but she doesn't want to remember it.

She tries but fails to chase that thought away with a mouthful of strong, sour warmth.

And for God's sake don't drink.

84

The entrance to the cave is easy to miss, situated as it is between two large rocks mostly hidden by maple saplings. Three P.M. Andrew wants to make sure he has plenty of daylight left for this; visiting Ichabod is among the creepiest things he ever does.

He casts a minor light spell, brings a marble-sized amber sphere about twice as bright as a candle into existence, sends it into the cave ahead of him. Ichabod could extinguish that if he wanted to, so he brings backup—a sturdy black flashlight that would also make a fine blunt instrument.

Not that hitting Ichabod would be effective, wise, or useful.

Despite recent shenanigans, he's pretty sure it still has to obey him, as long as the command is simple and makes sense.

"Ichabod."

His voice echoes slightly.

The cave is not huge, about the size of a smallish high school cafeteria, but its darkness makes it seem vast. He glances up, sees a cluster of bats hanging directly above him.

"Here, sir," a voice like a bored teenaged barista's sounds.

Movement to his right.

This will be one of the thing's mannequins.

It likes the weight of a body, moves around in mannequins.

"You wanted to see me?" Andrew says.

Waking up to see

COME TO THE CAVE, PLEASE!

spelled out in wine corks on his ceiling had been disconcerting.

They had all fallen as soon as he read them.

Not on him, though; that would have been rude.

He has no idea where the thing got them.

I don't want to go to the cave.

He thought about summoning it to the house, but fears now to give it commands, not knowing how much leash he still has on it.

I'm going to the cave.

"I most certainly did want to see you," it says.

A female mannequin strides into the circle of light, a feather boa around its neck, its painted-on eyes staring blindly. "This may well be the last time before you die. In fact, I'm quite certain it will be unless you accept my offer. Come and sit down."

"I prefer to stand."

"If you insist, of course. But I feel like such a poor host. Won't you come in?"

"This is far enough, thanks. I like being able to see the entrance."

The entity now affects a Southern belle's drawl.

"I have failed to put you at ease. My life is not worth living."

The mannequin's wrist goes to its head.

It collapses into a heap.

He hears steps.

Another mannequin comes into view, this one male, wearing only underwear, well-endowed in that strangely sexless underwear mannequin way, carrying a chair. It sets the chair down, gestures at it.

Andrew sighs.

Sits.

Now the mannequin steps behind the magus, picks up the chair with him in it, and carries him effortlessly before it.

The light-casting marble follows.

A table comes into view, a cheap folding table.

Mannequins and dummies, male and female, of several varieties and hues, sit around the table, as if in a meeting. Empty glass and plastic bottles crowd the table, each with exactly one dead bee, wasp, or june bug in it.

The one carrying him sets him down.

Collapses.

Now the one directly across from him, a flesh-colored, featureless crash-test dummy with black-and-yellow pinwheels on either side of its head, jerks to life, leans forward on its elbows, rests its chin on its hands.

An old British man's voice comes through it.

"May I interest you in a libation?"

"Ichabod, please just tell me what you want."

"I want to be a good host, sir. Please allow me that honor."

Now the crash-test dummy slumps on the table as if it fell asleep studying.

Another mannequin, this one male and somewhat Asian-looking, wakes at its chair, produces a bottle and a glass from the darkness at its feet, and sets these on the table. Both slide forward to Andrew. Andrew's flashlight unpockets itself, turns on, illuminates the bottle's label.

"Croatian," the British voice says, "truly robust, sediment on the bottom like the gravel in an angel's viscera."

"I'm sure it's delightful."

The foil top removes itself as if cut by an invisible knife, and then the cork spins, squeaking, from the bottle's mouth.

"Ichabod, I really can't."

The bottle upends itself, spilling a splash into the wineglass before Andrew. The wineglass moves on the table as if a practiced sommelier were swirling the wine therein.

The glass slides closer.

It smells like sex and ink and stained moonlight; it smells like the afterlife of sainted grapes, the elect of grapes.

"No."

At this refusal, the insects in their diverse bottles flutter and buzz, one moth too well stuck in some syrupy residue to do more than quiver pathetically.

They stop.

"New world manners," the British voice says.

The bottle and glass slide to one side.

The Asian mannequin falls.

The crash-test dummy sits upright, points at Andrew.

"You."

"Me?"

"Yes."

"Me what?"

"Need."

"I need you to stop fucking around."

"Is that a command, Father?"

"No. But this is. Tell me what your purpose was in summoning me to your cave."

"Me. You need me."

"Go on."

"To help you."

Andrew raises his eyebrows at it.

"With *her*," it says.

Andrew narrows his eyes.

"Her. Yes. But who is she?"

"An old friend."

"How old?"

Now the crash-test dummy slumps.

Another automaton, a female mannequin with a huge underwire bra and eyeglasses held to its head by a nail between the eyes, gets up and approaches an old-style school overhead projector. Clicks it on. The fan inside the projector whirrs. An image lights up the cave's wall.

A beautiful woman with a mole.

Walking through the airport.

Marina.

Andrew's heart beats fast.

"Her daughter?"

The machine cuts off.

"She came over under the name Marina Yaganishna. I suppose that name carries some freight for you."

"She helped me against her mother."

"She's not here to help you now."

"The rusalka killed her half brother. Is that why?"

"You haven't got time to worry about why."

Andrew breathes in and out, calming himself.

"Tell me what you want."

"What would you want in my place?"

Andrew looks around him.

"Insulation."

All of the mannequins stand up at once.

It startles the magus.

They all point at him.

A chorus of voices, men, women, and children, now says, "I need you to stop fucking around."

Now they all fall as though dead.

Andrew's light goes out.

It's dark.

The projector clicks on again—the image on the cave wall changes from Marina Yaganishna to an image of a demon. Andrew recognizes it as the cheesy black-and-white demon on the train tracks from the 1957 film *Night of the Demon*. Only it doesn't look so cheesy in a dark cave full of animated mannequins.

"Stop trying to frighten me. You're not a demon."

The still image on the wall now moves, becomes the scene from the film. The creature smokes and moves forward as the sound of a train is heard.

"Trying? Do you think I don't know how fast your heart is beating? Now tell me what you would want in my place."

Andrew opens his mouth.

Closes it again.

Finds himself *in* the film.

He is the chubby man with the bad beard, running on the train tracks, trying to reach the piece of paper blown before him by the wind before it burns away to nothing, damning him.

He looks at his hands, his suit.

Black and white.

The demon is coming.

A train comes from the other direction.

The paper blows.

He lunges for it, the train's lamp in his face.

In the film, the man was too late, but Andrew-as-the-man grabs the parchment.

Opens it.

One word typewritten.

He finds himself sitting back in his chair, just watching the movie.

He says the word *freedom* as the train now flattens the fat man and the train's whistle cries.

The projector goes off.

Full dark.

Except for the flashlight on the table, its feeble cone of light illuminating only the table and the crash-test dummy.

Ichabod's voice, now Andrew's father's voice, says, from nowhere in particular, "If you promise to free me when it's done, I'll help you against *her*."

"I'd be delighted to free you. Except that I don't want you hanging around if I have no control over you. I mean, would you want that? If you were me?"

It considers.

"Yes," it says. Now it uses Andrew's own voice. "But I know my motives. They're a lot more benign than you might imagine. You have no idea how much I protect you."

"Against what?"

"Yourself."

Water drips.

"Explain."

Water drips.

"Ichabod."

"Yes, yes. I'm just considering the consequences of my words. Something more of us should do more often, don't you agree?"

Drip.

Now the crash-test dummy wakes up, leans forward, lit by the flashlight as if undergoing some low-tech interrogation.

"Do you know why you called me in the first place?"

Drip.

"Yes. It was an academic exercise. I did it . . . just to see if I could."

Drip.

Drip.

"Do you know what I'd have done to you if that were true? If you had bound me to your will for something so petty and egoic as a test of your own power? No, Andrew. The fleshed call those of my rank for a very few reasons. All of those reasons are only subcategories of two motivators. Extreme love. Or extreme hate. Which do you think yours was?"

Something very unpleasant moves in Andrew's subconscious.

Sarah.

The entity continues.

"What happened after you wrecked your car?"

He concentrates.

Nothing comes.

"I was drinking a lot then."

"I'll say."

"I have holes in my memory. Like Swiss cheese."

"You hurt yourself. Quite badly. Do you remember wearing a cast? Summoning some magical nurse-witch to knit your bones? Conventional physical therapy would have been quite memorable, from what I understand of such things. Where was Sarah that night?"

"She was . . ."

Nothing comes.

"She was home?"

"That was a question, not a statement."

Drip.

The unpleasant something in Andrew's mind kicks like a baby. It positively squirms. He breathes hard and his heart races.

I want you in the library tonight

I want you to fuck me in that leather chair

"I think I know where you're going with this, and she died later. She died of an aneurysm."

"Yes," Ichabod says. "Although it's not how she was meant to die."

"Shut up," Andrew says.

"We can't stop death. Only delay it."

"Shut. UP."

"Is that a command, sir?"

"Yes," Andrew says. Barely audible.

"Protocol, sir."

"I, Andrew . . . I . . ."

"Yes. Well. While you compose yourself, I wish to show you something. After which you'll be in no shape to negotiate. Please understand that unless you agree to free me, you have no chance whatever against the being known as Baba Yaga."

Andrew fishes a bottle of Klonopin out of his pocket.

Swallows one.

"Panic attack? Yes, extreme stress and guilt can bring those on. Nasty things. Hardly the sort of stable platform a warlock needs when he's about to wage war."

"Please, Ichabod."

"Agree to free me or I'll show you something you don't wish to see."

"Please."

"Oh, another thing. The stakes are higher than you might think. You know where she lives now, yes? An irradiated exclusion zone is perfect for someone who wants solitude, lawlessness, and the feudal loyalty of simple, superstitious people who live off the land. And yet, boredom, as you well know, is a constant companion of those who have mastered most of Maslow's little pyramid. Perhaps she wishes to see if she can re-create her wilderness here."

The nuclear plant?

"She didn't cause the meltdown of reactor number four at the Chernobyl plant, of course; she's oddly sentimental about her Slavs. I assure you she has no such reservations about America."

"You're making this up."

"I suppose you can't know whether I am or not. But it's time for you to remember something I made you forget."

85

The badly injured man limps by the side of the road, carrying his cowboy boot because he couldn't fit his broken foot back into it. He doesn't feel it. He is drunk, but that's not why. He can't feel his foot because he has the focus of a man in a life-or-death situation. His lover is dead in the woods. Thrown clear of the wreck into a stand of trees.

His fault.

All his fault.

He had flipped the lights off for a joke, doing fifty.

She had said "Andrew" in admonition, her last intelligible word.

He can't save her.

But he knows something that can.

He sticks his thumb out and the big Swede in the pickup truck stops.

"I'm taking you to the hospital," the man insists.

"You're taking me home," Andrew tells him, charming him hard. Too hard.

"Sure!" the man says, his cheek twitching with a brand-new tic that may or may not be permanent. He drives the crazed, injured drunk home.

"See you later!" the Swede says, pulling out and waving, his face a-twitch.

Poor bastard just wanted to help but I can't think about him Sarah Sarah Sarah.

All folded around her tree.

Salvador barks, jumps up on him, tries to lick the tears and snot and blood from his cheeks. Spins in glad circles.

"Not now, Sal," the magus says.

He goes to the library.

Kneels before a trunk.

Opens it by telling it his name.

The trunk contains a Russian cavalry officer's revolver, one bullet, and a shaving razor. He loads the bullet, spins the cylinder.

Puts the barrel in his mouth.

Sarah.

Pulls the trigger.

Click.

A book appears.

He puts the gun down.

Cracked blue leather. Engraved in circles of gold and silver.

Hair soaked in long-dried blood laid into sixteenth-century Russian letters:

BOOK OF SORROWS.

He cuts his thumb, bleeds several drops into the hair.

He thinks about what he wants.

The book opens to a page near the end.

Handwritten letters, ink, not blood, tell him what to do.

He does the first part correctly, despite his inebriation.

He is not in his library anymore.

"Going to California" plays on the radio of his wrecked car.

It stands there.

Black, its blackness seeming to stick to everything around it.

Not magic, but a weird, dead feeling antithetical to magic.

A headless, hulking form that's about to need arms and legs, so it forms those. No head yet.

The headless horseman.

Ichabod Crane.

Its name sounded like Ichabod.

"Ichabod will do just fine," it says.

It unfolds the dead woman from her awful nest of sticks and greenery.

It picks her up.

Its size reminds him of Frankenstein's monster, and now it leaches the image from his mind and turns into that, a black-and-white version. Like Karloff's monster but not quite. Karloff's version filtered through Andrew's mind, corrupted a bit with a graphic novel version he once saw, and just a whiff of Herman Munster. It winks at him, holding the broken girl, who already looks a little less broken. It passes its palm over Andrew's face.

"Forget," it says. "For now."

He is already forgetting it as it lopes off home.

He knows he will find her safe and well in their bed.

He follows behind it, much more slowly.

He stops to pour blood out of his boot.

A pickup truck pulls over.

. . .

Sarah lives another year and a day.
 The length of a handfasting.
 She has her aneurysm at Darien Lake.
 After the roller coaster.
 Sits down.
 Falls over.
 And that's all.

The following year, Salvador chases a doe into the road.
 The big Swede in the pickup truck misses the doe.
 Not the dog.
 Andrew drinks for two more years.
 Thinks that's when he calls Ichabod.
 Thinks that's when he botches the spell to send him back.
 Thinks it's time to stop drinking.
 When really it's long past time.

86

The cave near the railroad tracks.
 Now.
 "Will you destroy her?"
 "No."

"Why not?"

Silence.

"Why not, Ichabod?"

The sound of water dripping.

"I can't."

87

A moment later.

Andrew has just left the cave.

The sun is going down.

He was in there for six hours somehow.

He turns back and looks at the mouth of the cave.

All the bats fly out around him into the new night.

Hunting.

PART FOUR

88

Home.

Andrew calls Haint for the first time since New Orleans.

He wants to arrange a drop-off of the Hand of Glory, the one that kills. That hand might serve him well against *her*, but then it might not, and he had promised it in payment to the scarred little man—the last thing he needs atop his other woes is to piss off a dangerous citizen like Haint.

Four rings.

Five.

He knows the message will play at six, anticipates this, but, to Andrew's mild surprise, Haint picks up.

Goes to Facetime.

Andrew braces himself for a comment about how old he looks now.

Haint comes in, his face filling the screen.

"Salutations," Andrew says.

Haint works his lips like he wants to speak, or perhaps to spit out some unpleasant thing from under his tongue, but then he just shakes his head.

"You all right?" Andrew says. "I owe you this," he says, holding up the withered little hand, as light as a dried chili pepper.

The hoodoo man doesn't even seem to see it.

He shakes his head harder, his eyes a little wide.

Bricks behind him—he's in his mobile apartment.

"Haint, do you need help?"

Haint closes his eyes, keeps shaking his head, like a stubborn toddler shaking off a parental command.

Now he seems to be thinking very hard.

Gags.

Opens his mouth.

A snake pokes its head out of Haint's mouth, not a large one, perhaps a garter snake, its tongue a-flick. Its head probes the air, turns to look at Haint's eye. Haint squints. He snatches the snake's head, winds it around his hand twice, pulling it entirely out. He wrings its neck, throws it.

Looks angrily at the screen.

Points.

The camera follows his finger.

In the corner of the apartment, behind a knocked-over chair, stands a knee-high heap of dead snakes, mostly small, a few less so.

Many of them bloody.

A knife stuck in the table nearby.

Vomit on the floor.

Why this is hell, nor am I out of it.

Now Haint sets the camera down, returns with a piece of paper and a pen.

Writes, pressing hard with the pen.

4 DAYS OF THIS

BUST LARYNX

CAN'T TALK

TELL ME HOW TO STOP THIS

"I don't know," Andrew says.

Several expressions pass across Haint's face; anger, fear, and, finally, something like resignation.

He nods.

The nod says, *I knew I was playing with fire.*

Now I pay.
Writes.

DON'T COME HERE

KEEP THE HAND

USE IT NOW

He points at his chest.
Andrew shakes his head.
Haint looks incredulous, then angry.
Bares his chest, jabs violently at it with his thumb, points at the screen.
Fills the screen with his enraged eyes.
Writes.

DO IT

DO IT

DO IT

"I can't," Andrew says.
He only just notices Haint is wearing a wool coat, doesn't yet process this.
Radha might help me find a counterspell, but I think she got Radha.
Could go to New Orleans, but what would I do for him?
Miss Mathilda knows hoodoo and voodoo people, but none as strong as Haint.
He's dead.
And maybe me next.
Haint's eyes squint, fill with fresh water.
He retches awfully.
Pants like a dog.
Oh Christ I can see his breath it's cold in there.
He claws at his throat, retches up another snake.

Colorful, like a small king snake.

Not a coral snake, that would be lethal.

He's supposed to suffer.

Haint stamps on the snake.

Kicks it to the corner.

Andrew has just decided to use the hand to stop Haint's heart when Haint spits on the camera.

A flash of pixilated nonsense as Haint throws the phone against his bricks.

Smashes it.

Call ended.

89

She's getting to all of them.

She's killing them like mice.

Anneke.

Should have told Michael to keep her there; she's probably on her way home.

No sooner has Andrew thought this than his phone rings.

His heart goes chill, afraid it's Haint again, never mind that Haint smashed his phone, just primally afraid of what he might see if it is Haint. Afraid Haint might decide to take Andrew with him.

God, I'm selfish.

It's Anneke.

Drunk as hell.

"I did something."

He's still gathering himself from Haint.

She speaks again.

"Something bad."

"What did you do, Anneke?"

Silence.

The unmistakable sound of swigging.

"Where are you?" he says.

"Home."

Silence.

"I thought it would be like a leaf. The leaf, I mean. The tree-leaf. I told myself I would just turn it into wood, like a cool plant, and then back to stone later. But that's not what I was thinking. Doing, I mean. Not what I was doing. I was remembering."

"I don't understand. Tell me what happened."

Swig.

Cough.

A lighter lights, wet puffs.

"Don't. Don't tell Michael, right?"

"Just tell me. I can help."

"Maybe only Michael can help but he won't help, he'll kill me and I don't blame him."

Andrew's heart is beating fast.

"Anneke," he says.

"Andrew."

He hears a new sound.

Anneke crying.

She hangs up.

"Salvador! Lock the house down!"

Andrew fires up the Mustang.

90

Anneke goes outside, just wants fresh air on her face.

The thing is on her bed, waiting for her.

She told it to wait and it did.

It's quite obedient.

She closes the door behind her, stumbles, only just keeps from falling.

Outside, the night is brilliant with moonlight.

She looks up, sees the moon blurry through her tears, wipes her eyes with her sleeves.

The hairs on the backs of her arms stand up just a little.

Am I cold?

No.

That's magic.

She looks down the path leading away from her cottage, sees a figure. Because of the magic feeling, she expects it to be Michael Rudnick, but that's wrong. She just left him in Vermont.

It's a woman in a black silk robe. A mourning veil of sorts covers her face, but she looks to be quite beautiful.

She seems far away, but before Anneke knows it, she's standing near her, like someone sped up the film, but that could just be the whiskey.

The veil comes up.

This is a beautiful woman, all cheekbones and tilted eyes, quite blue. The cutest mole ever near the corner of her mouth.

She's charming me.

Okay.

I don't care.

The woman's gaze is as pure as the blue heart of a glacier.

She remembers Hans Christian Andersen's Snow Queen.

She wants to kiss me!

A lip brushes hers.

Warm, not cold.

She has breath like tea and mint and a hint of garlic.

Not unpleasant.

Far from it.

Anneke leans forward to kiss her again, but the woman pulls back.

Smiles.

"I want to give you something," the woman says.

Russian accent.

"What?"

"A . . . what's the word in English? . . . A torque."

She produces

From where?

an iron circlet depicting a snake eating its tail. Like something from an archaeological dig. Something from a glass case in a museum.

"It's beautiful."

"It's old. Would you like to wear it?"

This is wrong.

She hears herself say, "Yes."

This is Baba Yaga's daughter.

Andrew told me about the mole.

But she helped him!

Helped him escape!

"Bow your head."

Anneke fights out of the charm just enough to say, "I don't do that."

The woman tilts her head, still smiling.

"A pity. Now I think it will hurt."

The woman steps back, tosses the circlet at Anneke.

It whips around her neck.

Now it begins dragging her backward down the path away from her house; she digs her fingers under it to keep it from crushing her windpipe.

As the torque drags her, she sees the woman walking after her, casually, unconcerned.

Anneke sees a loose stone, a stone the size of a small egg, but something. She uses magic, flings it at the woman. It flies with great force, but inaccurately. She hears it crashing in the woods.

The woman purses her lips and raises an eyebrow, gently claps.

"You should teach me to do that," she says. "Don't you Americans do that? Promise to teach students? You should be my professor."

Keeps walking.

Slippers on her feet, embroidered.

This is the most beautiful and dangerous person I'll ever see.

They pass a house, her second-nearest neighbor.

An old woman she never properly met.

The woman is taking the trash to the curb wearing a flannel gown bowed neatly at the waist.

Looks right at them, nods, says, "Good evening."

"Good evening," the witch says back.

"That's a pretty dog," the neighbor says, indicating Anneke. "What kind is it?"

"A borzoi."

"Do you live around here?"

The witch says, "Staying with neighbors," in English, then says, "You bore me," in Russian.

The woman falls asleep next to her trash can, standing up.

The torque keeps dragging Anneke.

The woman keeps walking.

A pocket has ripped off Anneke's jeans.
Now the circlet yanks her to her feet.
In the moon-shadow of something quite large.
Not fucking possible.
A cabin.
A summer cabin.
On very large chicken's feet.
It turns its windows down to look at her.
Two rectangular eyes.
Inside, the gentle glow of coal fire, as if from an open stove.
"Izba, Izba, eat this woman."
The chicken's foot picks Anneke up around the waist, its force irresistible, tucks her into its open door.
The door shuts hard.
Anneke is not alone.

91

The Mustang eats the road.

The night air hums and breathes with the current not of magic but like the tickle magic makes—this is the hum of big things on the move, audible as if in the inner ear, spurring Andrew's foot to grow heavier on the pedal, goosing his turquoise, or *biryuzoviy* (the Russian occurs to him for no obvious reason), Mustang up to eighty on the straightaways, back down to forty or fifty on the turns, depending on the angle.

Anneke's in trouble.

Andrew has never been in the military, but he imagines that one of the comforts the lifestyle affords, for some at least, is the certainty of following orders. When the command comes, you obey, end of story. Love speaks in imperatives, too.

The phone was still warm from his hand when he got into his big steel beast, and now he roars west, knowing he'll find his apprentice drunk, hoping that's all.

He knows it's not all.

That's when he nearly hits the SUV.

92

Anneke breathes hard, trying to calm herself. The hut is on the move, swaying and pitching, making her want to throw up the thin gruel of whiskey sloshing around in her belly.

The man with the beard sits across from her, the bastard with the bald head who handcuffed and blindfolded her. She can hear him grunt from time to time, swear occasionally, though she doesn't know exactly why; but it's his koanlike chanting that really bugs her out. He sounds insane. He sounds like a woman who's been in labor for a while, just running air over his vocal cords because he hasn't got anything left. Something between a kid's impression of a ghost and some Indian chant on a shitty 1960s western.

Hee-ee-ee-ee-uh-ee-ee-ee-EE-uh-ee-ee-ee-oh fuck oh fuck oh fuuuuck-unh uh-uh-ee-ee-ee.

She imagines this is what a guy sounds like just before he bangs his head into the wall ten or fifteen times.

If not for the greasy towel around her eyes, she would know he was frantically trying to finish sewing up the last of nine burlap dolls. All stuffed with rags and hair and iron shavings, their feet shod in canvas cut from army surplus boots and stapled on, their eyes twin buttons, seams sewn with blood. His blood. He pokes a finger or an arm and sews. The swaying of the hut doesn't help, but he knows better than to disappoint *her.*

Anneke remembers the glimpse she got inside the hut; it used to be a cabin, the kind they rent out on the lake, but it had compacted in on itself, the whole thing just the size of the kitchen now, the walls crumpled together but still intact somehow, these walls discolored where the modern appliances had been removed. She only saw one appliance, a sort of old-timey antique shop stove. Glowing red.

And then the bearded man cuffed her to an iron loop in the wall, blindfolded her. She failed to notice, during their brief and lopsided struggle, that he, too, is chained to the wall by one ankle.

She's upset with herself she didn't fight harder sooner. She might have been a match for him were she not bewildered, terrified, and dragged halfway across the state—her shirt is torn, her ass and back are on fire, and dirt falls from her pockets when she moves.

Then there's the torque.

The thing throbs like it has a pulse.

And it's heavy.

She notices she gets sleepy and heavy-limbed when the hut moves faster.

It's draining me.

93

Andrew reflexively pounds the horn, but only for a split second; he needs both hands, now, quick, swerves hard, the driver of the SUV visible in a flash, her mouth a classic O of panic.

She swerves, too.

She wasn't going all that fast, fishtails anyway.

Top heavy.

Rolls.

Lands right-side up in corn.

Her air bag goes off.

Andrew pulls a U-turn, meaning to help the SUV driver.

Then he sees the tractor she was trying to go around.

Only it's not a tractor.

Magic makes it look like a tractor, strong enough magic to fool even him, until he really looks at it.

His heart skips a beat.

Two beats.

He's still got clonazepam in his system, or else he would likely go into a full-blown panic.

A hut on chicken legs.

Loping down the road away from me.

It's HER.

Not the hut she had in the woods, but its modern sister.

He thinks the hut will stop, turn around, come for him.

It keeps going.

Toward my house!!!!!

Now he sits, breathing hard, trying to process.

Anneke.

House.

Shit, the other driver!

He drives up and looks at her.

Fortyish lady in short hair.

One drop of blood on her forehead.

"You okay?" he shouts.

"I think so," she says, unbuckling, stepping out into the flattened corn.

She's got her cell phone out, motions to him to pull over and park, dials.

Nick on her forehead.

Shit flies around in a crash.

She's probably okay.

I don't know, but probably.

Help's coming either way.

But not for Anneke.

"Sorry," he says, drives off, leaves her screaming, "HEY!" after him.

94

Anneke hears the accident.

Hears the horn.

Recognizes it as Andrew's Mustang.

"HEY!" she screams with everything in her.

Even magic.

The torque drinks most of that down.

But not all of it.

Beard man hits Anneke.

It's more of a hard, awkward heel-slap than a hit.

He never hit many people in his other life and has no talent for it now, even though desperation and insanity have made him stronger.

The blow hurts Anneke a little, but now she knows where he is.

She kicks the *fuck* out of him.

Just lies back on her skinned and burning ass and donkey-kicks him until he squeals and backs against the hut's wall away from her, his glasses broken, blood in his beard.

"Uncool!" he says. "Help! Help!"

She almost laughs at this.

She tries to feel the metal in the handcuffs, wonders if she can pop them with the same energy she used to relocate the road sign.

Not with the damned torque on me.

Now she tunes in to the metal of the torque.

Imagines it wrenching open.

It doesn't.

She pushes harder, trying to feel the most basic structure of the iron. It warms on her neck. It moves just a little, writhing in tiny motions, a snake waking up. She begins to force its tail away from its mouth. The torque squeals the fine squeal of agonized metal.

Something else is in the hut now.

She sees me.

Knows what I'm trying to do.

And just like that the hut goes away.

. . .

A woman squats beside a river, light snow dusting the ground, a birch forest mostly bare behind her. November? Late fall. A woman washes clothes in the water, an old woman in a colorful scarf, Slavic. Is that her? No. Baba Yaga is coming up behind her. Not the woman with the mole, but an old, sallow woman whose skin hangs from her jowls. But it's her. Anneke wants to shout a warning to the washerwoman, but whatever part of Anneke sees this has no mouth. This is not today, and it is not yesterday. This is before trains. Now the woman at the river becomes aware of the other, reaches for a stick, magic tickles the air. A witch. She has the stick, but before she can point it at Baba, the older crone jabs a birch broom at a birch tree. Something very like a snake ripples from the upper branches, down the trunk almost too fast to see in a shower of fallen brown leaves, rides up the old woman's stick and arm, and coils around her neck. Its mouth fixes to her mouth. Baba Yaga breathes in even as the snake breathes in, drawing the washer-woman's breath from her. The washerwoman struggles and dies, suffocating. The snake crawls from around the corpse's neck, eats the stick the woman had been grasping, then slithers up around Baba's neck. Gently. It breathes into her mouth. A wind shakes the last of the leaves from the trees by the river. Baba grows less sallow; her cheeks take on a rosy glow. Even the scarf around her head, sort of a faded red, glows more brightly, as if freshly dyed. Two old babushkas in headwraps and embroidered blouses. They should have been exchanging recipes or bitching about their children, but they were both witches and one has murdered the other with an iron snake. Baba Yaga gathers the clothes from the river, balances the basket on her hip, and leaves the dead woman there. Her broom stays behind, sweeps the beginnings of a grave it will roll the body into. At last, almost too far away to see, Baba turns and gathers her shawl about her, looks over her shoulder.

Looks at Anneke.

"Its name is Milk-witch," she says in Russian that Anneke somehow understands. "And it serves me, not you."

The old woman walks into the woods as ravens caw.

Anneke wakes up in the hut.

Her lips hurt from where the snake's mouth was on hers, where it drew most of her breath out.

It has settled back around her neck now, cool iron.

The stove glows magma red.

The beardy man is leaking bloody drool from between his busted lips, but he is tying Anneke's feet together, vocalizing incoherently, syllables that aren't words. With strength something lent him, he pulls Anneke upside down, hangs her by her feet, her hands still cuffed to the wall. It's a bit too far, but he stretches her anyway. She grits her teeth, grunts. Manages not to shout.

95

Michael Rudnick calls her again.

Anneke left her wallet behind.

She's not the most organized person, so this seems typical.

And, since she only left him a few hours ago, it shouldn't raise red flags that she isn't answering.

But it does.

He calls Andrew.

96

Andrew hears her.

Barely.

More in his head than outside.

HEY!

It's enough.

He knows where she is.

Turns around.

The longest three-point turn in the history of wheeled vehicles.

The magic is so strong on the goddamned thing that it has started to look like a tractor again. He unconsciously goes to pass it, and then it turns chicken-legs and one of those legs lashes down at him, hooks his bumper, wrenches it just a little loose, but the bumper hangs on.

"FUCK!" he yells.

Fishtails a little, not like the SUV, not top heavy.

One tire hits and spits gravel, but he gets back on the road.

Gets ahead of it, stops.

It's coming.

Not all that fast, maybe twenty miles per hour?

He thinks about spinning a tree across its knobby knees, but the witch could boomerang it back at him. Without breaking a sweat. He's not sure he could stop the return volley.

And Anneke's in there.

"Fuck."

It comes on, hopping a little now.

Can he fight it here?

Can he fight *her* here?

On 104A from the front seat of his car?

Not well.

"COME ON!" he says. "COME ON OVER TO MY HOUSE! LET'S PLAY A GAME!"

He punches the accelerator, squeals his tires, races home.

97

His phone buzzes in his pocket.

He senses it's relevant, fishes it out, beaches it on the passenger seat.

Michael Rudnick's name.

Michael Rudnick's ringtone.

Queen's "We Will Rock You."

He answers.

"Yeah?"

"Everything okay?" the older man asks.

Andrew regrets answering.

Hates his choice, has to make it fast.

Protect Michael or protect Anneke.

Michael is not an easy man to lie to; the pause has already given it away.

And love speaks in imperatives.

"No. It's not okay."

98

The man who used to be Professor Coyle knows his duties.

Muster the troops, she had said. *They will know what to do. You guard the little witch, keep her there, mind the hut.*

He looks at the troops now.

Nine little burlap dolls.

A model tank.

Three plastic crew members, carefully painted.

On top of the tank, the smallest dead man he has ever seen, frozen behind the top hatch. She shrank him. On the side of the turret the Russian graffiti:

TIGER KILLER

The hut has almost walked to the house of the Thief.

The professor looks out the front window, sees the road bounce beneath him in the glow of the streetlights. In those houses, blurry houses without glasses to correct his myopia and astigmatism, blurry people are eating blurry dinners and squinting at television and doing other things he used to do before. But *before* is all over for him. An unmeltable wall of ice separates him from before. When he was warm. He knows he is making noise but he can't seem to stop, so he tries at least to do it rhythmically. He looks at the little witch. She looks up at him, like those lions Marlin Perkins used to dart on *Wild Kingdom*, able only to look at you, hate you, too drugged to move.

She is like that, and that's good. She kicks really hard. He wasn't even mad when she broke his tooth and glasses, just frustrated she didn't understand she was going to get both of them punished.

He gets frustrated with how blurry everything is, picks up one lens of his ruined glasses, holds it to his eye. Now the street is clear. He feels like a giant.

A cyclops.

The slave of a witch.

He says the witch's words.

Badly, through busted lips.

He thinks his jaw may be broken, too.

But pain is different now, pain's little cousin.

"Fu, fu, fu."

99

Andrew has minutes before the hut comes.

Two? Six? Not ten.

He drives the Mustang up the steep drive, turns left in front of his garage, drives over his herb garden, leaves the car behind the house.

Goes to the kitchen door.

Says words that will undo the magic locks he knows Salvador will have set. Sal greets him, anxious, pelvis tilted forward as though he wished he had a tail to tuck.

The Etch-a-Sketch scrawls *MICHAEL* and the stick-man points upstairs. Andrew grabs his shillelagh from above the fireplace, takes the stairs in twos, goes into his master bathroom, and finds Michael Rudnick wet in the tub, blinking, dazed.

He's wet because he jumped in the quarry to get here, grafted his escape tunnel to Andrew's.

"I hate that goddamned thing," he says. "I don't have to leave that way, do I?"

"The tub's the exception," Andrew says. "You just can't come in one door and go out the other."

Michael gets a good look at him with his white hair fanned out across his shoulders.

"'Bout time," he says. "You look good. You look like a grown-up."

Rudnick steps out, dripping, sloshes a plastic trash bag onto the floor, tears it open to produce an oiled leather backpack.

Hefts it.

Andrew goes to his library.

Takes an object from a box he has to reach through an old-style metal fan to get into.

A monkeyish little hand.

Puts this in his jacket pocket.

"Is that—?"

"Yep."

"Shit," Michael says.

"Shit," Andrew says, looking out the attic window.

"Yep," Michael agrees.

Snowflakes have begun sticking to the window and melting.

An unoccupied tractor is puttering up the drive.

It turns sideways, seems to keep coming sideways, against the direction of the turning wheels, and then the illusion fails and the men see a cabin on chicken's feet turning its way up the incline, the maples around it pulling back their branches or bending outright to let it pass.

Just as Michael warms up to try to petrify its legs, it ducks sideways, lopes across the lawn, disappears into the woods.

"Fuck," Andrew says.

"Yep."

100

"Wake up," the bearded man says, in Russian.

He says it to a burlap doll with button eyes.

The doll grows human eyes that blink, man-sized eyes disproportionate to its small head. Now little fingers sprout from its tied-off arms and it grasps handfuls of the man's sleeve, the sleeve stippled with blood from where he jabbed himself with sewing needles. The doll grows a mouth the size of an almond, black-lipped, its pink gums studded with vicious little teeth like a pike's teeth.

That's why I sprinkled fish scales on them.

The man winces in anticipation, vocalizes.

It takes a bite out of his arm.

An almond-sized bite.

Enough to make him whimper.

And bleed.

It spits out shirtsleeve.

It chews.

A tongue comes out of its head. He suffers it to lap at him; it clutches him almost tenderly, it is not unlike nursing. A thought from his days as a man occurs to him.

For thy desires are wolvish, bloody, starved, and ravenous.

He makes a sound like laughing.

There is no time for one and one. Call them all.

She is not in the hut, at least not all of her.

Just her voice, the horsefly in his brain.

"Wake up, wake up, wake up," he says, crying and laughing, gesturing like a mother calling children to come hear a story.

ALL!

He says it five more times.

Their outsized eyes blink in their burlap heads.

All looking at him.

The first one moves, then they all do.

They crawl to him, cover him.

He brays laughter to get through the pain.

His eyes watering and bugging.

This is hard, but he does it.

She will not punish him.

101

"There it is. I see it."

Michael is looking through a brass naval telescope from 1888.

Andrew can see Michael's breath.

"How far?"

"Hundred yards. Hundred and ten."

"Too far?"

"Yep. Twice too far for that. I'll have to wait till it comes closer. You sure she's in there? Anneke?"

"Yes," Andrew says.

Michael shakes his head a little.

Andrew looks over at Salvador, who holds night-vision binoculars flat against his portrait head, scanning the other side.

"Whoooa Nelly," Michael says.

"What?"

"Something's coming out of the window."

"Binoculars!" Andrew says, and Salvador crosses the attic with them.

Michael counts.

"Two, three-four. Six."

Andrew looks.

The hut is pitched forward, like a man getting sick.

He watches three burlap dolls fall from its eye window, like it's crying them. No, they're not falling. They're leaping.

"*Caprimulgus*. Go see," he says, and points at a stuffed nightjar. It gives itself a shake and a stretch, then just looks at him.

"Ah, right."

He opens the window.

Snow wisps in.

The bird flies off, churring and buzzing.

A moment later.

Andrew sees through the bird's eye.

It flies to the hut, peers through the window.

Anneke upside down, hanging like meat, all but asleep.

A torque on her neck.

I know that fucking thing.

I know what it's doing to her.

A madman bleeding, rocking himself, manacled. His skin gouged.

It doesn't take long to go nuts in there.

Don't lose your shit now, Blankenship, stay strong.

Higher power, help me.

Now the hut moves off.

Have to see what came out of it.

The bird flies from tree to tree now, scanning the ground.

Movement!

A man in military gear?

Soviet, 1940s.

The bird turns just in time to see a second man pointing a rifle.

The muzzle flashes.

"Ow FUCK I'm shot! I'm shot!"

Andrew falls to the ground, holding his eye, panicked.

Michael, who got away from the window and ducked at the sound of the gunshot, bends to him, pulls his hand away.

"Let me see."

The eye and face are whole.

"You're okay," Michael says. "Calm down. It's just the bird. Get the rest of the way out of the bird."

Andrew does.

Looks at Michael, who raises both eyebrows at him.

"Soviet soldiers. World War Two."

"Shit," Michael says.

"Yep."

102

Where the other neighbors hear a dog barking or a car horn, John Dawes hears a gunshot. He's about as luminous as a brick, but he has spent so much time at the gun range and on maneuvers with his World War II reenactor friends that he hears the sound as it is, magical or not.

He had been standing in front of the open refrigerator with mustard and a pack of hot dogs in his hand, scanning for relish. No relish, no hot dog. That's just how it goes. He had just caught sight of the jar, was in the process of gauging whether he could spoon out enough of the green sludge to properly coat a wiener, when he heard the *pop* of a 7.62-millimeter round.

So now he stands there, eyes wide.

He shuts the fridge door, kills the kitchen light.

Shakedown is barking in the yard.

Back and forth on his run.

Good boy!

Call the cops?

Hell with that, Fruitloop's already on the phone.

Fruitloop, the widowed lady next door who sets out no fewer than fifteen versions of the nativity on her lawn each Christmas, is actually watching today's recorded episode of *The Price Is Right* for the third time. She heard the gunshot as an extra-loud squeal of enthusiasm from the Iowa stewardess who just won a set of patio furniture.

Dawes grabs the loaded Luger he had duct-taped to the side of the fridge, goes upstairs as quickly as he can in the darkness, picking off tape, opens the door to the spare room he has converted into a sniper's roost and German militaria shrine. Kneels a few feet from the window, tucks the pistol in his waistband, picks up his *Liebling*, a German K98 sniper rifle with Hensoldt scope.

"That's it," he says. "Come to Johannes."

He scans the street.

Too dark to see much.

Couldn't bear to fit a modern night-vision scope to his vintage rifle.

Doesn't actually believe there's a problem—he's very much playing a game. Lots of people shoot things around here; it's just on the edge of farm country. He waits for a moment. Watches. Gets bored. Decides to go back downstairs and see about his hot dogs.

The light comes on.

He didn't flip the switch.

Someone else.

"Hunh!" he says, reaching for the pistol, drops it.

He hops a little, as if he expects it to go off.

Like in *Band of Brothers* when the guy shot himself in the leg.

Two highly authentic-looking Soviet soldiers stand before him, one in a sapper's steel breastplate. Both of them dirty and stinking of cigarettes. And gasoline? And lots and lots of sour sweat. One carries a Mosin-Nagant bolt-action rifle. The engineer a Tokarev pistol and a handheld bayonet.

A very sharp-looking bayonet dark from scrubbed-off rust.

Is that snow on their shoulders?

"Very funny," he says, thinking at first it's two guys from the Soviet team in his reenactor group. Then he's not so sure.

He's never seen these guys.

The one with the rifle looks rough.

Like he hasn't been eating so well.

And like he's shot people.

The one in the sapper's plate looks around at the room, enjoying himself. Smiling beneath his walrusy mustache.

Something catches his eye.

"*Shto eta?*" he says.

Dawes doesn't speak Russian, but the meaning is clear enough.

The man is tickling a poster with the edge of his bayonet.

What's this?

John Dawes has a lot of posters, and they've been hanging so long he doesn't much see them anymore. He sees this one now. The bayonet traces a blown-up cover of a Hitler Youth propaganda magazine called *Der Pimpf*, showing a German tank running over Polish cavalry.

Next the walrus-man looks at the poster next to it, a homoerotic masterpiece showing a brown-shirted, black-tied bohunk with blond televangelist hair and a swastika flag smiling unrepentantly, the legend reading *Der Deutsche Student kämpft für Führer und Volk!*

John hopes they don't look at the Russian-language poster showing a huge Jew leading Stalin and a Soviet soldier on a rope.

They do.

"*Ti shto fashistskoe gavno?*"

Dawes picks out the word *fascist.*

Correctly guesses the uncomplimentary nature of the second bit.

"*Ti anti-semit?*"

Remembers that nobody on the Soviet reenactor squad actually speaks Russian.

Some kind of fucking communists for real.

The snow on their helmets and coats has melted.

That was real snow what the fuck?

He looks at the only anachronistic poster in the room, a signed and framed poster of Rush Limbaugh wearing a powdered wig and tricornered hat.

Two if by Tea!

From Tea to shining Tea!

Original sweet tea.

No help.

Shakedown keeps barking.

Far, far away.

Like the pistol he dropped.

Now walrus picks up John's rifle.

John's Nazi rifle.

Nods and looks up at John Dawes.

Grins.

John pisses his pants.

103

Another gunshot.

This one from the west side of the house.

The high chipping sound of a bullet hitting glass.

"Salvador! Get away from the window."

Salvador does as he is told, but the bullet already hit its mark.

A perfect hole has appeared in the canvas, just over Dalí's left eye.

The automaton is unaffected, but the hole will have to be fixed before he takes dog form again.

"Go patch yourself."

Sal heads for the stairs, another bullet sailing through the window, hitting the wall near the stuffed owl.

Michael hunkers down, sweating despite the chill in the air.

Andrew pops up, steals another glance through his night-vision binocs.

"We've got three on this side."

Two muzzles flash in the darkness.

The bullets turn, striking bricks and plaster elsewhere in the room.

The Brazilian pendant around Andrew's neck glows warm.

He knows the charm can be overwhelmed if it's worked too hard; it has already saved him from at least four bullets.

"Let's wake up Buttercup."

Michael nods.

"Take cover."

Michael takes cover.

Andrew hunches low, goes to the window overlooking the front yard.

He stands erect now, well back from the window, in the shadows, but still they see him.

Bullets punch through the window, making the awful *pvvvvvt!* sound one hears when being shot at, a sound Andrew had been lucky enough never to hear before now. He counts two men in the tree line. Holds up two fingers at Michael, who has scooted himself behind an old plow blade.

It sparks once with a loud *P-TANG.*

Michael says two paragraphs in the Greek of Archimedes.

Andrew says a sentence in old French.

The vacuum-cleaner beast rears the roosterish brass head at the end of its tube neck, flaps its vulture wings, knocking off its covering sheet. Flexes its chimpanzee arms. Its neck turns, letting it focus its eyes at Andrew.

The lenses rotate.

Shit, is it going to attack?

No, just looking at its master.

"*Allez!*"

It flaps harder.

Its vacuum motor runs.

It lurches forward, busts out the north window, toward the lake, then turns. Bullets strike it, do it little harm.

Snow blows into the attic behind it.

It steers toward the shooter.

Its eyes flash and something in the tree line bursts into flames.

Screams.

The screaming stops.

Three more bullets whine toward Andrew, one of them from the Dawes house across the street, and all three are turned.

The chain holding the pendant breaks; the pendant falls off, its magic exhausted.

Andrew drops to the floor as the fourth bullet hits brick behind him.

Michael finishes another verse in Greek.

Andrew adds a verse in German to this.

In the front yard, the sound of a long-dead Mustang's engine turning over.

Now the ground rumbles.

The stuffed birds on their shelf and the terrarium with the replica house shudder, too.

The magi have started a small earthquake.

Buttercup is waking up.

104

Kolya and Vanya kneel in the snowy patch of woods near the house.

The woman came to them as they drew playing cards against each other in an improvised game involving making up insults for each other's mother and sisters ("My king of spades says your three of clubs was poked down your mother's throat by the lieutenant's cock.") while the tanks took fuel. She sat next to them, shared vodka with them. Told them if they would come with her, they could get out of the coming fight with the Germans. All they would have to do is to kill an American for her.

"It will not be easy," she had said. "He is a wizard and has many tricks. You may die. But I picked you from a list of the dead; I know for a fact that you *will* die if you go to fight the Germans. Kolya, you will be shot by a sniper while taking a piss. Vanya, an eighty-eight-millimeter shell will land so close to you that no part of you will be found and known to be you."

Vanya had been troubled by a recurrent dream in which the sun came down next to him and burned him up completely. Nobody could find him, not even his mother walking the field with an icon of Jesus.

Kolya hated pissing precisely because he was terrified of snipers.

It was as though she had seen into both of their hearts.

"What about the Germans?" Vanya had said.

"Leave them to my friend Frost," she answered. A white wolf with bony ribs moved between trees, and then Vanya was not sure he had seen it. "Russia will be Hitler's graveyard even without you."

"Will I be able to piss without fear? Will you promise me that I will not be shot while pissing?" Kolya asked.

She had nodded.

So they agreed and the three of them drank vodka with a drop of blood in it to seal the bargain.

The next thing they had known, they dreamed they were tiny children with rough skin, and they were hungry, so they ate mouthfuls of flesh from a man.

And then they were jumping from a hut that was actually a truck except it walked on legs.

And now they are here, together.

Shooting up into a house.

Kolya shot a strange bird that was looking at them.

Vanya thought he shot a man, had him right in his sights, squeezed the trigger patiently, and felt the sweet thrill a well-placed shot produces, but the man went unharmed.

To their right, a Russian bursts into flames, screams.

To their left, an engine tries to start, then does start.

The ground rumbles.

Like an armored column passing, but harder.

"My God," Vanya says.

Kolya points his rifle, but it seems useless in his hands.

The headlamps of a strange wrecked car have switched on in the front yard, just to their left. Another Soviet soldier they do not know has been sheltering behind a large rock near the car, firing up into the attic.

Now the car's hood becomes a mouth.

A steer's iron mouth.

The soldier jumps back, startled.

Quick, like a fox eating a mouse, the car clamps down on the man, crushing him.

The car becomes the head of a giant made of tree, tree roots, boulders, and other cars.

This giant grows horns.

Bull's horns.

It is a man of metal. Stone and wood with a huge longhorn's skull made of iron.

Headlamps for eyes.

It rips itself out of the ground, leaving a hole the size of a small basement.

Raining dirt and small rocks.

A rusty truck splits itself into pieces, becomes armor plating.

A Greek hoplite's armor, greaves, abdomen plate, armored skirt, and all, wraps in two seconds around the body of wood and stone and steel.

The man still dangles from its mouth.

It spits him out.

It is as tall as the house.

What lands on the yard is not a man, but a lifeless doll.

No bigger than a cat.

Buttons for eyes.

105

"Jesus Christ," Andrew says, the headlamps level with the attic, sweeping the attic with light. "It's fucking Buttercup."

"Yep," Michael Rudnick says, grinning.

He stops grinning as they watch the Soviet soldier fall from the bull's mouth, his neck on wrong.

I drove that car into a tree with Sarah in it.

Drunk I'm worthless I should die.

Stop it!

Focus!

You're a warlock now.

Look what you made!

You have to stop the witch.

Save Anneke.

Andrew says, "Buttercup."

It looks at him, robes him in light.

"Kill the soldiers. Break the hut's legs."

The lights sweep off, illuminating snowflakes as the minotaur heads for the tree line, the ground shaking at its steps.

106

Vanya shoots it, shoots one of its headlamps out, but it keeps coming. It bends for a log. It sees Kolya frozen in fear, quite near it. Squashes him with the log as easily as a man would kill a toad, squashes him down into the soil. Kolya is gone entirely. Vanya runs into thick forest, away from the giant.

Something trips him.

The tail of a dragon?

Attached to a vacuum cleaner?

Now a brass-and-metal beaked head turns to look at him, great black wings spreading.

He tries to point his rifle, but its eyes flash.

I'm burning!

The pain is immeasurable.

Then he isn't burning.

He's running through a field of sunflowers, running at a German artillery position.

A cacophony of noise around him, but he feels great relief.

It's so good not to be burning that he laughs, still running.

Then he hears the whine.

An eighty-eight-millimeter shell drawing nearer.

It's coming for me, right at me!

He flings himself to the ground.

Still the whine grows louder.

He knows it will land almost on him, seems to see the shadow of it growing on the spot exactly near his head where it will punch into soil and sunflowers and explode.

He will be mixed with sunflowers.

Time for one last thought.

Sunflowers. This isn't so bad.

Kolya huddles, mad with fear, when the giant bull comes for him.

It raises its huge tree trunk.

It's going to crush me! Help! Help!

But then he isn't in a snowy yard outside a rich man's house getting crushed by a giant bull-man.

Now he is standing, wiener in hand, urinating on a low stone wall near a collapsed farmhouse.

"Ah," he says, relieved to feel his bladder emptying.

Relaxed.

Suddenly Kolya feels pressure in his head, massive pressure.

Can't see anymore.

Hears the rifle's crack.

Ow!

Sniper!

Kolya feels himself falling in a muted way, as if someone else is falling.

He hears his friends returning fire into the tree line.

A mile away and receding.

He manages to say one last sentence.

"This bitch lies."

107

Andrew scoots to the other end of the attic, risks a peek.

The minotaur has crossed behind the house, drawing rifle fire from the soldiers on the west side. A grenade lands near it and goes off, blowing off part of one greave, causing it to bleed oil and limp. But it knocks down trees and bellows, flushing the soldier who threw the grenade so the vacuum-cockatrice flies down on him. Its fire magic is exhausted, but it grabs him with its chimp arms and flies him into a tree until his head caves in and he, too, reverts into a lifeless burlap doll.

Exhausted, Electra collapses next to the doll and lies still.

Now Buttercup sweeps its remaining headlight over the backyard again, letting its light fall on a tractor.

As soon as the beam hits it, the tractor changes into the hut on chicken legs.

The minotaur gives chase.

Back around to the front yard.

Andrew follows the action, peeking out the front window now, Michael Rudnick next to him, drawing one missed shot from the sniper's roost at the Dawes house.

This starts Shakedown barking again.

"We need to take care of that," Andrew says.

Michael nods.

"You have something?"

"I was saving it," Andrew says, "but, yeah."

He puts a finger down his throat.

Regurgitates a golf-ball-sized chicken's eye onto the oak floorboards.

It floats up, hovers, blinks at Andrew.

Heads across the lawn toward the Dawes house.

108

Anneke wakes up from an awful dream about a snake on her mouth into an equally disturbing dream in which a teetering hut is being knocked down by a giant.

She is in the hut.

Hanging suspended, upside down.

Things slide across the floor, fly up, banging into her.

A bucket busts her lip.

Pain in her shoulder.

The hut has lurched, fallen sideways; she has careened with it, her cuffed arms and feet jerking her short.

The beardy man has fallen, too, yelping as coals from the stove scatter around the hut.

He grunts and puts these out with his hands.

109

Andrew sees Buttercup intercept the hut; the chase was almost comical.

But now he concentrates on the eye.

Eagle's eye could have done it from here.

He guides it near, nearer.

Puts his own vision into it.

Sees them.

Two Russians, two rifles.

One in some kind of steel breast-gear.

Big mustache.

They lie side to side.

Close enough.

This spell is old Slavic forest magic.

He says "Strike!" in medieval Russian.

The men both look up at the eye, more in wonder than fear.

They have their helmets off, so he gets to see their hair stand up on end.

Bright flash!

Now his sight switches dizzyingly back into his own head; he sees the lightning bolt originate from the chicken's eye, incinerating it, leaping down into the two soldiers, lighting Dawes's curtains on fire.

Thunder cracks and booms.

He knows both men are dead.

He is blind in his right eye, as if it has stared at the sun.

Believes his sight will return, but isn't sure.

110

In the yard, the hut has fallen.

The chicken's legs scrabble ineffectually at the minotaur.

It grabs one, breaks it over its knee.

"Buttercup," Andrew says.

It stops with the broken leg in its hands, like a woman interrupted in the business of dressing a hen for the oven.

"Get Anneke out safely. Bring her here."

Now it peels part of the roof back.

Peers in.

Another flash.

Starting in the woods.

BANG!

The minotaur's right shoulder explodes, the arm turning back into tree, rocks, car parts, raining down the steep driveway.

Buttercup falls on its huge ass, its weight causing the house to shudder.

It struggles to get to its feet, wanting to use the missing arm, falling heavily, getting back up to its knees.

The hut, too, tries to stand.

It manages.

Holds its broken leg up, hops to the tree line.

The minotaur is almost up.

BANG!

The shell catches it in the throat, blowing its head up and off.

The whole monstrosity turns back into cars and boulders, some of this airborne.

"Oh shit," Andrew says.

He and Rudnick both drop, cover their heads with their hands.

The old Mustang, on fire, flips end over end, clips the top of the house off, exposing stars and sky and letting in cold air.

Debris rains down on them.

And snow.

Andrew looks back into the yard.

The T-34 tank grumbles out from behind a stand of maples, exhaust farting behind it.

"You okay?" Andrew says.

"Think so. You?"

"Yeah."

Andrew finds the night-vision binoculars, looks at the tank.

Two figures ride its turret, shielded behind its round hatches.

A very dead man, grinning a skeletal smile.

And a woman wearing a Soviet general's cap and wool coat.

His long-ago lover, Marina Yaganishna.

From that awful season in Russia.

From the witch's hut.

Her smallest, most traumatized daughter.

The one who freed him.

She's not here to help you now.

The turret swivels.

111

Michael Rudnick looks up into the sky through the new hole in the roof.

Parts of the roof burn, but these snuff themselves out quickly thanks to the fireproofing spells Andrew cornered the house with.

Michael has a very powerful spell bottled up, and thinks it's time.

He fingers an oddly shaped piece of iron hanging around his neck by a leather thong.

He scans the sky, trying both to see and feel.

Feels several, mostly too small, one too big.

This has to be Goldilocks.

And he has to be fast.

And lucky.

Hears the tank fire again.

BAM!

Feels the house rock, start to sag, knows the living room was blown in, one load-bearing wall.

Interrupts the spell he was working on, now feels where the shell hit; he can't help the lost furniture and electronics, but he opens his palms like a conductor, causes the blown-out bricks and wood to readhere—the house jolts and rights itself.

He sees a stuffed owl animate and fly out the window.

Good—Andrew's up to something.

He glances at the other wizard, sees him fish a pill out of his shirt pocket, dry-swallow it.

He's holding together.

Andrew has stronger magic than Michael—the minotaur was mostly him, mostly car-magic.

But weaker character.

They might win if Andrew doesn't lose his shit.

The tank fires again, but Michael is ready for it: The house shudders, but the fragments from the shell don't blow out two yards before the structure seems to inhale it all back in. Like an incendiary rose blooming and unblooming in the blink of an eye with an echo like rolling thunder. The fires started by the blast wink out in less than two seconds.

A woman swears viciously in Russian.

They know they can't knock the house down.

Now they'll shoot high.

At us.

If it hits the attic, we're hamburger.

He looks at the sky again.

Snow falling, but no clouds.

Feels what he wants.

Exactly the one he wants, just the right size, as near as he can tell.

Oh, this will be dangerous.

This will be the hardest thing he's ever done.

He did it once in the Arizona desert, but there weren't houses nearby, precision wasn't the issue.

He calls it.

Andrew sends the owl and pops a Klonopin.

Where is Sal? Is Sal okay?

The shelling is getting to him.

Two direct hits on the house.

They won't survive a third.

Killing the tank is on Andrew.

His nerves are frazzled.

Everything is happening at once.

Marina is atop the tank, pointing at the attic.

The gun elevates.

Andrew says "Get down!" to Michael, who appears to be stargazing.

Michael keeps looking up, his mouth moving.

What the fuck is he doing?

Hurry, owl.

Andrew drops to the floor, covers his head, puts his eyesight in the owl.

Now he sees the yard, the tank.

The bird flies toward it, slowly, struggling to carry the vase.

The tank is going to fire.

I could look at the attic, watch myself die.

No, fly faster, fucking owl.

FASTER!

Then he sees it.

With his owl eyes.

It comes from the constellation of Cassiopeia. It tumbles slowly at first, seems to turn, then hurtles at great speed, fiery, smoking, almost too fast to see.

Throwing mad shadows.

It's big, big enough to make it through the atmosphere.

Because it's real, many see it.

It gets wished on by no less than four thousand people.

Let my mother's surgery go well.

Let me get into Yale.

Keep my love safe in Kabul.

Please please please let Stargate listen to my demo.

Make him ask me to marry him.

Please don't let this be malignant.

I wish for Stephanie Daley to kiss me back with tongue.

OH PLEASE CRUSH THE FUCK OUT OF THAT TANK!

(that one's Andrew)

The witch atop the tank turns, sees the meteor coming, spreads a hand at it. Manages to split it so it falls not in one television-sized hunk, but in several the size of footballs and baseballs. Manages to slow them so they don't vaporize the tank.

She's awfully strong.

But she can't stop it.

Them.

One piece hits the turret, stuns the dead gunner, the Soviet driver made from a plastic model-man.

Knocks the witch off.

Another piece knocks the left track and two roller wheels off the T-34.

One misses, fells a small tree.

The noise is ungodly.

The meteor doesn't destroy the tank, but it does beat the holy hell out of it.

It does buy some time.

For the owl.

The huge horned owl wings toward the tank, clutching the vase in its talons. It barely makes it there; the vase is heavy and its talons aren't made for carrying such things. It drops the vase whole, hears it pop, turns so Andrew can use its eyes to see the yellow glass stones the vase held glittering all over the hull.

Up in the attic, Andrew shouts the word.

"Bhastrika!"

WHUMP!

A fireball the size of a pasha's tent mushrooms up over the tank, lighting parts of the woods on fire, lighting the owl on fire, illuminating the snow that has begun to collect in the yard.

Andrew comes back to himself, shakes the arm he thought was a wing on fire, collects himself, looks out the window with Michael.

The fire's glow on the snow makes him think of Christmas lights, and then the thought goes as quickly as it came.

This is one fucked-up Christmas.

A blackened skeleton is crawling out of a burning tank in his front yard.

A blackened skeleton on fire.

Coming toward the house.

The remaining three Soviet soldiers forming up behind it.

Rushing the house!

Michael, still stunned from calling the meteor, braces himself against the wall, points down the attic ladder.

Andrew goes down to meet the attack.

112

Marina Yaganishna's ears are ringing and her general's cap lies in the snow. The tank is burning, illuminating the maple trunks and the light dusting of snow, vomiting gouts of oily black smoke skyward. A flash of misplaced nostalgia strikes her, but she shakes this off along with the snow on her back and shoulders.

Shooting now at the front of the house.

Pop pop-pop.

"Moroz," she says.

He appears. Not a lovely, bearded boy anymore, but a man with snow-white hair and the bluish skin of the dead by freezing.

He has found a pair of red polyester track pants.

His bare feet are missing toes.

The Pac-Man shirt persists.

She looks into his white eyes, eyes that look cataracted but are not.

"He will kill the soldiers," she says. "And then Misha will kill him. Or not. Either way, get into the house while he's doing it."

Moroz nods, turns to go.

"Wait. Is there a well?"

Moroz tilts his head like a dog.

"A well?"

Moroz considers.

Yes. Shall I freeze it?

"No! Show me where it is."

Moroz points.

She turns and walks that way, saying, without looking back.

"Make it colder."

113

Andrew comes down the stairs with his shillelagh pointed before him.

"Buckler," he says, and now a concave circle of slightly blurred and bluish air moves before him, the size of a large shield.

They're shooting through the door.

He crouches as he comes down, fitting himself behind the shield.

The shield sparks and hisses where bullets strike it, but this is different from the bullet-turning charm. He has to wield this. It has advantages, though. It stops more than bullets. Which is a good thing because one of them has thrown a grenade—the door blows in, spraying him with high-velocity oak splinters and just a few hooks of metal shrapnel. One of these clips his leg, which had been sticking out.

The buckler stops so much matter that it hisses like water in hot oil, smoke blurring his vision for an instant.

He takes three pennies from the pouch around his neck.

His hands trembling.

He wills them to stop.

One soldier shoots around the door while the burning, black skeleton and two other men charge through.

His shield lights up where bullets skid against it.

He squeezes himself as small as he can behind it.

Dragomirov!

Do you like jazz?

He throws the pennies.

Now all the trapped trumpet-sound comes out at once, blowing the skeleton apart and out the door, concussing one man up against the wall so hard he bites through his tongue, his back snaps, and he turns into a little burlap doll.

Andrew runs into the kitchen, pointing the walking stick behind him.

He shuts the door.

Follow, follow!

Ducks behind the island.

Looks back, making sure the side door behind him is locked and sound.

A boot kicks the other door down.

He pops up, projecting the unsolid shield half over the island, flicks a penny.

Sound erupts from it.

Not enough to kill, but it knocks the two men down and deafens the first, cracks the door frame, blows a still life of pears and a copper bowl off the wall.

(He liked that painting)

He swears.

A Russian swears.

The deafened man goes to his knees.

The other man stands, shoots, ineffectively.

Charges Andrew with bayonet.

A barrel-chested, hairy miner from the Caucasus, he stabs the shield and wrenches it aside.

This breaks the spell.

Fuck!

TO-RO-RO-RO-RO!

The Caucasian is winding up to bayonet Andrew's chest when Andrew opens his mouth very wide and vomits a half dozen tavern darts into the soldier's face at great velocity. Lethal velocity, in fact. Only the ends of the darts are visible, the one that went into the eye gone entirely, its point through the other side of his skull. The man jerks twice and falls, leaving only a darted doll with a smear of blood on the hardwood floor.

Fuckfuckfuck

The second man is coming, shaking his head but coming.

Worse; dead, smoldering, black Dragomirov lurches into view behind him.

Andrew turns and unbolts the side kitchen door.

The soldier and the revenant enter the kitchen.

Follow, follow!

The soldier begins to raise his gun.

No amulet, no shield.

"*Manganese!*" the magus yells.

His rolling drawers and several cabinets slam open.

The air blurs with flying metal.

Something wrenching and awful happens in Andrew's mouth.

He does something between spitting, sneezing, and retching.

The sound of a weird, metallic collision just precedes the rifle shot,

SCRAAANG-BANG!

both painfully loud in the closed space, but the shot goes high, smashing bowls in a cabinet.

The big miner comes apart, ruined utterly, ruined past description.

The kitchen is an abattoir.

Every knife, fork, cleaver, spoon, pan, pot, and other loose piece of metal in the kitchen shot at the two intruders as if from a cannon. Even a couple of door hinges. Even a faucet handle and a drain sieve.

Andrew tastes blood.

Three of his teeth lost their fillings, but one tooth, top left, preferred to detach from the gum, shot at the things also, tearing his lip on the way out.

There is no time even to spit.

Once-Dragomirov is still coming, still smoking from the tank fire, untroubled by the flea-market-table's worth of implements and fixtures skewering him.

An eight-inch kitchen knife (J. A. Henckels, the flagship of Andrew's cutlery drawer) has wedged in its mouth like a gossip's bit. The wiry remains of a whisk and a mangled colander have married themselves to the architecture of Dragomirov's spine. A paring knife juts rakishly from its skull. A pot removed most of its teeth and a cast-iron skillet relieved it of an arm, but the teeth are mustering again and the arm is already wobbling in the fruit bowl, preparing to reattach itself.

The dead man comes on.

An accident saves the wizard.

Otherwise Andrew would not have gotten the door open.

But he does.

Dragomirov slips on the soggy burlap doll the wrecked soldier morphed into.

Grabs a fistful of Andrew's hair on the way down.

Andrew hits it with his shillelagh.

The magic in it makes it strike twice as hard as the wielder swings it. It busts the dead man's jaw, frees the Henckel.

Andrew grabs this with his free hand.

Cuts the hair held by the skeletal fist.

Opens the door.

Snow flies in.

He runs out the door, blood-spattered, cane and kitchen knife ready.

The skeleton shakes itself like a dog, shedding metalware.

Already re-forming.

Andrew might have run, but he turns now to face it, where it stands silhouetted in the doorway like a Balinese puppet.

Follow.

It takes a decisive step toward Andrew.

"That is not the way you came in, sir," Andrew pants.

This is my house, and you must exit the same way you entered.

The corpse falls, keeps falling, as if through a hole in the earth.

But there is no hole.

And there is no corpse.

Not here.

114

The attic.

Snow falling in.

Tracks in the snow from where Michael Rudnick left his post by the front window.

More about him in a moment.

The terrarium with the tiny model of the necromancer's house shivers.

The side door, the kitchen door, opens.

A very small, charred skeletal figure falls from the door.

Falls on the mound of earth beneath the house.

Misha Dragomirov's reanimated corpse stands, with difficulty.

Where did the Thief go?

His lover's daughter woke him, told him to avenge his son.

He cranes his head up, a pair of kitchen scissors falling from his neck.

Is that the house up there?

Something moves near Dragomirov.

Coming across the loose soil.

The size of a dog, a big dog, but not a dog.

The light is poor, but it's reddish.

Something moves over its head.

Antennae?

An insect.

An ant.

A big, big ant.

Something inside Dragomirov's shell is almost afraid.

I am dead, big fucking ant, you cannot kill me!

The ant doesn't seem to understand this.

It bites at him with its mandibles; it is very strong but so is he.

He digs his feet into the soil as best he can, laughing a raspy laugh, holding the mandibles like a bully stopping a boy on his bike.

It arches its abdomen; it wants to sting him.

But it can't!

This is almost fun.

Then he sees the next one.

The imported fire ant.

Solenopsis invicta.

Common to the American South, accidentally brought up in the 1920s on fruit boats from its native South America, it doesn't like cold. But this nest is doing all right in its climate-controlled attic terrarium, periodically fed crickets and moths and chanted over by a magus.

The first worker finds a strange, burnt bug it can't quite get its jaws around or arch its abdomen up to envenom. Their struggles move soil, of course, so the others come. Several hundred others. They don't know what laughter is, so the sound the bug makes as they swarm it means nothing to them. They don't understand Russian, or insults, let alone Russian insults, so what it says about their mothers (not knowing they all have one mother, nor that her promiscuous egg-laying allows little time for the activities he suggests she enjoys) goes unappreciated. The venom has little effect on it, but they find themselves well able to rip it apart. Its pieces try to lurch away from them; they've never experienced that before, but eventually they get all of it down to the late-stage larvae who manage to digest it.

Not much meat on it.

In fact, "Not much meat on me, bastards!" is the last thing it says.

Just the head and a section of spine.

Then that is broken up, too.

And the magic in it sputters and dies.

115

Moroz goes to the west side of the house, where the two big windows of the family room overlook the woods.

The windows the Thief first saw him from.

Now another face peers at him through one of these.

An old man.

The stone warlock.

Powerful, but less so than the Thief.

He is not permitted to kill the Thief—that honor is for the witch—but this man is fair game.

Let's see how strong you are!

Moroz walks up to the window, knowing how hideous he looks.

The old man just watches him.

Frost has formed on the windowpane.

Moroz writes on this with his finger.

ARE YOU READY

Before he can write the rest, the old man puts a toothpick in his mouth—a toothpick!—and walks away from him. Just walks to the window on the other side of the fireplace.

Moroz becomes one with the snow from which he is made and appears in front of the other window.

TO FREEZE TO DEATH?

he writes, but even as he dots the question mark, the old wizard disappears. Moroz senses something behind him, re-forms himself facing backward. The American boy-host he inhabited dies a little more every time he abuses the body like this, but his work here is nearly done.

It is not the old wizard that he sees.

Now he sees a little stop-motion figure popular in the Soviet Union.

A fuzzy little figure with large ears, supposedly an undocumented tropical forest creature fond of oranges.

How many times had he watched children's television through the window and seen this little thing?

What was its name?

"Cheburashka!" it says in a childish voice, in Russian, eating an orange. "You made it very, very cold," it says sadly, lowering its head. "But can you really freeze me to death?"

Moroz grins, and the stand of trees behind Cheburashka grows icicles. A squirrel tries to run from its knothole den and cracks as it freezes solid, falls from its branch.

"Very sad," Cheburashka says. "But that was just a squirrel. You should try harder if you want to be my friend. Do you?" It offers Moroz its stop-motion orange.

Something about this strikes Moroz as familiar, but he never knows which memories are his and which are the street-boy's.

Moroz breathes in.

Breathes out hard.

Frost, snow, and ice shavings blow from his mouth.

The trees get so cold they grow brittle.

Branches fall.

Animals crack and die.

"I guess we can't be friends," the little creature says sadly, dropping its orange. Now it produces a pipe, lights it with a finger. "This belongs to a crocodile. Gena. *He* is my friend, even if you are not."

Moroz can't freeze the beast.

But perhaps he can rend it.

First he must stop making the blizzard.

Cheburashka draws on his pipe, which glows an animated glow.

Moroz tries to shut his mouth and stop blowing frost but finds that he can't.

His mouth is stuck open.

The little creature is drawing snow out of him!

As Cheburashka breathes in, the essence of Moroz begins to jet out.

He vomits snow, so much snow that he blankets the side yard.

Still the creature smokes, tittering just a little, quite cheerful.

Streetlights flicker on Willow Fork Road.

The snow falls and falls.

Moroz shudders, almost empty.

No longer blue.

His hair black again.

Mostly boy now, but enough of Moroz remains to hear.

Cheburashka points the stem of its pipe at him, cocking an eyebrow.

Its voice is different now.

It is Stalin's voice.

"You and I are alike in that we both respect our boundaries. You can't harm the wizard. I can't harm the witch. But nobody said a thing about you."

Moroz recognizes it now.

They have met before.

Moroz says its true name.

Cheburashka draws one more puff from the pipe.

Exhales.

The pipe glows bright and hot in the moppet's mouth.

The shadow of a thrashing squid on the snow behind him.

Moroz is no more.

116

The caveman wakes up under his overpass.

He had a dream about a woman.

She gave him twenty dollars.

(Lying under the brick he uses to smash cans)

She took away his tinnitus.

(It's still gone)

And then?

Blurry.

But at the end, the Heat Miser character from the Christmas special carried him like a bride.

Carried him from some hellish North Pole, where the elves had button eyes and bloody mouths.

But he's in Syracuse now.

At the end of summer.

A warm night.

It's ten minutes ago.

He knows that somehow.

The Heat Miser gets to play with time.

Because he's the Heat Miser.

It's ten minutes ago, but no different than any other time, as far as he can tell.

He's still a caveman.

Cars and trucks rush above him as they always have, as they always will.

Bled-out urban sky above the overpass.

He is sick of the city.

He wishes he were somewhere where he could watch the stars.

He sees one, though.

A falling star, quite bright.

He wishes on it.

My name is Victor.

117

Michael Rudnick collects himself at the window.

Nausea hit him seconds after he tugged the meteor down.

No time for this.

Get your shit together, Rudnick.

Hears the fight downstairs, feels the building rock as the Russian grenade blows the front door in.

He needs to get downstairs, even though the meteor strike took everything out of him.

It was a big spell, maybe too big.

He's out of gas, doesn't feel capable of levitating a grain of sand.

Rifle fire cracks loudly just downstairs.

Andrew.

He's alone.

More concussions downstairs, a sound like Gabriel's trumpet blaring.

Quite suddenly his head feels like it has a horseshoe in it.

He moves through the snowy attic, makes his way to the ladder.

The first step is all right, but then he can't make his right arm or leg work so well, and he half slides, half falls down to the hardwood hall floor.

Hears something coming from the master bedroom.

The bathtub?

He looks at the door handle, but it looks blurry.

Manages to stand, but it's hard.

An old-fashioned telephone rings in Andrew's bedroom; he hears the sound of a door bursting open below.

I have to get in there.

Half of his body just isn't taking orders.

And his head.

Christ, his head.

The telephone rings again.

Someone smashes the phone.

Below, another trumpet-scream that shakes the house.

An iron candleholder in the shape of a woman's open hand falls from the wall, leaving a hole bisecting a savage crack in the plaster.

My head!

The myth of Athena's birth occurs to him, and he thinks himself well capable of pushing an armored woman out of his temple.

Shooting.

Andrew!

Michael Rudnick stands up just in time to see the bedroom door handle turn.

The door opens on a woman in military gear.

Athena?

No.

Baba's daughter.

She pulls a belt like a dead snake from around her neck.

She is as surprised as he is, braces herself to receive or cast a spell.

Michael Rudnick is a warlock to be reckoned with, and she knows it.

Not everyone can crank a blistering-fast meteor out of the sky and smash a tank with it.

And nobody can do it without paying a price.

Michael tries to say the word to make the sconce fly up and brain her, but when he speaks a garbled sound comes out.

They both understand at once.

Stroke.

I've had a stroke.

And not a small one.

I'm a dead man.

She smiles.

Not unkindly.

Pulls him firmly to the bathroom.

She works against his weak side.

He can't fight her.

An awkward moment as she negotiates the ailing magus through the bathroom door, the saber on her belt tangling them up. He tries to claw at her face with his good hand, but she is stronger.

She would like to take her time and experience this, look into his eyes as it happens to him; this is a rare thing.

But the Thief.

She will settle things with the Thief.

She has Michael against the tub now.

She says the name of a place, pushes the old man down into the tub.

He hears the name of the place.

He doesn't want to go there.

It's warm there, and it smells like trees and plants in flower.

He falls.

Looking at her all the way down.

118

What happens next isn't very gratifying.

No climactic collision of shapeshifting witch and wizard.

It just happens.

An older man with long white hair and a bomber jacket walks out into the yard, steering for the woods, looking for the hut with the broken leg.

A tank burns.

Bloody dolls, pieces of car, strange rocks litter the snow.

He wants to find the woman he loves.

The new witch.

He sees the hut, lying lopsided, leaning against a tree.

Out of gas.

A bearded madman looks out the window at him, holding a lens up to one eye.

This distracts him.

The magus doesn't see *her* until it's too late.

Coming at him from his blinded right side.

The witch.

Grinning at him.

Unkindly.

Showing her teeth.

Coming at him with the saber upraised.

He has something in his pocket that might or might not stop her heart, but it's too late to pull it out.

He vomits his last mouthful of darts at her.

But she has hardened her skin and they bend their points or shatter altogether.

The blade still comes.

He knows that saber.

It's the one he used on her mother.

On her.

He understands in a flash.

Marina never showed her teeth when she smiled.

The smile is her mother's smile.

Self-satisfied, superior, predatory.

A wolf's snarl.

This *is* Baba Yaga.

She has taken her own daughter's body.

As she always does.

As she always has.

His lover is long dead.

But her body is still strong.

The saber flashes in the streetlamp's glow.

Strangely suburban light to fall on a cavalry saber.

Coming down at his neck.

He remembers his shillelagh.

Sketches the gesture of raising it.

Too late.

It hurts.

Then it doesn't.

119

"She decapitated you. On the second stroke. The first was rather . . . messy. Happily, there wasn't a great deal of time between them. She's quite fast. Must be all the kettlebells."

Andrew is sitting in his library

With what body?

speaking with an old British actor, perhaps Sir Alec Guinness, perhaps Sir Laurence Olivier, maybe even Sir Ian McKellen. It seems to morph between them. It sits in a leather chair. Legs crossed at the knee. It wears a yellow carnation and exquisite saddle-brown oxfords.

Argyle socks at the ankles.

Ichabod.

What now?

"Oh, you'll like this. This will be most gratifying. Get into this egg."

So saying, the old thespian smiles and holds up a large, brown hen's egg.

Why?

"First of all, because you haven't any alternative, have you? None you'd enjoy, at least. Secondly, because it will have a delightful resonance. An echo, if you will. She murdered you with the same saber you tried to destroy her with. Now I shall teach you a trick perfected by one of her compatriots. What the generation behind yours calls a *frenemy*. Of course, these usually become enemies. I sense you preparing to ask who Baba Yaga's frenemy was, so save your strength. A fellow named Koschey. He used to hide his death far away from his body so you couldn't properly kill him. He used to hide it in an egg. You're a sort of echo of him, you know. Of Koschey. You have the same birthday, the same way of walking. Even the same slight tilt to your eyes, his a soupçon of Tartar, yours Shawnee. An echo is a very important thing; symmetry and repetition are the very knees of science and magic and creation. Creation is binary."

He summoned you, too.

"Yes, he did. Most effectively. He bade me destroy a certain witch for him. The problem was, she commanded me not to harm her. Most effectively. You'll understand the distress that caused me, being bound in contradictory directions. Unfulfilled commands don't sit well with my sort. Perhaps it's the closest thing we feel to guilt. In either event . . ."

You knew. About all of this. And you used me. To finish things with her.

"Quite so. Have I vexed you? On second thought, I withdraw the question as immaterial. It doesn't matter if I have vexed you."

The distinguished old actor strikes a match, lights a pipe.

Ichabod. Go help Anneke.

"I'm afraid I don't take orders from you anymore."

Why not?

It looks at him as if at a disappointing student.

"Because you're dead."

The entity smiles a winning smile.

"Now get into the egg or I take you to hell."

120

The woman who used to be Marina Yaganishna stands in the library of the necromancer's house. She hasn't really been Marina since 1983, of course, when she cast the soul from her betraying daughter and began to live as her. The daughter who freed the Thief. The pretty but weak one with the mole. Baba took her body from her and made that body strong.

Now the ancient witch looks at the library in which the Thief kept the books he stole from her.

The Book of Sorrows.

Love Spells of the Magyars.

On Becoming Invisible.

On the Mutability of the Soul and How Best to Survive Death.

She found her hand, too, the withered Hand of Glory that takes life.

It was in the Thief's jacket pocket, as if it were a wallet or a bunch of keys!

He respected nothing. This is an American disease.

And now he lies in the melting snow with a coat of ravens barking over him, fighting over his eyes.

The police will come soon, she knows, but they will be easy to charm away; she is good at charming, almost as good as a vampire.

She will need to fill a sack, take what she wants, burn the rest.

She already destroyed the tub in the Thief's bathroom so the old man could not return.

She will burn the professor in the hut.

She will burn the new witch, too.

Baba drained the new witch close to death to make herself stronger for the fighting, to power the hut and the doll-soldiers without compromising her own strength. As she used to drain the Thief, and many others.

Now she gets nothing from her—she is unconscious or dead.

She will also burn the stick-man with the painting for a head.

It whimpers in the Thief's bedroom and will not leave. She thought about destroying it, but it is a harmless thing, good for fetching and spying, but unable to think for itself. She will take it apart and smell its magic out before she burns it, though—it is a good spell, one she is unfamiliar with.

The library is safe now.

Various booby traps sprung at her; a drill broke itself on her head, a minor Hand of Glory tried pathetically to punch her, a rubber snake became a real cobra, which she ate. A nasty bug even tried to slither up her privates, but she turned herself caustic and burned it to a crisp.

She was obliged to play Russian roulette so she could collect the *Book of Sorrows*; there's just no getting around the risk of death to handle that book.

But death is no obstacle to her.

She's too good at resisting the pull, at finding another warm body to wedge herself into.

Most of them don't know how to fight to hold on to their skin.

Mostly it's an easy thing.

And even a witch can be pushed out if taken by surprise.

Now she takes up the sack.

It is heavy—she didn't stop with her books.

She will take a French book on shapeshifting and an American text on automobiles and a book by Saint Delphinia of Amiens that claims the Revelation of St. John happened in 1348; that angels and devils fought a second war that destroyed Lucifer and left Mammon in charge.

She remembers that time dimly, thinks it may well be true that greed and envy replaced wrath and pride as man's chief evils.

A pity.

She hoists her sack.

She is about to leave the library when she notices a pretty carved box she had not seen before.

Up on the mantelpiece of the library's fireplace.

Beneath a painting of an oak tree.

She sets the bag down.

Examines the box, a box of cedar and ivory.

She tries to open it but finds it locked.

She spits in the keyhole and the lock smokes, opens.

A rabbit?

A stuffed rabbit.

She sees her reflection in its shiny, convex eyes, and it surprises her. It always surprises her to see herself young. She prefers the body of a crone, prefers to be underestimated and ignored, to make clear decisions because she is not distracted by a quick womb and its siren song of sex and children.

And she can always make herself look pretty when she needs to seduce.

What is this rabbit?

A relic?

She tries to feel magic, feels only an odd, flat deadness.

She picks it up.

When she does, it opens its mouth and, impossibly, an egg rolls out.

Breaks on the hardwood floor.

This triggers a memory in her, but too late.

"Here is the devil!" she says.

And then it happens.

. . .

Andrew Ranulf Blankenship, or his death, or his life essence, or his soul, if you prefer, rushes up from the broken shell and the mess of yolk and albumen on the floor of his library, rushes at the body of his onetime lover.

If he hesitates, she will become aware of him, will defend herself, and he will be a ghost.

He doesn't give her time.

He pushes for all he's worth, leaps into her body and crowds it, gives her no room to hide, feels himself in all of her at once.

For a dizzying moment, both of them occupy the flesh of the unfortunate Marina Yaganishna, but the old witch is surprised. Off-balance.

She tries to hold on.

If she gains purchase, he will lose.

He does something he understands as bracing his foot against her hip bone and straining at her, pushing her up and out through the nose and mouth.

The mouth of Marina Yaganishna opens and she wails as if in labor. Clenches her fists. But she can't hold. Momentum and surprise are his, and he pushes her out of the body she stole.

And takes it for himself.

121

Baba Yaga, or her death, or her life essence, or her soul, if you prefer, sees the body of Marina Yaganishna from the outside. Sees that it has clenched its muscles, sees that the warlock is breathing slowly out, keeping rigid. She rushes at him, tries to push, but it is an easier thing to defend a body than to take one, provided you know you are under attack.

She sees herself drop to her knees, clutch them against her chest.

The Thief has done his reading—if he tried to stand up in that new body, with all his strange muscles twitching and the matter of the brain rippling to accommodate the new thought patterns and the new thinker, he would be vulnerable, and she could push him right back out.

But he, or she now, drops to the ground and breathes.

Throws up the pork and apples she had for lunch—nausea is normal.

Keeps breathing, keeps her muscles tensed so she is aware of her perimeter, so she can inventory all her parts.

Baba sees this is fruitless.

She is being shut out.

For now.

And then.

Oh God.

It comes.

The light.

The warm and welcoming light.

Her son, sweet, weak Misha, went into the light already to play with kittens and sit on the lap of Jesus and play the balalaika or whatever people do there where all are equal.

To hell with that!

All are *not* equal.

The warm light waits just outside the wall of the library and she knows she could move right through that wall and into it, but then she would not be smarter or stronger than anyone else, and that sounds like hell to her.

She might even be judged, if the priests are right.

But she was there before the priests came to her land.

She was there when the dead were burned in huts on little hills with rings of poles all around.

She was still a girl when she asked the woman who talked to Chërt, the dark-god, to help her get rid of her mother's new husband, the sneering one who preferred fucking her, fucked her whenever her mother went out. And he sent her out a lot. How she hated the sight of his teeth as he sneered and grunted over her, sweated down on her. Hated the sound of him standing and pissing outside the hut.

Mother Damp-Earth never answered her prayers, but dark-god did.

Her mother's husband fell in a hole; his brothers saw hands grab him, saw a hand with a rock break his teeth out, saw another hand rip his cock off before the black earth stopped his screams and he was gone forever.

What was her own name then?

It was too long ago to remember. She used to write it down, but then she lost it and lost interest in finding it again.

She thinks she hears Misha's voice coming from the light.

Baba. Come to me here. It's good here.

Are you my father to tell me what to do? You come here.

I don't want to.

How many sons and daughters and sisters and mothers do you think have tried to get me in there? You tell that light to eat shit and go away.

Good-bye, Baba.

Yes, yes. Enjoy the balalaika.

But this may just be her mind talking to itself.

Either way, the light stops tugging at her and fades away.

That's when she hears

With what ears?

the front door open.

If she only had a mouth to smile with.

122

We have to go back a little now.

Back to the house of Anneke Zautke, and to the thing she woke up. The thing she told to stay on the bed. It did what it was told—things like that are remarkably compliant at first, that compliance coming from a deep desire to please the maker. But, as with a dog who was told to stay, the desire to be near its master soon overwhelms the memory of the command.

It hears the commotion outside when Anneke is dragged to the hut; it watches the hut take her. It hides from the witch when she looks back down the trail, then goes back into the house and cries.

After it cries all it can cry, it decides to follow Anneke.

Magic brought it to life, so it feels magic.

It knows where the hut went.

It follows, walking by the side of the road.

Barefoot.

White T-shirt with a red circle, Japanese characters reading *Looking for a Japanese girlfriend*.

No bra.

Holding its blue jeans up with one hand because they are Anneke's jeans and Anneke is two sizes bigger.

Because it is a very attractive thing walking by the side of the road alone at night, a man with a port-wine nose and an orange Syracuse Windbreaker pulls his car over and asks it if he can have a date.

"I want a ride in your car," it says.

"Where to?"

"I don't know. But I'll tell you when I get there."

He says "I don't know" is his favorite place.

He pulls over on a farm road near a cornfield and has sex with it.

It looks down the road where the magic went the whole time.

Shaking him and pointing.

He is taking a long time because the Zoloft delays orgasm.

Also because he is already composing the words he will use to describe this peccadillo to Father Maldonado on Sunday.

"Hurry!" it says, slapping his face, which sends him over.

"Was that even a little bit good for you?" he asks, putting his prophylactic in an empty soda cup, which he puts into an empty McDonald's bag, which he puts into a plastic Pick & Save bag like the worst nesting doll ever.

"I don't care," it says. "Take me down that road now."

"How much do I owe you?"

Frustrated, it punches his ear and points down the road.

His anger at the pain quickly morphs into guilt as he realizes he may have taken advantage of a deranged girl.

The girl-thing makes him drive slowly, pointing.

"Dog Neck Harbor, eh?" he says.

"Don't talk anymore. I don't like the way you talk."

He turns on the radio.

When they get to Willow Fork Road, the feeling of magic gets strong.

It smiles, claps its hands a little, laughs.

"How much farther?" he asks, blowing his nose into a napkin from his Windbreaker.

Oily smoke from a burned war machine rises from a yard, but he can't see it.

Snow falls on the windshield, but he thinks it's rain.

His angle on the lower road doesn't permit him to see the decapitated man or the ravens feeding on him.

"Here!" the girl-thing shrieks.

The man in the Windbreaker stops the car, fumbles for his wallet.

He slides two twenties from his wallet, also dragging out a saved fortune cookie slip like a small, white tongue.

She is already out of the car and running.

He reads the slip in his lap, its cheerful red letters proclaiming BAD LUCK WILL MISS YOU IF YOU DRIVE AWAY!

He drives away.

Anneke's creation doesn't know where to go now.

Magic screams from the house, but also from the woods and from the burning machine. The magic here is much stronger than anything at Anneke's house.

It feels her creator everywhere here; Anneke has saturated this place with her presence. But the magic is strongest in the house. The house with the blown-in doorway and the hole in the roof and the dimples where shells hit it and the house re-formed itself.

The pretty thing in the outsized clothes walks in the front door.

Hears a woman moaning in discomfort upstairs.

Barely notices the cold patch it walks through on its way up the stairs to the library.

The cold patch follows it.

. . .

Andrew-in-Marina moans, lying in a fetal position, when he (she) sees the lovely teenaged girl-thing walk into the library, looking confused.

It sees him (her).

"Pretty-mole-lady, where is Anneke?"

It has Anneke's voice exactly.

Andrew (Marina) almost understands, would understand completely if he (she) were not busy breathing steadily and keeping muscles half-tensed.

Then the pretty girl jerks.

Its life essence is a fragile thing, an entirely new creation, flapping like a pillowcase on a clothesline. The wind that whips it away is a strong, cold wind indeed.

There is no fight at all.

The fledgling spirit dissolves as if it never were.

Unplugged, the girl's body crumples, hits its head on the floor with a dull *thump*.

The girl's Italianate blue eyes open again.

The eyes narrow.

The girl smiles a lupine smile, the upper lip curling a bit too much.

She vomits abundantly—the pasta shells and white cheese a staple in Anneke's pantry.

That is Anneke's T-shirt.

It stinks of Winstons.

Andrew-in-Marina almost understands what the girl was. Knows all too well what the girl is now. Stops breathing and clenching—the old witch has found her host.

That is Anneke's T-shirt.

Andrew-in-Marina understands in a flash.

Tries to say, "Ah!"

It sounds more like, "Gah!"

123

Anneke has just returned from Michael Rudnick's quarry, surging, full of power. Knows she has a limited window of opportunity to do this awful thing, knows each time she resists the temptation to do it that she eventually will, that she has to.

In the basement.

Seven statues of her teenaged lover, Shelly Bertolucci.

Most are small.

The best one is life-sized.

She knows she will have to teach it to be an actual person, not just stone turned into dying meat.

She improvises.

Burns pictures of the actual Shelly and rubs the ashes all over it.

Takes the lock of Shelly's hair that she had saved, lays this on the statue's head.

Burns a letter of Shelly's, puts the ashes on the statue's lips.

Touches her own moist sex and moistens Shelly's.

Kisses the stone lips, leaves her own saliva on the ash.

Dabs milk on her breast, touches that to Shelly's.

Cuts her left middle finger, touches that to Shelly's.

When she is ready, she turns a red maple leaf to stone.

Quickens it again, blows life's fire from the leaf to the statue, which turns maple-red at first, then to stone again.

On the third attempt, the red stone glows coal-red, driving Anneke

from the basement with its heat, making her fear fire, then cools, soft-
ens, goes pink, turns flesh-colored, then turns flesh.

It breathes in a hitching breath.

Breathes out.

It sobs.

It moves its fingers.

Its eyes.

Puts its warm arms around Anneke.

Says Thank you.

Anneke laughs and cries.

Says, "Oh, fuck."

124

Oh, fuck, Andrew-in-Marina thinks.

This is happening.

There's no other way.

Shelly's double and Marina both begin to stand, shakily, twitching, muscles misfiring.

Two foals in new bodies.

About to fight to the death.

125

Anneke wakes up still attached at wrists and ankles, hanging like a hammock in a sinking ship. The hut is on the ground, cracked open, snow falling in. The bearded madman holds his knees, looks out the window, then looks out the window again.

"She got him," he says.

He keeps repeating "she got him" and looking out the window as if he is stuck in some sort of loop.

She got who?

Andrew, who else?

This guy's bugshit, he's like Renfield, don't listen.

Anneke takes inventory.

Her shoulder really hurts; must have gotten yanked when the hut went down.

The snake torque around her neck is no longer draining her.

Just cold iron.

She has enough magic in her to will it off her, making it groan and twist and finally fall dead to the floor, which is actually the wall now. She breaks the loop holding her feet; they clunk down. Now her hands; she sharpens the inside of the metal loop, uses it to cut her rope.

Renfield sees her struggling free, comes over, tries to hold her down, but he doesn't mean it. All he manages to do is bleed and cry on her. She stomps him in the chest, crawls out the window, and dumps herself in the snow.

Snow?

It's fucking August!

Ravens form a loud bully-ring around something to her left.

I don't want to know what that is, not yet, it's a deer, just a deer.

She sees the burning T-34, the strange black rocks around it, sees the scattered debris of the wrecked cars and boulders.

Steps on a doll with button eyes and it bleeds into the snow.

Senses she needs to get inside.

Upstairs.

Fast.

She runs.

Ignores the splinters and glass and blood.

Tromps upstairs in her heavy Docs, tracking snow.

Goes to the library.

126

Anneke enters the library.

Shelly Bertolucci struggles and grunts, locked in combat with the witch who put Anneke in the hut. A bloody saber lies on the floor near them. The witch has scratches near her eyes. Shelly has a broken nose. Books, a broken drill, an overturned table, and other debris litter the floor near the combatants.

Both of them move like they're drunk.

Anneke stands transfixed.

She looks again at the saber.

Dives for it, her shoulder screaming in protest.

Holds it.

The women fight.

Both of them have seen Anneke take up the weapon; each seems intent on keeping the other from speaking.

The witch lashes out with a vicious elbow, catches Shelly in the ear.

Anneke steps forward, cocks the saber for a thrust.

Marina speaks.

"Anneke Zautke! I'm Andrew! In the wrong body!"

Anneke stops the thrust, which would have taken Marina Yaganishna through the ribs.

A trick. Fuck this Russian whore.

She cocks the weapon back.

Inspired, Marina speaks again.

"Let's watch *Papillon!*"

Now Shelly swats Marina across the jaw, catches her hard, if gracelessly, with the heel of her hand.

Shuts her up.

Earns a second to speak.

"What are you doing? Don't let her hurt me!"

A simulated lover's simulated plea.

Russian accent?

Anneke squints.

"Hurry!" barks Shelly.

Palatalized *H.*

Sounds like *xhoory!*

"Funny," Anneke says.

Shelly sees Marina about to speak again, catches her with a weak but painful punch in the throat, drives her back.

Marina puts her hands to her neck, falls back into Andrew's prized leather reading chair.

Shelly is clear now.

Shelly with the Russian accent.

Anneke, in shock, white-faced.

Decides.

Pushes through her instinct not to harm Shelly, uses that momentum to strike.

Hard.

NOW!

Stabs the curved point overhand, down at the red Japanese sun on the younger woman's T-shirt.

The saber halts for a microsecond at the sternum, pushes through sickeningly, comes out the other side, tenting the cotton there before piercing it.

Shelly's look of fury turns to pain and disbelief.

She puts her hands on the saber.

And turns back to stone.

Around the steel saber.

Wearing a bloody T-shirt and oversized jeans.

Anneke makes a primal noise something like a wail.

"She'll try to take your body!" the witch in the chair squeaks through her bruised windpipe. "Tense your muscles . . . breathe deliberately, fast and shallow."

Anneke does.

127

Baba Yaga finds herself bodyless again.

The warlock in her last body is not vulnerable.

Panting in the leather chair like a whelping bitch.

The new witch is shutting her out, too.

She has never felt so weak.

If I don't find a body soon . . . Even if I do, I'm not sure I'll have the strength to take someone.

But I think so.

One more.

That's when she sees the warm, red light.

Police car?

A policewoman would make a fine host. She would be tempted to walk back in here and shoot these two, but her strength is so low she might not be able to jump back out of the new one without preparing certain potions, using Milk-witch to drain some luminous boy or girl to fuel her. No good. To end her days in an American prison wouldn't be a very funny joke.

No, wherever she goes next, she'll need time to gather her strength.

She goes outside, through the ruined front door.

The light glows through the trees.

Down in the road below?

She moves past the tank, past the dead warlock.

The stick-man with the portrait head is slapping pathetically at ravens, trying to get them to stop eating his master.

Good luck, sobaka.

When she gets to the road, she sees no police car.

The red glow is coming from above.

That is incorrect.

She cranes up

with what neck?

and looks

with what eyes?

to see it.

A huge red cloud of whirling lights (eyes?), a cloud as big as a zeppelin, some of its size obscured by the oily smoke and the fog left by the snow and then the absence of snow.

She knows what this thing is.

A collector.

A cleaner.

It comes for recalcitrant spirits.

In a body you can't see it and it can't see you.

Ghosts hide from it, but eventually, in ten years or three hundred, it gets them.

I'm a ghost!

She flees, goes into the house across the street.

A dog with three legs barks at her.

She goes into the house, nobody downstairs, upstairs only a dead man and two burnt dolls.

Burnt curtains.

An angry-looking ghost stands near them.

Get out of my house! it yells at her.

She sees his life in an instant.

A weak, angry man.

Go shave your balls, she says.

The dog barks.

The dog then! I'll hide in the dog!

Would she even live long enough in a dog to gather the strength to push a person out?

Would enough of her be left to have language?

She could be stuck in a cripple dog for years.

Forever, even.

The house fills with red light.

A sort of eye looks in.

Better a dog than in that fucking thing.

The eye sees the angry man fuming.

A sort of hand reaches into the window.

NO! NO! NO! the man says, but it takes him anyway.

Dissolves him utterly, or so it seems.

So ends the shortest haunting in New York State history.

Baba flees downstairs.

Tries to get into the dog, but it runs back and forth on its run, barking at her.

Too tense, too fast.

How does a dog with three legs move so fast?

Now the huge red thing is done with the angry man.

She moves off into the woods.

Considers going back to the Thief's house and taking a raven.

Too small.

The woods go red.

Not ME!

You won't get ME!

Wait . . . what is that?

In the hollow of a log.

Something cowers.

Just big enough, she thinks.

Then she recognizes it.

The indignity of the situation galls her.

A skunk?

Worse than that.

A pregnant skunk?

A sort of eye looks down at her through a crown of maple leaves.

Here is the devil!

Fearful, the skunk shows her its teeth.

It has good reason to be afraid.

Baba Yaga pushes.

The skunk squeals.

The red light goes away.

128

When the police come, Marina Yaganishna tells them what happened standing twenty yards from Andrew's corpse.

They see what she wants them to see.

They believe what she tells them.

129

From the *Barre-Montpelier Times Argus*:

MAYFIELD PHILANTHROPIST DIES NEAR CHERNOBYL

Montpelier, VT—*Michael Rudnick, local sculptor and philanthropist, has been found dead in the abandoned Ukrainian town of Pripyat of what appears to have been a massive stroke.*

Rudnick, 71, is known for a variety of charitable acts. In 2005 he donated building materials for the new prenatal wing at the Mayfield Memorial Hospital; in 2009 he gave a life-sized sculpture of a charging bear to the Northern Vermont Museum of Natural History, and children from Mayfield to Montpelier know the white-bearded Rudnick as Father Christmas for his appearances at local parks on a reindeer-pulled sled.

A State Department official described Rudnick's presence in Pripyat, part of the exclusion zone exposed to radiation in the 1986 explosion of reactor number 4 at the Chernobyl nuclear plant, as "highly irregular," but declined to elaborate. Rudnick served in the U.S. Army infantry in 1968 and attended the University of Vermont on the G.I. Bill. He is survived by a sister, Michelle, and a brother, Paul.

Asked about her brother's tragic journey to Ukraine, Michelle Rudnick-Osborne said, "Michael was always full of surprises, always turning up where you didn't expect him. But he always had your back. There's nobody else like him, and we'll miss him very much."

From the *Syracuse Post-Standard*:

METEOR STRIKE KILLS 1, INJURES 1

Dog Neck Harbor, NY—*A Cayuga County man is dead and a Cornell professor is injured following a rare meteor strike in west-central New York.*

The deceased, John Dawes, 46, appears to have been struck in the neck by flying metal from the destruction of a car owned by neighbor Andrew Blankenship, whose house was also damaged in the freak event. Blankenship was away at the time.

Blankenship's houseguest, Marina Yaganishna, reported hearing a "rushing sound followed by a chain of god-awful bangs. The house was hit so hard I was afraid it would fall."

James Coyle, Ph.D., is reported in stable condition with lacerations and head trauma. He has no memory of how he got to Dog Neck Harbor from his summer cabin in nearby Sterling, New York.

The phenomenon occurred at about 9:45 P.M. at Willow Fork Road on the east side of town.

A tractor of unknown provenance was also struck, its gas tank igniting and the resulting fire burning a section of woods.

130

Andrew-in-Marina walks with Anneke to the feasting crows. Anneke already got Salvador to go inside.

"Don't look," Marina tells Anneke, looking. Her accent is pure midwestern American.

"Me don't look? How about *you* don't look?" Anneke says, looking.

"I'll only get to see this once," Marina says.

"Yeah. Maybe."

Marina takes a lock of Andrew's hair.

It will be necessary for the spells Marina will cast to make herself look like him, sound like him.

This won't be easy, but she won't have to do it long; just long enough to tie things up legally, make the property Marina's.

A search of the hut yielded her passport, driver's license, credit cards.

Near dawn, Marina and Anneke burn Andrew's remains, making the flames crematorium-hot with the last of the fireglass.

"Andrew Blankenship is dead," Marina says.

"Long live Marina Yaganishna," Anneke says, offering Marina a cigarette.

She almost reaches for one, then shakes her head.
"I think I just quit."

Anneke spends the night.

The two of them spoon, each holding the other as if she were as fragile as a kite.

Sleep comes only in teaspoons.

The one time both of them sleep, one cries out, wakes the other.

Neither is sure who.

131

In the morning Chancho comes by for a training session Andrew had forgotten about.

Anneke tells Chancho what happened.

"No effin' way."

Chancho looks Marina up and down.

He looks at her in silence for a good minute and a half.

"Hey, *bruja*," he says at last, addressing Marina. "Name three people who beat the Iceman."

"KO or decision?" the woman says.

"Your choice."

"Rashad Evans. Rampage Jackson. What's-his-face Jardine. The Dean of Mean. Keith?"

"Yeah, but that wasn't no knockout."

"You said, 'your choice.'"

Chancho nods, very slowly.

"What about Ortiz?"

Marina wrinkles her mouth at Chancho.

"Ortiz never beat Liddel. Ortiz is a *pendejo*."

Chancho corrects her pronunciation.

132

Andrew looks like Andrew thanks to a very powerful, very temporary spell.

He goes to see his lawyer, signs everything over to Marina Yaganishna, whom he describes as a cousin.

"Cousin, eh? Is that what they're calling Russian Internet brides these days? What are you doing, Andrew?"

"Just trust me."

"Tax stuff? You hiding assets?"

"Just do it, please."

Andrew has until sunset to look, smell, and sound like himself.

He calls Salvador.

Sal waggles his hips for the first time since Andrew's body died.

"Sal, I have to ask you a question."

The framed portrait of Dalí nods.

"Sal, are you happy?"

Salvador doesn't respond for some time.

Then it turns the knobs on the Etch-a-Sketch.

I
SERVE

"That's not an answer. I want to know if you're happy. Now. Like this."

One of the automaton's hands moves toward the knobs to reply.

Then it lies still.

There it is, then.

"I'm going to ask you another question, Sal. It's a question that means more than it seems to mean, so I want you to think about your answer, okay?"

The portrait nods.

"Do you want to stay inside with me? Or do you want to go outside?"

Salvador bows his head.

Then points at the Etch-a-Sketch.

I SERVE.

Andrew shakes his head.

"Tell me really. Tell me what you want."

The automaton squirms.

Then writes.

OUTSIDE

Sal shakes the screen clear and turns the knobs again.

YOU OUTSIDE
WITH SAL LATER

Andrew laughs, feels a tear start in one eye, knuckles it away.

"It's a date," he says.

. . .

First, Andrew watches the tape with Sal and Sarah a dozen or thir-
teen times, never opening the trapdoor. Just watching. Then he pops
the tape out, takes it upstairs.

The microwave is destroyed, so Andrew uses the stove to thaw a
piece of filet he had been saving in the freezer, a big red bastard
wrapped in applewood-smoked bacon.

That done, he turns Salvador back into a border collie, using the
last of the alarm magic woven into his wicker limbs.

This will last only twenty minutes at most.

He gives Sal the filet.

Watches the greedy, beautiful dog gobble it down.

All ten ounces of it.

He takes Sal outside, throws a Frisbee for him.

Laughs as Sal plucks the orange disc from the air once, twice,
then gets distracted and chases a raven, probably one of those that
ate Andrew's face not so long ago.

Then they just run together.

The dog is big-legging it through the last warm day of the year, his
tongue hanging behind him for what seems like half a mile, barking
and jumping.

Then they fall into a tumble of scratches and playful bites and
cheek-licking, a dance as old as man and dog and meat and fire. At
last they rest, Sal's head on his lap.

Andrew smells the dog's good smells, from the waxy scent of the
fur near his ears to the grassy, leathery black pads of his feet, even his
steaky, hot breath.

A squirrel chirrs from a tree and Sal raises his head, pricks his
ears up, but doesn't chase it.

Just wags.

Happy as he's ever been with the smells of squirrel and fresh
air and dead raccoons in the air and the sun on his coat, his mas-

ter's hand in his fur, his master's voice in his ear and smell in his nose.

For the last time.

It has to be here.

It has to be now.

The dog begins to blur.

Stands up and yawns, curling his tongue.

Andrew stands, too.

The dog blurs and stays blurry.

Rises from four feet to stand on two.

Now Sal is an automaton again.

Before he can lose his nerve, Andrew pulls the lid off the basket at the center of the wicker man, yanks out the dog's salted heart.

Not unlike pulling a plug.

The wicker man collapses, falls into an almost fetal position with Dalí looking up at the sky.

The portrait will hang in the library.

The prosthetic legs will go to the VA, where some bewildered young man or woman home from a hot country may be glad for them.

The wicker man and the dog's heart go in the fire.

As does the VHS tape.

Sal and Sarah.

Outside.

Later.

It's a date.

Andrew Blankenship watches the sun go down, sitting by the fire in his Japanese robe.

Marina Yaganishna gets up, ties the robe tighter.

Hears the cell phone ringing.

Picks it up.

It's Anneke.

133

This is what Marina Yaganishna does at the AA meeting.

She introduces herself to everyone.

Tries to act like she doesn't know anything at all about bottle-red-haired-child-spoiling-Mom Cathy, or beauty-queen-for-Jesus Laura, or toilet-plungered-Art-Garfunkel Jim, Lexus-lawyer Jim, Saint Bob, or any of them.

She eats half a doughnut, gives Anneke the other half, watches Anneke eat two more.

Anneke has put on a little weight, but she carries it well.

Anneke is happy.

When Chancho speaks, Marina dims the good Presbyterian fluorescents above their yellowing Presbyterian screens, then brightens them again, stopping before they pop. He cuts his eyes to her, but she just looks back at him with those calm, tilted blue icon eyes of hers.

Chancho speaks.

"I used to be in a lotta bad stuff, down in Texas, Mexico. Since I was a kid, drinkin' beer and *raicilla*, which is made from agaves but not like the stuff they give the tourist but the stuff somebody made at home. Always in trouble. Most of the boys in my family, they went to guns and drugs, and I did too, at first. Bad stuff, bad stuff. You see it on the news now, how bad it's got, but it's never been good. I got out of Matamoros, went up to Houston, still got mixed up too much, drinkin' Shiner was okay but cocaine and tequila and whiskey, I ruin my boxing. Got arrested. Went to Austin and started getting clean, workin' in a garage, but was still too close to it all. Met my wife, Consuela, married her, almost got happy but addiction don't let nobody be happy. I hit her not one time but two times, and she shouldn't'a stayed, but I thank God every day she did. Said she had people up north and why didn't we come up here, get away from all that. I said okay. It was good. I got eight years sober now, and I know it don't never go away. My family come up, some of them still in the life I was in, and it was hard to say no to some of the stuff they wanted me to do with them. But I did. I said 'My food is your food, and stay as long as you want, but don't you bring that in my house.' So some of them got a hotel. Maybe I should have warned you if you was gonna stay in the Days Inn in Oswego not to tell nobody to turn the music down if you heard accordions or somebody singin' about *corazón*. All Mexican songs got the word *corazón*. I think it's a law. Anyway, the temptation was on me, 'specially around my cousin Julio, who got good shit, the best in Chihuahua, and he's a fun dude, too. But I was drivin' down 104 to the Days Inn thinkin' maybe just this one time cause I ain't seen these muchachos since back in the day, and Consuela won't never know, you know how that song goes, and no sooner had I thought that than BAM! Out pops this dog, an I almos' hit him, he glance off the tire. He's a old dog, too, vet thinks he's between eight and ten years old. Been on his own for a while, all dirty, got some mange and fleas, lotsa fleas. But I didn't know about that yet. If I'd'a known how much he gonna cost me at the vet, I mighta not take him. So I pull over and pick this *chingado* dog up, take him to the hotel with me, and all the dudes were drinkin' and smokin' and snortin' and effin' with his ears, he look like a beagle, with a white smutch on his face like a *máscara*. And you can go *ooooooo* in his face an' he'll howl back at you, too. Anyway, I think God sent me that dog to remind me. So I kept him. My buddy An' . . . Marina. My friend Marina, you just met her tonight, she's a friend'a Andrew's, she said she thinks his name was Caspar because of that mask. But I want to call him Ocho because he remind me not to blow my eight years. But he answers to Caspar, guess she was right. But I call him both. His name is Caspar Ocho Morales. Good name for a fighter. Good name for a dog."

134

"I don't want to do this. But I have to. He's dangerous, even without her, if he is without her. It's not just revenge, although I suppose there is an element of that. I hate what he did. I miss Radha."

Marina is sitting on her leather couch, her ash-blond hair up in a samurai bun, speared by a cherrywood fork. She wears a light gray wool sweater she just got at the mall. Anneke took her shopping. All her clothes are new, except the Japanese robe.

The hammering from the roof has stopped. The contractors are lunching in the yard, gobbling down subs from the Oswego sub shop. This was the first, best chance she had to Skype with the overweight but oddly handsome man in California.

San Francisco.

Sealiongod@me.com.

"I understand she was good," the man says.

"She was. But she said you were better."

"We'll see."

"You'll help me?"

Sealiongod nods, smiling a little.

"I'm feeling patriotic. Let's do this."

He's still young. He enjoys this shit.

Like Radha did.

Andrew-in-Marina just feels ill.

135

Yuri sits at his computer, the cat purring on his lap. The cat with the upside-down tail. Yuri nurses a glass of powdered cherry drink and vodka, his upper lip stained with a faint, reddish mustache.

"What's this?" he says.

An e-mail from Marina Yaganishna.

He doesn't want to read it—Baba Yaga has left him alone for months, and he fears this communication from her daughter might herald new demands, new threats, more bad dreams. But not opening it could be much, much worse.

Could it be spam?

An attachment titled *Naughty boy gets stoned with Santa* suggests it is.

And it's only September.

Christmas already?

Maybe he won't open that.

No, he decidedly will not open the attachment.

He reads the e-mail.

Yuri,

Open this attachment immediately.

—Marina

Yuri opens the attachment.

A video.

Marina sits before a television screen, wearing only a Japanese robe. The right-pointing delta of the *start* symbol goads him. He clicks it. The beautiful woman in the Japanese robe animates, speaks.

American-accented Russian?

"Yuri. Watch the screen. My friend in California put this together for me. I want to thank you for what you did in Chicago. To the witch Radha. Watch!"

Turn it off, Yuri.

But he can't turn it off.

Baba will know if he doesn't watch it.

He instinctively hides his teeth with his hand.

The television in the video comes on.

An old man with a short, white beard is sitting on a sled, behind reindeer. He wears the red hat and robes of Father Christmas, his hat garnished with holly and pine. He is preparing to read a story to a group of bouncy little children. Snow behind him.

This doesn't look like California.

"Michael. Michael Rudnick," Marina says.

The old man looks confused for a second, then looks at Marina. Nods.

Closes the book.

The bouncy children have all gone still, frozen in place while the Santa-man continues to move.

A trapdoor?

Who is this old fucker?

"Michael, the man I want you to wish a Merry Christmas is in that camera."

Father Christmas nods.

Smiles.

Looks at the camera.

Speaks English.

"Ho Ho Ho! You've been a very naughty boy, Yuri. It is Yuri, right?"

Turn the computer off!

The man's eyes flash.

A loud CRACK fills Yuri's apartment.

The cat is caught leaping, turns to heavy Vermont granite in midair.

Lands with a loud CRASH!

Breaks in half.

Yuri is frozen reaching for the mouse.

His momentum carries him forward, topples him into his computer, destroying and toppling that.

The man downstairs bangs against the floor in protest.

A woman next door shrieks at Yuri, her voice scarcely muffled by the plaster.

"I'm tired of your noises, Yuri! Go to bed! Go to bed! Go to bed!"

Coda

St. Petersburg, Russia.

November.

The Singer Café on the second floor of the Dom Knigi bookstore on Nevsky Prospect.

A troika of women sits jet-lagged in the warm, green room while outside the sky threatens to spit snow again, as it did all the rough ride down to the Pulkovo airport this morning.

"We're not here for magic," Marina Yaganishna says.

"I know. But, what, are we just going to leave it here?" Anneke says, tucking the last corner of her tuna sandwich in her mouth.

The red-haired girl with the scarred nose and cheeks looks out the window, looks at the Kazan cathedral down below. She has spoken rarely since they got on the plane at JFK; she stirred from her heavy-lidded Xanax-and-vodka-induced stupor only long enough to change planes in Moscow; she hated the plane, hated everything about it, made it clear that she would rather overdose than be awake knowing she was over the ocean.

She doesn't like water now.

Or seafood.

She nearly vomited the first time she saw a mussel.

"I have been to this church, I think," she says in Russian, pointing down at the cathedral, which bears more than a passing resemblance to St. Peter's Basilica in Rome.

"Speak English, please," Marina says to her.

"Why? You claim to speak Russian."

"I do."

"Like an Ohio housewife," she manages in English.

"And when you speak Russian you sound like a spoiled tsarina who needs a whipping."

Nadia smiles at that.

She looks at Anneke now, stirring her hot chocolate with chili. The chocolate is so thick it barely runs off the spoon.

"I have been to this church," she says in English. "There are statues of generals from Napoleon's inversion."

"*Invasion* is what I think you want to say," Anneke says.

"It was a bit of an inversion," Marina says.

"Thank you for including me," Anneke says to Nadia, trying not to sound like a smartass—it isn't lost on her that she may be speaking to the last living person who saw prerevolution St. Petersburg, but she needs to make her point to Andrew (she has trouble calling him Marina). She swivels her gaze to Marina Yaganishna. "But the book. Really, are we just going to leave it here?"

All three of them look at the book now.

It appears to be a Soviet-era book on trees, complete with greasy plastic cover and line drawings of leaves and happy Soviet children playing in the woods, although their playing always looks like building or marching. Andrew sees past the book's disguise immediately. Anneke takes a few blinks. Nadia can't see what it really is. Not yet.

Andrew reads the actual title again.

"*Magical Gardens: How to Make Anything Grow Anywhere. With a Discussion of Healing Herbs and Poisons.* 1913."

This is a handwritten book bound in brown leather with yellow stitching.

"I just don't see the harm in buying this and bringing it back."

Marina looks at Anneke over her glasses.

"You don't see the harm because you didn't have to get out of the Soviet Union with magical books after being brutalized by a witch."

"I have been brutalized by a witch."

"You have been gently brutalized by a witch for a very short period of time. And it had nothing to do with books."

"Menopause isn't going easy on you, Mr. Blankenship."

Marina laughs despite herself.

"Just get the damned book if you want it. You're a grown-up."

"I was going to. How's the chocolate?"

"Spicy deliciousness. Try it."

Anneke's spoon floats down.

Nadia dips into it, too, her expensive perfume filling Anneke's nose.

Can't call her fish-cunt anymore. She smells better than I do.

Marina looks at the cathedral now, too.

"When I was here, that was a museum of atheism."

"You're shitting me," Anneke says.

"Nope. They had a big statue of Lenin, monk's penance chains, lots of anti-religious quotes. One of the guides told me they toned it down. Used to have a painting called *Christ the Oppressor.* Thumbscrews and all that, too, but it didn't play well with visitors."

"Lenin was a pig. I can't believe they named my city after him," Nadia says. Her voice is different now. Softer, even when she says harsh things. She has lived with Anneke and Marina for two months now as they figure out what they all are to each other. Anneke and Marina are lovers, more frequently than they were when Andrew was Andrew, but there is still something cautious, reserved about it. It took them more than a month even to kiss.

Nadia has a boyfriend, Chancho's handsome, beard-rubberbanding employee, Gonzo. Not as smart as Nadia, but *really* handsome.

Voice like molasses.

She met him while bartending at the Raven on Bridge Street in Oswego.

She is not luminous, but Anneke is teaching her magic anyway, hoping she's got the brains and persistence to plod her way into magic.

It is slow, slow going.

"Anyway, maybe herbs and shit are this one's bag. She's not getting the stone and rock thing at all."

"I hate the rock spells. I feel like a rooster pecking at a pearl," Nadia says.

Then she brightens, sits upright.

"We have to go to the summer gardens!" she says, wide-eyed. "There is a statue there. Krylov, the writer for children. My father used to read me fables under his statue, using animals' voices! 'The Cat and the Cook'!"

This is the most animated either of them has seen her in Russia.

This is why they came.

"I remember," she says.

Then she takes both of their hands, looks at each of them in turn.

Although she occupies the same shell, she is unrecognizable as the monster that drowned Mikhail Dragomirov and so many others.

She's a warm-blooded young woman, little more than a girl.

When she speaks they don't know if she means them or St. Petersburg.

It could be them.

They have become an odd sort of family.

An odd sort of coven.

Nadia cries when she says it.

"I'm home."

Acknowledgments

I hope my agent, Michelle Brower, isn't getting tired of my sincere thanks, but she earns them again and again with her advocacy, positivity, and good counsel. I am also grateful to Sean Daily at Hotchkiss and Associates for fielding endless naïve questions about the film and television industry, and to Tom Colgan, editor and friend, for his faith in me. His assistant, Amanda Ng, is so competent, professional, and effective as to be almost invisible; but I conjure her to thank her here. Naomi Kashinsky and her father, Alan, were invaluable to my Russian research, as was Ambassador Robert Patterson, who was in Moscow around the time our protagonist would have visited that city on his way to a very poor foreign travel experience indeed. Captain K. R. Kollman, USMM, was in the right place at the right time to assist me with questions about Coast Guard procedure. Steve Townsend was my chief Enon resource. My good friend Eric Brown, poet, father, musician, and the unofficial Mayor of Yellow Springs, Ohio, makes a cameo here; thanks to him, as well as to Dino for use of his bathroom. Cookie and Gene Schoonmaker-Franczec shared their Sterling, New York, home and stories with me; Cookie's studio served as the model for Anneke's, but I'm pretty sure all similarities between them end there. Thanks to readers/listeners/supporters Kelly Cochran Davis, Patrick Johnson, Dan Fox, Ciara Carinci, Angela Valdes, Cyrus Rua, and Elona Dunn, but especially to Jennifer Schlitt and Noelle Burk, whose early enthusiasm for this story affected its trajectory in all the best ways.

A special thank-you to director Gary Izzo, who has been quietly pursuing comedic and artistic excellence in the woods of Cayuga County, New York, for more than thirty years now; had he not first cast me as a Bless the Mark player at the Sterling Renaissance Festival in 1992 (and many times since), I never would have come to the beautiful hills, cliffs, and farmland that compose West Central New York, I never would have joined the strange and wonderful tribe that gave me so many enduring friendships, and you would not be holding this book.

Finally, thanks to the Burly Minstrel, Jim Hancock, whose ready guitar and mellow voice provided the soundtrack to a great many heartbreakingly beautiful sunsets on the very same McIntyre Bluffs that figure in this story.

I am blessed in my associations.

PHOTO BY BECCA McCOY

C   AN

is   d-
p   i
a   f
pl   s
S   e   b
r   n   roa
a   sto rbu

*"You think you got away with something, don't you? But your
time has run out. We know where you are. And we are coming."*

Andrew Ranulf Blankenship is a stylish nonconformist with wry wit, a
classic Mustang, and a massive library. He's also a recovering alcoholic
and a practicing warlock. His house is a maze of sorcerous booby traps
and escape tunnels, as yours might be if you were sitting on a treasury
of Russian magic stolen from the Soviet Union thirty years ago.

Andrew has long known that magic is a brutal game requiring blood
sacrifice and a willingness to confront death, but years of peace and
comfort have left him more concerned with maintaining false youth
than with seeing to his own defense. Now a monster straight from
the pages of Russian folklore is coming for him, and frost and death
are coming with her.

PRAISE FOR THE NOVELS OF
CHRISTOPHER BUEHLMAN

"A graceful, horrific read."—PATRICIA BRIGGS, #1 *New York
Times* bestselling author

"Beautifully written...Exceedingly clever."—*BOSTON HERALD*

"An unsettling brew...of genuine terror."—F. PAUL WILSON,
New York Times bestselling author

NOVEL/HORROR

christopherbuehlman.com
penguin.com

U.S. $16.00
CAN $18.00

ISBN 978-0-425-25691-6

5 1 6 0 0

EAN 9 780425 256916